Kelly Elliott is a *New York Times* and *USA Today* bestselling contemporary romance author. Since finishing her bestselling Wanted series, Kelly continues to spread her wings while remaining true to her roots and giving readers stories rich with hot protective men, strong women and beautiful surroundings.

Kelly has been passionate about writing since she was fifteen. After years of filling journals with stories, she finally followed her dream and published her first novel, *Wanted*, in November of 2012.

Kelly lives in central Texas with her husband, daughter, and two pups. When she's not writing, Kelly enjoys reading and spending time with her family. She is down to earth and very in touch with her readers, both on social media and at signings.

Visit Kelly Elliott online:

www.kellyelliottauthor.com
@author_kelly
www.facebook.com/KellyElliottAuthor/

Also by Kelly Elliott (published by Piatkus)

COWBOYS & ANGELS
Book 5

Blind
Love

NEW YORK TIMES & USA TODAY BESTSELLING AUTHOR

KELLY ELLIOTT

piatkus

PIATKUS

First published in Great Britain in 2018 by Piatkus

1 3 5 7 9 10 8 6 4 2

A CIP catalogue record for this book
is available from the British Library.

ISBN 978-0-349-41848-3

Printed and bound in Great Britain by
Clays Ltd, Elcograf S.p.A.

Cover photo and designer: Sara Eirew Photography
Editor: Cori McCarthy, Yellowbird Editing
Proofer: Amy Rose Capetta, Yellowbird Editing
Developmental/Proofer: Elaine York, Allusion Graphics
Interior Designer: JT Formatting

Papers used by Piatkus are from well-managed forests
and other responsible sources.

Piatkus
An imprint of
Little, Brown Book Group
Carmelite House
50 Victoria Embankment
London EC4Y 0DZ

An Hachette UK Company
www.hachette.co.uk

www.littlebrown.co.uk

This book is dedicated to Tanya.
Thank you for giving me the idea for Harley.

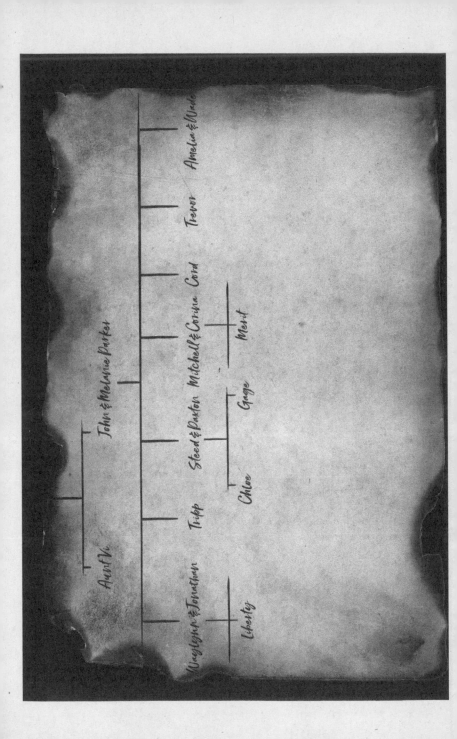

A Note to Readers

Blind Love is book five in the Cowboys and Angels series. The books in this series are not stand-alone books. Stories intertwine between books and continued to grow within each book. If you have picked up this book and have not read *Lost Love, Love Profound, Tempting Love, and Love Again,* I strongly suggest that you read them in order.

For a list of characters in the series as well as other fun extras, please visit the series website: www.cowboysandangelsseries.com

PROLOGUE

Spring break, Senior year in college

I pulled in next to Harley's father's truck. I smiled when I saw Harley standing in the middle of the field looking out toward the west. The sun still had a few hours to set, and her eyes closed while she soaked in the sun. This was her favorite spot to come on her folks' place, and I'd known she would be right here. Something hadn't been right over the last two days.

"Hey there, beautiful."

Glancing over her shoulder, her mesmerizing light-emerald eyes lit up. Those eyes had haunted my dreams for months after she left for college. They were a stunning green with specks of gold.

"What are you doing here?" she asked, her arms unfolding and dropping to her sides.

"Your folks said you needed some air, so I figured you'd be here."

Her smile was soft, barely reaching her eyes. I knew Harley Carbajal like the back of my hand. We'd been friends forever and had dated since high school. I already had an engagement ring ready for after our college graduation. I promised both her daddy and mine

I'd wait until we'd finished before I asked her. We only had a few more months; they never said I had to wait until after graduate school.

"Yeah, I needed some fresh air."

I nodded and walked up next to her. "Feel like company?"

"If it's you? Always."

Pulling her into my arms, I leaned in and kissed her. It didn't take much to get Harley to melt in my arms. If I wanted her, all I had to do was talk a little dirty, and she'd be begging for me to take her right here. She was my first, and I was hers. It didn't take us long to figure out we both liked to have a bit of fun when it came to sex. Harley liked it romantic—and sometimes a little rough.

"What's going on in that pretty little head of yours?"

She smiled, but this time I knew it was a forced one. "Nothing, really."

I decided to let it go and tell her my good news.

"Dave Hassell was pretty happy about me getting in UT's law school. He's offered me a position at the law firm this summer. I mean, I won't be doing anything major. More like an intern, but I'm going to take it! This is a great step toward starting my own law practice."

This time her smile was real. "That's amazing, Tripp! I'm so proud of you."

"The even better news? He's going to offer me a partnership in his law firm when I graduate from law school. I know it's a few years away, but just knowing I'll be able to come back home and start practicing law right away means a lot. We can build that house we dreamed of, and you can start building up your veterinary practice, and who knows? Maybe kids will be in the picture a few years after that."

Her eyes filled with tears.

"Doc Harris already has a practice in town," she said softly.

"Then you can work for him. Who knows, maybe he'll offer you a partnership as well. He's gotta retire one day, right?"

Her eyes drifted to the ground. "I don't think that's going to happen."

I pulled her into my arms. "You never know."

"Tripp, have you ever thought about *not* living in Oak Springs?"

Laughing, I replied, "No. Never. This is our home. I can't imagine leaving my family and moving away. Besides, our dream has always been to own one of those old houses off Main. I'd love to have my law offices out of one."

Harley pulled away from me. "That's the whole thing. It's your dream, Tripp. Not mine."

My heart felt like a brick as it fell to my stomach.

"What?"

She folded her arms over her body. "I don't want to settle down in Oak Springs. I want to travel and see the world. I want to know what it's like to live in a big city. Maybe a loft overlooking the hustle and bustle of everything. My Aunt Tanya told me about some of the amazing places she's traveled, and I can't stop thinking about how fun that would be."

My brows pinched together. "So, is this something you've just decided, Harley? We've always talked about settling down in Oak Springs."

"No, *you've* always talked about it. I've just listened."

I swallowed hard and turned away from her. My head was spinning. Racing through the catalog of endless conversations we'd had had about our future—I realized she was right. The conversations were always one-sided, and I'd been too caught up in the excitement of our future to notice that she'd not been participating in the plans I was making.

What in the fuck happens now? I can't lose her. I won't lose her.

Facing her again, I forced a smile. "Then, that's what we'll do."

Her eyes widened. "What do you mean?"

I shrugged. "If you want to live in the city, we'll live in the city."

For a quick moment, I saw excitement in her eyes. There wasn't anything I wouldn't do for this woman. Even if it meant putting my own dreams on hold for a while. Harley had been my number one dream—the rest was just the icing.

"You would do that? Leave your dreams and family behind just like that?" she asked. I could see the guilt pooling in her eyes.

"I'd do anything for you."

My phone rang, causing both of us to jump. I pulled it out of my pocket and went to hit ignore.

"It's my dad. I better get it."

She motioned for me to answer.

"Dad? Everything okay?"

"Tripp, where are you?"

Something was wrong, I could hear it in his voice.

"I'm at Harley's. What's wrong?"

"Son, I need you to come home."

My heart was racing. "Dad, what's going on?"

"Steed thought it would be a good idea to make a ramp over the creek and jump the four-wheeler over it. You boys are going to be the death of us, you know that."

I rolled my eyes. I'm sure my folks loved it when we were all back home for Christmas break. "Did he get hurt?"

"Might have broke his arm. Your mother is freaking out. Would you mind meeting us in Uvalde at the hospital? Your mother wants me to tell you to be careful on the roads. It's a mess out there."

"No, I don't mind at all, Dad. I'm on my way. Tell Mom not to worry. I'll be careful and will be there soon."

I could hear my father sigh in relief. "Thanks, son. Don't speed."

"Yes, sir."

Hitting End, I gave Harley a weak smile. "Steed might have broken his arm, and they're on the way to the hospital. Dad said it would help Mom if I was there. Can we talk about this when I get back?"

She nodded and looked down at her hands.

"Want to come with me?"

"Yes, of course."

The silent resignation on her face should've been my first warning, but I was only imagining our future...all the while choosing to ignore our present.

My father and I stood in line to get Mom coffee. They were setting Steed's arm in a cast, and it felt like it was taking forever. Harley had stayed back in the hospital room to keep Mom company.

As we walked back to the elevator, I mentioned to my father about Harley wanting to travel.

"Harley doesn't want to settle down in Oak Springs."

"What?"

I swallowed hard as we came to a stop, and he motioned for us to sit down.

"How do you feel about that?" he asked.

"I don't know. I'm upset about it, but I love her, Dad. I'll do whatever she wants and if she wants to travel...that's what I'll do."

"What about your internship this summer? The partnership you were offered."

"I guess I'll do it until she's finished with vet school and maybe take some time off?"

"Tripp, I know you love Harley, but that is not the smart thing to do. I won't tell you not to do it, but you've been talking about starting a law practice in Oak Springs since you were ten and went on that field trip to the courthouse in Austin. What about wanting to run for mayor someday?"

I blew out a deep breath. "I don't want to do this...but I will. For her."

My father rested his hand on my shoulder. "Son, you both need to sit down and talk about this. If you give up your dreams, you risk ending up resenting Harley. And the same can be said about her dreams."

"I'd never do that, Dad. It'd just be putting things off a few years. We'll make it work. Harley is my life and without her in it, all the internships and partnerships in the world wouldn't matter." Raising the cup of coffee we were carrying and not wanting to face the uncertainty, I added, "We better get this to Mom."

We headed back to the elevator. Glancing over my shoulder as we stepped in, I swore I saw Harley standing right where my father and I had just been sitting. Straining to look around the closing doors, I missed getting a better look.

The drive back to Oak Springs was silent. Harley sat in the passenger seat, her hands folded neatly in her lap. Something in her eyes had changed at the hospital. She was quiet and I couldn't help but wonder if she might be changing her mind about this whole travel thing. I knew her aunt filled her head with loads of stories. She was married to a rich husband who could afford it. How in the hell did she think we would be able to do it? Hell, we were both going to have student loans to pay off and would need to have serious jobs to do that.

Pulling into her driveway, I pulled off the side of the road and parked. Her house was about a half-mile down the dirt driveway.

"Harley, have you thought about what we're going to do for money? I mean, for traveling and all of that?"

Her response was not what I was expecting.

"This isn't going to work, Tripp."

"What isn't going to work?"

Her head jerked up and our eyes locked. "You leaving Oak Springs. Us traveling the world. I'm making you give up a dream and that isn't fair."

"Harley, we can make it work. There's just some things we have to figure out. We'll both be in debt. How long are you wanting to travel for? We need to plan it out. That's all."

She shook her head. "I don't want to plan it all out. That's the adventure part of it, that's what makes it so thrilling. But that's not how you live your life. You're a planner and what I want is the opposite of planning. I want to live and be in the moment."

My brows pulled together, the gravity of her words weighing down my thoughts. "I can do it, Harley."

Her eyes pooled with the threat of tears. When her chin started to tremble, I went to pull her toward me, but she jerked away.

Her voice was barely audible as she whispered, "This won't work. You'll end up hating me."

My heart fell to my stomach.

Harley jumped out of my truck, and I followed her.

"What in the fuck are you trying to say?" I demanded.

"Maybe we should take a break. Until after graduation."

I was nearly knocked onto my ass. Surely, I wasn't hearing what I thought she was telling me. I had law school, graduation, an internship, a partnership in my future... Hell, I had Harley and she was the reason for my future. She was my future.

"Take a break? Are you fucking insane? I love you and I'm not walking away from this. I've already told you, we can make this work. We'll figure it out and I'll...I'll start a law practice after we travel some."

Tears filled her eyes. "I, um, I met someone, at school. He... he's just a friend, but we have been talking and he wants the same things I want. I can't...pretend like everything is okay with us when we want such different things."

It felt like someone had just sucker-punched me in the stomach. "Harley, I just fucking told you! I'll do whatever you want. I just want you."

I watched tears roll down her cheeks. She slowly shook her head.

"It won't work, Tripp. Maybe I'm...developing feelings for him. I don't know. I think we need to take a break, so I can work this all out in my head."

My entire world felt like it was falling apart. The only woman I'd ever loved was standing before me dropping the biggest bomb, and all I could do was stand here, angry and yet willing to beg her to stay with me.

"Have you been cheating on me?"

Her chin trembled, and she looked away from me for a quick moment. She dragged in a shaky breath before facing me again.

"I'm not cheating. I mean...I haven't acted on my feelings. I'm confused."

All I could do was stare at her. "I can't believe you would do this to me."

She opened her mouth, regret filling her emerald eyes. "Tripp, wait. I...I...I can't do this!"

Harley turned away and ran as fast as she could down the driveway while I stood there. Stunned. Unable to move.

"Harley!" I shouted.

She ran faster. Never once looking back.

My legs trembled as I forced them to take a few steps. With as much energy as I could muster, I cried out after her.

"Harley! Harley! You can't go. Please, please don't go!"

Falling to my knees, I dropped my head and let the tears fall. I felt the anguish of what had just happened when a few short hours ago we had—no, *I* had—been planning our future and staring at an engagement ring that Harley would one day wear.

"Why, Harley?" I whispered.

CHAPTER 1

Tripp

Present day

"Hey, you seem a little withdrawn. You okay?"

I forced a smile and nodded. Mallory was sitting across the table, smiling. We'd been dating since December. I liked her and her daughter Laney a lot. She was the first woman who had actually made me feel like I was possibly getting over Harley. That was, of course, until Harley came back to town.

"A long day at work, that's all."

"You still planning on making the announcement tomorrow?" she asked.

"I am."

She started to chew on the left side of her bottom lip. "Do you want me there?"

My chest squeezed. I'd always pictured Harley standing next to me when I made the announcement of running for mayor. It was a fair question from Mallory, I guess. Four months of exclusive dating... I hadn't done that since Corina, and honestly, after the first month, it had been clear to both of us that we were better off as friends. Especially since she was in love with my brother, Mitchell.

Sitting up a bit straighter, I spewed out some bullshit. "I think Charles felt like it would be best if I was alone. It would keep you and Laney out of the spotlight and free from potential harassment."

"That's true. Good call on his part."

Sighing internally, I looked down at my sandwich. That was a dick move to use Mallory's daughter as an excuse. Laney was about to turn four, and I knew how much Mallory enjoyed her privacy. I adored Laney, and I was pretty sure she was at the top of the small list of reasons I stayed in the relationship with Mallory. The other reasons just made me seem like a cocksucker.

Mallory was good in bed.

Mallory had a body that made men salivate.

Mallory liked her space and wasn't needy.

And the best reason of all, I knew it drove Harley crazy to see me with Mallory.

Yep. I'm a cocksucker alright.

The bell on the door of Lilly's Café rang and I knew it was Harley without looking up. I could feel her eyes on me, making the hair on my arms and neck stand up. Lifting my eyes, we stared at each other for a quick second before Harley's gaze drifted to Mallory and then away from both of us.

Walking to the counter, Harley slid onto one of the stools and smiled at Lucy. They talked for a few seconds before Lucy left. I caught myself before I watched her too long. Mallory knew our history, and I knew any acknowledgement of Harley in her presence wouldn't be a good thing.

"So, have you been very busy?"

Mallory's voice pulled my gaze off Harley.

"No, not really. Things have been quiet at the office. Just preparing for the mayoral announcement."

She lifted her brows. "Does that mean you have to go straight back to work?"

A lump formed in my throat. "What did you have in mind?"

Her tongue rolled over her lips, and if Harley hadn't been sitting a few feet away, I'm pretty sure my dick would have been hard as a rock. Mallory was my kind of girl. She liked her sex like I did—a little naughty and a lot of dirty talking. She had a way of making me forget everything that was happening around me.

"A little restroom sex, maybe?"

I looked toward the hall that led to the restrooms. Was she serious? Fucking in my office was one thing, but doing it in a restroom at the café I ate at nearly every damn day? No. That wasn't going to happen.

"You want to fuck in the restrooms here?" I asked with a chuckle. Not thinking she was serious.

She leaned over the table, a whisper meant only for me—but I silently wondered if it was loud enough for Harley to overhear. "If you could feel me you'd know how wet I am just thinking about it."

My eyes darted over to Harley again. She was talking to old man Potter. I could almost bet they were discussing his cows. The man was obsessed with the damn things. Here I was, being propositioned for bathroom sex by my girlfriend, and all I could think about was Harley and old man Potter discussing the dairy business. What the hell was wrong with me?

When I looked back at Mallory, she was still giving me that sexy-as-sin smile. There was something in her eyes, though, and for a split second, I wondered if this was a game. Her own personal vendetta against Harley that directly involved me and my dick.

There was no way I was doing this. One, it was too risky, and two, Harley was here. I couldn't get my dick to stand at attention, even with Mallory talking about how wet she was.

"As fun as that sounds, there's no way. Too risky."

She rolled her eyes and dropped back in the chair. "Party pooper."

Lifting a brow, I leaned in closer. "You do realize we live in a small town, and I'm fixin' to announce I'm running for mayor. How do you think it would look if I had you bent over a sink at Lilly's Café and someone walked in while my cock was pounding into you?"

Mallory squirmed in her chair.

"Tripp," she whispered. "You're teasing me."

Yep. There was one thing for sure about Mallory: she liked to be fucked. With her it was simple. We fucked fast and furious, then one of us left. I don't think I'd ever cuddled with the woman once. She always had some excuse as to why she had to leave. Laney, the store, something. It was fine by me. The less emotionally attached I got, the better. Especially since I didn't really see a future with her.

At some point, I was going to have to break things off with her.

I opened my wallet and threw some money on the table before standing and reaching for her hand.

"Thanks, Tripp and Mallory!" Lucy called out.

Lifting my hand, I called out, "Later, Lucy." I didn't dare look that way. If I saw Harley, I wouldn't be able to do what I was about to do to Mallory. Still, I felt the weight of her stare heavy on my back. Guilt ripped through my body before I remembered that day in her driveway.

She'd met someone.

"Where are we going?"

"You'll see," I said while we walked down the street toward Cord's Place, closed today so that Cord could paint the bar. He wanted to give everything an extra day to dry. Since I had keys to the place, I was going to give Mallory the bathroom fuck she wanted.

Walking up to the front of the bar, she asked, "Why are we here?"

I pulled out the key and unlocked the door.

"It's closed today."

A smile spread over her face.

"Are you sure no one will come in?"

Laughing, I shut the door and locked it. I grabbed her hand and pulled her to the ladies' restroom.

"Oh, someone's going to come. And when you do, I want to hear you screaming my name from that pretty little mouth of yours."

The second we were in the bathroom, I unzipped my pants and pulled out my cock. Mallory dropped to her knees and took me in her mouth but I pulled her up. I wasn't in the mood for that. I never liked women going down on me. The only one I'd ever let was the woman sitting back at the café. The one whose emerald eyes I couldn't get out of my fucking head.

Shit! I needed a second to clear my thoughts. I wasn't about to screw Mallory while I was thinking of another woman.

"Tripp, why are you making me wait?"

Looking into her eyes, I lifted her skirt and slipped my hand into her panties. She was soaking.

One quick rip and the panties were gone. I reached into my wallet and took out a condom, rolling it on as I stared at her for a few moments. Once my head was clear, I lifted her and lowered her onto my cock and pressed her against the door.

"You ready?" I asked.

"Yes," she hissed. "Fuck me hard."

I gave her exactly what she asked for.

The knock on my office door had me looking at my watch. Shit. It was seven.

"Come in."

The door opened, and Cord walked in. "What in the hell are you still doing here this late?"

I shrugged. "I guess if I was being honest with myself, hiding."

He sat down in one of the chairs facing my desk. "From?"

"Hell, I don't know. Everyone."

He nodded. "You want to talk about it?"

I dropped my pen onto the desk and scrubbed my hands down my face while leaning back in my chair.

"Fuck, Cord. I'm twisted up inside. I'm really trying to give this thing with Mallory a go."

"What's keeping you from doing that? Her kid?"

"No, hell no. I love little Laney. She's precious, and I honestly hardly ever see her. Mallory is pretty strict about that. I'll go over to pick them up for dinner or a movie, but I rarely hang out at their house. Mallory says she doesn't want to confuse Laney."

Cord lifted his brows. "Really? I would think Mallory would want you to get to know each other better."

"Yeah, who knows. Maybe it's for the best anyway."

"So, what has you holding back?"

I stared at him. He already knew the answer. The five-foot-two, gorgeous brunette with the sun-kissed skin, and crystal-clear eyes that sparkled like emeralds was the reason I was so fucked up.

"I think you already know."

He smiled. "Harley?"

I pointed to him. "Right, as usual."

Pulling in a deep breath, Cord said, "She is looking damn hot. I heard Todd Schneider has been asking her out."

My brows pulled together. "Steed's old high school buddy?"

He nodded.

"How do you know this?"

"Corina told me."

My jaw dropped. "She told you, but not me?"

Tossing his head back, he let out a roar of laughter. "Dude, why in the hell would she tell you?"

"I don't know. Maybe because she's my best friend, and she knows I dated Harley."

"She also knows, like everyone else in town, that you're now dating Mallory."

"Still, she should have told me."

"Why? Would it have made a difference to what is happening between you and Mallory?"

"To know that Harley is dating? No."

I was getting better at telling myself that lie. Each night I laid in bed and thought about that fucking letter she wrote me. I had torn it up without even reading it. I had regretted it the moment I put it in the shredder.

"She said she had Milo in for a check-up, and Todd was in there with his new puppy. She overheard him asking Harley to dinner."

I swallowed hard. "And Harley said no?"

He gave me a look that said I was pathetic. "Harley said no."

Letting out the breath I hadn't even known I was holding, I leaned back in my chair.

Cord stared at me. "Tripp, are you over her? Are you really able to say you can move on with another woman?"

"If you had asked me that *before* Harley came back I would have said probably. Maybe."

"That shouldn't make a difference, Tripp. What does her being back in town have to do with it?"

I let out a gruff laugh. "For starters, when I see her a flood of memories come rushing back. If Mallory is with me I can't focus because I'm afraid she'll catch me stealing glances at Harley, or she'll ask me if I still have feelings for her."

"Do you?"

"Yes. No. Yes."

With a lift of his brow, Cord gave me an incredulous look. "Which one is it?"

Closing my eyes, I sighed. "Listen, there will always be a part of my heart that belonged to her. That will *always* belong to her. But she made it clear when she told me she'd met someone else that she didn't feel that way about me. So I know there isn't a chance in hell with her."

Cord leaned forward and rested his elbows on my desk. His chin went to his hands, and he shook his head. "Have you ever sat down and talked to her since that day?"

"No."

"All those years she came to the house when she was visiting her parents, looking to talk to you, or asking us to please have you call her. I mean, Tripp, there were times I was ready to see her fall to her knees and beg us to tell her where you were. You never once thought that maybe you should call her back? That y'all needed to talk?"

"Why? She made her choice, and she picked some jerk she met at school who would live happily ever after with her in a goddamn loft apartment in downtown Dallas after they saw the world."

Cord stood. "You're an idiot."

I laughed. "Me? You're the fucking idiot. You haven't even pieced it together yet that Maebh is the owner of the new restaurant…and that it's not a bar. Remember the city council meeting?"

His eyes widened. "You told me it was a pub!"

Standing, I folded my arms over my chest. "Maybe if you hadn't been staring at her tits while she was talking you would have heard that she's opening up an Irish restaurant with a bar. Not the kind of bar you run, you stupid shit."

"You motherfucker. How long have you known it wasn't a bar?"

"A few months," I replied with a smug smile.

"And you let me believe it was a bar. I saw her at the corner store and ignored her! I thought she was the enemy!"

I couldn't help but chuckle. "That's your fault. You're afraid of a little competition."

Cord started for the door. He turned and pointed to me. "I'm not telling you anything else Corina tells me! Ever!"

"Ha! I'm her best friend, asshole. All I have to do is give her a call and get the information myself."

He shot me an evil grin. "Good luck with that."

As he shut the door I closed my eyes and let out a long groan. "Fuck. My. Life."

CHAPTER 2

Harley

The trees swayed back and forth as I stared out the window at the beautiful sunset.

"Harley, sweetie, are you okay?"

My mother's voice pulled my eyes from the reds and pinks that danced across the sky. With a half-hearted smile, I nodded. "I'm fine."

"No, you're not fine. You haven't been fine in years. I thought moving back to Oak Springs and taking over Doc's practice would have made you happy."

"I am happy, Momma."

Her eyes looked at me with pity. I couldn't stand it.

"Then why do you seem so sad? Is it because of Tripp and Mallory?"

Just hearing their names in the same sentence made me feel ill. My stomach knotted each time I saw them, nearly knocking me to my knees.

I was so stupid to let him go. So. Damn. Stupid.

"I don't know what I expected when I came back. All those years of knowing he hadn't settled down with anyone and then I move home hoping for something—anything—and now he's dating someone."

"Are you ever going to tell me why you lied to the boy and told him you met someone?"

My chest ached as the memory of that day rushed back. I'd never spoken about it to anyone, not even to my parents. The day I broke the heart of the only man I had ever loved.

"Come on," she said softly. "I have a couple horses saddled up. Let's go for a ride. The horses always have a way of taking away the pain and heartache for a bit."

I followed my mother through the house and down to the barn. The moment I climbed onto Starlight, I felt the tension start to leave my body. Horses used to be my life. I rode competitively when I was younger with my good friend, Lori. Her family owned some of the most expensive show horses in the county.

We rode in silence for a bit before we came to a ridge that looked out over the hill country. It was my favorite spot on the ranch. The place I went to when I needed to get my thoughts in order.

"Do you want to talk about it?"

"There's nothing wrong, Momma."

She groaned. "You have that stubborn Latino blood flowing in you, Harley, with a head as hard as the land we are gonna ride through."

I chuckled. She was right. I took more after my father in my personality and my looks. My mother had beautiful blonde hair and the most gorgeous blue eyes. My father was Latino. Brown hair and beautiful cognac-colored eyes. My hair was brown, and I had green eyes. Emerald-green eyes. My mother used to tell me they were Rose's eyes. My great-grandmother.

The ranch I had grown up on was my mother's parents' and they, in turn, gave it to her and my father. Daddy was the son of two Mexican immigrants who worked on another ranch here in town not far from this one. My mother always said she would never forget the moment she saw my father for the first time. It was in elementary school. She said he was the most handsome man she'd ever laid eyes on. It was love at first sight.

Just like with me and Tripp.

"You're right on that. I am my father's daughter." Releasing a sigh, I looked out toward the horizon, wondering how in the hell I ended up so lost. Confused. Lonely as hell.

"Talk to me, Harley. *Please.*"

Years of holding in my secret came rushing to the surface, and I instantly started crying. Sliding off my horse, I paced while she stood there, giving me the time I needed to find the words.

I'd always known my parents knew I had lied to Tripp. The last thing I would ever do to him was cheat on him.

"I didn't know what else to do, Momma. He was going to give up everything, and I wasn't about to let that happen. I even heard him telling his daddy he didn't want to leave. He was only going to do it for me!"

She reached for my arms and held me still. "Take a deep breath. Slow down."

I tried to do as she said, but I was ready for the first time in almost ten years to tell someone other than Tripp the truth. I wanted him to be the first, but since he wouldn't even talk to me, I had no choice. I had to tell my mother everything.

"You a bit calmer?" she asked.

Nodding, I took in one last shaky breath and started at the beginning.

"That day it happened, I knew Tripp had been asked to join Dave Hassell's team at the law firm. I'd overheard him telling Tripp's daddy he was going to offer Tripp a summer position and that he would work around any days Tripp would be needed at the ranch. I had planned on asking Tripp if he wanted to move to Dallas with me after vet school. I just didn't want to come back here, Momma. At least, not right away. I love Oak Springs, but I wanted to see things. Travel around the world like Aunt Tanya. Live in a big city for just a bit."

My mother rolled her eyes. "Oh, Harley."

I wiped the snot that was now running from my nose with the back of my hand. My mother snarled.

"I wanted to explore what else was out there besides Oak Springs and College Station, Texas. But I knew Tripp had other dreams. I guess a part of me thought that maybe he might want to do those things, too, once I finally voiced them. At least, I was hoping like hell he would."

Her eyes glassed over with tears.

"But he didn't?" she asked.

Closing my eyes, I dropped my head as the memory of the day hit me full force.

"He started talking about our future. Him opening up a law practice and me going to work for Doc at the vet clinic. I wanted so badly to want that, Momma, but I didn't. At least, I didn't want it right then. When he mentioned starting a family after school, I had to tell him what I wanted."

"Of course. A relationship is based on two people, not just one."

I wiped at my tears. "I know that, and I know he knew that. He just thought I wanted that, too, because I was never open and honest with him. If I had been, from the beginning, maybe things would have been different. Oh, God."

My hands covered my face and I started to cry. My mother put her arm around me and led me closer to the giant oak tree that had fallen over years ago.

"Sit down, sweetie."

Doing as she said, I dropped my hands to my lap.

"What happened after he mentioned kids?"

With a hard swallow, I went on. "I asked him if he would ever want to leave Oak Springs, and of course he said no. Then, I told him I didn't want to live in Oak Springs. It sort of all came out at once. He replied by saying he thought that was what I had wanted, too, and then he brought up how I never said anything about wanting to live in a big city."

I looked at her. "I told him I wanted to live in a big downtown city. In like a loft or something, just for a bit. We could travel and see things."

"What did he say?"

I cried harder.

Pulling me to her side, she rocked us back and forth. "Did he say something hurtful to you and that's why you made up the relationship about the other boy?"

"No! Just the opposite. He said he would move anywhere I wanted because he loved me. For a few moments I was so over-the-moon happy. He was going to let me live out my dream and I'm ashamed to admit I was greedy enough to want him in my life and I was going to let him."

"Oh, Harley."

I reached up and wiped my nose. I hadn't cried this much in years.

"Then what happened? I'm trying to figure this out in my head."

Pulling away from her, I stood. Facing her, I took a deep breath.

"Steed broke his arm and we ended up going to the hospital. His momma needed him…that was my first clue that if I took him from his family, not only would Tripp resent me, but Melanie and John would too. I overheard him telling his father he didn't really want to travel and had doubts about how we would make it." Tears rolled down my cheeks faster. "But he said he would do it. For me. John told him if he didn't talk to me about his feelings, he'd end up regretting his decision."

I dropped back down next to my mother. "I loved him too much to have him give everything up only to have him hate me years later. I made up the other guy because I didn't have the guts to tell him no. I so desperately wanted him to follow me around the world like a puppy dog, living out my dream while he left his behind, that I couldn't tell him no. As a matter of fact, I didn't want to tell him no. At least, not at first."

My tears started again, and by the look on my mother's face, I knew she already knew what had happened from that point on.

"So, instead of telling him that you wouldn't let him give up his dreams, you made up another man."

"At first I told him we should break up. Take some time apart. I didn't know what else to say. I panicked and all the emotions running through my head and heart were confusing. Tripp wasn't about to let that happen. That's when I knew he would follow me, no matter what. Give up everything for my stupid, silly dream. So, I made up the guy I had met at school. And the hurt in his eyes made me want to throw up. But I couldn't take it back. It was too late. And I knew, if I told him no, that I would come back to Oak Springs and we would start our life later, he wouldn't have let me do it. He would have followed me, Mom. He would have left school, moved to College Station and then he would have resented me. I wasn't going to let that happen, so I came up with the other guy theory."

My mother stood. "Harley, you broke that boy's heart! Why didn't you just tell him you overheard his conversation with his father?"

Massaging my forehead, I groaned. "I don't know! I panicked and did the only thing I could think at the time. Every single time I came home to visit I tried to track him down to talk to him. Each time I wanted to tell him the truth. That there was never another guy. That I was stupid for walking away from him that day and that I should have just let fate play its role."

"He won't talk to you still?"

I shook my head. "No. I've called his cell, left messages at work, asked his siblings to have him call me. Nothing. Then, when I came back this last time, and he was dating Mallory, I gave up."

"A Carbajal does not give up." She stood with her hands on her hips. "If you want him to at least know the truth, you force his ass to listen. He's being a stubborn bastard, as well. You two are perfect for each other, both as hard-headed as they come."

I chuckled. "Why, Maddie Carbajal…listen to you swear!"

Shaking her head, she looked me right in the eye, and with as much determination as I've ever seen any one person have, she whispered to me, "Don't give up."

The rush of sadness I'd come to know like a best friend swept over me. With a single tear rolling down my cheek, I replied, "I think I'm too late."

CHAPTER 3

Harley

I stood staring at the cat before looking back at Corina.

"Corina, there's nothing wrong with Milo. I promise you."

She shook her head. "Are you sure? He was limping earlier."

"Yeah, maybe you should check his temperature," Paxton added with a concerned frown.

Smiling, I replied, "I did. It was normal, y'all."

"Mmm…weird," Corina said.

A knock on the door of the exam room drew my attention away from the two of them.

Poking her head in, Julie, my very sweet vet tech, said, "Um, Harley? The Parker sisters are here."

I glanced back to Corina and Paxton before turning back to Julie. She was sharp as a whip when it came to the animals, but she seemed to be lacking common sense today considering two of the Parker sisters were already right here.

"I know, Julie. They're standing in front of me."

She shook her head. "No, the actual *Parker sisters*."

"*Oh*." The last time I had talked to Waylynn she made it clear I wasn't welcome at their place. It had destroyed me. We were once the best of friends. Her, me, and Paxton. Three peas in a pod.

"Are they here with y'all?" I asked.

The look Corina and Paxton exchanged told me these ladies were up to something. It was time to see exactly what.

"Why don't you have them come on back to this room," I told Julie.

"Will do."

Paxton and Corina avoided my stare.

"Thank God you were here today!" Waylynn busted out as she walked into the room and went straight to Milo who was still sitting on the exam table, taking everything in. The poor thing was just as confused as I was. Even he knew there was nothing wrong with him.

"Well, I did have the day off, but Corina called about an emergency with Milo," I said. Waylynn and Corina exchanged smiles. "So, ladies, what brings you by?"

"Milo, of course! When Corina said she was bringing him in for an emergency, we knew we had to rush right over. Thank goodness Jonathon was home to watch Liberty."

I stared at Waylynn. Had she lost her damn mind? My mother had told me about Waylynn's accident last year. She'd swerved to miss a turtle and lost control of her car. My heart broke in two when I found out she wasn't able to have kids…but now I was wondering if she might have hit her head also and was now having residual effects from that.

Clearing my throat, I looked up at the four of them. "From what I can tell, he's perfectly fine."

"Oh, good!" Waylynn exclaimed while clapping her hands. "I was *so* worried."

I gave her a grin. "Is Milo like the Parker family pet?"

Waving her hands all over the place, she laughed. "Oh, hell no. That would be Patches. Chloe's pet goat."

"Yes, I've had the pleasure of meeting Patches."

I glanced at Julie, who wore a shit-eating grin on her face. Yeah, maybe she wasn't lacking common sense today. More like she was in on this so-called *emergency visit*. I was going to have to have a long talk with her.

"Well, Julie here can take Milo and give him a little snack."

"Oh, that would be just perfect and so sweet," Corina said.

I nodded. "Julie, why don't you take Milo and get him settled back into his crate."

She scooped up Milo and grabbed his carrier. "Let's go, Milo. I've got a tuna treat with your name on it."

Spinning on my heels, I walked over to the sink and started washing my hands.

Paxton cleared her throat. "So, Harley, how do you like being back in Oak Springs?"

When I turned and faced the four of them, I couldn't help but smile. They were all hanging on my next set of words.

"I'm beyond happy to be home. I'd have come home a lot sooner, but..." I left my sentence dangling in the air. They already knew the reason why I had waited so long.

"But what?" Waylynn asked. "What kept you away?"

I tilted my head and gave them a hard look. They wanted me to say the words that would rip that wound open even more, yet I knew there was some underlying motive for the four of them being here today. "Do you want the truth? Is that why you ladies are here?"

"Yes, always," Amelia replied.

Expelling an obnoxiously loud sigh, I decided to throw caution to the wind and tell them what they wanted to hear—and what I sort of wanted them to know—with the hopes it would get back to Tripp. If there was one thing I knew about the Parker clan, they were tighter than the ticks I removed off of animals. Anything I said to these ladies would most definitely make its way back to him...

Besides what remained of my dignity, what the hell else did I have to lose?

"Your brother. When he wouldn't talk to me or let me explain, I couldn't bear the thought of living in this town and having him ignore me."

It looked like Waylynn's eye twitched and her jaw clenched. She was holding back from laying into me.

"Tripp? Why?" Corina asked.

I stared down at the floor and let out a laugh before focusing back on them. "Listen, I don't know why y'all are here, but if you want to lay into me about leaving your brother, there is nothing you can say that I haven't already said to myself. You couldn't possibly make me feel any worse than I did the day I walked away from him."

At least Amelia and Waylynn's cold stares melted a bit.

"Tell us why you did it," Paxton said kindly.

"Why?" I scoffed. "What difference does it make? Your brother has moved on and doesn't want to speak to me no matter how many times I've begged him. I even wrote him a letter, hoping he would read it. I'm positive he never did."

Paxton and Waylynn exchanged looks.

"Listen, do y'all want to tell me what's going on here? I know you're up to something so let's just get this over with, okay?"

"Harley, we're not here to lay into you," Paxton said with a sweet smile. "We wanted to talk. Listen, we all used to be close, and I speak for all of us when I say I want to be friends again."

"Well, you and I were never friends because I didn't live here," Corina said while she rubbed her stomach. When I glanced down, my heart physically ached. I longed for a baby so badly. My eyes lifted to hers and I was positive she could see my pain.

"I'd love to get to know you better, Corina. I have a feeling we'd be great friends."

Her smile grew bigger, and I knew I was going to fall in love with her. The kindness dripped off of her.

When I peered over to the other three, my heart dropped. Waylynn and I had been the best of friends. Paxton and I had been a bit closer, though. We did nearly everything together when I wasn't with Tripp.

"I know you all hate me for hurting Tripp. I only did what I thought was right at the time, and I knew the moment after I did it that I'd made the biggest mistake of my life."

Waylynn walked up to me. "I ran into your mom yesterday. She told me you were having a hard time adjusting, and to be honest, I told her it was your karma coming full circle. When she told me I had no idea what really happened that day and that I should speak to you about it, I started putting two and two together. I know how much you loved my brother, Harley. I also know you both had different dreams and that you never told Tripp yours."

I swallowed hard and looked at the floor.

"You lied to him, didn't you? You threw yourself on the sacrificial sword for Tripp's dreams," Waylynn asked in a whispered voice. My head snapped up and my mouth fell slightly open.

She stared into my eyes. "There never was another guy, was there?"

"What?" Amelia gasped from behind Waylynn. "Waylynn, what are you talking about?"

Waylynn continued to look into my eyes. A part of me was relieved that someone had figured it out. I had just always hoped it would be Tripp.

"No. There was never another guy."

The gasps from the women in the room made me turn around and wrap my arms around my body. *Damn it all to hell. The flood gates of tears are threatening to spill over.*

"What in the hell, Harley! Why would you do that to him?" Amelia cried out.

"Wait, don't yell at her. Let her explain first," Paxton added.

They gave me a few moments to gather my wits before I faced them. Leaning against the sink, I took a deep breath.

Here we go again.

"The day I left I found out that Tripp had been offered a job at the law firm here in town during the summer. I had been on my way over to y'all's house to finally be honest with him about my dreams for after we graduated—to tell him I wanted to travel after graduating from vet school. For years Tripp had dreamed about settling down in Oak Springs, opening up his own law firm, one day running for mayor, and I honestly wanted that for him, and for us, too…just not on the same time schedule as he did. My aunt had filled with my head with stories about the world and being the stupid, naïve girl I was, I longed for those adventures."

I pressed my lips tightly together and closed my eyes while taking another deep breath in through my nose.

"I know if I had only been honest with him and told him I wanted to travel before we settled down, things would have been different. At the time, he wanted one thing, and I wanted something else. But I loved him so much I told myself that I would want the same things he wanted and before the time came, our paths would align. I asked him that day if he would ever want to live outside of Oak Springs and he said no. That's when I knew I had to tell him the truth."

"Oh, Harley," Waylynn whispered.

I kept going. "That day I was planning on asking him to come to College Station after law school. Once I graduated I wanted to travel around Europe, Asia, lie on beaches in the Caribbean, anything for a few months, before the responsibilities of adulthood weighed on us. I wanted to live in a big city like Dallas for a bit. When I told him this, I could see the disappointment in his eyes and it nearly killed me. That was the reason I kept my mouth shut all those years. I wanted to avoid hurting him." My eyes stung with the threat of tears. I knew once they started, I wouldn't be able to stop.

"Then he…he told me he would go with me. Wherever I wanted to go he would be there because he loved me."

Tears streamed down my face, the reality of what I'd given up like a punch to the gut, and I heard a few sniffles in the room but I couldn't look at any of them. I was too ashamed of what I was about to say.

"And even though I knew it was wrong and it wasn't what he wanted, I let myself be happy. I was going to let him give up his dream so that I could follow mine. Then he got a phone call from John. Steed had gotten hurt and broke his arm. John told Tripp he needed him to come to the hospital to be with your mom. We went, and I overheard a conversation Tripp had with John. He told him he didn't want to travel and that he worried about how we would afford everything. Your dad mentioned that he'd resent me in the long run."

I forced a smile and took a few seconds before talking again. I had held this in for so long, waiting to explain it all to Tripp, and here I was spilling it all out again. And *not* to Tripp.

"It just sort of hit me. I could never live with myself if I took him away from Oak Springs, away from his own dreams and hopes. I panicked and knew if I told him now that he should stay and I would come back to him, he would follow me. He would give up everything to make me happy. So, I did the only thing I could think of. I lied."

My heavy gaze lifted to see four sets of eyes staring at me. I couldn't read their expressions.

Would they hate me even more now? Probably.

I looked away, the guilt and shame eating at me like it had for so many years.

"Every time I came back into town, I tried to talk to Tripp. I wanted to tell him there never was a guy. I wanted to come back to Oak Springs and start the life we had always dreamed of. At least, I wanted to try if he would forgive me, if he would understand the why of what I did."

"But you couldn't because he always left. The moment he found out you were in town, he would leave," Amelia said softly.

I nodded. "I can't tell you how many times I've called and left him a message. In the beginning I begged him to let me explain. But I don't even know if he ever listened to those messages. As the years went on, the messages kept getting shorter. I asked him to talk to me, he ignored it. I wrote him that letter I mentioned, hoping he'd read it, but I doubt he did."

"All those times you were in town..." Amelia's voice cracked.

Grinning, I added, "A few times I managed to sneak in without him knowing I was there. I went to his office but he refused to see me. He was always in a meeting or Karen would tell me he was out of town. I never got the chance to try. He never gave me the opportunity to explain that I'd always known I'd come back to Oak Springs."

Waylynn walked up to me and took my hands in hers. "That's why you showed up on decorating day. You knew he would be there and you thought he wouldn't make a scene around the rest of us."

A small sob slipped from my mouth, and she pulled me into a hug.

"Oh, Christ. I was so rude to you!"

I cried harder. "I deserved it for hurting him."

The next thing I knew, I was engulfed in a giant hug from all the Parker women.

When they stepped back, Paxton and Amelia were wiping my cheeks.

Paxton gave me a sweet smile. "I did the same thing when it came to Steed. It was easier to forget him than to even talk to his family. I avoided them for years."

"Don't cry," Amelia said.

"He's the only man I've ever loved—he's the only man I'll ever love—and I've lost him."

"Did you not date anyone after Tripp?" Corina asked.

With a half shrug, I replied, "Nothing serious. One guy I dated off and on exclusively for about a year. He wanted something more, but I couldn't give him my full heart. I cared deeply for him, but I didn't love him. Not like I love Tripp."

"Because your whole heart belongs to Tripp," Waylynn declared.

I smiled at her. "Yeah. It does. But I've decided I'm going to stop trying to explain to him what happened that day. He's moved on, and I'm glad he has found someone who makes him happy."

Waylynn laughed. "Oh, my gosh. Harley, if you think Mallory makes him as happy as you did, you are wrong. I think it's more physical. They like having sex. A lot."

Paxton, Amelia, and Corina all looked at Waylynn. "Waylynn!"

Laughing, I grabbed a tissue and blew my nose.

"It's okay, y'all. I'm not naïve. I know they're sleeping together. I need to move on. It's just…hard…ya know?" I forced the tears back down.

"We're going out tonight," Amelia declared.

Waylynn held up her hands. "Well, hold on. Some of us have kids we have to deal with."

"Oh, speaking of, Waylynn, congratulations on the baby," I replied, a little bit of melancholy in my voice that I tried to tamp down.

She gave me a breathtaking smile. "Thanks, Harley. She's an absolute joy."

Amelia went on. "We can make this happen! I'm sure Steed and Jonathon wouldn't mind if we hit Cord's Place for a couple of hours. We need to get Harley back in the game of dating. If Tripp can do it, so can Harley."

The other three looked at her, unsure that this was such a good idea.

I snarled. "Date the guys here in town?"

"Hey, we've had a few hot ones move in. You should see the new fire chief. He's smokin' hot!" Waylynn said with a laugh. "See what I did there?"

We all chuckled. It felt good to have my friends back, and to make a new one. A little bit of weight lifted off my chest.

"Yes, I see what you did there," I replied with a chuckle as I wiped at my still-damp eyes.

"Okay, it's settled," Amelia announced while clapping her hands. "Y'all get your kiddos taken care of and then let's meet at Harley's place at seven. Early night for all of us."

I chewed on my lip. "I don't know."

Taking my hand in hers, Corina smiled. "Tripp won't be there. He and Mallory are never there. The bar scene isn't Mallory's thing. You won't even see him, I promise!"

"But the hot fire chief will be there for sure," Waylynn said with an evil laugh.

"How do you know that?" I asked.

She merely winked. "Trust me."

I had a feeling I was going to have a terrible night, or the best night I'd had in a long, long time.

As they all started piling out of the exam room, Corina looked back over her shoulder. She was the last one out of the group I thought would ever utter the words she said next. "Wear something sexy! And make it red. With your hair and tan skin, it will make your boobs and A-S-S pop!"

My mouth dropped as my eyes widened.

As if two Parker women were not enough in this town…now there were two more.

"Good Lord, be with me tonight. I have a feeling I'm going to need you to take the wheel."

CHAPTER 4

Tripp

"Well, look what the cat dragged in," Trevor mused while pushing a beer my way.

With an eye roll, I sat on the barstool. "Yeah, it's been awhile."

"You get in a fight with Mallory?" he asked, a hint of a smile playing at his lips.

"That's an understatement," I scoffed.

About that time Cord walked up. "What's up, big brother? Mallory get a babysitter for the night?"

I had to laugh. Mallory hated coming to Cord's Place. She didn't like to dance, and she didn't like to go out to bars, period. About the only things she liked to do were fuck and shop. The first one I enjoyed, the second not so much.

"No, we sort of got in a fight."

He lifted his brows. "About?"

"Her lack of ever wanting to do anything. All she wants to do is sit home and watch movies. She uses Laney for an excuse and I'm growing tired of it. Then, there is the on-call fucking. When she's in the mood I'm supposed to drop everything."

Trevor shot me a look like I was insane. "I wouldn't be complaining about the fucking." He glanced to his side and winked at two young girls who were now sitting next to me at the bar. Tourists, for sure. It was spring break; I hated this time of year. March had never been one of my favorite months for that reason alone.

"Speaking of," Trevor mumbled as he took a step over and started up a conversation with them.

Cord let out chuckle as he watched Trevor flirt with the two girls. I wouldn't be surprised if my brothers ended up hooking up with one…or both.

"So, do y'all argue a lot?" Cord asked, focusing back on me.

"I wouldn't say a lot, but probably more than we should."

"That's not a good sign. You figured anything out more about how you feel about her?"

"I don't know. I mean, I like Mallory. She's the first woman to make me actually want to give it a shot."

"There is a 'but' in there somewhere."

"Yeah, there's a *but* and I have no fucking clue what it is."

He studied me carefully. "I think I know and you just don't want to admit it. Your 'but' is Harley. Hell, maybe you are thinking of Harley's 'butt' and that's the problem." That caused him to laugh at his own wit, until we heard Trevor speak up.

"Holy shit."

Cord and I looked over to Trevor. He was staring at the front door. I swung around and saw our two sisters, Paxton, Corina, and…

"Holy shit."

"Dude, your ex is looking mighty fine tonight."

Spinning back at Trevor, I shot him a dirty look. "You stay the fuck away from her, Trevor."

He laughed. "Like I'd ever do that. Seriously. I'm not that much of a douche. But looking ain't the same as touching."

I seethed inside as they all walked in. "What in the hell is Harley doing with them? Those traitors!" I muttered.

Cord was now on the other side of the bar standing next to me. "Obviously they know something you don't. Harley and Waylynn seem to be pretty chummy. Didn't you say Waylynn gave Harley the cold shoulder the day she came over to the house around Christmas time?"

"Yes!" I exclaimed. "She practically shut the door in her face. Now they're acting like best friends again."

I couldn't pull my eyes off of Harley. She was wearing cut-off jean shorts, cowboy boots, and a red shirt that looked too damn small. I could see the hint of her toned stomach. My dick instantly got hard and dirty thoughts ran rampant through my mind.

"And now our sister is introducing Harley to the new fire chief, Toby Warner."

"What in the hell?" I mumbled as I watched this Toby asshole shake my girl's hand and look at her like he wanted to fuck her in front of everyone in my brother's bar.

"Hate to say it, dude, but she ain't your girl anymore."

My head jerked back to look at Cord. "What? Did I say that aloud?"

"You just said he was shaking your girl's hand. She's not your girl...unless you want her to be?"

Pinching my brows together, I stared at my brother. The idea that I could walk up and claim Harley was insane. One, she wasn't the type of woman any man could claim, and two, I was still pissed at her. Plus, there was Mallory. Damn, my brain was all over the map tonight. I came in because I was pissed at Mallory, and brooding over Harley, and in walks Harley, my very own kryptonite looking sexy as fuck.

I glanced back to where Harley was standing, still talking to Toby. The rest of the girls had somehow managed to get a table and were sitting down. If I had to guess, I would say Waylynn pulled the

'Corina is pregnant and can't stand' stunt to make a group of guys give up their seats.

Cord slapped me on the back. "Don't worry, Tripp. He's not Harley's type."

My jaw dropped as I watched Toby lead Harley out to the dance floor, his hand dangerously low on her back with most of his hand on her skin and only a small amount on her shorts. It took everything in my power not to go all caveman, beating my chest and screaming at him, "Get your fucking hands off of her, she's MINE!"

Fucker.

Cord let out a rumbled laugh that I barely heard over the music. "Or…maybe he is."

Standing, I leaned in so he could hear. "Time for me to find out what our sisters are up to."

"Good luck with that. You know they are always ten steps ahead!" he called out.

I made my way over to the table and when all four of them looked up, their smiles vanished. Clearly they weren't expecting me to be here tonight.

Waylynn jumped up. "Tripp! What are you doing here?"

With a half shrug, I replied, "Thought I'd stop by and get a beer."

Waylynn looked behind me. "Where's…um…Mallory?"

The way she chewed on her lip told me that Harley wasn't expecting me to be here either.

"We had a fight."

Waylynn's eyes lit up. "You did?" she practically screamed.

"You seem pretty happy about that, Waylynn. Why's that?"

An awkward laugh slipped from her lips before she turned to the rest of the Parker clan. "He got in a fight with Mallory!" she yelled.

The three of them tried—and failed—to hide their smiles.

"Was it serious?" Amelia called out.

I shook my head. The look of disappointment on her face was another clue these girls were up to something.

"Why are you here with Harley?" I shouted.

Waylynn opened her mouth and then clamped it shut again.

"Are we not allowed to be friends with her? We're just a couple of ladies wanting a night out to blow off some steam," Paxton yelled out.

Fuck, the music was loud.

"Y'all can be friends with whomever you want to be friends with," I replied with a smile. I made the mistake of looking out onto the dance floor. Clenching my jaw, I tried like hell to keep my shit together. That asshole was holding Harley close as they danced to a slow song.

"Listen, we told Harley you wouldn't be here because you and Mallory are the stay-at-home-type of couple," Waylynn said as I glared at her. "So, if you could just…you know…leave before she sees you and resume your stay-at-homeness so you don't ruin her night."

There was no doubt my mouth was hanging open. "So, now you're championing Harley?"

Waylynn lifted her shoulders. "Listen, I actually took the time to listen to what she's been trying to say to you for the last however-many-years. So, yeah, I'm hoping she can finally find happiness…like you have."

I took a step back and looked at all four of them. "You talked to her about *what*?"

Paxton shook her head. "That's her story to tell. If she even still wants to. She seems to have given up, especially with you being with Mallory and all."

"Yeah, she said now she knows you're happy with Mallory she's decided to leave you alone. Move on."

My stomach felt sick. *What in the fuck? Move on?*

"So, that's it? She's moving on with Toby?" I barked out.

Waylynn narrowed her left eye at me like she did when she was fixin' to get mad. "Tripp, the woman has been trying to talk to you for years and you've avoided her like she's got the plague. Now she is moving on like you did and you're pissed?"

"You're the one who told me to date, Waylynn!"

"I didn't tell you to ignore Harley all those years. I said maybe dating other women would help. You're the one who got into a serious relationship with Mallory."

I threw my hands in the air. "I give the fuck up. You want me gone so she can enjoy her night, fine. I'm gone."

I did the only thing I knew to do. I turned and headed straight to Cord. I knew he had security cameras in his office. I was the one who'd told him to install them so he could see if there were any shenanigans with patrons. If they didn't want Harley to see me, fine, but there was no way I was going to leave with that asshole hanging all over her after one damn dance.

"Hey, can I go sit in your office for a bit? It appears our sisters don't want me around to ruin Harley's night out."

Cord raised his brows. "Wow. You gonna watch her on the cameras...like a stalker?"

"Hell yes, I am."

He laughed and motioned for me to head to his office. I had keys to the bar and his office so I started in that direction, careful to go around the dance floor so Harley didn't see me.

After I pushed my way through the crowd, I pulled my keys out and opened Cord's office door. Shutting it, I locked the door and made my way to the wall of TVs that displayed every angle of the club. It didn't take me long to find her. She was now back at the table and holding a beer, talking to the traitors I called sisters. Toby was nowhere to be found.

Good. Maybe the asshole left.

I leaned my head back and closed my eyes, a deep breath escaping from my lungs.

Harley was back in town and I still couldn't wrap my head around having these feelings for her. Feelings that were all over the damn place…anger, lust, frustration, desire, resentment, possessiveness, and countless others that had my mind so muddied that I couldn't think straight.

She was moving on, and I couldn't blame her. She had slowed down on the calls to my cell phone and hadn't called my work since she'd moved back for good. My mind drifted back over the past years to all the voicemails. The one where she had said she hadn't been honest nagged at me the most. The unread letter she'd sent to me that I'd destroyed simply because my pride couldn't take another beating. A large part of me wanted to know what she meant, what she wanted to tell me, but the other part—the one that could still see her running away—didn't care. I was hurt and pissed. The only woman I had ever truly loved had walked away from me and I didn't think I would ever be able to forgive her. No matter how much seeing her caused my body to ache in both pain and desire.

Leaning my head back, I closed my eyes and was quickly lost in a dream.

The door to Cord's office burst open, causing me to jump out of the chair. Spinning around, I stared at Harley standing in the doorway.

"Harley?"

"Tripp," she purred, making her way over to the front of my chair.

My eyes roamed over her perfect body.

"I'm sorry. I didn't know you were in here."

I opened my mouth to speak, but nothing came out.

Harley's eyes wandered down my body and stopped on the bulge protruding in my pants. Her tongue quickly darted out and ran over those plump lips of hers.

"Come here," I whispered.

Her eyes turned dark, and for a moment, she seemed unsure.

"Harley, I want you."

A smile slid over her face. "Finally," she gasped. She quickly walked up to me, and I grabbed her hips, pulled her to me, causing her to straddle me in the chair.

My face leaned in as I placed a kiss on exposed neck. Her warmth pushed into me, causing my cock to swell even more.

"I've missed you so goddamn much."

Her hands rested on my shoulders, emerald eyes staring into my blue.

"Make love to me, Tripp. Please."

My body jerked, and my eyes snapped opened. I was still in Cord's office. Alone. And with a major fucking hard-on.

"Shit," I whispered. I'd fallen asleep and got lost in a dream. About Harley.

After dragging my hands up and down my face to wake myself up, I scanned the TVs again. The girls were all sitting at the same table, but Harley was missing. Maybe she'd left.

I could only hope.

Less than a minute later I found her. Sitting up, I swallowed hard as I watched her dancing with that asshole Toby.

I'd forgotten how fucking sexy she was when she danced...and she was almost dirty dancing with that dick. I could barely hear the music coming from inside the bar. I stormed out and started to make my way back to the bar after locking up Cord's office.

Fuck this bullshit. If she wanted to move on then she would have to get used to seeing me. I was no longer running.

The song "Buttons" was playing as I made my way through the crowd. This time I didn't give a shit if she saw me or not. As I worked my way through I saw her. That fucker had his hands all over her...

She didn't see me, too busy grinding on the fireman, so I made my way to the bar.

"Give me a whiskey," I yelled to Cord.

Without a word, he poured me two shots and walked away. After downing both, I scanned the dance floor again, hoping like hell my being here made Harley just as uncomfortable as I was watching her dance with that son-of-a-bitch. The dance floor was lowered a bit so from the bar and you could see practically the whole floor. It didn't take long for our eyes to meet. Harley's smile faltered for a second before she turned away. Leaning in, she said something to Toby. He laughed and nodded as he grabbed her hand. I watched as they walked toward the exit.

"What in the hell is she doing?" I almost screamed to anyone who would listen. I jumped up and made my way to them.

"Tripp! Don't!" Waylynn called out from behind me, grabbing my arm.

"Let go of me, Waylynn."

She gripped me harder. "You have a girlfriend and it's not Harley. You go after her now, and she's going to be pissed."

"She's fucking leaving with him!"

Waylynn shook her head. "No, she isn't. They're going out for air. She sent me a text. She's not leaving with him."

"Fuck that! She's outside with him, Waylynn. Anything could happen."

She laughed and shook her head. "Listen to yourself. Tripp, you can't have it both ways. You've made your feelings clear with your silence toward her."

I pushed my hand through my hair before shooting daggers at my older sister. "This is your fault, Waylynn!"

Taking a step back, she shot me a dirty look. "Come again, Parker?"

"You told me to date!"

"*Again*, I know that the XY chromosomes you have prevent you from differentiating reality from fantasy, so let me remind you, I told you to try to get over Harley by dating other women. I didn't tell you to ignore her, Tripp. That's all on you. So the next time you're fucking your new girlfriend, remember it was you who decided to stay in that relationship and push Harley away by not responding to her. I had *nothing* to do with that. The least you could do is let Harley talk to you. You're the asshole who has to own up to that. Not me."

Waylynn pushed me in the chest and stormed away. I let out a frustrated groan before heading to the exit.

I walked straight out and didn't bother looking around. The last thing I wanted to see was Harley making out with that dick. I jumped in my truck and started it up. With a frustrated growl, I hit the steering wheel over and over before resting my forehead on it.

"Why are women so damn confusing!" I yelled.

First, Waylynn tells me to be careful with Harley. Go date, have fun, make her see you've moved on. Then she's mad because I did the very thing she told me to do. There was only one person who understood the Parker women.

My father. I needed his sage input on how to navigate these treacherous waters. I made a mental note to reach out to him and schedule lunch. If I ever needed advice, it was now.

CHAPTER 5

Tripp

I stared at my computer trying to concentrate. It had been a few weeks since I'd seen Harley at Cord's Place dancing with that jerk. Karen informed me this morning that she saw Toby join Harley for breakfast at Lilly's place. I'd stopped going on Fridays because Harley ate there. The vet clinic didn't open until later that day so she made it a habit to stop into the café.

The phone on my desk buzzed. Glancing down, I saw that it was Mallory. Things hadn't been the same with us since the night we got into a fight nearly three weeks ago. I was distant, and she could tell. I had hardly even touched her since the last time we fucked in the bathroom at Cord's. It didn't feel right. Not when I was so conflicted with my feelings for Harley.

Reaching down, I slid my finger across the screen to answer it.

"Hello?"

"Hey there. I was wondering if you might like to have lunch today. I'm closing the shop for a couple of hours, and I can come meet you at your office."

I chewed on my lip, trying to think of a reason I couldn't, but a small part of me wanted to just bury myself in Mallory and not think about what Harley was doing with Toby.

"Having a bad day?"

She chuckled. "After the morning I had, yes. A very bad day. I wouldn't mind spending some time with you. I feel like we're drifting apart."

"I'll let Karen know you'll be stopping by."

I'm such a fucking asshole.

Anytime Mallory stopped by for lunch, that meant Karen was free to have an extra-long lunch break. One that she took full advantage of. She wasn't stupid; she knew what in the hell we were doing.

"Perfect. I'll stop by around eleven forty-five."

With a quick peek at my watch, I replied, "Great. I need to finish looking over this contract for a client of mine and then I'm free."

"Wonderful! See you then, handsome!"

A lump formed in my throat. I was about to tell her I just noticed I had a meeting, but instead I replied, "See you then."

I hit End, a part of me wishing I had called my father this morning and set up that lunch date.

Damn it. I can't put this shit off any longer.

Hitting the red button on my desk phone, Karen came on the other line.

"Yes, Mr. Parker?"

"Karen, Mallory is going to be stopping by at eleven forty-five for lunch here in the office. Feel free to take a long break today."

"Okay, shall I just send her straight in when she arrives?"

"Yes, please."

"Will do."

The phone clicked and went silent.

Leaning back in my chair, I blew out a long breath before reaching for my phone and pulling up my father's number. It only rang three times before he picked it up.

"Tripp, what's going on?"

I couldn't help but smile when I heard his voice.

"Not much. Is now a good time to talk?"

"Of course, it is."

I heard him muffle the phone and excuse himself.

"Dad, if you're in a meeting or something, we can talk later."

"Nonsense. You kids always come first."

My smile grew bigger. That's how my folks were. Always putting us kids first, no matter what.

"Are you free for lunch tomorrow?" I asked.

He paused for a few seconds, probably going over his schedule.

"I believe the only thing I have tomorrow is a meeting with Steed, Trevor, Mitchell, and Wade to talk about the spring fling."

The spring fling was my father's way of saying branding. It was when the ranch branded, vaccinated, castrated, and if need be, dehorned the calves. Branding was still a big thing in these parts, an excuse to have everyone over for a party. That was the whole reason my folks called it a fling. There would be enough food to feed an army. Luckily, though, it wasn't how it used to be when I was younger, when we had to rope the calves and have a whole team helping out. A good crew would consist of at least twenty. You had to rope 'em, wrestle them to the ground, brand, vaccinate, castrate, and dehorn. It was a hell of a lot of work. Now it only took a few people to herd them into the chute and take care of it all at once.

"Y'all still moving over to the tag system?"

"Yeah, Mitchell's got some fancy-ass program that will track it all. Probably even tell ya when the damn thing shits."

I laughed. I was glad to see Mitchell was settling right into the ranch. He was meant to be there and we all knew it. He'd gone off to be a cop as a way of separating himself from Steed, even though they were two completely different people. But somehow he'd found his way back to the ranch, and my father and brothers couldn't be more thrilled.

"How about I come out there? Sit in and listen in on the meeting. Wouldn't hurt to be kept up to date with things. Then afterwards we could talk a bit. I need some advice and you are the only one who can help me."

"I think that sounds like a plan. We're meeting in Steed's office at ten and can go for lunch afterwards to talk."

"I'll be there."

"Sounds good, son. Talk then."

"Okay, Dad. See ya tomorrow."

Hitting End, I set my phone down and got back to work. Talking to my father about the ranch must have been what I needed. I was soon lost in the contract. When my work phone buzzed, I glanced up to see it was nearly time for Mallory to arrive.

"Mr. Parker?"

"Yes, Karen?"

"There's, um, someone here to see you."

"Do they have an appointment?"

"No, she doesn't."

I smiled.

"Is it Mallory?"

There was a slight pause. "It's not Mallory. It's Harley Carbajal."

Sitting back in my chair, I then cursed under my breath. My heart started to race, and my hands shook.

What in the fuck is wrong with me? So what if Harley is here. Maybe it's time I just got this shit over with.

I stood up and made my way to the lobby.

When I walked out and saw her, I almost stopped breathing. She was beautiful, even dressed in scrubs covered in cat and dog fur. Her hair was pulled into a ponytail, and she looked…panicked.

"Harley, is there something I can help you with?"

She looked nervously at Karen and then back to me. I could see the worry—or maybe it was fear—in her eyes. "I know you don't want to talk to me, but I need your help, and it's sort of an emergency."

My stomach lurched when she said I didn't want to talk to her. I'd been a dick the last few weeks. Hell…the last few years. Shit. It had been nearly ten years. Glancing at my watch, I knew Mallory would be walking through the door any minute for our lunch date.

When I focused back on Harley, our eyes met. It killed me to see the way she was looking at me. Pleading with me to give her five minutes for an emergency.

"I'm meeting someone for lunch. I have about five minutes. Why don't we head into my office."

I could feel Karen's stare as I let Harley walk by. When I looked at her, Karen lifted a brow and crossed her arms.

Pointing to her, I muttered, "Stop giving me that look."

"What look? The one that says you're taking your ex-girlfriend into your office when your current girlfriend will be here any moment for *lunch*?"

"Hush!" I whispered as I followed Harley into my office and shut the door. Karen shook her head from side to side. I couldn't stop this freight train that was approaching. It wasn't like I could kick Harley out of my office. I was running for mayor, she was a constituent, and I had to talk to all of my constituents, right?

Stealing a breath before I went through the door, I realized this was the first time in almost ten years we had been alone together. A part of me wanted to run away, but the part that wanted to know what the emergency was—and also how Harley had won over Waylynn—was taking the lead.

"What's going on?" I asked.

She stood there wringing her hands, staring at the floor. My chest clenched. Something was wrong. I knew Harley, and she wasn't the type of woman who got scared easily.

"Harley? What's going on? What's so important that you needed to see me?"

When she started pacing, I grew more worried. I had the urge to help her, but I was now worried Mallory would be showing up any second.

"Harley! I don't have all day, for Christ's sake. What's the emergency?"

Stopping in front of me, she took a shaky breath and blew it out.

"I think he's found me."

My eyes widened. "He's found you? What, do you have a stalker or something?"

She closed her eyes and shook her head.

"Sorry, that came out all wrong. It's Doc Harris's brother. He's..."

In that moment, the door to my office opened. Harley paused, not wanting to finish her sentence as Mallory stepped in. From the angle she was standing, and with the door wide open, Harley was blocked from Mallory's view. She was wearing a long jacket and the moment I looked at her, she undid the belt and let it fall open.

"Ready for our lunch date, Mr. Parker?"

"Um..." I said as my eyes swept across her body. She was wearing heels, black barely there panties, and a matching bra. I could see her nipples through the thin lace fabric. Any normal man would have had a hard-on if his girlfriend showed up dressed like this, but not me. Nope. I stood there with a limp fucking dick because of the brunette standing a few feet from me.

Before I had a chance to stop her, Mallory shut the door and shrugged the coat off. I quickly walked up to her and picked up the coat, draping it back over her.

"What's wrong?" she asked. It didn't take her long to catch Harley out of the corner of her eye.

When I turned to her, Harley had her mouth open and the look in her eyes screamed something along the lines of sadness, regret…and pain.

"I'm so sorry. I shouldn't have stopped by without an appointment. I'll, um…I'll check with a lawyer in Uvalde. Sorry to have bugged you, Tripp."

When she rushed by Mallory, Harley gave her a warm smile and whispered, "I'm so sorry."

Mallory opened her mouth to speak, but nothing came out, and honestly, Harley didn't wait long enough; she was out the door so fast.

Mallory shook her head. "Well…that was awkward. Karen told me to come on back. I'm so sorry, Tripp. I would *never* have done that had I known you were with someone."

I clenched my jaw together. I was going to have to have a little talk with Karen after lunch.

"It's okay. She didn't have an appointment and she looked pretty upset. I was just trying to figure out what was going on. It's, ah, it's fine. If she needs to talk to me she can make an appointment like everyone else."

Tilting her head, Mallory stared at me for a few seconds.

"You sure you're okay?"

I nodded. The need to get the encounter with Harley out of my mind, I pointed to her. "I'll be better when you take that jacket off."

Jesus, the levels I'll stoop to.

With a sexy grin, she did just that, letting it fall to the floor.

"Is Karen gone?" I asked.

"She got up and grabbed her purse as I walked in."

I brushed my thumb over her nipples causing her to let out a little moan. "Had a bad morning, huh?"

With a frown, she nodded. "Very bad. I feel like being naughty."

Mallory reached down and rubbed her hand across my dress pants. My cock had finally woken up and was ready to come out and play.

"I can do naughty really well," I promised.

Her tongue ran across her lips. "*Very* naughty."

She squeezed my dick, and I let out a groan. Gripping her hips, I pulled her to me and pressed my mouth to hers.

"I want you from behind," I whispered against her lips.

"Then take me from behind."

Spinning her around, I pressed her to my desk.

"Hands on the desk and don't move. I'm going to fuck you fast and hard."

Mallory peeked at me from over her shoulder and flashed me another sexy grin as I rolled the condom on.

I knew why I wanted her from behind.

Fucking asshole. That's exactly what I was.

Mallory didn't deserve this but my mind rationalized that she wanted me for sex as much as I wanted her as a distraction. It didn't take me long to get lost in our fucking. The sounds of Mallory's little whimpers and moans mixed with my balls slapping against her had me coming right along with her.

Slowly pulling out, I leaned over her and kissed her back. "Let me go get this off, and I'll bring you back a wash cloth."

The nice thing about having my office in an old historical house, I had a private bathroom.

"I'm okay. I need to get back to the shop. I thought I could take longer, but I'm meeting with a supplier."

Standing there staring at her, I frowned as she put her jacket back on. "So, that's it? A quick fuck and then back to work?"

She shrugged. "Isn't that what our little lunch dates always are? I was worked up from a bad morning. I needed a release."

In that moment it hit me: when we hooked up at lunch it was because she was stressed and needed a quick release—or because I was. My office or her back storage room at the store. There was nothing romantic about any of it. Was there anything romantic at all about our relationship? Was there any substance outside of the bedroom...or my office, the storage room...the other odd places we ended up fucking?

Nothing. At. All. It was purely sex. And lately, it was hardly even that. This was the first time I'd fucked her in almost three weeks.

"Tripp? Are you okay? You seem a bit lost."

I was standing in the middle of my office, my dick hanging out of my pants with a condom on it. To say I was lost in thought was an understatement.

"No, sorry, I'm good. Are we still on for dinner tonight?"

She made a face and scrunched her nose. "I thought I told you I had to take this supplier out to dinner. He's flown in from Dallas to meet with me. Their company doesn't sell to very many boutiques so if I land this it would be amazing."

"A guy, huh?"

Mallory walked over to me. Smiling, she reached up on her toes. "You have nothing to worry about. Now go take off that condom and toss it before you fill your office with the scent of sex."

I laughed. "The scent of sex?"

"Yes!" she said, hitting me playfully on the chest. "I swear when we have sex in the stock room I can still smell our sex hours after you leave."

Snarling, I added, "Hell, I hope Karen can't smell our...sex."

She chuckled again. "I've got to run. I'll call you tonight once I get back home. Lucy is babysitting so I won't be out too late."

Spinning around, Mallory headed for my office door. "Talk to you later!"

"Yeah, I'll see you later," I called out as she walked through the door and shut it.

I made my way into the bathroom and discarded the condom as I began to clean myself off. Leaning my hands against the sink, I stared at my reflection and spoke to him like he was a long-lost friend.

"You're an asshole. You just fucked your girlfriend to forget about your ex-girlfriend. How did that work out for you, dick?"

After splashing water onto my face, I made my way back into my office when something caught my eye. It was a single key on a little key ring. The moment I bent down and picked it up I knew whom it belonged to.

I thought for a few moments before making the decision to head over to the vet clinic. No sense in making Harley drive all the way back over here, plus I'd be able to find out what in the world she was talking about earlier.

Writing a note to let Karen know I would be gone the rest of the afternoon, I placed it on her desk and locked up the office. The entire time I drove to the vet clinic I kept trying to talk myself into turning around. All I really had to do was call her and tell her she dropped the key. Maybe I was tired of running from her. If she was going to be living in Oak Springs, we needed to make peace.

By the time I pulled up and parked behind Harley's SUV, I had successfully talked myself into dropping the key off with the front desk and leaving. I wasn't ready to face Harley after just having had sex with Mallory.

What a douche I am.

Unfortunately, there were no other cars around but Harley's.

Shit.

I pushed the truck door open and slid out. Glancing around, I smiled at the small touches Harley had already made to Doc Harris's place. I guess it was her place now.

My feet felt like lead as I made my way up the steps of the porch. I reached for the doorknob and turned. As I walked in, I could hear Harley talking to someone. Remembering where Doc's office was, I headed that way.

"I know you told him to leave me alone, but he came by the clinic today. He said he was going to take it from me. I panicked and went and saw Tripp but he was…well, he was busy. I need to look into getting a lawyer. I don't think he is going to walk away from this like you thought he would. Doc, we're missing something if he is making this claim."

Frowning, I stepped into her office. She was standing with her back to me, looking out the window. Doc Harris had opened his practice on a couple of acres right outside of town. It was perfect because it had room for larger animals, as well as small ones.

"I'll go to San Antonio on Monday to try and find a lawyer. I know, Doc, I know it would be easier to have him help me, but that's not going to work. I'll go to San Antonio on Monday."

My heart started beating faster. Harley was in trouble. And there was no way I was going to let her find another lawyer, no matter what this was about. Not when she came to me first.

Clenching my fists together tightly, I prepared to jump off the ledge, right into the fire.

Hell, I was fixin' to jump into the abyss.

"No, you won't. You already have a lawyer."

Harley spun around and stared at me with a stunned expression. She tried to hide it, but I saw the corners of her mouth lift before she looked away from me.

"Doc, let me call you right back."

She hung up and focused on me. I smiled wide, expecting her to return it. But this was Harley. And even though she'd been initially happy to see me, she was now far from pleased.

In fact, she was downright pissed.

CHAPTER 6

Harley

The sound of his voice made me jump. When I spun around and saw Tripp standing there, for one brief moment, I was happy. He came to me. Finally.

Then I remembered what I'd just walked away from in his office, and I turned from him. A sickness rolled through my stomach.

"Doc, let me call you right back."

"Okay, Harley."

When I'd placed my phone on my desk I stared at him. He had the nerve to smile that damn smile of his. The one that normally would have my knees shaking and my stomach dropping. His dimple on the left cheek that you rarely saw unless he was giving you a genuine smile, yep, there it was. There he was…in all his handsome glory. After years of begging him to talk to me, now he shows up and thinks he's going to be my knight in shining armor. Well, fuck that.

My knees were far from shaking. Right now, his smile made me feel more pain than anything. He'd given *her* that smile when she walked into his office. Dressed like an on-call whore, with Tripp's dimples on full display not that long ago. When I realized I had dropped my key in Tripp's office, I went back in.

As I walked down the hall I heard Mallory moaning as she called out Tripp's name. They were screwing in his office. It wasn't like I didn't know they were having sex...but to actually *hear* it nearly destroyed me.

Now he wanted to help? He couldn't wait for me to leave so he could have his little *lunch* date. Well, no, thank you, Mr. Parker. I don't want your help.

"What do you want?" I bit out.

His smile faded. "Well, first off, I'm here to finish the conversation you started when you barged into my office earlier."

My hands went to my hips. "Oh, you mean when I interrupted your lunch fuck date."

His brows pulled together.

"Excuse me? I was having lunch with my, um, girlfriend."

Ouch. That hurt more than I thought it would.

Rolling my eyes, I pushed out a frustrated breath of air as I dropped into my chair.

"Well, if fucking your girlfriend in your office is your version of lunch, then lucky her." I looked away quickly. I hadn't meant to say that last part.

"I wasn't fu—"

"Save it, Tripp. I realized I'd dropped my key and came back to your office to get it. I heard you both going at it like rabbits. So, please, I'm not really in the mood for this."

His eyes filled with what looked like regret. "I'm...I'm sorry about that."

Forcing a smile, I shrugged. "Why? Like you said, it's your *girlfriend*. Not really something I expected from someone who is running for mayor, but then again, I guess I don't really know you all that well anymore."

I couldn't help but notice how he cringed a little when I said that. Interesting.

I wonder how many more times I can get the word girlfriend *into this conversation.*

Tripp broke eye contact and walked to the window. He was totally lost in thought. I didn't have time to deal with his issues. I had bigger problems of my own.

"Did you come to bring me back my key?"

He nodded and turned to face me. "Yeah. Here ya go."

After he dropped it on my desk, I expected him to turn and leave. He had avoided me for so many years, I couldn't believe one lost key would bring him around. It was almost laughable. I would probably have laughed if I didn't want to cry so desperately.

I opened the file on my desk and started to read it.

"Why did you come to my office earlier?"

Lifting my gaze, our eyes met. He had aged into an even more handsome man. His dark hair, unshaven face, and finely sculpted body were enough to make my stomach pool with warmth. When my eyes went back to his hair, the feeling vanished. He had that just-fucked hair. Her hands had probably been pulling at it as he screwed her. I quickly dropped my head.

Damn it. He still has such a strong effect on my body. Both bad and good.

"It doesn't matter anymore. It was a mistake and I should have known better."

He sat down in the chair that faced my desk.

Shit.

"What does that mean?"

Staring at him, the anger grew quickly. I wanted to tell him what an asshole he was. How much I hated hearing him having sex with Mallory. How it had killed another part of my heart. How I wished it was me having sex with him behind that door. I wanted to say it all now that I had a captive audience.

So. I did. In Spanish. I blurted out how much it had hurt to hear him with his girlfriend. And how I didn't think my heart could possibly hurt anymore, but walking back into his office had nearly destroyed me. How I wanted to scream his name out as he made me come over and over again. Damn him.

He sat there, watching me as I yelled in a language he didn't know. A few times his body jerked, as if he knew the words I was screaming out to him. For a brief moment I pondered if he might have learned Spanish. My voice raised a few times…catching him off guard. When I had mentioned him making me come, I thought his eyes turned dark. But I knew I was only dreaming it.

I finished and dropped my face into my hands. I was emotionally exhausted.

With a knowing look, he simply said, "Please, Harley. I want to help you."

I scoffed. I felt like I was defeated in more ways than one. "Tripp, please. You've avoided me for years, no matter how many times I begged you to talk to me. Why I thought you would help me with a legal problem is beyond me. I panicked and you were the first person I thought to go to."

He smiled.

Ugh. He actually had the nerve to smile.

"That's because I'm the best lawyer in Oak Springs."

Sitting back in my chair, I lifted a brow in contempt. "You're the *only* lawyer in Oak Springs, Tripp. Sort of like me saying I'm the best vet in Oak Springs. It's an esteemed honor, to say the least."

His head tossed back as he let out sexy-as-hell laugh.

"I wish that were true, Harley. There are three other lawyers in town."

Well…that was an interesting bit of information.

"That's good to know," I said. Crossing my arms over my chest, I watched as his gaze fell to my chest, then rose back up to my eyes. "I'll be sure to look them up and reach out to them."

The small chuckle that came out of his mouth was clearly a sign that he was not happy.

"That's how you want to do this, then?"

Swallowing hard, I started wringing my hands. I wanted to cry out that, *no*, this wasn't how I wanted to do this. I wanted to beg him to forgive me for walking away all those years ago. Tell him the truth about how I've been miserable ever since.

But I didn't. I simply nodded.

Tripp nodded and stood. "Fine. Then I would contact Pete London. He's a good lawyer."

My heart dropped to the ground. He was giving up just like that. My chin trembled, and I felt the tears threatening to spill out. I wasn't sure if he noticed my reaction; he didn't falter at all.

"Good luck, Harley."

I tried to respond, but I couldn't. He started for the door, and I jumped up. Ready to spill the truth from my lips.

He opened the door and walked out, softly closing it behind him.

He left.

Sinking back into the chair, I covered my mouth to keep the sob in that wanted to bust free.

He left.

He truly doesn't have any feelings for me at all.

With a spin of my chair, I turned and stared out the window.

I should never have come back to Oak Springs. It didn't take very long for the tears to slip out and trail down my cheeks. Closing my eyes, I dropped my head against my chair and cried.

I cried so hard, the only thing I could hear was my heart pounding in my ears.

"Harley?"

Jumping up, I tripped over the chair and fell flat on my ass.

The pain in my lower back nearly made me sick to my stomach as I attempted to get up off the floor.

"Christ! Are you okay?"

Tripp lifted me up, and my head started to spin. My sadness mixed with the pain—and the excitement that came with him touching me. My world felt like it was tilting over, and there was nothing I could do to stop it. All the strength I'd used over the years to keep moving on was quickly fading away.

"I'm...fine. I'm f-fine," I said between sobs.

"You're not fine. Please tell me why you're crying, Lee."

His pet name for me nearly had me falling back to the floor. I hadn't heard it in years and all the memories of us came flooding in.

My eyes lifted to his beautiful baby blues. I'd forgotten how blue they were. They reminded me of a summer sky after a heavy rain when everything gets washed away and you're left with nothing but a crystal clear day.

"I never cheated on you. There was never another guy," I blurted out. The moment the words left my lips, I wished I could take them back.

His grip on my arms got tighter.

"What?"

I closed my eyes for a brief second. "I didn't want to tell you like this, Tripp. I've tried so many times to tell you the truth, but you've been pushing me away."

Confusion washed over his face while his gaze searched mine for answers.

"What are you talking about?"

I tried to step out of his hold, but he held onto me.

"Let me go, Tripp."

"Tell me what in the fuck you mean, Harley...*now*."

Standing straighter, I pulled in a deep breath and attempted to steady my voice.

"Let. Go. Of. Me."

His hands instantly dropped to his sides, but his voice stayed hard. "Talk. Now."

I turned away and stared out the large window. All those years I had practiced how I wanted to tell him, and now I had nothing. My mind was completely blank.

"That day I told you I met someone? I lied."

"Why?" his voice was laced with hurt and anger.

I faced him. "You were about to give up your dreams to help me chase mine, and I wasn't going to let that happen."

He stared at me like I'd lost my damn mind. "You fucking asked me to come with you! You asked me to leave Oak Springs. I told you I would."

"I heard you talking to your father at the hospital! I heard what you said. You wouldn't have been happy if you had left. It took me a while to realize I couldn't allow you to follow me. For a few minutes I was going to let you. I had every intention of letting you leave Oak Springs because in my mind I thought we could have a few years of seeing the world together and then we'd moved back here. Start the life you wanted after we lived the life I wanted."

He let out a confused chuckle. "And what the fuck happened? Your mind just switched like that and you decided you didn't want me with you?"

"No!" I cried out. "I heard you tell your father you didn't want to leave, that you were only doing it for me. When I heard him say you would resent me…I couldn't bear the thought. I knew if I asked you about that conversation, you'd deny the possibility of ever resenting me."

He started pacing before walking right up to me. He was so close I could practically hear his heart racing.

"So you decided to end us right then and there. You made that choice for both of us?"

Tears streamed down my face.

"I panicked, Tripp! Once I realized what I'd done, I wanted to take it back but it was too late. I tried calling you and came to town to talk to you…I planned on telling you the truth. I was going to move back to Oak Springs after vet school. I wanted to tell you how stupid I had been and beg you to forgive me, but you refused to even talk to me. For years I begged you and you constantly ignored me! It wasn't something I wanted to leave on your goddamn voicemail."

He shook his head. "I would think not. You fucking destroyed us, made my life a living hell for years! All because you *panicked*."

"*Your* life? How do you think I've felt? I've had to live with the regret of walking away. At the time, I did what I *thought* was right. I knew the only way to keep you from following me was to lie about a guy. I stupidly thought I could explain it away later. That didn't happen because you never gave me the chance. For Christ's sake, Tripp, you were leaving town whenever you heard I was here! Did you even read the letter I sent you?"

He gave me a look of pure hate. I gasped at his expression and took a few steps back. He was beyond angry, and I didn't blame him, but damn it, so was I.

"Who's Al?"

My brows pinched together. "What?"

He pointed at me. "Don't fucking lie to me anymore, Harley! Who the fuck is this guy Al you moved to Dallas with."

It took me a few seconds before it hit me.

"Alison? I moved to Dallas with a girl named Alison. Her nickname was Al. We rented a two-bedroom loft apartment downtown until she started partying and getting into drugs. I kicked her out not long after we moved."

Tripp stared at me as he processed what I was saying. All those years he had thought I moved to Dallas with a man? That explained the ignoring me, to some degree.

"Who told you I moved to Dallas with a guy?" I asked.

He raked his hand through his hair and paced again. "It doesn't matter. How could you have done this to us, Harley? I wouldn't have regretted going with you."

"Really? Can you honestly tell me that putting off starting your life and your career wouldn't have made you a little resentful? I heard you telling your father you were only doing it for me. I couldn't risk you hating me...or your family hating me for taking you away. I was young and caught up in stupid stories my aunt filled my head with. I did what I thought was right at the time. Can you honestly tell me you wouldn't have regretted leaving in some way?"

"I don't know! I never got the fucking chance to find out. So what if I had been? A few fights about it and we would have been good. You took that chance away from us and destroyed everything we ever had. What hurts more than anything is that you didn't trust that my love for you—that our love—would've been enough."

My gaze dropped to the floor. I couldn't argue with him on that.

"I've lived with that knowledge since that day. From the moment I walked away from you, Tripp. It has torn my heart in two, and I don't know what I can do to make it up to you."

Something in him snapped and he punched the wall, causing his hand to go right through the drywall.

"Tripp!" I screamed.

I started to make my way to him, but he held up his hand.

"You can't make it up to me. You can't fix what you did. You lied to me, Harley. That's almost worse than me thinking you cheated."

I stood there, my entire body shaking.

He mumbled under his breath and started to the door.

"Tripp, wait."

"I don't have anything else to say to you, Harley."

His words hit me like a brick wall and I stumbled back, wincing while the ache in my chest grew ten times stronger.

My body felt cold as I cried out.

"Tripp! Tripp, please don't do this!"

The bell on the front chimed, sounding his departure.

My legs gave out, and I fell to the floor. Everything Tripp must have gone through when I left him coursed through my mind as my heart broke into a million more pieces. I never thought this situation could get any worse, but I was wrong.

Now I knew for a fact that the love of my life was gone forever.

CHAPTER 7

Tripp

Walking into Steed's office, I stopped when I found three of my brothers, as well as Jonathon and Wade, all on the floor...making a pyramid.

"What the fuck are y'all doing?" I asked, making my way into the room.

"Christ, don't ask," Mitchell spat.

Steed was climbing to the top of the pile as Trevor bitched. "Your foot is on my damn face, Steed!"

"Just shut up and let's do this damn thing," Wade called out.

I crossed my arms over my chest and let out a roar of laughter. "What are you cheerleaders up to? Practicing a show you're gonna put on at the branding?"

They all looked at me. If looks could kill I'd be dead five times over.

A strong slap pushed me off balance, causing me to stumble forward. Glancing over my shoulder, I saw my father. "It's team building, Tripp. Good for them to learn to trust each other while they're on the job." He gave me a wink, and I knew he was full of shit. Jonathon didn't even work on the ranch.

Focusing back on the pyramid, Steed was at the top. He got on his knees and spread his arms wide open.

"Look at me...I'm flying!"

Wade and Jonathon lost it laughing.

"Don't laugh, assholes. You're making it unstable," Trevor shouted.

"I'm king of the world!" Steed went on, a huge smile on his face.

Mitchell joined the laughing. I saw it happening before they even knew it; the pyramid was collapsing.

"Great...they're gonna fall," my father said. "No one better get hurt."

And fall they did.

Jonathon and Wade took the brunt force of it.

"My ribs. I think I broke my ribs," Trevor cried out.

My father walked over to them. "You better not have. We've got a lot of work to do, son."

Reaching out a hand, I pulled Jonathon and then Mitchell up.

"Seriously, Dad. What in the hell was all that about?" Trevor asked, rubbing his hip.

My father walked over to the conference table and took a seat at the head.

"No reason. I just wanted to see if you would all do it. I guess I really am still in charge." Holding his arms outstretched, my dad said, "Look at me, I'm king of the world."

I couldn't help it, I lost it laughing as the five of them stared.

"I don't understand this family. Not one bit," Jonathon said. "I was just stopping by to pick up a lasagna your mom made and I got suckered in."

My laugh turned into a full-blown, tears streaming down my face, bent over at the hip, trying to catch my breath guffaw.

"Fuck you, Tripp," Trevor said, giving me a hard push and causing me to fall to the ground.

Jonathon bid his farewell and took off out of Steed's office—probably before he got suckered into doing something else. I got up and held my sides while I made my way over to the table. Wade, Trevor, Mitchell, and Steed were all pouting.

"Oh, come on, y'all. It looked fun," I stated.

Trevor snarled at me. "Yeah, too bad you got here late. You could have joined us."

I sat down at the far end of the table. "That's the difference between me and you, Trev. I don't fall for Dad's pranks. Never have. Never will."

My father lifted his brows. "Is that a challenge, Tripp Parker?"

With a grin, I stated, "If you want it to be. Sure."

When he leaned back and steepled his fingers under his chin, I knew I was fucked.

"I accept," he replied.

"If y'all are finished with your tea party, we have a lot to talk about," Steed said.

They were soon lost in the planning of the spring branding. I usually skipped the planning meeting and showed up ready to work…and eat. In high school I used to love this time of year. It meant a day off on Friday to get everything set up. Saturday was spent working our asses off, only for the kids to head out to one of our pastures and have our own party. My folks always pretended like they didn't know, but they did.

I smiled thinking back to those days. We used to pitch tents and camp out. Mostly because we had paid one of our older siblings to buy beer and our parents would kill us if they knew we were drinking and driving. But then there was the fun in the tents. My body felt warm thinking about Harley crawling into a sleeping bag with me butt ass naked. We never had sex, it felt too awkward with other peoples' tents near us, but man, did we make each other feel good more times than I could count. I could practically feel the stroke of her warm hand on my cock now.

"Tripp?"

Something hit my boot, drawing me out of the memory.

"You wanted to talk, son?"

I looked around, noticing the rest of the room had emptied out. "Hell, where did everyone go?"

He chuckled. "You seemed to be withdrawn into your own world. Steed said goodbye, but you were staring out the window."

I forced a grin. "Yeah, I was thinking about all the past brandings."

The way he looked at me, I could tell he knew I was a damn liar.

"Let's go to my office. Steed will be back soon and will want his office."

The chair pushed back as I stood. Following my father out, I reached into my pocket and checked my phone. My shoulders dropped when I didn't see any missed calls or messages.

"Expecting a call?"

"More like hoping for one."

He opened the door to his office and motioned for me to walk in. "Mallory?"

I let out a gruff laugh. "No."

At the bar in his office, he poured each of us a glass of scotch. He handed it to me and gave me a questioning look. "Trouble with you two?"

"No, not really." I half shrugged.

"Mallory is the first real girlfriend you've had since Harley. It's got to be an adjustment."

"I dated Corina," I added.

He chuckled. "Yeah, okay. Keep telling yourself that, son. You know the only reason you were 'dating' Corina was to make your brother jealous."

Smiling, I sat down in one of the two large, leather armchairs facing my father's large oak desk. He sank into the chair opposite and took a drink while staring me down. "What's on your mind, son?"

I blew out a breath. "Women."

He laughed. "That's usually the answer. That, or politics, with you."

I let out a slight chuckle, then frowned. "Dad, I'm so confused right now… I don't know whether I'm coming or going."

"Well, take it from me, son. Women will do that to you."

I finished off my drink and set it on his desk. Leaning forward, I let out a frustrated groan. "Yesterday Harley told me she lied about there being another guy. There never was one. She claimed she told me that because she knew I would have left Oak Springs and ended up resenting her for it. She said she heard us talking at the hospital and she panicked."

My father's eyes widened. "Wow. That's a bombshell."

"Sure is."

"And she never thought to tell you the truth?"

I looked down at the floor. Guilt had been tearing me apart since yesterday when I was in Harley's office.

"Tripp?"

Clearing my throat, I sat back and lifted my brown cowboy boot over my leg to rest it on my knee.

"She said the first time she came back into town after graduation, she was going to tell me the truth. But I've avoided her completely…for years."

He waited for me to continue, but I knew he already knew what story I was going to tell. The moment I found out she was in town, I convinced Cord and Mitchell to go camping with me. We packed up and left town and I turned off my phone the entire weekend.

"She must have called my cell over a hundred times. Begging me to meet so we could talk."

"You went camping, if I remember right."

"Yeah, I did. I went with Cord and Mitchell and then deleted every one of her messages without listening to them or reading them. I was still hurt, thinking she'd left me for another guy."

"Well," he said before taking a drink. "I also believe every time Harley came into town, you had some excuse to leave. She stopped by the house a few times, never told your mother and me what really happened, but we certainly saw the pain in her eyes and the regret in her voice."

"Yeah, she said she wanted to tell me before anyone else. She never even told her parents the truth until recently. Also said it wasn't something she wanted to leave on a voicemail. Not that I listened to them anyway."

I stood up and scrubbed my hands down my face and cursed under my breath.

"Fuck."

Turning back to face my father, I shook my head. "All those years we wasted because she didn't trust that I knew what I wanted."

"What prompted her to make up the fake love interest?"

Dragging in a breath, I told my father everything.

"So, she lied about this guy because she knew you would follow her and you were certainly not going to let her break up with you."

"Yes, sir. That's what she did."

"You did tell me that day, son, you didn't want to do what Harley wanted. Would you have?"

I shrugged. "I guess I would have. I mean, at the time, I would have followed her to the end of the world if it meant she was happy."

"Tripp, would that have made you happy?"

I looked my father in the eyes, wanting him to help me out of this mess, not wanting him to make me doubt my feelings for Harley.

"Dad…" A sigh spilled out.

Leaning forward, my father placed his forearms on his knees and shot me a serious look. Like his life depended on the next words out of my mouth.

"Why do you think Harley was afraid to tell you what she wanted to do?"

My breath caught in my throat. I knew where he was going with this. "Because I always talked about my dreams as if they were hers."

"And why do you think she never said anything?"

With a harsh laugh, I threw my hands up in the arm. "Fucked if I know, Dad."

"She didn't tell you, son, because she didn't want to ruin your dreams. When she finally mustered the courage to tell you, she overheard our conversation. She didn't want you to resent her for making you leave."

"That's the thing! She wasn't making me do anything. I offered to do it. I mean, it was a few years away. I still had law school and she still had vet school. She made a choice for both of us, Dad, without thinking, without trusting that my love for her was enough."

Leaning back, he nodded. "You're right. She did. Sort of like your brother, Steed, when it came to Paxton. Or Mitchell when it came to Corina. We make mistakes, and sometimes we live with the regret of that mistake. Now I'm not excusing what she did, but I'm also saying you need to see that she tried to make it up to you, and you're to blame for the separation all these years."

My jaw dropped. "Me! How in the hell am I to blame for this, Dad?"

His brow lifted. "If you don't know the answer to that, nothing I say matters. You're better off moving on and forgetting about Harley. You seem to be somewhat happy with Mallory."

I swallowed hard. *Forget about Harley. Is that something I can even do? I honestly don't think that after almost ten years it's even a possibility.*

Sinking into the leather chair, I let out a defeated breath. "I don't know what to do. For once, I met a woman I enjoy being with. And Harley comes back into town and messes with my head. I pretty much told her yesterday I was done with her. That I had nothing left to say to her."

"Did you mean it?"

I focused on the large painting on the wall behind him. My mother had painted it years ago and had given it to my father on their first anniversary. It was my father on a horse smiling down at my mother. She said she knew the moment she saw him she was madly in love. My mother believed in one true love, and that no matter what the problem, love would overcome.

My muscles tensed, and I cut my eyes over to my father. "I don't know. Maybe at the time I said it I meant it. Now I'm not sure what to think."

"Tripp, I think you came here with the hope and expectation that I would tell you which woman to pursue. I can't tell you that. You're going to have to decide on your own. Sounds like you told Harley things would never be the same, and like I said, you must care about Mallory or you wouldn't be conflicted. Only you can find the answers."

All I could do was nod in agreement. My father stood.

"One piece of advice I will give you: if you truly believe you cannot forgive Harley, let her go. Give her forgiveness so she can also move on. It seems to me she waited for a chance to explain her actions to you, and you offered her no hope. Be prepared for her to move on."

"Move on?" I pulled in a breath. It felt like a ton of weight had settled on my chest.

He rested his hand on my shoulder and gave it a squeeze. "It isn't fair to either of those ladies if you hang on to old feelings."

He headed toward the door. "Where are you going?" I asked while standing.

"I have a tea date with my beautiful granddaughter, and I don't intend on missing it. If I do, Patches will get my scones."

Letting out a laugh, I lifted my hand to say goodbye to my father.

He headed out of his office with a smile on his face. My father loved his grandkids with every ounce of his being. I was glad to see him letting my brothers run the ranch more each day, giving my father time to spend with my mother and the grandkids.

Running my hand through my hair, I rubbed the ache in the back of my neck.

"Hell, I'm *still* confused. Maybe even more."

My phone buzzed in my pocket. Pulling it out, I saw her name. I wasn't about to admit that it wasn't the name I wanted to see, though.

Mallory: *I've got a mommy's night out with the other moms planned for tonight. We're heading into Uvalde for a painting party. Were you going to stop by the house in a bit? I could use a bit of attention before Laney gets home.*

I stared at the message. Was she fucking kidding me?

With a shake of my head, I cleared my thoughts and responded.

Me: *I'm out at my folks' and will most likely be here for the rest of the day helping out. Have fun tonight.*

Mallory: *I'm sure I will. Talk tomorrow!*

Me: *Sounds like a plan. Bye.*

I headed out of the office and made my way down the hall. I stopped when I heard Amelia talking to Wade.

"She was really upset. I'm worried."

"Just make sure y'all stay out of it, Amelia. That's Harley's business, not yours."

My chest tightened at her name, and I found myself holding my breath.

"I know. We promised her we wouldn't tell my folks or the boys. She wants to handle it on her own."

Wade laughed. "And I suppose I'm not a *boy*?"

Peeking around the corner, I saw my sister up on her toes, kissing Wade. "You're all man."

I held back the gag.

Pulling back around the corner, I didn't move. Amelia clearly knew why Harley came to my office that day. She was in trouble and was now hell bent on me not finding out what it was.

But I knew exactly where to go to get answers.

Karen.

CHAPTER 8

Harley

Lady looked up at me with a sigh as I flopped onto the couch.

"Sorry, girl. Didn't mean to disturb your slumber."

My golden retriever lab mix stared for a moment before settling back into the couch.

"Here we are, girl, on a Friday night sitting at home fixin' to watch an *Outlander* marathon. We're party animals."

She let out a whine.

"I know. We're losers."

My doorbell rang, and I froze for a moment. What if it was him? Here to harass me some more…

I pulled up my security cameras on my phone and smiled when I saw Paxton and Amelia standing outside my door. Waylynn and Corina walked up, and I knew my Friday night had just taken a turn for the better.

Turning my alarm off on my phone, I rushed to my front door.

"What are y'all doing here?" I asked as I hugged and kissed each of them on the cheek and ushered them in.

Amelia walked in holding a dress bag. "We had a free night off and decided you deserved a night out."

"Yep, I'm kid-free for the evening. Steed and his folks are having movie night tonight."

"And Jonathon insisted I get out for a few hours while he watched Liberty."

My cheeks burned from smiling. "Y'all don't have to cheer me up. I'm fine. Honestly."

Corina rolled her eyes and let out a *humph*. "You've got another person claiming to be the rightful owner of the vet clinic, and Tripp is being...well..."

"An asshole," Amelia and Waylynn said together.

I'd told Paxton all about how Doc's brother was making a claim on my vet clinic, and she had shared the information with the rest of the Parker women.

"I can't blame Tripp. It's my fault. Maybe I didn't try hard enough to tell him the truth. I could have left it on his voicemail or something."

Paxton hooked her arm with mine while she guided me to my bedroom. "You sent him a letter. He obviously never read it."

I nodded. That was true. I had sent a letter to Tripp two years ago, explaining everything and begging him to call me. He clearly hadn't bothered to open it. "A part of me wonders if I should have come back to town. I've always wanted to settle in Oak Springs. Raise a family here. But maybe it was a mistake to come back."

Waylynn grabbed my upper arms. "Don't say that. You stayed away long enough, and now that we know the truth, we're glad you're back. If Tripp wants to be an ass about it then let him. It's his loss."

I tried to smile. "Then why do I feel like it's my loss too? Maybe he's in love with Mallory."

They all laughed. Waylynn brushed my comment off with a wave of her hand.

"Please. Tripp panicked because you were back, and he's using Mallory as another one of his places to hide." She pulled the plastic off the dress and held it up while studying it. "Now don't get me wrong, I think he cares about her. Otherwise I don't think he would have stayed with her as long as he has. But love her? No."

Her blue eyes looked over to me. "But there's another reason he's kept dating Mallory."

My head tilted as I waited anxiously for her to keep talking. "And that is?"

Paxton jumped in. "He announced he's running for mayor of Oak Springs, and he sees her as a good addition. Someone stable by his side. Successful politicians are rarely single, the public likes to see a family man running things."

"He's long since stopped his man-whoring days and has found someone who is pretty much squeaky clean. No dirt to dig up," Amelia stated.

I cringed at Amelia's words. To know Tripp had slept around made me feel ill. I'd had a few boyfriends off and on, and of course, had sex with them. But nothing like what I'd shared with Tripp.

Dropping my head, I tried to take in a few breaths to calm my sick stomach. "I wouldn't say she was squeaky clean. She showed up at Tripp's office dressed in lingerie when I was there."

They all snarled, then the snarls morphed into *ewwww* faces.

"For real?" Amelia asked.

"I had dropped my key and had to go back." Tears filled my eyes. "I heard them…you know."

They all gasped.

"I'd love to chop my brother's dick off and shove it down his throat sometimes!" Waylynn huffed.

Warm hands rubbed my back. It was Corina and Paxton. "Let's forget all about Mallory and Tripp and the clinic for tonight. Let's go have fun."

Forcing a grin, I asked, "What are the plans?"

"Dinner first, then we're off to do some dancing at Cord's Place."

Waylynn held out a black dress that looked like it wasn't finished being made. "And you're wearing this."

I cocked my head and narrowed my eyes. "It looks sort of...revealing."

An evil grin appeared on Waylynn's face. "It's going to showcase this curvy rocking body of yours. Now, let's go get you ready."

Glancing down once again, I sighed. "Seriously, I feel like this dress reveals a whole lot."

"My dress shows cleavage," Amelia said as we walked into the restaurant.

"You're a lot younger than me! You can get away with it."

I looked at Paxton, Corina, and Waylynn again. "Okay, Corina is dressed in a darling dress that showcases her pregnant tummy."

Corina grinned and rubbed her bump.

"Paxton and Waylynn, y'all have on dresses that are more...age appropriate. They say 'I'm married but out having fun.'"

Waylynn pointed to me. "Watch it, Carbajal. I only just let you back into the circle of trust. I can kick you out again. Age appropriate, my ass..."

Paxton chuckled. "Harley, you have a smoking hot body. You're single, and you need to get out there and start a new life. Showcase it, girl!"

I couldn't help but laugh. Paxton had two kids and a body to die for. She could easily get away with wearing this dress. Me? I was never the one to wear sexy outfits, but I had to admit, I felt pretty good for the first time in a long time.

"Well, I still feel like my dress is screaming 'Hey, I want to get laid!'"

Of course, the second I had said that, the hostess walked up. She eyed me up and down and then looked at everyone else. "Do you have reservations?"

We all looked at each other.

Sighing, Amelia said, "Um, no, I didn't realize we needed them."

The hostess lifted her chin. "We've become very popular and require them on Friday and Saturday nights"

Amelia huffed behind me.

"Seriously? Since when?" Waylynn asked.

The girl shrugged. "If you don't have a reservation I cannot seat you."

"Screw this!" Amelia said. "I'm down for Lilly's. We'll be the best dressed there."

We all agreed and started to walk off.

"Wait! You can't be serious. You want to go to Lilly's dressed like this?"

They looked at their dresses and then back to me. A wide grin moved over Corina's face as she said, "Jacob will certainly be happy to see you!"

When the rest of them started laughing and walking toward the parking lot, I started after them, moving the best I could in these damn heels.

"Okay, wait! Who is Jacob?" I shouted as their giggles grew louder.

"Corina!" I shouted.

A truck came around the corner and the driver had to slam on the brakes to miss me. Throwing my hands up in the air, I yelled, "Slow down, *asshole*!"

"Um, Harley. That's Tripp," Amelia said, grabbing my hand and pulling me away.

"Oh, shit," I mumbled.

"What in the hell, Harley!" he yelled out the window. I turned to face him and give him a piece of my mind, but I saw Mallory sitting in the truck and froze.

"Sorry, Tripp. You better have a reservation or you'll be joining us at Lilly's," Amelia said.

My eyes were locked on Tripp. He quickly looked my body up and down before focusing back on Amelia.

"Yeah, we have reservations."

Pulling my arm free of Amelia, I walked away. Amelia went up to Tripp's window. I did a quick glance over my shoulder and saw her talking to him. I slid into the back of Corina's car and closed my eyes.

"I'm never going to get used to seeing him with her, and I know I have no right to feel that way. Not with what I did to him."

Paxton took my hand in hers and gave it a squeeze.

"You'll get used to it," Waylynn said, crawling behind Paxton into the third row of seats. "Besides, did you see the way he looked at you? Oh, yeah, my baby brother still has the hots for you."

I threw my arm over my eyes as I leaned my head back. He may look at me with lust in his eyes, but he had no plans to act on it, and I just had to resign myself to that fact.

"Lilly's then?" Amelia asked, getting into the front seat.

"Let's do it!" Corina replied.

Chewing my lip, I wanted to ask Amelia what she'd talked about with Tripp, but I looked out the window instead. Were the girls all friends with Mallory? Had they gone out together? A part of me hoped not, and I felt so guilty for that. They didn't have to forgive and take me back into their lives like they had and here I was hoping they weren't friends with Mallory. Christ. How shallow could I be?

"Penny for your thoughts," Paxton said.

"Thinking about the problem with the vet clinic," I lied.

"It's all going to be okay, Harley."

I dragged in a deep breath. "I wish I could be so optimistic. I'm still waiting for Chuck White to call me back."

"I've heard he's a good lawyer," Paxton said with a smile that screamed she'd heard the opposite.

Shit. I am so screwed.

Doc Harris had a brother who was an investor. After Doc had retired and sold me his practice, his brother showed up claiming he owned part of the practice and Doc had no right to sell it to me, and he wanted his share back. It was so messed up. If there was any truth to his claim, I'd never be able to buy his brother out. Hell, I was in debt for buying the vet practice as well as paying off my school loans. I'd already squeezed every ounce of blood out of the turnips that I could. And I hadn't been able to sleep in days.

It didn't take long before we were all walking into Lilly's. Jacob, I quickly found out, was one of the cooks. Apparently he had let it slip to Amelia he thought I was hot. He couldn't have been over twenty. Thankfully, Lilly's was so busy he never noticed I was there.

After eating our dinner and laughing more than I had in years, we walked across the square to Cord's Place.

"So, how's the work going on the new Irish pub?" Paxton asked Waylynn.

"It's good. Jonathon's almost done. He said Maebh should be opening up soon."

"Who's Maebh?" I asked.

Waylynn rubbed her hands together and laughed. "Oh, just a pretty little Irish thing who happens to have caught the eye of Cord. Although he claims to detest her because she's his competition."

"I thought she was opening up more of a restaurant, fine dining-type place," I said.

"Oh, she is," Amelia said. "But Tripp keeps feeding Cord lies to get him fired up."

"Steed said Cord knows the truth now, I guess. But I think the poor guy doesn't know what is up and what is down. He's not sure what to believe."

We all laughed.

"*Maebh*. That's such a pretty name."

"It's spelled pretty, too. It's Irish. M-A-E-B-H, pronounced like may with a v on the end," Corina added.

Waylynn stopped walking and put her hand up for us to stop.

"I looked it up," she said with a huge grin. "I means…ready for this? She who intoxicates."

We all let out a gasp. "Wow," I said as I looked over to the entrance of Cord's Place and then back down the street to Maebh's restaurant. The sign read *Aisling*.

"*Aisling*?" I asked as Waylynn shook her head.

"It's pronounced, Ash-ling. Jonathon said it means vision or dream."

"That's beautiful…" Corina and I said at once.

"Y'all should see the inside. You feel like you're stepping back in time. The mahogany is amazing. Jonathon had to hire a guy from Dallas to come down and bring Maebh's vision to life. There are shelves she plans on filling with books."

"Books?" Corina asked, confused, just like me.

Waylynn nodded and motioned for us to follow her. "Come on. Let's see if we can peek inside."

When we walked up, the lights were on but you couldn't really see into the place.

Waylynn cupped her hands around her face as she peeked into the windows. "Her vision is for people to come during the day, grab a coffee, a sandwich and relax. Hence, the books."

The front door opened and a beautiful woman stepped out. Her brown hair was pulled into a ponytail. She wore overalls that had paint covering almost every square inch. She didn't look to have on even an ounce of make-up, and she certainly didn't need it. She had the most beautiful green eyes I'd ever seen.

She smiled the sweetest smile ever. "Hello. How are you ladies doing?"

"I love your accent!" I blurted out while the other girls all laughed.

"And I love yours!" she replied.

"Sorry to bug you, Maebh. I was trying to give the girls a peek. We were headed to Cord's Place."

Her eyes lit up. "Really? How fun."

"Would you like to join us?" Paxton asked.

Maebh's cheeks flushed. *Interesting.* Was that excitement about being asked to hang out with the girls, or was that because she would get to see Cord?

Amelia squealed. "Yes! Please do, I'd love to get to know you better! Plus, you haven't met Harley. Our town vet!"

I chuckled and stuck my hand out to shake Maebh's.

"It's a pleasure to meet you. I hear you're adding a restaurant!"

She nodded. "Would you all like to come in for a tour?"

The five us responded with an overly excited, "Yes!"

Maebh laughed and motioned for us to follow her in. The first thing I noticed were the old, wide plank floors. I remembered them from the pharmacy that used to be here. As a little girl I would try and keep my feet on one plank as I walked.

Lifting my gaze, I took in the beautiful blue walls. They matched the paint on Maebh's overalls.

"These bookcases are stunning!" Corina said as she made her way over to them.

"Thank you! My inspiration came from a picture of some bookcases that are in our home back in Ireland."

Corina faced her. "You still have a home in Ireland?"

"Oh, yes. It's been in my father's family for years."

"Wow, that's sort of cool knowing you have a place to stay if you want to go back."

Maebh smiled and nodded. "There will be a bit of a sitting area here in front of the cases. I want to open for a few hours in the mornings a few times a week, for those who'd like to come in for coffee and relax."

"Great idea!" Paxton said.

We moved through the place, taking it all in as Maebh gave us a tour.

Amelia turned to Maebh. "It seems like it will be really cozy, yet have an elegance to it."

"I hope so. That's the look I'm going for."

Looking up, I couldn't help but notice the amazing crown molding. "This used to be the old pharmacy, but I do not remember that crown molding."

Maebh laughed. "It had been covered up. Jonathon's workers discovered it. You should see it up in the sitting room."

"Sitting room?" Amelia asked.

With a wide grin, she motioned for us to follow her up the old wood steps. "This part of the restaurant is nearly finished."

The moment I stepped off the last step, I was in awe.

"Holy shit," Waylynn gasped. "Jonathon told me it was beautiful, but he didn't say it was stunning!"

"What is a sitting room, Maebh?"

"I guess it would be like your bar, not like Cord's Place. It's more of a cocktail bar. So, if you are early for dinner, or even after dinner, you would come up here and order perhaps my father's famous whiskey and have a bit of craic."

"Crack? What kind of place are you running, Maebh!" Paxton said with a wink.

"It's spelled, c-r-a-i-c, but yes, pronounced like your *crack*. It means good conversation. High-spirited fun."

"I love this idea!" Paxton said. "For those who don't really want the atmosphere of Cord's Place, you can come here. I can totally see me and Steed coming up here and relaxing on a date night."

"I agree!" Waylynn and Amelia said at the same time.

"It's simply beautiful, Maebh. Was this fashioned after your house in Ireland again?" I asked.

She nodded. "Yes. One of the ballrooms."

I lifted my brows and couldn't help but notice how Maebh tried to cover up what she clearly hadn't meant to say. "I'm thinking here in the fireplaces we can put candles when there isn't a fire going."

"Beautiful idea," I said as I gave her a wink. I was pretty sure I was the only one who caught that she'd said *ballroom*.

"Do you have a culinary background?" I asked.

Maebh nodded. "After school I worked for a two-star restaurant in Dublin. I found myself moving up and was soon running the back-end. I loved it, maybe even more than cooking."

"So you decided to open your own place?" Amelia asked as she sat down in one of three oversized leather chairs. I was guessing Maebh had them up here to plot out where the furniture would go.

Letting out a laugh, she shook her head. "No. That's a bit of a long story."

"Well, you'll have to tell us about it someday. Jonathon said you and your father are living on the third and fourth floor?"

She nodded.

"Then I say go get cleaned up while we dip into your father's whiskey and come out with us tonight."

Her eyes lit up like Christmas morning.

"Really? You'd let me come along with you?"

Paxton took Maebh's hand in hers. "Of course! Besides, you look like you're getting more paint on you than the walls, sweetie."

Maebh glanced at herself and laughed. She chewed on her lip for a few seconds before saying. "Yes! I'd love to join you. I'll not be long!"

Waylynn had made her way behind the bar and somehow found a bottle of whiskey. "Take your time. We're not in a hurry."

"Maebh, I hate to ask, but do you have a restroom?" Corina asked. "The baby pushes against my bladder, and I swear I pee every five minutes."

She took Corina's hand and led her to a door. It opened and led to a set of stairs. "We'll be back!" Maebh called out in excitement.

"Geesh, poor thing. Do you think she has any friends here?" I asked as I walked up to the beautiful wood bar. Running my hand along it, I slid onto one of the matching stools.

"I don't think so. I never see her out. I think she puts every spare second into this place."

"Hmm. Well, we're going to have to change that. The girl is too pretty to be hiding out."

"Agreed," Paxton said.

The four of us held up our shots of whiskey and downed them.

"Holy...shit!" Waylynn stuttered between coughing. She held up the bottle and read it. "Sona Single Pot Still Irish whiskey. Motherfucker, this shit is strong."

"I think I grew a few hairs on my chest," I said as I shook my head to help chase the burn away. Picking up the bottle, I turned it around and read the information on the label.

Created and produced by the O'Sullivan Distillery, Cork.

"What's Maebh's last name?" I asked.

Waylynn was pouring each of us another shot. "O'Sullivan."

My eyes drifted back to the bottle. "Does her father make this whiskey? Is that what she meant when she said *my father's whiskey*?"

"I don't know, why?" Waylynn asked.

I pointed to the bottle. "It says it was created and distilled by O'Sullivan Distillery in Cork."

"Isn't she from Cork?" Paxton asked.

We all looked at each other. Waylynn's mouth opened before she said, "Shit. She said ballroom and then tried to move on. You don't think they're from money, do you? I mean, the money she is sinking into this place would likely say yes."

Corina came rushing into the room. "Y'all, get Maebh to spell her name!"

"What?" Amelia asked. "Why?"

"Trust me! Just do it!"

Corina looked at the shot glasses and pouted. "Dang. That looks good."

Waylynn grabbed the shot and held it up to Corina. "It will grow hair on your balls."

Corina snarled. "I don't have balls."

"You will after you drink this," Amelia added with a giggle.

"Drink up, ladies! Well, not you, Corina!" Waylynn added.

"Oh, no! Let me show you how to take a shot of Irish whiskey," Maebh said, walking up to us. She had changed into a darling little green cocktail dress. It looked like the only make-up she'd put on was mascara.

Maebh poured a shot and lifted it up. "Take a breath through your mouth first."

She tilted her head back and drank it in one smooth go. The damn shot glass was nearly upside-down when she finished.

"You have to tilt your head and the glass back as one. It makes it go down easier. Then you swallow it immediately while keeping your jaw and throat relaxed while you swallow."

"Why does it sound like we're getting a blow job lesson?" Waylynn said.

We all laughed, and Maebh's cheeks flushed. She let a huge smile play across her face before saying, "Anyway, a shot is best enjoyed when taken with others!"

"I can't do another one. I'm already feeling it," Paxton stated.

"Hell, I'll do another one with you, Maebh," Waylynn proudly announced.

"Count me in!" I added.

Amelia shook her head and bowed out along with Paxton.

"Ready?" Maebh asked. She poured three shots.

Waylynn's eyes widened. "Hell, girl, those are double what I poured."

With a laugh, she handed Waylynn and me our shots. We did as she instructed and the cool burn rushed down my throat.

"Damn, that's strong. How can you drink it like that?" I asked.

Maebh laughed. "My father owns the company that makes this whiskey. I've been drinking this since I was about ten."

Waylynn got an evil grin on her face. "So, you can hold your whiskey, then, right?"

She shrugged. "I guess so. Why?"

"No reason. Just an observation. Wow, you shine up pretty nice, Ms. O'Sullivan."

"Okay, it looks like I'm still the only one dressed like a hooker." I pouted.

Maebh shook her head. "I think you look amazing."

"Thank you," I said as I laced my arm with hers. "Then you can help me down the damn stairs in these heels."

By the time we got out of Aisling's we were ready to dance and have a good time. The whiskey had hit me like a Mack truck, and I was pretty sure it had hit Waylynn just as hard because she told Corina not to let her take any more shots for the rest of the night.

CHAPTER 9

Harley

The bar was packed like usual.

"Do you see a table?" Waylynn shouted over a Dierks Bentley song.

I shook my head while I scanned the place. Amelia grabbed our hands. "There should be one reserved. I told Cord we were coming."

"Thank goodness!" Corina shouted.

Glancing over my shoulder, I saw Corina and Maebh lost in conversation as they made their way through the crowd, trying to keep up with us and chat over the music.

When we made it to the table, Amelia and Waylynn high-fived each other.

"Okay! Drinks! Corina, water?"

She nodded and sat down.

Waylynn pointed to each of us and got our order. "Want to come with me, Maebh?"

With a huge smile, she jumped up and followed Waylynn.

"She totally did that on purpose so Cord would see Maebh with us," Paxton stated, shaking her head and speaking to no one in particular. "Cord's going to see right through that ploy."

When they came back, the music had stopped so that the DJ could take a break.

"Maebh! Spell your name!" Corina said all giddy.

"Again?" Maebh chuckled.

"Yes! Listen y'all."

We leaned in. "M-A-E-B-hayche."

"Hayche?" I asked.

Maebh shook her head, "No, *hayche*."

"H," Waylynn said with a giggle.

Maebh nodded. "Yes! Hayche!"

We all started laughing. "Maebh, your H and our H is not the same. You're pronouncing it like hay-che."

She agreed again. "Right. Hayche."

I felt a hand on my back and jumped. When I looked up, I was looking into the eyes of Toby.

"Hey! Fancy meeting you here." The music started back up with "Problem" by Ariana Grande. "Dance with me?"

I let him lead me to the dance floor. The whiskey was flowing through me. Toby was a good dancer and handsome for sure. My neglected body was certainly happy to have a man touching it.

Toby drew my body into his. His mouth against my ear, he purred, "You look hot in that dress, Harley."

I felt my cheeks heat. It wasn't the same feeling Tripp instilled in me, but it was nice to have my body reacting to a man. "Thank you, Toby! I feel a bit exposed."

He gave me a sexy wink. "No way."

I was lost in dancing with Toby and noticed Maebh was dancing with the guy I had seen with Toby. I pointed and yelled, "A friend of yours?"

He nodded and moved his mouth to my ear again. "Another fire-fighter."

My stomach pulled as his hot breath hit my ear once more. Toby wasn't bad looking, by any means. He was fit, a firefighter, and knew how to dance. I hadn't been with a guy in over a year. My last on and off boyfriend had been a doctor who never seemed to have time to fit *us* in. I didn't complain, though. He was really only good for the occasional hook-up we managed to squeeze in. We both knew it would never go anywhere, so it worked out for both of us.

I smiled and let Toby wrap his arms around me for a slow song. I was in heels so two-stepping was out of the question.

"It's great being able to see you again," he said as he tugged gently on a loose piece of hair.

I did the only thing I knew to do. I flashed him a wide grin. "I feel the same."

Do I?

He certainly was a lot of fun to dance with, and I could see my-self dating him. Maybe it was time for me to move on, like the girls said. Tripp had made it clear he had no intention to forgive me, and was angrier with me now more than ever.

Toby's hand moved to my lower back, pulling me in tighter. My body shivered, but it wasn't because I was getting turned on...it was because I knew *he* was here. I felt him before I even looked around.

Tripp.

My eyes filled with tears as I watched him and Mallory slide across the wood dance floor. When his eyes met mine, my breath caught in my throat. I wanted to run over to him. Beg him to forgive me. It wasn't Toby I wanted to be dancing with; it was Tripp.

I let my eyes roam over him. Tripp held Mallory close to his body. Her head buried in his chest. My eyes cut back to his, but he was looking down at Mallory and no longer at me.

It was really over. I'd lost my chance of ever winning Tripp back. The reality hit me full force. Everything ached. My head, my stomach, and most of all, my heart. Taking a risk, I glanced back at them. The look on Tripp's face appeared to be pained. But then again, it was probably my own stupid hope that I kept holding on to. I jerked my gaze away.

"Toby, I'm sorry I feel a bit sick."

"Are you okay? Is it too hot in here?"

"I think I just want to go home."

He nodded. "Okay, let's take you back over to your friends."

I let him guide me through the crowd of people over to the table, but I pulled him to a stop before we got there.

"Wait. I don't really want to ruin their night. Would it be horrible of me if I asked you to drive me home?"

He gave me a sweet smile. "I don't mind taking you home."

"I don't want to ruin your night either."

Toby laughed. "Trust me, you're not. Plus, this gives me a chance to get to know you a little better so I can ask you out to dinner."

My heart melted. Most men would think this was their chance to hook up, but Toby was being a gentleman, and I appreciated that more than he knew.

"I would love that," I replied.

He motioned for me to walk first. Corina was the only one sitting at the table. I had a feeling she didn't want to be here either. She looked like she wasn't feeling well.

"Hey, are you okay?" I asked as I took her hand in mine.

Shaking her head, she said, "No. I called Mitchell to see if he wouldn't mind coming to pick me up. Paxton offered to drive me home, but I know they're having fun and getting to know Maebh, so I told her I had called Mitchell already."

"I can drop you off at home, Corina," Toby said.

Her eyes bounced from Toby to me and then back to him.

"Harley isn't feeling well either so I'm taking her home."

Her brows lifted.

"It's not like that, so push those thoughts aside," I whispered.

She glanced past me, and I knew what she was doing. Looking for Tripp and Mallory. She must have seen them because her eyes turned sad. I knew the girls were rooting for me and Tripp, but they had to see he wasn't interested in forgiving me, let alone dating me again.

When she looked back at me, I could see it in her eyes. The pain, the pity, the regret.

"It's okay. I made my bed and now I have to lie in it." There was no other way to get through this situation unscathed except by facing the harsh reality, as much as that gutted me.

"Harley…"

Giving her hand a squeeze, I forced a grin. "Would you mind telling the girls I bugged out?"

"I'll let them know. Text us when you get back to your place."

Corina flashed a look at Toby. "Drive safe, Toby."

He tipped his cowboy hat and replied. "Yes, ma'am. Tell Mitchell I said hi, and I hope you feel better."

"I will, and thanks!" she responded with that sweet smile of hers.

I nudged Toby. "Let's get before the crew gets back and tries to talk me into staying."

Taking my hand in his, he led me through the crowd and to the exit. My heart was racing for some reason. I could feel the heat of Tripp's eyes. Glancing over my shoulder, his blue gaze pierced into me as I made my way out the door with Toby.

I wasn't trying to make him jealous by leaving with Toby, and it appeared by the way he was looking at me that he wasn't jealous. It was almost like he was relieved I was leaving. Mallory whispered something into his ear. He looked down at her and nodded, before giving me one last look.

Swallowing the lump in my throat, I turned before he could see the tear that slipped free and rolled down my cheek. I wiped it away and took in a deep breath of the cool spring air. My body shivered. Toby wrapped his arm around me, pulling me closer. He had mistaken the chill for me being cold. It was actually the truth hitting me right in the middle of my chest. Breaking yet another piece of my heart off. I honestly didn't know if there were any pieces left. The pain in my chest was the only indication that there was still something keeping me going.

Mallory is the one Tripp wants.

Not me.

The drive back to my place was filled with chatter. Thank God. It was almost like Toby knew I needed to have my mind somewhere else.

By the time he had pulled into my driveway, we had both gotten to know each other a bit more. Toby grew up in Dallas, went to college at Texas Tech, became a firefighter in the Dallas area and then took this job in Oak Springs a few months back. He wanted out of the big city and into a smaller town.

"Well, you got what you wanted. Oak Springs is pretty small," I said with a chuckle.

He returned the laugh. "It is, but I love it here. The community is amazing. Well, besides the fact that everyone knows everyone…or at least acts like they do."

"Yes!" I said with a chuckle. "You got that right. Don't let the town gossip get to you though."

"I won't."

We sat for a few awkward moments before he cleared his throat. "So, how do you feel about having dinner with me tomorrow night?"

I chewed on my lip before replying. This was it. It was fight or flight time. I either sat home with a pint of Ben & Jerry's ice cream or I took the leap back into the real world of dating.

The way his schoolboy smile appeared, I couldn't help but get a few flutters in my stomach. It had been a long time since a man looked at me like that. It wasn't the man I wanted making my stomach jump, but the reaction was still the same. Clearly it was time to move on.

"Tomorrow night sounds amazing. I'd love to have dinner with you."

He clapped his hands together. "I'll pick you up around six? Is that too early?"

I shook my head. "Nope. That's perfect! I'll see you then."

Opening the door to his Toyota truck, he reached for my hand. "Wait, let me walk you up. If that's okay."

Again, the stupid little flutter as I was about to accept his offer. My poor pathetic body was overjoyed with the slightest attention from a good-looking guy. "I'd love for you to walk me up."

I waited for Toby to get out of his truck and jog around to my side. I'd taken in his body before when dancing with him. His tight Wrangler jeans and gray T-shirt made him look even nicer. He had a broad chest that my fingers were suddenly itching to touch.

Christ. What is wrong with me? I'm boo-hooing over Tripp, yet fantasizing about Toby's body.

His hand went to my lower back and a zip of desire raced through my body.

Down, libido. Yes, he is a very good-looking guy, and I know it's been forever. But you need to stow your little horny ass away.

But he's looking at me and touching me the way I want Tripp to. My heart wants one thing but my mind and body want another.

I stopped at my door and took in a deep breath. A part of me knew that Tripp and Mallory would most likely be ending the night together, but that was no reason to jump into bed with another man. Screwing him wasn't going to make me forget about Tripp. It would make my body happy, but certainly not my heart.

"Have I told you how amazing you look in that dress tonight?"

My heart started to race. I wanted him to touch me...I couldn't deny that. I'd be lying if I said I wasn't attracted to him.

"Thank you," I softly said.

Our eyes met, and I was positive we were both holding our breath.

Taking a step forward, Toby cupped my face within his hands. He leaned in and kissed me gently on the lips. It was soft and caring and the perfect kiss I needed to end this night.

When he drew back, we both smiled. "I'll see you tomorrow night."

"See you then."

His hands dropped to his side and he took a step back and winked. I lifted my hand and waved.

"Night, Toby."

"Night, Harley."

With that, he turned and headed to his truck. The perfect gentleman. My fingers swept over my lips. Would a man ever be able to make my body feel the way it did with Tripp? Sure, there were flutters with Toby, but with Tripp the flutters turned into burning desire. Would another man be able to replicate that same passion in me?

Never.

I sighed and watched Toby drive off.

Maybe he would be the one to help me move past that. It was going to take time. Now that I knew Tripp wasn't going to forgive me, I needed to start my own healing process. I smiled thinking about tomorrow night's dinner.

"Little steps," I whispered to no one in particular, silently hoping my heart heard the words as I unlocked my door. I was greeted by Lady who barked and rushed past me. She did her business and zipped by me again. She went straight for my bedroom, ready to call it a night.

Sighing, I kicked off my shoes and made the way to my bedroom. I was greeted by Lady laying not so lady-like on my mattress, on her back, paws in the air, ready for a good night's rest herself. Geez…if life were only that easy.

"I know girl. It's past our bedtime."

I stripped out of my clothes and got into sweats and a T-shirt. With Lady snuggled in my bed, I reached for the Kindle on my nightstand. I needed to escape the real world for a bit. Sliding books from right to left, I finally settled on a historical romance. My favorite genre.

For one brief moment, my mind wandered to Tripp. Would he spending the night with Mallory? Maybe they would go back to his place before he took her home. Or maybe he stayed with her at her house. The thoughts were starting to make me feel sick. Pushing him as far out of my mind as I could, I was soon lost in my book.

All my problems would have to wait. Tonight was all about the perfect love story—two characters who were destined to be together forever.

Something I thought I knew about...once upon a time.

CHAPTER 10

Tripp

I stared at the paperwork on my desk. My mind raced with everything except what I was supposed to be working on.

It had been days since I'd seen Harley and Toby leave Cord's Place, and of course, it was all I could think about. Mallory had ended up getting a headache and asking me to take her home. We were both having a miserable time anyway, so it wasn't a big deal to call it a night early. Plus, she could tell I wasn't in the mood for staying out. After I dropped her off, I had been tempted to drive by Harley's house. Luckily, I got my wits about me and went home.

Three knocks on my office door had me looking up while I called out, "Come in."

Karen walked in with a piece of paper in her hand. She slapped it down on my desk and raised one brow. "You owe me."

With a grin, I folded my arms and waited to hear what she had found out.

"I'm sure your next bonus will more than make up for the one favor I asked of you."

She huffed. "According to my source over at Pete London's office, they confirmed Harley met with Mr. London."

I learned forward, my arms on my desk. "What else did she find out?"

"I didn't say it was a she."

Rolling my eyes, I blew out an exasperated breath.

"Karen, I know it's your sister, Riley. She works for Pete. That's not a secret."

She shot me a dirty look. "And if you so much as breathe a word of where you got this information, I'll quit."

I held up my hands and then crossed my heart. "I swear. Not a word. Now spill it."

"Okay, well, apparently Doc Harris has a brother who is a big time investor in Texas and beyond."

I nodded. "I knew that."

"I guess when Doc was opening up this clinic in Oak Springs, he borrowed money from his brother or something along those lines. Doc says he paid his brother off, but the brother is saying that isn't the full story and that Doc Harris had no right to sell to Harley. He's trying to take the vet clinic away from her. Said that he was the rightful owner and that he intends on taking over and booting Harley out."

Anger raced through my veins. "Where was this guy all those years Doc was running the clinic? Has he put any additional money into it?"

She shook her head.

"Any major decisions he was a part of?"

"The brother? Not that I know of. Might be they just haven't found out yet."

I nodded. "What's Pete's game plan?"

Giving me a shrug, she replied, "I don't know. Pete has set up a meeting with the brother's lawyer and a mediator."

I dropped back in my seat. *Damn it.* Pete wasn't going to be able to help Harley like I could. He wasn't that great at this type of thing.

"There is a bit of information I got that you might also be interested in."

"What's that?" I asked, knowing the second the words were out of my mouth I would regret it. I never let myself get caught up in gossip.

"Harley had dinner with Toby two nights in a row."

My brow lifted. *Okay... maybe just this once.* "Why do you think I would be interested in that? I have a girlfriend. Harley and I are old news."

Karen tilted her head. "Really? So then what's the reason you can't focus on your work?"

"What?" I nearly shouted.

"You've been staring at this deposition for hours, Tripp. I've worked with you long enough to know your mind is somewhere else."

"It's on the race."

Her left brow raised like it always did when she was calling me on my bullshit. "The race?"

"As in the mayoral race?"

"The one that hasn't started yet? Planning out your strategy on a race that isn't on anyone's radar for months, at least? That one?"

If I could have shot daggers out of my hands I would have aimed right for her.

"By the way, I can't believe you sent Mallory into my office when I was in with Harley."

She looked at me like I was insane. "What do you mean? I told her you were in there with Harley, and that when she came out Mallory could go straight in. When I left, she was sitting in the waiting room."

Why the fuck would Mallory lie about that? Did she purposely come into my office and drop her coat because she knew Harley was there? What the fuck?

Before I had a chance to question Karen any more, Cord walked in.

"It's Wednesday! That means banana nut bread day!" he declared.

Karen stood. "Hello there, Cord. Sorry, no banana bread today."

Cord's face fell. "W-what? But…Wednesday is banana nut bread day."

She shrugged. "I had to do a favor last night for your brother and it took longer than I thought, so blame him. I'll leave you boys be."

Karen turned to walk out of my office. When she looked back to us, she grinned. "I guess you wouldn't be interested to know that I also overheard Harley telling Maebh something worth knowing. By the way, those two seem to have struck up a friendship. They've had lunch together the last two days."

"Karen!" I warned.

With an innocent look, she went on. "What? I was just gonna say I overheard them saying they were going on a double-date this Friday."

I scoffed. "Well, good for them."

A smile moved over her face as she gave us the evil eye. "I do think they're lucky. Both girls going out with such handsome firefighters."

"What the hell?" Cord said as his eyes bounced from me back to Karen.

"Did you know there's talk of a calendar that those boys are gonna do to help the senior center's annual fundraiser? I'd pay good money to see our local firefighters with no shirts on."

I knew for sure Cord was about to blow a gasket. "It's not just the firefighters! Trevor and I were asked to do it, as well."

My head jerked, and I glared at him. "What!"

Wiggling her eyebrows, Karen let out a chuckle. "Now that is something I could go to sleep with every night."

I nearly gagged. "Seriously? I just threw up in my mouth, Karen."

Cord, on the other hand, puffed out his damn chest.

"I'm just saying, two beautiful women like that up for grabs. It's no wonder those boys are moving in fast."

"Who's moving in fast?" Cord's head jerked over toward Karen, almost in disbelief.

"Nobody," I mumbled.

"Toby and Jackson. They're the ones going on the dates with the girls."

"Jackson? Maebh is going out with him?" Cord asked with a fake-as-hell laugh. I knew it pissed him off because I'd seen the way he couldn't tear his eyes off of Maebh when she came into the bar with the girls. It wasn't lost on me that my sisters were up to something with both Maebh and Harley, but what exactly, I didn't know.

Karen glared at Cord. "Well, at least those boys know what they want and aren't afraid to go for it. Unlike *some* men in this town." She eyed both of us before spinning on her heel and marching out. She slammed my office door behind her.

"What the hell did she mean by that?" Cord asked.

"I've stopped trying to figure out years ago what that woman is trying to say to me."

Staring at my door, I shook my head. Here I had thought Karen was Team Mallory. It appeared she'd switched sides, and I wanted to know why.

"Well, since I'm here, you want to grab lunch? There's a new food truck in the parking lot of Hank's Hardware. Joe's BBQ."

"Joe? As in Joe Maynard?"

Cord smiled big. "Yep. He's finally gone off and done it. I guess enough people told him his ribs were the best in Texas, and he decided to take the leap."

I stood. "Well, I'm happy to know he followed a dream. I had seen an application to sell food had been presented to the city council a few months back, but I didn't pay attention to it. Heard rumors that the food trucks were making their way to our little town."

Following me out of the office, Cord slapped my back. "Looks like our sleepy little town is growing. You sure you still want to be mayor?"

My chest tightened at Cord's question. I had no idea what in the hell I wanted anymore. For as long as I could remember, I'd wanted to run for mayor. It was all I ever thought about and had been one of my long-term goals I had set for myself my senior year of high school. Among other long-term goals. Some which were coming true. Lately I was feeling like the most important ones were not.

I found Karen typing away at her desk.

"Hey, give me a few seconds. I need to talk to Karen about something."

With a nod, Cord tipped his cowboy hat to Karen. "Have a good one, Karen."

She lifted her head slightly to give him a smile. "I will. You do the same, Cord."

After Cord walked out the door, I stood in front of her desk, but she ignored me. "Karen?"

"Yes?" she answered while she kept typing.

"May I ask you a question?"

When she stopped, she shot her eyes up to mine. "You may. I, however, may choose not to answer it."

I frowned. "What the hell does that mean?"

She half-shrugged. "I'm upset with you, Tripp Parker."

"I see that. Why?"

Standing, her hands went to her hips. "You're stupid. Blind. Unforgiving. Stubborn. Ignorant." Her brows lifted, and she gave me that look that all southern women have perfected. That one that says she's going to speak her mind and you should pay close attention cuz shit's about to go down. "And a man. I don't think I need to say anything else."

My mouth opened to speak, but her look challenged me to disagree with her.

"Fine. I'm all those things. You want to tell me why you're all of a sudden on Harley's side?"

"Sides? Oh, are we pickin' sides now?" Her Texas accent hit full force. It always did when she was angry.

I rolled my eyes. "No, we are not *picking sides*. It's just before you were pretty clear you liked Mallory. Now you seem to…like Harley a bit more."

Her arms folded across her chest and her chin lifted.

Fuck. I pissed her off. Now I won't hear the end of it for a week.

"Tripp Parker, let me tell you something. I am not pro or con about either one of those girls. They're both nice. I thought Harley had done you wrong, but from what I've heard, she has apologized to you, and you have not accepted."

"What! How in the hell do you know that?"

"I have my verified sources which I will not disclose."

I narrowed my eyes at her. One of the Parker women was behind this. No one else could possibly know that information.

"I take it, though, you do not deny it."

Letting out a frustrated sigh, I scrubbed my hands down my face. "That is none of your damn business!"

She huffed. "Fine. Then I won't tell you what I know about Mallory that has knocked her down a few pegs in my graces."

My eyes widened, and I was pretty sure my jaw dropped to the floor.

"Mallory? You have information on Mallory?" I laughed. "What could you possibly have on her?"

The woman stared like we were in a pissing contest, and she was hell-bent on lasting longer. She finally broke the stare.

"I need to get back to work. If you want to find about the young man who visited her house and stayed for hours before leaving, you'll have to ask her yourself."

My stomach dropped. "What? When was this?"

She shrugged. "My memory seems to be strugglin' on that bit of information."

I pointed to her and was about to demand she tell me, when she glared.

My hand dropped, and I stormed outside and past Cord.

"What's wrong with you?" he asked, attempting to keep up with me.

"Women. That's what's wrong with me."

CHAPTER 11

Tripp

I walked up the porch steps and took a breath before knocking on my sister's door.

Three taps and I stepped back. The door opened. Waylynn was holding her daughter, Liberty, in her arms.

"Hey, Tripp! What brings you by on this fine April day?"

I smiled and took my cowboy hat off as I followed Waylynn into the house.

"Hadn't seen Liberty in a week or so and wanted to stop by. How is my sweet little niece doing?"

Waylynn beamed with happiness. "She's amazing. Can you believe she's a month old?"

"No," I replied with a light-hearted chuckle.

"Hey there, Tripp!"

I turned to find Corina standing there. My eyes immediately went to her stomach. She had gotten bigger in the last week.

"Hey, you." I kissed her on the cheek and pointed to her stomach. "May I say hi?"

She giggled. "Yes! The baby is super active today."

My hands gently touched her six-month pregnant belly. Leaning closer, I started talking to the baby.

"Hey there, baby Parker. How are you today?"

Instantly, I felt a kick.

"Wow!" I said with a laugh.

"I know. Baby Parker is for sure an active one."

Moving my hand on her stomach, I felt another kick. "That's incredible. Still not finding out the sex of the baby?"

"Nope. Keeping it a surprise.

"I love that y'all are doing that," Waylynn added.

After a few more seconds of baby talk with Corina's stomach, I stepped away. The ache in my chest was pretty clear as I looked at both of them.

I wanted kids. For the first time ever, the urge was strong and the pain in my chest very real.

"Have you talked to Liberty Senior lately?" I asked Waylynn as I took my niece out of her mother's arms. Liberty Senior was Liberty's birth mother, who she was named after.

"I have. She's doing amazing and only has a few weeks of school left in the semester."

"She still working for Mick and Wanda?" I asked.

"Yep. They have taken her under their wing and are treating her like their own daughter."

Corina smiled. "That doesn't surprise me in the least bit. They are such amazing people."

As I gazed down at my niece, I couldn't help but wonder what things would have been like if Harley and I hadn't gone down the paths we did. Would we have kids by now? If so, how many would we have wanted? Would I still be wanting to run for mayor, or would I be content with my job?

"You're deep in thought, little brother. What are you thinking about? The kid bug hitting you?"

Corina and Waylynn both laughed, but when I looked up at them, their smiles faded.

"Oh. My. God. It is."

I laughed. "I guess it is, Waylynn."

"Are you and Mallory…um…are y'all talking about kids?"

"What?" I asked as my gaze bounced between the two of them. "Why would you think that?"

They looked at each other and shrugged. "People talk," Waylynn stated.

"People talk? Who's talking and what are they saying?"

"Nothing," both of them said at once.

I shook my head. "I think I've heard enough small town talk for a while. I got an earful from Karen yesterday."

Turning, I headed over to the living room and planted myself in the rocker. Liberty was staring up at me, those big blue eyes gazing into mine.

"What do you think about all of this?" I asked her in a sing-song voice.

Her mouth rose into a smile.

"Waylynn! She's smiling at me!" I softly yelled.

"It's gas, Tripp. Just gas."

Corina chuckled.

Running my finger along Liberty's cheek, I smiled bigger. "That wasn't no gas, was it, baby girl? You love your favorite uncle, don't you?"

Liberty smiled again. This time it was followed by a rumble in her diaper.

"Oh, dang girl. What are you trying to say?"

I sat there for another few minutes until it was clear to my nose that my precious little niece had just shit in her diaper.

Heading back into the kitchen, I cleared my throat. "I believe your child needs a diaper change."

Corina plugged her nose. "Whew! Man, oh man, can that kid stink up a room."

Waylynn chuckled as she took Liberty from my arms. "Come on, you can help me change her."

"Hard pass," I stated.

Rolling her eyes, Waylynn walked off.

I stepped farther into the kitchen, grabbed a grape and popped it into my mouth.

"How are you feeling, Corina?"

Her cheeks flushed and an adorable smile appeared on her face. My brother, Mitchell, was a lucky son-of-a-bitch. His wife was so incredibly sweet and loved my brother like he was the reason the sun rose and set each day.

"I feel amazing, Tripp. I honestly do. I don't think I've ever felt so happy."

A rush of happiness for her and Mitchell ran through my body. Even though we once dated, I always knew we were better at the friend's thing. "I know Mitchell feels the same. Every time I see him he looks even happier."

She bit her lip. "He's so happy working at your folks' ranch. I was worried he would regret his decision to leave the Texas Rangers. I know he also loved being a cop."

"All's well in that department?" I asked, knowing the answer already. Mitchell didn't have a single regret. His life was the ranch and Corina—and not in that order.

"Yes. He's helped out on a few cases that were still open that he was investigating, but other than that, he loves working on the ranch."

I nodded while picking up a strawberry. "I know he does. That ranch is in all of our blood. There's something about working on it that seems to soothe the soul."

"Maybe you should stop by and give them a hand sometime. Lately, you look like your soul could use some soothing."

I let out a gruff laugh. "You hit that on the head."

"Anything you want to talk about?"

Glancing at the floor, I took in a deep breath and blew it out before catching her eyes.

"I guess I'm just a bit confused."

"Mallory and Harley?"

With a nod, I sank onto one of the stools at the kitchen island.

"Well, it seemed pretty clear to everyone the other night at Cord's that Mallory and you are an item. Especially to Harley."

A lump instantly formed in my throat. "What?"

"Well, I mean, it's pretty obvious you don't intend on forgiving Harley and that you told her you were moving on. I think she saw that the other night at Cord's Place. We were hoping by forcing her to go out that y'all might run into each other, but our plan sort of backfired when we saw you with Mallory."

Giving her the stink eye, I said, "I knew y'all were up to something. What do you mean your plan backfired?"

"I can answer that one," Waylynn stated.

She handed me a clean Liberty whom I gladly accepted. I glanced down at the baby and my heart melted once again. I lifted her and took in a deep breath of her smell. There was something about the way babies smelled. It was like a happy pill.

"We had this grand plan to get y'all together and I thought maybe we could make you a little jealous. I introduced Harley to Toby, and well…now they seem to be hitting it off. They've gone out a few times."

"Yeah, and Maebh has gone out with Jackson a few times, as well. So much for getting Cord to notice her," Corina added.

"Trust me, Cord has noticed Maebh and is not too happy about her and Jackson."

Waylynn looked at me with a dumbfounded look. "Then why doesn't he ask her out?"

I shrugged. "Cause he's Cord."

She shook her head. "I don't understand men. Especially my brothers."

Clearing my throat, I asked, "So Harley and Toby are dating? As in exclusively?"

They turned to look at each other again and shrugged.

"What was that?"

Waylynn did it again. "It's called a shrug. I have no clue what's going on with them. I know she said she enjoys his company and he makes her laugh."

Fucker.

"Paxton and Harley talk every day. If you want the scoop, you'll need to ask her," Waylynn added.

I let out a scoff. "I don't want any scoop. It's none of my business."

A sadness settled into Waylynn's eyes. "Yeah, I guess so."

I spent the next two hours at Waylynn's helping with Liberty while Waylynn and Corina cut up a bunch of fruit for trays they were making for Mrs. Johnson. Something about a luncheon. I tuned them out and played with Liberty most of the time until she finally crashed out on me for her nap.

Before I headed out the door, I turned back to Waylynn. "Do you know about Doc Harris's brother trying to take the clinic away from Harley?"

She nodded. "Yeah. Pete's trying to help her, but I think he's in over his head with this one. Harley is getting ready to find a lawyer in San Antonio. Someone with a bit more experience."

Guilt hit me right in the gut. "I'll stop by the clinic and see if there's anything I can do. Besides, I owe Harley an apology for acting like an asshole."

A wide smile took over her face. "It's about damn time you realized that."

Kissing her on the cheek, I pulled back and winked. "I'm a man. What did you expect?"

"Touché."

The drive over to the vet clinic took about thirty minutes from the ranch. When I pulled in to park, I noticed an older couple walking out of the clinic. Harley was behind them, holding a cat carrier. She was dressed in jeans, a white blouse, and cowboy boots. Her hair was pulled up into a sloppy bun that was piled on top of her head. I was left breathless by the sight of her. That was never going to change. She held a piece of me that would always be attracted to her. Guilt ate me up inside as I thought about my feelings for Harley, and the fact that I was with Mallory.

When she turned and saw me getting out of the truck, she smiled. And my knees damn near went out from under me. After the way I'd treated her, she still rewarded me with a smile.

I'm such an asshole. Maybe if I think it enough times it will sink in.

"Thank you so much, Harley. I don't know what we would have done if you hadn't been able to figure out what was wrong with Snuggles."

I tried like hell to cover my chuckle.

"No worries at all, Mrs. Poteet. Now that we know she has a food allergy, she should be feeling better soon."

The older man took the cat carrier and set it in the back seat before shutting the passenger side door to his car. "Thanks again, Harley!" he called out before climbing in and pulling off.

As I walked over, our eyes met. Her green eyes sparkled when the sun hit them just right. An urge to pull her into my arms hit me, causing me to pause for a moment before I continued on.

"Snuggles, huh?"

She nodded while pressing her lips together. "Yep. A six-month old calico kitty who is the apple of Mrs. and Mr. Poteets' eye."

We both grinned.

"Do you have any more clients waiting on you?"

"No, I'm finished for the day. I was about to head into San Antonio."

A hard squeeze in my chest reminded me what I was here for. "May I talk to you first? Before you leave?"

The hint of a smile at the corner of her mouth offered me a bit of hope. I didn't deserve this, not after the way I'd stormed out of here the last time.

"Of course. Come on in. Everyone's already left for the day so I have to clean up, if you don't mind chatting while I clean."

Motioning with my hand for her to lead the way, I replied, "I don't mind at all."

Harley gave me a once over, and I was wondering if she was thinking the same thoughts I had been only moments ago. She headed into the clinic and down the hall to one of the examination rooms.

I decided to get right to the point. On both reasons I was there.

"Harley, I'm sorry for reacting the way I did when you…well…when you told the truth about everything. I was angry."

She gave me a soft grin. "You had every right to be angry. I lied to you and made a decision about our relationship without giving us a chance to make things work. I hope you know that is a decision I'll regret for the rest of my life."

Her eyes filled with a sadness that seemed to spill into the room and swallow me up. After a deep breath, I looked at her. She was spraying the counter with something and wiping it.

"The other reason I'm here is to offer you legal help on your problem with Doc's brother."

She stopped cleaning and looked at me. "You know?"

I nodded. "Yes, and it won't be long before the whole town knows too."

With a deep sigh, she dropped down onto a stool. "Shit. The last thing I want is drama. Pete isn't really offering much hope…or help. I was heading to San Antonio to find another lawyer."

My hands started to sweat, and I prayed she couldn't hear my heart pounding.

"Well, that's why I'm here. I want to help you."

Her eyes widened with hope. "Really? You'd do that for me after everything I told you?"

"Of course I would, Lee."

A beautiful smile spread over her face but quickly vanished. Tears sprang up in her eyes and I hated that I was the cause of them. I hated seeing her upset. I always had.

"What's wrong?" I asked, walking over and lifting her chin so our eyes met.

"I'm going to lose everything, Tripp. Every penny I've saved for ten years was spent on this practice."

My brows pulled together. "What?"

She sniffed. "After college, I was home and helping Doc Harris at the clinic. He asked me if I ever planned on moving back home and I said yes. He told me that when he was ready to retire, I could buy him out."

"How long have you known you were going to move back to Oak Springs?"

She looked away. "Since…not long after that day. It didn't take me long to realize the mistakes I'd made in my life."

I realized I was holding her arms. I let her go and took a few steps back.

"Anyway, every bit of money I had saved went into buying Doc out. I have a feeling his brother is going to drag even more money out of me. Money I don't have."

I shook my head. "I won't let that happen. Finish up here and then let's grab something to eat at the café. You can follow me if you'd like."

She chewed on her lip for a few seconds before giving me a slight smile. "Okay, let me finish up."

CHAPTER 120

Harley

As I cleaned up the clinic, I told Tripp about Doc's older brother, Gerald Harris, and how he had started sending me harassing notes soon after I purchased the clinic.

"What did the notes say?"

"At first they said things like the clinic belonged to him. He was the rightful owner. Then they got angrier when I ignored them. He accused me of stealing from Doc, forcing him to sell out to me for under-market value. Trust me when I say that I paid fair market value for this place."

Tripp turned out the lights as we made our way out of the clinic. "What does Doc say about all of this?"

I stopped at my car and sighed. "At first he told me to ignore the notes. He said it was his older brother causing problems. I guess they had a falling out a few years back. He told me it would all blow over once he contacted him and they talked."

"Did that help? Doc talking to his brother?"

"For a few weeks. Then I got served with the papers that said Gerald was suing me for illegally buying out Doc and that he was also part owner and deserved to be bought out."

"Is that true?"

I shrugged. "I don't know. Doc claims it isn't true, but I feel like he's hiding something. That or he truly doesn't remember borrowing money from his brother and not paying him back."

Our eyes met, and we stared at one another for what seemed like an eternity. I finally managed to tear my gaze away. Trying to break the awkward silence that surrounded us as we stood alone in the parking lot, I began to shift uncomfortably.

"Well, um, I'll meet you over at Lilly's?" I asked.

A few moments passed while Tripp simply stared at me.

"Tripp? Are you okay?"

He took a step back. "Yeah, sorry. I got lost in a thought for a moment. We'll get this figured out. I promise."

My stomach dropped at his promise. He was being so kind, and I was so thankful he had forgiven me, although I was sure it wasn't forgotten.

"Thank you, Tripp. I appreciate you helping me on this."

With a hard swallow, he replied, "Of course. I'll see ya at the café in a few minutes."

My teeth sank into my lip as I reminded myself not to reach up and kiss him. Tripp's eyes looked so empty. It made me sad because I was positive I'd caused that. I couldn't help but wonder why he had done a one-eighty. Maybe Waylynn had threatened him. It didn't really matter. I was just happy he was talking to me.

I gave him a small smile. "Okay. See ya there."

The moment we walked into Lilly's, all eyes were on us.

"Oh lawd, let the rumors start flyin'," I whispered as Tripp took me by the elbow and guided us over to a table.

"Gives them something to talk about tomorrow."

I chuckled as I slid into a booth in the far back corner of the café. One quick scan of the restaurant, and it was confirmed. We would indeed be the talk of the town by morning.

"Karen's here," I whispered.

Tripp rolled his eyes. "I take that back. Gives them something to talk about tonight. She's already on the gossip text."

"Gossip text?" I asked.

Leaning in closer, he spoke softly. "There is a group of women who are on a text message chain. It started as a 'prayer chain.'" He used his fingers to do air quotes around prayer chain. "But in reality, it's really the modern-day gossip mill."

"Great," I huffed as I sat back. "I hope Mallory won't be upset with us eating dinner here together."

Tripp's eye appeared to twitch. "Mallory?"

Nodding, I said, "Yes, your *girlfriend.*"

When he opened his mouth to respond, I let my heart believe he was about to tell me they weren't dating. That they were only friends. But I knew better.

"Evening, y'all," Lilly said with a wide-as-Texas grin. "Fancy seeing y'all two in here together."

Turning my attention to Lilly, I grinned, but it faded when Tripp spoke.

"We're only here for business. That's it."

I tried not to let those words hit me in the gut like a hard punch. I had made my bed, and now I had to lie in it.

"Business, huh?" Lilly asked with a wink.

"Yes. Business only, Lilly. I'll take a water and a coffee, please."

Lilly's eyes bounced between the two of us. For a brief moment she looked confused. I tried to force a smile and act normal, but the way Tripp was acting bothered me more than it should. It's true; we were there for business. But the way he stressed it...*twice*...made me feel like I was doing something wrong.

"What will you have, Harley?"

"Water, please."

"Y'all want to order some food?"

"No."

"Yes." Tripp looked at me confused. I had said no because all I wanted to do in that moment was run from the café and back home to the safety of my house.

"I thought we were having dinner?" he asked.

"Just the drinks for right now, Lilly," I said.

She nodded and headed away.

"What's wrong?" Tripp asked.

"Listen, Tripp, if you're worried about people getting the wrong impression and this getting back to your girlfriend, then maybe we should only talk at your office during office hours."

"What?" he asked with a stare.

I shook my head and looked down at my nails. For some reason, in that moment, I noticed how much I had let myself go since coming back to Oak Springs. I no longer went and had my nails done. I didn't even remember the last time I'd worn my hair down...or washed it, for that matter. Okay, not true. I'd washed it two days ago.

Why would Tripp ever want someone like me when he had the perfectly polished Mallory? She owned her own business, was a successful single mom. Beautiful and always dressed to the nines. She was the perfect match for the future mayor of this town.

"Harley? Harley?"

When his hand touched mine I jumped back.

"Jesus, what's wrong with you?"

I could feel the tears burning at the back of my eyes. *Jesus, I've turned into a crybaby.* "I, um…I just think we should talk at your office."

"Nonsense. I meet with clients here all the time. I'm not worried what people will say."

"It didn't seem like that when Lilly said something. You were very defensive."

He leaned back in the booth, took off his cowboy hat, and pushed his fingers through his hair. He let out a frustrated sigh as he set the hat down next to him. My stomach pulled with desire and all I could think about were the days my fingers went through his brown hair, giving it a small tug when I needed him to be deeper inside of me.

My tongue slid over my dry lips. Tripp's eyes immediately landed on my mouth. I'd give anything to feel those lips on my skin.

Closing my eyes, I dropped my head and cursed. *Christ above, Harley Carbajal. Knock it off and stow the dirty thoughts. He's made it very clear he's not interested, and he's dating someone.*

"I'm sorry if I made you feel like I didn't want to be here."

I held up my hands to stop him. "You don't have to apologize. My emotions are just all over the place right now because of Doc's brother, and I don't know which end is up and which is down."

He reached for my hand again but I pulled them both back and rested them in my lap.

Clearing his throat, he said, "I am seeing Mallory, yes. But we're not…I mean, we *are*… It's sort of…"

"Here are those two waters and a coffee. Are we getting food?" Lilly seemed annoyed. She looked at me with sympathy and at Tripp with frustration.

Before I could answer, Tripp did.

"Yes. I'll take the special."

Lilly faced me. "And for you, Harley?"

I wasn't even sure what the special was, but I ordered it as well. "I'll take the same."

Scooping up the menus, Lilly gave me a wink. "Two specials it is."

Watching her walk away, I wanted to call out to her. Ask her to sit down and join us. The thought of being alone with Tripp suddenly scared me to death.

"Do you even know what the special is, Lee?"

His pet name for me sounded so good. My eyes met his. I shook my head.

"I didn't think so."

He gave me a smile that melted my heart and had it breaking even more. Just when I was positive it couldn't possibly break anymore, it kept proving me wrong.

"Doc's brother came back into the picture claiming he has stakes in the clinic. Is that all you know?"

"Yes. I've been putting off talking to him and his lawyer for weeks now. I'm afraid my time is up. We're meeting in the courthouse tomorrow at eleven AM."

Tripp pulled out his phone, and I guessed he was pulling up his calendar.

"I'm free, so I can attend. I'll get everything from Pete first thing in the morning and go over what he has. Once we meet with them we'll be able to find out what in the hell is going on with the clinic, and you can go back to doing what you love."

Tears formed in my eyes. "Th-thank you, Tripp."

"Don't cry. God, Harley, please don't cry. You know how much it kills me to see you cry."

Wiping the tears from my cheeks, I looked down at my folded hands. "I'm sorry. It's just…I thought things would be so different when I moved back here. Honestly, I don't know what I was expecting or even thinking. Nothing has worked out like I thought it would and a part of me wonders if I should give him the clinic and just slip away."

"Look at me."

His voice was strong and commanding. Like it was when we were together. Memories flooded my mind all at once and I couldn't have stopped the tears even if I tried. I knew people were staring at us. The gossips were probably typing out their text messages and snapping their clandestine pics now.

Harley is crying. Tripp's told her to leave town. Oh, Harley's now on the floor in a fetal position sobbing like an idiot. Click, click, click.

"I'm sorry for the way things worked out. But we can't change the past."

I swiped the tears away again and took a shaky breath. "We can't," I said. My voice shaking.

"But we were best friends at one time, Harley, and I don't want to lose your friendship."

A sick feeling settled in my stomach. *Friends.* He wanted to be friends.

Forcing a smile, I replied, "I don't want to lose that either. Our friendship."

His sweet, gentle smile should have made me feel better, but all it did was serve as a reminder of the terrible mistake I had made.

I'm an idiot. How could I ever think he would take me back after the pain I caused him?

"We're going to figure this out, Harley. I swear to you. Once we meet with Gerald and his lawyers tomorrow and see exactly what proof they have of his claim, we'll get this taken care of."

Lilly walked over with two plates of meatloaf, mashed potatoes, and fried okra. "Two specials. Anything else I can get y'all?"

Her eyes met mine. She could tell I had been crying. I could see the sympathy in her eyes.

"No thank you," I said with a smile.

For years Lilly would hardly speak to me because of what I did to Tripp. I was pretty sure Waylynn had told her mother, Melanie, the truth and Melanie had spread it over town like wildfire. Probably like wildfire on the gossip text. I no longer got stares of anger, now they were looks of pity. The silly girl who lied to Tripp thinking she was doing the right thing only to have him ignore her for years…

"Are you going to eat?"

"What?" I asked as I looked over to Tripp.

"Your food, Lee. You're just pushing it around with your fork. You need to eat."

After taking a few bites, I set my fork down.

"What if he takes it away from me?"

"He won't."

I shook my head. "How can you say that? It's a possibility."

Tripp leaned back and gave me a hard look. "It is a possibility, yes. But if you give up before you even try, then why even bother? Where is the fight in you? This is something you have dreamed about and although we haven't seen each other in almost ten years, I know damn well that fight is still in you. You're not a quitter."

Warmth spread through my entire body. He was right. I was going to fight—with Tripp by my side. I could feel it deep in my soul.

"You're right. I'm going to win this."

For a brief moment, staring at Tripp across the table, I wasn't sure what I wanted to win more—the legal mess I was in or the battle for Tripp's love.

He reached his hand across the table and I set mine in it. The instant rush of tingles sweeping through my entire body almost had me gasping out loud, but I somehow managed to keep the sound back. I could have sworn Tripp reacted the same way, judging by the way his body shuddered.

"*We're* going to win this."

We smiled at one another as my heart raced. Tripp squeezed my hand three times before letting it go and motioning with his fork.

"Eat up. The meatloaf is damn good."

I had to bite the inside of my lip to keep my emotions from getting to me. It was becoming clearer with each passing day that Tripp Parker had indeed slipped through my fingers. I was going to have to be happy with simply being friends. Now I just had to convince my heart of that.

I picked up my fork and forced myself to eat.

This was going to be a long, hard road to navigate.

CHAPTER 13

Tripp

The knock on my office door had me standing up. My heart was racing and my damn hands were sweating.

Christ Almighty. Get it together, Parker.

"Come in."

When my mother walked in, my entire body sagged.

"Clearly you were hoping for someone else."

I rounded my desk and walked to her. Extending my arms, I pulled her in for a hug.

"Nonsense. I love seeing you anytime, anywhere."

She gave me that look that said she wasn't buying my bullshit. "Who were you expecting?" she asked with a sly grin.

"A client."

One brow raised. "It's a small town, son, and you're the talk of it currently, courtesy of the 'prayer chain'. I'm going to guess you were expecting Harley. The mediation is today, correct?"

A chuckle slipped from my lips. "I thought you didn't get into all the town gossip, Mom."

With an evil look, she replied, "I don't participate in it, son." She shrugged. "At least, not all the time. That doesn't mean I don't like to hear it."

"You're impossible. I don't suppose you had anything to do with the whole damn town finding out about the real reason Harley left?"

She wore a fake surprised expression. "You mean the made-up boyfriend story because she loved you so much she didn't want to take you away from Oak Springs? That *real* story?"

Now it was my turn to give her a surprised look...but mine wasn't fake. "Wow. You really kicked up the story there, Mom."

She gave me a wink. "I try."

I shook my head. "You do remember Mallory, right?"

"She's a very nice girl, but Tripp, even I can see the two of you are not serious. Unless you've talked about a future together?"

"No, not really. But I do care about her and Laney."

She smiled. "I know you do. But do you love her?"

I was frozen by those five words. *Did I love Mallory? Did she love me? I enjoyed spending time with her, but did I see a future with her?*

"I care about her. We've only been dating since December."

"Uh-huh. Well, I'm not here to talk about Mallory *or* Harley. I'm here on other urgent business."

Motioning for her to sit down in a chair, I leaned against my desk.

"Is everything okay?"

"Oh, yes, everything with me is fine. It's your brother, Trevor."

I jerked my head back. "Trevor?"

Her lips pursed in a hard line, and she got a fiery look in her eyes. Oh, hell. My mother was on a mission and my poor baby brother was part of it. Unbeknownst to him, I was sure.

"The spring fling is this weekend, right? Well, that means my annual benefit dinner is the next evening and everyone is going to be there."

"Yes," I replied with a slight grin. I had a feeling I knew where this was going. After a hard day of work on the ranch, my parents always hosted a dinner party the next night. It was a benefit dinner and the one time of year my father let my mother go crazy with party planning. It was a black tie event and cost a few hundred dollars to attend, but one hundred percent of the money collected went to the American Cancer Society. My mother's parents both died from cancer so it was a cause very close to her heart.

"Well, I've been begging Trevor to escort Scarlett Littlefield and he refuses to."

"Sounds like Trevor just doesn't want to be tied down to a date. You know how he is about that."

"Oh, please. I know that boy has a reputation for being a ladies' man. It's one night, for Pete's sake. That's all I'm asking for. The last few years he's brought the most dreadful girls. If I didn't know better, I'd say he picked them up at the bar the night before."

He probably had, but I wasn't about to tell my mother that.

"Mom, you know what you have to do to get him to agree."

She sighed. "I know, but I feel like that's a low blow."

I laughed. "Why do you want Trevor to go out with this girl so much?"

"She's adorable and if he would entertain the thought of a girlfriend, they would be perfect for each other."

"Methinks our little Trevor is not going to be entertaining the thought of a girlfriend any time soon, Mom."

She brushed me off with her hand. "Nonsense. I see the restlessness in his soul. He needs a woman like Scarlett."

"And how does Scarlett feel about Trevor?"

Fiddling with her hands, she mumbled something.

I leaned closer to her, cupping my hand around my ear like I was hard of hearing. "I'm sorry. What was that? I didn't really hear you."

"She doesn't want to be fixed up with anyone. She's stubborn like her mother and insists on going to the dinner stag. Stag! Can you believe it?"

"What's wrong with that? I'm sure lots of people will be there without dates."

"My son will not be one of them. I let it go in years past because he and Amelia were both younger. Now that Amelia is married, Trevor is going to have to escort a proper young lady."

"Just tell him that, then. He can pick his own date."

"No!" my mother nearly screamed. "It *has* to be Scarlett."

"Mom, you do know if you push them together, Trevor will fight tooth and nail. What you need to do is make it seem like it was his idea. Not yours. Has he seen Scarlett since she moved back from Boston?"

"I'm not sure. Her mother did say she hadn't been to Cord's Place yet."

"Trevor will be working Friday night. If you can get Scarlett there, I bet Cord and I can get Trevor interested in taking her to the dinner."

My mother's eyes lit up. "Really?"

I couldn't believe I was doing this. A small part of me agreed with my mother, though. It was time both Cord and Trevor gave up the endless sleeping around.

"Yep. My sisters aren't the only ones who know how to play matchmaker. And I have a feeling they learned from the best. Their mother."

She stood and straightened her hair before smoothing out her pencil skirt. "Why...I have *no* idea what you're talking about, Tripp."

With a wink, she reached for a hug. "I'm counting on you. Don't let your mama down."

Holding her close to me, I replied, "No, ma'am. I wouldn't dream of doing that."

"Now, you do all you can for Harley. Whatever it takes. You hear?" she stated as she messed with my tie and patted me on the chest. "I love you, Tripp."

"Love you, too, Mom."

Once she left the room, I started back for my desk when I heard her exclaim, "Harley! Darling! What a nice surprise seeing you here!"

I rolled my eyes and headed out of my office to save Harley from my mother. She was on a roll today.

"Melanie, it's so great seeing you. How are you doing?"

"Oh, I'm doing amazing. I know you'll be at the spring fling this weekend, but are you coming to the benefit dinner?"

"Well, um, actually I was asked to attend with Toby."

I slowed my pace and stopped just shy of where my mother and Harley were standing. A heaviness traveled over my chest as I let Harley's words sink in. Why was I so bothered by this? I had planned on taking Mallory.

"Wonderful. I'm so glad you'll be there."

My mother had Harley's hand in hers. "I am, too."

"It is so nice having you back home. I know I told you that before." My mother pulled Harley in for a kiss and then a hug. She whispered something that made Harley's cheeks flush.

"Good luck today!" she called out while rushing past Karen's desk. "Bye, Karen!"

"Bye, Melanie!" Karen called out. A huge smile was on her face when she turned to me.

"Next time, a heads up it's Mom, will ya?"

She threw me a snarky grin and sat back down.

"You ready to go?" I asked a very nervous-looking Harley.

"Yeah. I guess so."

"Let me grab my jacket and briefcase and then we'll head over to the courthouse."

After rushing into my office, I headed back to the lobby where I found Mallory talking to Harley.

"Mallory?"

She flashed me a smile. A very fake smile that said she was pissed rather than happy. "Hey. I guess you forgot we were having lunch today?"

Shit.

"Mallory, I am so sorry." I gave her a quick kiss on the cheek. I caught her frown but looked at the floor for a quick second. I could feel Harley's eyes on me, and I wished I hadn't just done that.

Christ Almighty. I don't know what in the hell I'm doing anymore. I feel like I'm in the middle of a love triangle but I'm not, at least I don't think I am. I can't even think straight with both of these women within an arm's length from me.

I'd barely even touched Mallory in the last few weeks, and we certainly hadn't had sex.

"This came up last minute yesterday, and I forgot to let you know."

Her brows lifted in question. "Yesterday? I talked to you on the phone last night, Tripp. Why didn't you mention you had a court *date* with Harley?"

The way she stressed date pissed me off.

Harley cleared her throat. "Um, I'm just going to meet you over there, Tripp. It was nice to see you again, Mallory."

"You, too, Harley." Mallory gave her a condescending smile.

Once the door shut, I asked, "Again? When did you see Harley?"

"She stopped in to the store with Paxton and the kids."

"When was this?"

"I don't know, Tripp. A couple of days ago. Does it really matter?"

I closed my eyes and shook my head. "Of course not, but why the hell did you make it seem like we were heading out on a date? We're going to a mediation to see what can be worked out before this thing goes to court."

Mallory forced a grin. "I don't know what you mean."

"You stressed *date*, Mallory. Don't play coy. It's not like you."

With a huff, she threw her hands up in the air. "Well, I'm sorry if I was a bit taken aback by the fact that you blew off our lunch date to help out your ex-girlfriend."

"Hmm…" Karen mumbled as she swiveled in her chair. I turned to her and shot her a warning look.

Focusing on Mallory, I said, "I am not blowing you off. I took this case on yesterday afternoon and I meant to tell you. Why are you making such a big fucking deal about it? You know the second we were finished with…lunch…you'd rush out of here and back to the store."

"Mmm-hmm," Karen added softly.

This time both Mallory and I shot Karen a look. Turning her back to us, she started typing on her computer.

"It's fine. I'm sorry if I got snippy about it, and I certainly didn't mean to make Harley feel uncomfortable."

"Well, you did and now I'm going to be late."

She stepped out of my way. I felt like a complete ass because the only thing I could think about was getting to Harley. Even with the woman I had been dating-slash-having-sex-with standing in front of me, I couldn't shake the image of Harley talking to my mother out of my head. She had on black dress slacks, high heels, and a tan blouse. Her brown hair was down but the sides had been pinned back. She looked beautiful.

I started to walk off when Mallory grabbed my arm. "Tripp, wait. I'm sorry for overreacting and causing a scene."

"Good thing there wasn't anyone else in here," Karen added, somewhat under her breath but loud enough that her intentions didn't escape either one of us.

"That's enough, Karen," I snapped.

"I better get back to the store. I'm sorry about the misunderstanding." Mallory reached up on her toes and went to kiss me on the lips, but I pulled back. "I'll see you later?"

I nodded. "See you later." One quick kiss on her cheek, and I was out the door and rushing over to the courthouse.

It had taken me a few minutes to find out which room the meeting was being held in, but I got there with two minutes to spare.

Walking in, I cleared my throat and said, "I'm sorry I was held up."

Harley stared at me, and there was no way in hell I could miss the sadness in her eyes.

Fuck, this is all such a goddamn mess.

I opened my briefcase and took out the file Pete's office had sent early this morning, along with a notepad and two pens.

"Are you ready to begin?" the mediator asked.

"Yes," all parties answered at once.

"Then, let's start. Mr. Harris, please state the reasons you claim to be co-owner of the Oak Springs veterinarian clinic."

To say I wasn't prepared for what came next would be an understatement.

Harley and I sat on the bench in the town square and stared off into the distance.

"This is bad, isn't it?" she finally said.

"Yeah. It's for sure not good."

"How could Doc not remember his brother gave him cash to buy the land that the vet clinic was on!"

"It was probably so long ago he didn't think about it. We need to find out for sure that he never paid his brother back."

"If he didn't?"

"Then he owns the land the clinic is sitting on. That would explain why he's been harassing you about it. He probably wants to develop it."

Harley stood and started pacing. "I cannot believe this. I'm going to lose everything I've been working for."

"You will not. I won't let that happen, Lee."

She faced me. "Tripp." Tears flowed freely down her face. "I put every penny I had into buying that place. I can't ask Doc for the money back!"

Burying her face in her hands, she started crying harder. Standing, I pulled her into my arms. She felt warm against me. When she grabbed at my perfectly pressed shirt, my stomach dropped. It had been a long time since I'd held her in my arms like this. I missed it. Missed her.

"You're not going to lose everything. You legally bought the clinic. If anything, Gerald will have to buy you out. He would have had to buy out his brother. Just probably not for the same price since he owns the land."

"Oh, God. You heard what he said. If he was going to buy me out he would deduct the cost of the land."

Reaching up, I pulled the piece of hair pasted on her cheek away and tucked it behind her ear. I lifted her chin so her eyes were locked on mine.

"Listen to me, Harley. You're going to be okay. I swear to you, I won't let him take away your dream. I'll figure something out."

When she buried her face into me, my chest tightened. I hated hearing her cry, but damn it if I didn't like feeling her body against mine. My dick certainly took notice too.

Asshole. Asshole. Asshole.

I fought the urge to pull her closer. To stroke her hair and tell her everything was going to be alright. The urge to place a soft kiss on the top of her head was almost unbearable. I could have sworn I felt her rubbing my chest with her hand, but maybe that was wishful thinking.

My fogged-up mind was starting to clear up. My confusion, piece by piece, was being chipped away. I cleared my throat as I tried to regain some clarity, although the moment ended just as quickly as it began.

With an awkward step back, Harley wiped her cheeks. "I'm sorry I broke down like that."

"Don't be," I answered.

Our eyes met again, and we stood in silence. Her breaths started to accelerate before she broke the intense staring contest.

"I'm going to head on home. Thank you for being there for me today."

"We're still going to win this thing."

With a look that said she wasn't as sure as I was, she forced a grin and walked away. I was rooted to my spot as I watched Harley walk to her car. She slipped in, rolled the windows down and drove off. I sat back down on the bench and scrubbed my hands down my face.

This was all kinds of fucked up. First thing on my agenda for Monday morning was a talk with Doc Harris. Maybe he could offer up a miracle piece of paper that said he'd paid his brother off long ago. I had a terrible feeling that wasn't going to be the case...but I could at least hold out hope.

CHAPTER 14

Harley

The door flew open, and Chloe and a goat came rushing out. It wasn't Patches, so I was assuming this was Lincoln, Chloe's show goat.

"Harley! You're here!"

I was nearly knocked over when she plowed into me and wrapped her arms around my waist.

"Hey there, sweetie! How are you?"

"Great! I'm so glad you're here! I need you to look at Roy!"

"Roy?" I asked as I bent down to look her in the eye.

"My rabbit," she whispered.

The way she looked at me like I should have known who Roy was made me giggle. "Oh, right! Roy!"

Grabbing my hand, Chloe pulled me into the house with Lincoln hot on our trail.

I glanced over my shoulder to look at the goat. "Chloe, does your grammy know you have a goat in the house?"

Patches came tearing around the corner. Wearing a shirt that had the acronym G.O.A.T. down his back. Realizing what it stood for in the sports world—Greatest Of All Time—I just cracked up since Patches was her first, and obviously her favorite.

"Patches!"

Next it was Waylynn who went running by screaming the goat's name.

"Oh no, Patches got into Liberty's diaper bag again," Chloe stated.

"Again?"

She nodded. "Yeah. He likes the blanket Mommy bought for Liberty. He ate Gage's blanket, too."

Patches ran by again and this time Lincoln followed. Waylynn came running up and stopped next to us. With her hands on her knees, she dragged in a few deep breaths.

"Chloe. I'm going to kill Patches."

She laughed. "Oh, Aunt Waylynn, you're so funny! Meet me in Daddy's office, Harley!"

I leaned down to look at Waylynn. "Are you, um, are you okay?"

Blowing a long strand of her blonde hair from her face, she shook her head. "No. He ate Liberty's blanket! Next thing I know he'll be eating the baby! It's too early for this shit!"

"Waylynn, I got them out!"

I looked over to see Paxton walking up, holding Gage.

"Oh, my gosh. He's getting so big!"

"Nine months old and trying like hell to walk."

I looked from the drooling baby to Paxton. "Already?"

She nodded. "Yep. Already."

"Wow!"

Gage held his arms out to me, and I didn't waste any time taking him from Paxton.

"Hey there, handsome cowboy!" I cooed while tipping his little black cowboy hat. "This is the cutest darn thing I've ever seen."

Paxton chuckled. "He has to have it on all the time. I guess he sees Steed, Mitchell, and Wade wearing theirs so much he thinks he's supposed to wear his too."

"This little guy is going to be so smart, Paxton. You better watch out."

She sighed. "Well, if he's anything like his sister, I'm in for a ride."

"Paxton, honestly, those goats can't be coming into the house. They're getting too big," Waylynn said, now fully recovered from all the running.

"I know! I know! Steed is having a long talk with Chloe. They're allowed in her playhouse and she assumes they can still come into the house. Melanie is about to have a fit with them in the house because of all the food for the Spring Fling."

A small puppy howl came from down the hall.

"Was that a…"

"Dog," Waylynn and Paxton said at once.

"Y'all have a dog?" I asked.

"No," they both answered.

Another bark-howl.

I had to keep from laughing as I asked, "Do we know whose dog is barking?"

"Oh no," Paxton mumbled. "This is bad. Really, really bad."

"Why?" I asked, switching Gage to my other hip. This little guy was heavier than he looked.

"Wooof! Wooof!"

"There it is again!" Waylynn shouted as she hit Paxton.

"Why are you hitting me?"

Waylynn shrugged. "I don't know. It seemed like the right thing to do at the time?"

Cocking her head and putting her hands on her hips, Paxton asked, "Really? Hitting me seemed like the right thing to do?"

"Yes. At the time."

"Y'all…there is still the slight problem of a strange dog howling from down the hall. And your daughter took off down that hall and told me I had to look at 'Roy'."

"Roy?" Paxton asked with a puzzled expression.

"Oh dear," I whispered. "I'm going to guess Chloe doesn't have a pet rabbit named Roy?"

She shook her head. "Nope."

Handing Gage back to Paxton, I ushered both of them back toward the kitchen. "Y'all go take care of your kids and help Melanie. I'll find Chloe. She told me to meet her in her father's office."

Paxton's hand slapped over her mouth before she dropped it. "She's had it in there all night."

"Don't worry. Whatever it is…I'll, um, take care of it."

Another bark followed by a puppy howl had Paxton nearly in tears. "No wonder she wanted to spend the night over here last night."

"Woof!"

"Did you hear that? Oh my God," Paxton gasped.

"I didn't hear a thing," I stated.

"Neither did I," Waylynn added.

Paxton spun on her heels and said, "Damn liars!"

If I knew better, I would have sworn I heard Gage say damn.

With a groan, Paxton cried out, "This isn't my day!"

Waylynn stood in front of me. "I feel like I need to warn you. Chloe begged Steed and Paxton for a puppy. They saw them in town at the feed store…last night. Little blue tick hounds."

"Oh. No."

"Yep. It appears Chloe has dognapped a hound dog and hid it in her dad's office."

I covered my mouth and laughed. "How?"

Waylynn pointed to me. "That's for you to find out and some-how get that dog out of here before Steed finds it."

"Me?" I asked with wide eyes. "Even if it's been in there all night?"

Another little bark came from the hallway.

Waylynn turned and headed toward the kitchen. "Holy hell. Goats, dogs, babies. This place is a nuthouse!"

"Wait! Waylynn! Waylynn!"

She retreated, leaving me to deal with the great puppynapping.

Quickly making my way down the hallway, I stopped when I realized I had no clue which office would be Steed's. It had to be next to John's. Then I heard the muffled whine of a puppy and Chloe whispering very loudly.

"Shhh! You're gonna get us in trouble, Roy."

"Oh, Lord," I whispered as I opened the door and walked into the room. The most adorable blue tick coonhound puppy came run-ning up to me.

His snout was mostly white with the trail moving up between his eyes. He had a small black dot at the top of his head and coming down the sides was the same beautiful black coloring. He had brown on his eyebrows and on his cheeks.

"Chloe! This is not a rabbit!" I stated as I dropped to the ground, instantly attacked with puppy kisses.

"I just couldn't leave him, Harley! I told the man selling them that I'd have my daddy come back today and pay for him. He laughed and told me this was the last puppy left who wasn't going to a home. That if I promised to make sure he would be okay, I could have him."

"So, you didn't steal him?"

Chloe gasped. "I wouldn't steal! Ever!"

Relief washed over me. "I didn't think so, but you understand I had to ask."

She nodded. "I understand. But I don't know what to do. Daddy won't let me keep him, and I already asked Grammy if she was in the market for a puppy, and she laughed and said no. He's a good puppy and barks at the door when he has to go potty."

I let out a sigh. "Chloe, you've been taking care of this dog since you brought him home?"

Her chest puffed out. "I sure have. I'm going to make a great veterinarian."

"Really? Is that what you want to do when you grow up?"

"Yep. And be a goat farmer, and take over the ranch. Of course, I'll have to have a dog to watch over the goats. That's where Roy comes in. He'll have a job and will earn his keep, as I hear my dad say."

Holding up the puppy, I gave him a once over. He looked to be about eight weeks old. Flipping him over, he went limp. He'd be a good docile pup. "That's a good baby." I looked again and chuckled.

"Um, Chloe, honey. We can't name him Roy."

"Why not?" she asked, her eyes filled with sadness.

"He's not a *he*. He's a she."

Chloe jumped up in excitement. "It's a girl?"

Laughing, I nodded. "Yep. It's a girl."

"Oh, that's even better! We need a name for her!" The little puppy started barking again. "She needs to go potty, then we need to hide her!" Chloe said. "At least until you can come up with a plan."

"Me?"

What was it with these Parker women?

The pup started up again.

"Okay, um, let me think."

I stood and picked up the puppy.

"We can take her to the barn. There used to be a small room where Tripp would hide presents. We can put her in there for the time being."

"Will she be okay?" Chloe asked, tears filling her eyes.

"Yes. She'll be perfectly safe, and there isn't anything in there that can hurt her."

Chloe thought about it for a few seconds, but once the puppy started howling, she made up her mind. "Okay! Let's do it!"

"Is that her little blanket?"

Chloe nodded. "The man said her momma's scent was on it."

"Perfect. Let's wrap her up in it and try to sneak her out to go potty, then take her to the barn. Folks are already starting to arrive for the spring fling."

After we got the puppy wrapped, I opened the door to Steed's office. Looking both ways, I started toward the door I knew was at the side of the house. John had used it as his business entrance.

"Chloe, we need to go out the back door down this hallway."

"But that's granddaddy's door. I'm not allowed to go in or out of it. In case he has folks coming in to see him or the boys."

I smiled at her referring to her father and the other guys who worked on the ranch as boys. I could hear Melanie telling Chloe to go tell the boys lunch was ready, or that there was a delivery truck waiting for them. Memories of being on this ranch came back to me in a rush and I couldn't ignore the pain I felt in my chest.

God, how I missed this place and these people.

"I promise this time it's okay. No one will be using that door so we can sneak out. I'm sure they're all down at the..."

Once I turned the corner I ran into something solid and knew I had spoken too soon.

"Harley? Darling, what are you doing?"

Taking a step back, I looked up into the deepest of blue eyes. They almost left me breathless.

John Parker. The man was the older image of all of his five sons. Handsome. Built. And a smile that made your knees week.

"Oh shit," I mumbled.

"Hell, shit, fuck," Chloe whispered next to me.

"Chloe Lynn!" John said.

"Hey, what's going on?"

My eyes darted to Tripp.

Great. Just great.

"Oh hey. I was, um, just showing Chloe your *new* puppy."

Tripp's eyes about popped out of his head. Of course, the little rascal who had started all of this was standing next to me giggling.

"Ah. Come again?" Tripp asked.

"You got a dog, Tripp? That's amazing," John said as he turned and smiled big. "I've been telling him for years he needed a dog."

I let out a nervous laugh. "Well, he's got a cute one!"

"Wait. *What?*" Tripp said as he shot daggers at me.

"Who's got a cute what?" Trevor asked, walking in behind Tripp and his father. Of course, the whole damn family would be walking through the very door I was trying to escape out of. We would have been better off going out the front door.

"Tripp's got a new puppy!" Chloe called out as I hit her on the arm as a warning.

"Wait!" Tripp cried.

I panicked and did the only thing I could think of. I unwrapped the puppy and shoved it in Trevor's face. When he was little he was a sucker for a cute puppy; I was hoping things hadn't changed.

"Oh, my gosh! Look at this little guy," Trevor said in a baby voice as he took the puppy from my hands.

"Great, you want him? He's yours," Tripp said.

"It's a girl!" Chloe said with a clap of her hands. I hit her a few times to get her to take it back a few. We weren't out of the woods yet.

"Aww, he's so cute. Don't worry, Tripp. I won't steal your girl." Trevor looked at me when he said that and winked, causing my cheeks to heat up.

"Now wait a second here," Tripp started. I knew I had to cut him off.

"Tripp mentioned he wanted a hound dog, and when I saw this little girl in town, well, I had to get her."

I could feel angry eyes on me, but I kept going.

"I mean, she was the last puppy and I felt so bad, I had to take her." Looking at Tripp, I motioned with my head to Chloe, hoping he would catch on. "He was afraid y'all might be mad if she was in the house so I was fixin' to take her to the barn."

"What? Nonsense. Tripp, we don't mind your puppy being in the house," John stated.

"Hell, Patches is always in the house," Trevor said with a deep rumbling laugh.

John sighed and lifted his cowboy hat to run his hand through his dark hair. A sigh of resignation escaped his lips.

"What's her name, Tripp?" Trevor asked.

Chloe grabbed onto my hand and squeezed it hard as I held my breath.

It felt like forever before Tripp finally spoke. "Hemingway's Whiskey. Hemi, for short."

I pinched my brows together as I tried to figure out how in the hell he came up with that name off the top of his head. I knew it was a Kenny Chesney song, and Tripp liked his Kenny Chesney. But *Hemi*?

"What the hell kind of name is that for a girl?" Trevor asked.

Tripp forced a smile. "The moment I found out the dog was mine, I wanted to drink a fifth of whiskey."

I laughed. Awkwardly. "Ha! That's a good one." I hit Tripp on the chest as Chloe belted out a fake laugh of her own. She had no clue what Tripp even meant.

"Hemi is a cute name!" Chloe pipped in.

Tripp ruffled her hair and said, "Then that's her name. You like it, Harley?"

"Me?" I pointed to myself. "Yeah. I love it!"

An evil grin spread over Tripp's face. "That's good, considering we have shared custody of Hemi."

"Yes," I said without thinking. My eyes jerked back to Tripp. "Wait. What?"

"But y'all aren't even dating," John said.

"Well, Harley has agreed to help me out with training little Hemi."

"I'm confused," Chloe stated as her eyes bounced from me to Tripp.

"It's called karma, Chloe," I replied as I took her hand in mine. "Tripp, you want to take Hemi out with us to go potty?"

He shook his head. "Nope."

"Karma?" Chloe asked as she looked up at me. "What's that mean?"

"Hey, little bit, I want to show you something for the spring fling today!" John said as he reached and picked up his granddaughter.

"You two can take care of the puppy, right?" John asked. I was pretty sure he had already caught on to the little game we were playing.

Swallowing hard, I replied, "Um, yeah. Sure we can."

John flashed us a smile. "Great. Make sure to get the pen that we used for your mother's old dog. It's down in the main barn. You'll want to make sure Hemi has a safe place to be."

Tripp and I looked at each other as John walked away with Chloe.

"Classic. Where in the hell did the dog come from?" Trevor asked.

"Chloe's soft heart just couldn't bear to leave the puppy. She's been hiding him in her dad's office since last night."

"I knew I heard a dog barking last night," Trevor said. "I thought I was hearing things. Was that Chloe taking her out? I heard the front door alarm chime a couple of times but thought it was Aunt Vi coming in and out."

"Aunt Vi's here?" I asked with a huge smile.

"Yep."

"Listen, someone is going to have to have a talk with Chloe about this. It was dangerous for her to be taking that dog out last night," Tripp stated.

I nodded. "Paxton knows about it so I'm sure she'll talk to Steed and they'll handle it."

Trevor slapped Tripp on the back. "In the meantime, looks like y'all got yourselves shared custody of one fine looking blue tick coonhound."

Hemi barked and Trevor laughed. He pushed the dog into Tripp's chest.

"Listen, I'd love to stand here all day and watch you two fight over this, but I got a branding to get down to. So do you, Harley."

Tripp held up his hands. "I'm not taking this dog."

"Tripp, look at how cute she is," I pleaded.

"No! I work all day."

"You can bring her to work."

He looked at me like I was insane. "What the fuck? So can you! You have a damn vet clinic."

I shook my head. "Until she has all her shots, it's best if I don't have her at the clinic."

"What!"

Trevor started walking out the door they had come through. "Ah hell, this is the best thing ever."

"Shut the fuck up, Trevor!"

After the door closed, Tripp cursed under his breath. "I'm so glad I set him up for tomorrow night."

"Huh?"

He brushed off his comment. "Nothing. Listen, Harley, she's cute and all."

Handing Hemi back to me, he brushed off his shirt. "But I don't want a dog."

I held her up and pushed her into his face. "Twipp, Daddy... Pwease take care of me until momma can keep me? Pwease!"

His lip snarled. "Mallory is allergic to dogs."

My smile faded, and I held Hemi close. Making my way down the hallway, I opened the door and stepped outside. Tripp followed me and was practically on top of me when I set her down.

"It's only until I can get all her shots. I know who the breeder is, Hank Philips. I'll see what shots he's already given her and give him some money for her. After that, I'll take her and you don't have to be bothered with her. Heaven forbid we make Mallory suffer."

He frowned, and I knew I had just acted like a bitch. "How long are we talking?"

"Well, it's about every three to four weeks, and they get their last shots around sixteen weeks."

He frowned. "How old is she?"

I shrugged. I wasn't about to tell him I thought she was only eight weeks old. "I'll have to ask Hank."

"What kind of a vet are you? Shouldn't you be able to guess how old she is?"

Anger pulsed through my veins. "Fuck you, Tripp. Don't worry about it. I'll take care of the dog *your* niece took, and I'll figure out a way to deal with it. Wouldn't want to put you or your *girlfriend* out."

I picked Hemi up and left, walking backwards. "By the way, she's about eight weeks old. Dick."

"Harley, wait!"

I made my way around the house to get the portable crate I had in my trunk. It was only by luck I had the damn thing in there.

"Harley!"

"Just leave me alone, Tripp."

"Let me talk to Steed and Paxton. They might be able to help."

I stopped and faced him. "Paxton doesn't want the dog. She already told me."

He removed his cowboy hat and raked his fingers through his hair and said, "Shit."

My stomach pulled. Which pissed me off even more. I was mad at him. Why was my body reacting like this?

"Like I said, don't worry about. I'm a vet, I should be able to figure it out. Right?"

"Wait, Harley."

Picking up my pace, I almost started running to my car. When I walked around the corner all the air was knocked out of me when I saw Mallory and her daughter. The little girl took off running and ran straight to Tripp.

I tried like hell not to let my emotions out as I forced a smile and walked by Mallory.

"Hi Mallory."

She returned the gesture. "Hey there, Harley. You're here for the branding?"

It wasn't lost on me that she didn't seem very happy.

"John likes to have a vet here during the process."

She nodded. "Makes sense."

Glancing at the puppy in my arms, she took a few steps back. She wasn't just allergic to dogs; she was afraid of them.

"Whose puppy?"

I huffed. "I guess mine. If you'll excuse me, I need to get her settled and down to the corral."

"Oh yes, of course."

Walking around her, I didn't bother to look behind me. I already knew what was happening. Tripp was taking her in his arms and kissing her good morning, I was sure. I wanted to hurl. I wanted to scream. I wanted him to be kissing me good morning. Damnit, when would this pain lessen?

I set Hemi on the ground and opened my trunk. Pulling out the crate, I sighed in relief when I saw the samples of puppy food in a box. I was taking them to donate to the shelter and was so glad I hadn't dropped them off yet. In the back seat was a blanket I could use to cover the crate in case I didn't find shade.

"Let me help you carry that down to the corral." I was shocked to find Tripp standing behind me when I assumed he'd have accompanied Mallory.

His voice was starting to physically cause me pain. My chest ached and my head spun.

"I don't need your help."

"Come on. You're being ridiculous over a stupid comment."

Looking up into his beautiful blue eyes, I took in a sharp breath. His cowboy hat was back on and he looked so handsome I wanted to cry.

"You insulted me, Tripp. This is all I have. Being a vet is my *life* and the *only* thing I've ever gotten right. I'm sorry that doesn't mean anything to you, or if you think it's a stupid career. We all can't dress to the nines and own cute little boutiques and look the part of the perfect woman for the town's mayor, now can we?"

"What?" He looked like I'd slapped him.

"Hey, what's going on out here?"

I turned to see Mitchell and Corina walking up.

"Oh my gosh! A puppy!" Corina screamed as she took Hemi from my arms.

"Sorry we're late. Corina wasn't feeling very good." Mitchell looked from Tripp to me. "Is everything okay?"

With a nod, I replied. "Everything is fine. Mitchell, can you help me carry this stuff down to the corral so I can get it all set up?"

"Of course," he answered. He looked at Tripp and frowned.

"Where did she come from?" Corina asked.

"Chloe snuck him into the house last night after she saw Hank selling them in town last night."

"She stole it?" Mitchell asked.

"No. Hank told her to take the last puppy. I'm going to take care of her…I guess."

"Harley—" Tripp started to say but I cut him off.

"I really need to get down there. Thanks, Mitchell."

Corina handed Hemi back to me. "She's so cute. I wish we could take her, but a new dog *and* a new baby? I don't think so."

"Plus, Milo would be pissed," Mitchell added with a chuckle.

Laughing, I shook my head. "Yes. Milo would not be too thrilled with the idea of a dog."

I ignored Tripp as I walked away. "Corina, I believe Melanie and everyone else are in the kitchen still preparing the food."

She gave me a sweet smile. "Great. I'll see you down there soon." Turning, she gave Mitchell a kiss and they exchanged *I love you*s. When Mitchell bent over and kissed her stomach, my eyes burned with the threat of tears. It was the sweetest thing I'd ever seen—and yet it was cutting me to the quick.

"Don't do too much, Corina!" he warned.

"I'm pregnant, Mitchell, not dying. I can very well help out in the kitchen."

"Make sure you drink lots of water, Corina! You threw up earlier. It's supposed to get up to the low eighties today."

She tossed me a wink. "Yes, doctor."

Mitchell started to head around the house and down to the corral. Tripp grabbed my arm and pulled me to a stop.

"Harley, please let me talk to you."

I jerked my arm free. I could see Mallory standing on the porch waiting for him. Her little girl had followed Corina inside the house, and she was watching our interaction, as if she was waiting to see one of us show all our cards.

"There's nothing to say, Tripp. Mallory is waiting for you."

"I don't give a damn about her right now," he whispered.

I sucked in a breath at his admission. *Does he even realize what he just said?*

"Do you really think I don't care about what you do, Lee?"

My eyes bounced around his face. I couldn't form any words. All I heard on repeat was....

I don't give a damn about her right now.

Breaking the tension that surrounded us like a blanket, we turned as Mallory called out, "Tripp? Are you heading down to the corral? Should I go in with your mom or come with you?"

Lifting my gaze back to Mallory, I smirked. "Your *girlfriend* needs you."

Spinning around, I walked away as fast as I could. Hemi let out a few puppy barks at Tripp, and I pretended she was telling him to fuck off.

I snuggled my face into her and whispered, "Good girl."

CHAPTER 15

Tripp

Riding up on my horse, I looked at the cattle. Yesterday, Wade, Jonathon, Steed, Trevor, and a few other local cowboys rode out in the pastures and gathered up the cattle. We were getting off to a late start this year. We normally started at six AM, but it was already eight.

"About damn time you showed up," Steed said with a huge grin. He lived for this shit. So did my other brothers.

"Yeah, well, I'm here for the best part."

Trevor walked up and shoved a bag in my chest. "Throw this feed into the pasture to entice them, then we'll get them into the sorting corrals."

I took the back of feed and headed over to the holding pasture.

It didn't take long before there were about fifty people helping out. Most were herding the first batch of calves into the tub. Once they were in that smaller corral, Mitchell pushed them into the calf shoot where they stood on a scale. Paxton recorded each calf's weight and tag number before the next gate opened and they went into the calf table. The process took only about a minute and a half for each calf. We had about three hundred to do. The day would be a long one, to say the least.

Chloe was following Harley as she vaccinated each calf. Steed was banding the bull calves, Wade was tagging, and I was branding them. Not all of the volunteers would help. A lot came for the experience. You could guarantee to see about a dozen kids running around watching and asking when they would be old enough to help. It was something I still loved being a part of and knew I would forever love it. It was in my blood.

This was Chloe's first branding. Last year she wasn't feeling good and had to miss it, so she was even more excited than usual.

"What's that spray for, Uncle Tripp?" Chloe asked.

"It's so they don't get an infection after we brand them."

"Does all of this hurt them?"

"It only hurts for a minute, sweetheart," I replied.

"Then they get to go back to their mommy?"

I nodded. "Yep. Then they go back to their mommy."

Everything was moving along smoothly until they tipped one of the cows over for Steed to band. Harley was looking at something on the calf, and it kicked, hitting her right in the chin. When she fell to the ground it felt like my entire world stopped.

"Harley!" I cried as I rushed over, leaning close to her face.

Everyone started calling out, "Is she okay?"

I lifted her chin to look at the cut. Our eyes met and Harley drew in a quick breath.

"Baby, are you okay?"

Her eyes filled with tears; I hadn't been thinking when I called her *baby*.

"I'm o-okay," she whispered.

"You're bleeding."

Blinking away our intense stare, she moved back. Her anger from earlier returned.

"I'm okay. I'm alright," Harley repeated.

"Harley, are you okay?" her father Gus asked, pushing me out of the way. I stood there and watched Gus fuss over Harley.

"I'm fine, Daddy. Honestly. It just stunned me. He barely got me."

"Barely got you? Your chin is cut open, Harley!" I cried. She shot me a dirty look that clearly said fuck off.

"It's fine, Tripp. I'm fine." Looking from me back to her father, she gave him a beautiful smile. "Daddy, I'm fine. It's not the first time an animal has hurt me."

"You're sure you don't want a break? Jonathon can vaccinate," my father stated from next to me.

She shook her head. "I'm good. I promise."

"That's my tough girl. Takin' it on the chin like a trooper," Gus said with a huge smile.

When she kissed Gus on the cheek and headed back over to the table, I wanted to scream. Why was she so damn stubborn? She'd always been that way. I knew she was in pain. I could see it in her eyes.

"Damn it, Dad. You should have made her stop and rest."

He laughed. "Son, do you remember at all who this is we're talking about? Harley Carbajal has been doing this since she was ten years old. The woman knows what she can and can't handle. You'd do best to remember that." He glanced over to Mallory. "And remember your girlfriend is watching."

I cursed under my breath. I found Mallory sitting on the fence, watching me. Lifting my hand, I smiled and waved. She waved back and looked over to everyone at their respective posts. Mitchell had taken over the branding so I headed over to Mallory.

"Hey, so what do you think about all of this? Want to join in?"

She scrunched up her face and shook her head. "Um, no thanks. Looks a little too dirty for my tastes."

I forced a grin. Mallory was indeed a high-maintenance kind of girl. I had never even seen her in a pair of old jeans and a T-shirt.

And her cowboy boots were in perfect condition. More fashion than function.

"Where's Laney?"

Mallory rolled her eyes and pointed at Hemi. There was a group of kids all sitting in a circle playing with the puppy. Waylynn was sitting there, as well, watching over the kids.

"My sister certainly looks happy, doesn't she?"

Mallory glanced back. "Yep. Motherhood looks good on her."

"It does," I replied with a smile. Scarlett walked up, and my smile grew bigger. Turning back to look over my shoulder, I found Trevor. He was on his horse getting the next round of calves into the tub.

"I think I'll go take over for Trevor with getting the calves in the tub."

"Question, why do you call it a tub since they aren't being washed?"

I shrugged. "I don't know. That's what it's always been called. I guess because it's a small area."

"You said this will take all day?" Mallory asked, boredom evident in her voice.

"Yeah, but you don't have to stay. Or you could head up to the house. They're making a feast for after all this is over."

She looked around and brushed off her jeans. "I may do that, if you don't mind."

"Of course not," I said, climbing down.

"Um…no kiss?" she asked.

I paused. "I just figured I was too dirty to kiss you."

Her forced grin spoke volumes.

"I'll see ya in a bit," I said.

"Okay, see ya."

I headed around to my horse and made my way over to Trevor.

"You want a break?" I asked coming up alongside him.

"Nah. I'm good."

I glanced over to the oak tree where Scarlett was sitting next to Waylynn. Liberty was in her arms.

"Who is that next to Waylynn?" I asked, knowing damn well it was Scarlett. Somehow my mother and Scartlett's mother had gotten her into Cord's Place the other night. It was my job to point her out to Trevor. I knew the moment he saw her, he'd go to her like a moth to a flame.

Trevor looked to where I was pointing. I couldn't help but notice he sat up a little taller.

"That's Scarlett, you idiot."

With a look of pretend recognition, I replied, "Oh yeah. Mom's friend's daughter. Isn't she the one Mom was getting on you about dating?"

He rolled his eyes. "Yes. I asked her to the dinner tomorrow night."

"No fucking way. What did Mom bribe you with to do that?"

Trevor laughed. "Nothing. I hadn't seen Scarlett since she got back home from Boston and she mentioned she was at the bar looking for Joey Meed. I guess her friend from work set her up on a blind date with the idiot. He was planning on asking her to Mom's dinner tomorrow night, so I decided to save her from his endless talking about *Star Wars* and I asked her myself."

"You're bringing a date?"

"I figured I could do something nice for both Mom and Scarlett. Get our mother off my back by taking Scarlett out, and save Scarlett from the most boring man in Oak Springs."

Laughing, I asked, "And the fact that the woman is hot as hell and has a body to die for had no bearing on your decision?"

He turned and gave me a shit-eating grin. "Oh, it did. I'm neither stupid nor blind. I did it just as much for me."

"Trevor, don't screw her."

Glancing toward Scarlett, I saw her look over and smile.

"Yeah, sorry, big brother. If she gives me the green light, I'm proceeding."

"Christ, Trevor. You better be careful. It's Mom's friend's daughter."

He motioned his horse to turn and face me. "Dude, I'm always careful. The stick is always wrapped, and the ladies are always smiling."

I rolled my eyes. "Yeah, well I have a feeling one of these days your whoring ways are going to catch up with you."

A whistle from behind made us turn to Jonathon. "Next batch coming in!" he shouted.

"Open it up!" I called out and went to work alongside my brother. Best damn place to be.

Two large tents covered my parents' back yard. Some of the folks from around the neighboring ranches had helped set everything up while we did the branding. Rows of tables were lined up with chairs on each side. Another table had coolers filled with drinks, and small bags of every kind of chips and pretzels you could think of.

It was always the same meal each year. Barbecue catered from one of the local restaurants, while my mother and her friends spent most of the day baking desserts and sides. My mom's baked beans were one of the favorite items on the menu, along with her grandmother's famous potato salad.

"Tripp! Grab this before I drop it!" Waylynn called out.

I ran up and took one of the large plastic bowls out of her hands. "Damn, that smells good."

She nodded. "Tell me about it. I've been smelling barbecue and beans the last two hours while Liberty napped. Look at my hand!"

Shoving the back of her hand in my face, I laughed. It was red.

"That's from mom slapping my hand every time I went for a brownie, or a rib."

My mouth watered at the thought of Johnny G's dry-rubbed ribs.

"Fuck. I'm going for the ribs first."

Waylynn chuckled. "Well, they will be placed on the far right. I heard Mom telling some of the girls how she wanted the food table set up."

We set the two bowls of potato salad in the middle of the sides table. Even with Saran wrap over them you could smell the heavenly dishes.

"Hey, what are you doing up here anyway? Dad's not making you clean up?" Waylynn asked.

"We're done. They're all down there drinking beer before heading up. I wanted to check on Mallory. Has she been having fun?"

Waylynn frowned.

"What? I thought you liked her."

"I do like her…as the owner of one of my favorite little boutiques, but honestly, Tripp, what do you see in her?"

"What do you mean?"

She shrugged. "She doesn't seem your type and she doesn't fit in with this motley crew."

A long sigh came out of my mouth. "Are you saying that because you and Harley are BFFs again?"

Waylynn shot me a dirty look. "No, but I'm not going to lie. It would be nice to see you two back together."

"Christ, Waylynn, not now."

"I'm not pushing you, Tripp. You asked. And back to Mallory. She is fucking boring as hell. Amelia said she acted like she'd never even been in a kitchen before."

"That's crazy. Mallory cooks all the time."

"Well, then, she didn't want to be bothered with helping. I mean, you'd have thought she would have told Corina to sit down, and she would take over peeling the potatoes, but she just sat there and watched, Amelia said."

"She probably just didn't want to get in the way. You know as well as I do that everyone has a role. If Mom needed her to do something, she would have asked."

She shrugged. "Maybe. But Amelia said she hardly spoke two words. Just smiled every now and then and only spoke when someone asked her something. And she sure is private."

I laughed. "That she is. Did you ever think she's just shy?"

Sighing, she turned to face me. "You're right. I'm trying to find reasons to not like her. I'm sorry. If you really like her and see a future with her, than you know we'll all support you."

My brows pinched together. It was like she could read my mind and see every doubt floating around my head.

"What's wrong? Are things not going well with y'all?" The smirk on her face spoke volumes. She wasn't rooting for Mallory.

"We've both been busy and not spending much time with each other. Plus, it's still hard when Mallory refuses to let me stay the night at her place. I mean, I get it, but I could also sneak out before Laney wakes up."

"Does she stay the night with you at your place?"

"Sometimes."

Waylynn crossed her arms over her chest. "So, excuse my frankness, but where do y'all fuck?"

Someone cleared their throat, and we both turned to see an older couple walking by.

"Oh! Sorry, Mr. and Mrs. Jacks!" Waylynn called out and then covered her mouth and chuckled. "Ooops."

"Not that it's any of your business, but either my house or my office. Or her office at the store."

"Gross! In your office?"

I grinned. "Yep. The desk, chairs, sofa. Even against the door."

"I sit on that sofa, you sick motherfu…"

Waylynn clamped her mouth shut and looked around before placing both hands on my chest and pushing me back. "Jerk. You've ruined your office for me forever."

"Hey, what's going on?" Mallory walked up to us with Laney trailing behind.

"Nothing. We were just talking about how it's time for me to redecorate my office."

"Amen," Waylynn whispered.

"Why? I love your office," Mallory said.

Waylynn mumbled under her breath, and I was almost positive she said, "I bet you do."

"Don't you have to go back in and help Mom?" I asked as I gave my sister a buzz-off look.

"I'll take that as a hint to leave."

"Please do."

Mallory hit me in the stomach. "That wasn't nice."

She motioned for me to kiss her. I leaned over and kissed her cheek. "How was your day?"

I picked up Laney and kissed her on the forehead. "Did you have fun with Hemi?"

"Yes! She's cute!"

"Harley must love animals," Mallory said.

Tickling Laney, I replied, "Well, she is a vet so…"

"What's a vet?" Laney asked.

"Someone who works with animals every day," Mallory said quickly.

"Oh! I want that job," Laney exclaimed.

"No, you don't, darling," Mallory stated.

"Why not?" Laney asked.

"You have to go to school for a long time. Longer than a doctor!" I said.

Laney shook her head. "Ferget it."

"Seriously, Tripp. A vet cannot be compared to a doctor." The way she laughed rubbed me the wrong way. She was putting down Harley's profession. The way Harley had reacted to my earlier comment flashed through my mind. I was just about to comment when I was saved by the bell, literally.

My mother rang the dinner bell on the back porch, and within seconds, people started piling in.

"You ready for some good food?" I asked, forcing a smile and pushing away Mallory's last comment.

"Bring it on!" she said, with a happy face. I could tell she was over branding day.

CHAPTER 16

Harley

"You can't keep your eyes off of him."

I turned to Amelia.

"That's not true. I'm not looking at him now, and I wasn't looking at him a few seconds ago. Besides, they're right there in front of us. How do I not look over there?"

She grinned and whispered, "He keeps looking at you too."

"Stop it!"

I pushed her away with my shoulder.

"I'm okay…honestly. It's pretty clear that he's happy with Mallory. I'm ready to move on."

"Easier said than done. I know," Corina said.

"Once you get a taste of a Parker brother, you're done for," Paxton added.

Amelia held up her hand. "Okay. *Yuck.* Those are my brothers y'all are talking about."

Taking my hand in hers, Amelia gave it a light squeeze. "If it's worth anything, I don't think he loves her. It doesn't even seem like he likes her that much anymore. I've never seen Tripp look so pained to be sitting and talking to someone."

I tried not to look over at Tripp and Mallory, but my eyes wandered. They were laughing at something Jonathon had said, and I noticed that Amelia was right. Tripp looked like he wanted to be anywhere but where he was.

"If he's not happy, why does he stay with her?" I asked.

Amelia shrugged. "Well, I don't think Mallory is the type of girl to keep Tripp's interest. She's boring as hell."

"Amelia!" Paxton, Corina, and I all said at once.

"What? It's true. Do you know how many times I tried to strike up a conversation with her today? She sat there with her nose turned up like she was too good to be there. Don't get me wrong, she is a nice person, but you can tell she clearly comes from a fancy background and is repulsed by what we do on the ranch."

"But she was here...for Tripp," I added.

Amelia rolled her eyes. "I guess."

We got quiet as the reality set in for all of us. No matter what we said, Tripp and Mallory were a couple.

"How are things going with Toby?" Paxton asked.

Shrugging, I replied, "I think he feels like our friendship could lead to something more."

Corina gave me a sweet smile as she pressed for more information. "And you? How do you feel?"

"Like I only see us being friends. He's a great guy, and I have to admit he made my stomach drop a time or two and made my libido sit up, but I don't think I'm interested in going past friendship."

"Not even for a little friends with benefits kind of thing?" Amelia asked, wiggling her eyebrows.

"Nope. I don't think so. It wouldn't be fair to him. I need to get Tripp completely out of my head and heart before I can even think of moving on with another guy."

They all nodded like they knew exactly what I was talking about.

"Like you said, Corina, easier said than done. I know Tripp will always hold my heart like no other man could. That will never change, and I have to accept it."

Three pairs of eyes stared back at me with sympathy. Forcing a smile, I grabbed my plate. "I'm going to go check on Miss Hemi, and a calf that got hurt earlier. I'll talk to y'all later?"

"Sounds good," Paxton responded.

I dared to take a quick glance at Tripp and Mallory. Tripp was lost in a conversation with Jonathon and Mallory looked bored as hell. I honestly didn't know what Tripp saw in her. She seemed like a stick in the mud. Correction, she wouldn't do mud; that much was obvious.

As I walked down toward the barn, I thought about Tripp and Mallory. She seemed like the perfect woman for a guy who was running for mayor, and I kept telling myself that was why Tripp was with her. But I knew it was more than that. When I overheard Karen telling her friend how she had to leave the office because Mallory came over for those lunch fuck fests, I knew Tripp was into Mallory for the sex. It probably thrilled him taking her in his office.

My hand came up over my mouth to keep me from losing what I had just eaten. The memory of overhearing them made me physically ill.

"Christ above. Why are you even thinking about it again, you idiot?"

A small bark came from inside the barn. Stepping in, I smiled at Hemi running in circles inside her crate.

"You didn't think I forgot about you, did you?"

She jumped up and whined.

"Settle down, I'm coming to let you out."

Once I opened the gate, she took off running around me and jumping up.

"That's a sweet girl. I can see why Chloe dognapped you."

Picking her up, I held her in front of me. "Hemi. Should we keep that as your name?"

"Yes."

I let out a shout as I jumped.

"Jesus, Tripp. You scared me."

He leaned against the doorway looking hot as hell. When he took off his cowboy hat I nearly dropped to the ground. His hair was messy and he had a bit of dirt on his face. Lord, could this man look any finer? I could see his broad chest through the T-shirt he had changed into and my hands shook as I fought the urge to slip my fingers under it and feel his hard muscles. Muscles I had explored years ago but knew would be more defined than ever.

Good Lord, Harley. Stop this.

"Wh-what are you doing here?"

His brow lifted, and he pushed off the doorframe and walked my way.

"This is my parents' barn."

I let out a nervous laugh. "Right. But why are you here right now?"

He looked down at the puppy in my arms.

"I figured we needed to work out our custody agreement for Hemi."

My heart soared. I wasn't sure if he was doing this because I had gotten angry, and he felt guilty, or if he was just doing it for me. I hoped the latter.

"Really?"

With a nod, he scratched under Hemi's chin. "It only seems fair since it was my niece who got you in this predicament. Besides, I already begged Steed to take the damn thing and he said no. She could go back to Hank."

I pulled Hemi closer to me, and Tripp laughed.

"He can't take her back. That would be terrible."

"That's what I told him. So what do you propose we do with this mutt?"

My cheeks hurt from smiling so big. It was wrong of me, but I knew if Tripp took Hemi, it would give me an excuse to see him more often.

Yeah, that is a pretty shitty thing to do to Mallory, but right now I don't care.

"Okay, well, I'll keep him Friday afternoon until Tuesday morning. I usually use Mondays for surgery so Hemi could come to the vet clinic that day since it's slow and Julie or Louise can watch over her."

"So, I'll have her Tuesday morning through lunchtime on Fridays?"

"Yep, if that works for you. I can get you a crate for your office. She seems to do great in it. If you have to leave or go out or anything you can keep her crated. Just make sure she goes potty first and don't leave her in there for long periods of time."

Tripp stared at me for a few moments. When his eyes dropped to my mouth, I instinctively licked my lips.

"I'll, um, give you food and everything."

"I can buy the food." He stepped closer to me, or to Hemi, I wasn't sure.

My gaze drifted down to the dog. If I kept staring into Tripp's baby blues I was going to combust.

"O-okay. I'll get her some toys."

Hemi was now looking back and forth between me and Tripp.

"Anything else I should know?" Tripp whispered, reaching a hand toward me...or the dog, surely.

I love you more than life itself.

"No, I can't think of anything."

Lifting my gaze, our eyes met once again. It felt like a secret moment between the two of us. I could feel the intensity we'd always had. Swallowing hard, I took a step back to break the heat between us.

"Hurry, Mommy! Here she is."

I looked past Tripp to see Laney pulling Mallory into the barn. When I turned back to Tripp, he was no longer looking at me. The ache in my chest grew stronger.

"Laney! You are pulling my arm out of my socket."

"Harley! Can I hold Hemi?"

"No!" Mallory stated, just as I said, "Sure!"

I stopped handing the puppy to Laney.

Tears built in her eyes. "Mommy, why?"

"His fur will get on you."

I wanted to roll my eyes, but I really wasn't sure if she had an allergy or not. "I can brush any hair off of her if you'd like."

She shot me a fake smile. "I don't want her getting attached because she won't be seeing Hemi again."

"You don't have to worry about that," I said. "With Tripp watching Hemi for me during the week, I'm sure Laney will get to see her."

"What?" Mallory glared at Tripp. He had his eyes closed for a few seconds before popping them open and sending me death rays.

Oops. Looks like Mallory doesn't know about Tripp's new house guest.

"You're taking the dog?"

Tripp walked closer to Mallory. "Not permanently, just for a few weeks."

Her mouth fell open. "Weeks? How many weeks?"

When Tripp didn't answer, I did. "Only about six or so."

I had to admit it, I was smiling inside, and I knew it was so wrong. I may or may not have done a mental fist pump at the look on her face.

So. Wrong. But it feels so right.

"Six weeks!" Mallory shrieked as Laney jumped up and down in excitement.

"Or so," Tripp added with a smirk.

"Tripp, we cannot deal with a puppy for six weeks."

He cleared his throat and moved closer to Mallory. "*We're* not dealing with her, *I* am. She won't ever be at your house."

"Damn right she won't!" Mallory whispered. "You know I don't like dogs and am allergic."

"Yep. I know."

Mallory's death stare was now on me.

"Was this your idea?"

"Yes. Considering I don't even want another dog, it was only fair that Tripp help me out with her."

"If you don't want a dog, why are you keeping her? Take her to the pound."

My blood burned hot. "The pound? Are you seriously telling a vet to take an animal to the pound?"

"Yes! Unless this is your way of spending more time with Tripp!"

I wanted to smile at her. I knew it was wrong, but damn it all to hell. I was starting to dislike this woman even more as the seconds ticked by.

"Okay, let's just calm down here. Mallory, I owe it to Harley."

I could see the anger in her eyes, but she pushed it down and gave Tripp a smile that screamed fake. Then she looked at me. "You know what? It's fine. I'm sure Laney will *love* going over to your house to play with her."

Ouch. That was a sucker punch in the gut.

"So, we have it worked out then?" Tripp asked.

I forced a grin. "Great. Well, I'm exhausted, and I think Hemi and I are going to head home. I have to stop at the clinic to pick her up some food."

"I was going to buy her food."

"I'll get it this time. You can get the next one."

"Isn't that cute, you have a little custody agreement…for a dog," Mallory snickered.

I winked and whispered under my breath. "Better a dog than a kid!"

Mallory's smile faded.

Clearing my throat, I bent over and let Laney pet Hemi. "Laney, say goodbye to Hemi. She needs to go potty and then off to home."

"Bye bye, Hemi! See you soon!"

"Mallory, I'm going to help Harley take the crate back to her car. Give me a few minutes?"

"Can I take her to go potty with you?" Laney asked as she reached up for my hand.

"Sure! If your mommy is okay with that."

"Of course, you can, sweetie."

Laney and I started for the barn exit.

"Laney's new nanny starts tonight, so I can pay you a late-night visit," Mallory said, louder than she needed to.

I swallowed the bile in my throat as I picked up my pace and turned the corner, heading to a large oak tree. The last thing I wanted to hear about was Tripp and Mallory making plans to have a midnight rendezvous.

CHAPTER 17

Tripp

Mallory reached up and ran her finger down my chest.

"So? What do you say? You in the mood for a visit later?"

"You know what, Mallory, I'm exhausted. Today has been a long fucking day, and all I want to do is fall into a bed and crash."

"Well, the things I want to do to you require you to be in a bed, so that makes it easy."

I forced a smile. "Sounds nice, but honestly, I'm barely keeping my eyes open as it is. I'm probably just gonna crash here at my folks' place."

"Oh," she said with disappointment in her voice. "Well, that sucks for both of us. You can make it up to me tomorrow night after the benefit dinner."

"Sure."

Mallory stared for a few moments before reaching up on her toes to kiss me. I gave her a quick kiss on the lips and stepped back.

"Y'all better get going before it gets too late."

"Right, we do need to get going. By the time I get home and give Laney a bath to get all that grime off of her, it will be past her bedtime."

"That grime is called dirt, and it's what happens when kids are allowed to let loose and play."

Mallory scoffed. "Maybe for ranch kids, but not my Laney. I'm glad she had an older outfit on since that one is ruined."

I pinched my brows together. "Mallory, that was a snobby ass thing to say. These kids out here are no different than Laney."

She sighed. "I know, I'm sorry. I've never told you this, Tripp, but I come from a very well bred family. They own a few companies back home, and to be honest, I grew up very differently from you. Finishing schools, nannies, butlers...the whole thing. I moved to small-town Texas because I didn't want my daughter to grow up with a silver spoon in her mouth or have a mother like mine."

"But you do see you're slowly going down that path, Mallory? You just hired a nanny for Laney."

Her eyes filled with frustration. "I'm a single mom living away from my family and I need to have some form of childcare. I guess with my choice for a nanny it shows the apple didn't fall far from the tree."

"Can you make it up to your car okay?"

She stared at me and shook her head. "Why don't you ever touch me anymore, Tripp?"

"What?"

"Come on. It's clear that you're pulling away. Is it because of...the race?"

I stared at her for a good minute. I was sure she'd wanted to ask something different.

"The race has been on my mind a lot lately."

She nodded. "Right. At least you know the woman standing next to you when you've won the mayoral race will be a polished, well-rounded woman."

My stomach dropped. I needed to be honest with Mallory, and the sooner I did it, the better. I didn't see the same future as she did. I had to stop lying to myself and admit that I was still very much in love with Harley.

"Mallory, I need to—"

Harley and Laney came walking back to us.

"Well, she went potty!" Harley said.

"She pooped!" Laney added.

We all laughed, everyone but Mallory.

Mallory picked up Laney. "Say goodbye, sweetie. We need to head home."

Laney waved. "Bye, Hemi! Bye, Harley! Bye, Tripp!"

"Bye, Laney!" Harley said as I waved and said goodbye too.

After they'd started to walk toward the house, Harley broke the silence.

"You don't want to walk them out?"

"Nah, they can manage. Let me get this crate taken down, and I'll bring it up to your car."

Harley's cheeks turned a slight pink. "Thank you. I just need to check on this calf. Trevor put her and the mom in one of the stalls."

"Okay."

I headed over to the crate and started taking it apart. Harley was talking to the calf in the stall, and I couldn't help but smile. It made me think of all the times she would sit in her daddy's barn and sing to the animals. She'd always been a sucker for the four-legged creatures.

After taking the crate apart, I walked outside and set it up against the barn. When I walked back in, Harley was standing on top of the stall reaching for something.

"What in the hell are you doing? You're going to fall."

"No, I won't. There's a cat up here. I think she's stuck."

"Harley, get the fuck down before you break something."

She reached up on her toes. "I've almost got her."

"Harley!" I said firmly. All I could think about was the time she fell and broke her arm trying to help a damn baby bird back into the nest.

"Just. A. Little. More."

"Son-of-a-bitch," I said as I headed over to get her down. Before I got there, her foot slipped. My heart fell as I watched her tumble into the stall next to one of dad's new stallions.

"Harley!" I cried out as I ran and pushed the stall door open.

"Wait!" she said. "Don't come in here, Tripp."

"What?"

I looked at the horse standing over Harley.

"Back out slowly so you don't spook him."

"But…"

"Tripp, please!" she quietly urged.

Slowly backing out, I watched as Harley stood. She appeared to be okay.

"Are you hurt?"

She held out her hand, and the horse took a step closer to her. *What in the hell was she doing having him move closer to her?*

"Harley, Dad said that horse is not the least bit tamed."

"*Shhh*. It's okay, baby. I'm not going to hurt you."

I groaned internally at the softness in her voice. My heart raced.

"What happened? I heard a scream," Trevor called out as he ran into the barn.

"It's okay, Trev. We just need to talk softly and not spook him."

Trevor's eyes about came out of his head as he looked at Harley in the stallion's stall.

"What in the fuck is she doing in there?"

"She fell in."

He jerked his head to look at me. "That horse kicked Ryan yesterday and broke his damn jaw, Tripp. We need to get her out."

"Would the two of you…*please*…shut up."

We both looked back into the stall. I held my breath as I watched Harley move closer to the horse.

"Hey there, handsome boy. Looks like we're gonna get to know each other."

He snorted and bounced his head a few times.

"Oh, I know, big guy. You're the boss."

Hemi whined at my feet. I reached down and picked her up.

When the horse put his mouth against Harley's hand, Trevor grabbed onto my arm.

"Do you want some oats? Is that what you want?"

I turned to look at my brother. "Dude, did you grow a pussy overnight? Get the fuck off me and get her some oats," I whispered.

He looked at his hand and jerked it back like he had just gotten bit. "Right."

Trevor got a small bucket and walked into the other stall. Harley was backed against the wall.

"Move slow, Trevor, and shake it a bit so he knows what it is."

Trevor did exactly as she said. Harley reached for the bucket and the horse jumped some. He kicked at the ground, and I swore my heart rate went through the roof. I was going to kick her ass when she walked out of that stall. Because she *would* walk out. It was Harley. The fucking animal whisperer.

She took a handful of oats and put it to her mouth as the horse watched her. He nickered and she responded with a sound of her own as she held her hand out for him to eat the oats.

Taking a step closer, Harley ran her hand down his neck. Trevor and I shared looks. We both shook our heads and smiled.

"There ya go. You going to be my new boyfriend?" Harley asked while he bopped his head up and down.

I rolled my eyes and let out a deep breath.

Slowly moving alongside the horse, she ran her hands along him. She stepped away and casually moved to the stall door. The stallion turned and followed her. When Harley put her hand on the door, the horse nudged her back.

"Oh, you're not ready for the date to end?"

He dug at the floor with his hoof.

"Fine, one more kiss it is."

Taking the oats, she again put it to her mouth and then reached it out to him. When he finished eating the oats, he turned and walked away.

Harley slipped out of the stall and looked at me. I could see tears building in her eyes, and her breath sounded shallow. "I think I broke a rib."

"What?" Trevor and I both said at once.

CHAPTER 180

Harley

"It's not broken, just bruised."

The three of us let out a sigh of relief.

"Thank you so much, doctor," I said, extending my hand.

"No worries. Remember to keep icing it once you get home and take the pills I'm prescribing for the pain. No heating pads, no compression bandages."

With a nod, I replied, "Got it."

"And rest your body."

I laughed. "Well, I've got a dinner and dancing tomorrow that I have to squeeze into a dress for…"

He lifted a brow at me and gave me a stern look. It reminded me of my father.

Shit. Speaking of, I forgot to call them!

"We'll make sure she gets plenty of rest," Trevor said.

"Good. The nurse will be in to get your discharge papers, and you'll be all set to go."

The second the doctor was out the door, Tripp was standing in front of me. "I'm so angry at you for doing that!"

"She's not hurt, so will you let it go? Jesus, Tripp. You sound like her husband."

Tripp and I stared at Trevor.

"What? He does. I'm going to call Dad and Mom and let them know Harley is okay."

"Hey, my phone must have fallen into the stall, can you have your folks call mine? They left earlier today and didn't stay for the barbeque. I told them I would call them."

Tipping his hat at me, Trevor flashed that smile I'm sure landed him a lot of women. "Sure thing."

I couldn't help but chuckle.

"Still the same ol' charmer."

Tripp let out a frustrated sigh.

"You haven't changed a damn bit, have you? Always doing something to save a damn animal."

I didn't respond. There was no sense in arguing with him. It had been a stupid thing to do, and I knew it. The worse part was the stupid cat had jumped down and walked out of the barn like nothing had happened.

"I'll need to stop by the clinic after I pick up Hemi from your folks' to get her some food."

Staring at me like I had two heads, Tripp started laughing and took off his cowboy hat. Pushing his hand through his hair, he shook his head and plopped the hat back on his head.

"Did you hear the doctor say you had to take it easy?"

"Yes. And I will. But I have things that I still need to take care of."

"You're not going in there getting a damn bag of food."

"I'll have my dad get it for me."

He looked directly at me for the longest time. There was something in his eyes, but I couldn't read what it was. The door opened and the sweet older nurse walked in.

"Harley Carbajal?"

"That's me."

She gave me a warm smile. "You look like a beautiful girl I used to know back in college. She had the same last name."

"Really? What was her first name?"

"Tanya. Oh…she used to turn the heads," the nurse said as she winked at Tripp. "Especially when she got out on the dance floor. The poor men didn't stand a chance as soon as she started to dance the salsa."

I let out a chuckle, but quickly stopped when a pain shot up my side.

"Tanya, you say? My father's sister's name is Tanya."

"No!" the nurse replied.

"Yes! Let me show you a picture of her. She went to the University of Texas."

"Oh my goodness, that must be her. I went there, as well."

My Aunt Tanya was a world traveler. She and her husband had been to almost every country. We only ever saw her at Christmastime.

"She's in Africa right now with her husband. They're on a safari for their anniversary."

"Well, how exciting."

I pulled up a picture from Facebook and showed her.

"That is her. What a small world. I just adored her. Lord, was she fun to be around."

"She still is."

"I bet," she said with a warm smile. "Tell her LoriBeth Williams from UT said hello. Did she ever pursue her desire to be a photographer?"

One quick swipe of my finger, and I pulled up a photo Aunt Tanya had taken in Iceland.

"Yes. She works for *National Geographic.* That's how she met my Uncle Bob. He's one of the editors."

"Well, what an exciting life she must lead."

I nodded. Aunt Tanya was the reason I had caught the travel bug when I was in college. The irony of this situation—me being in the hospital with Tripp here and Aunt Tanya being brought up again—wasn't lost on me.

After going over everything, I was finally discharged and walked out to Tripp's truck.

One quick stop at the Walgreens in Uvalde, and we were heading back home to Oak Springs. It was only a forty-five-minute drive, but the second I leaned my head back, the pain meds took over and I was out.

The feeling of warm arms carrying me caused me to let out a contented sigh. My entire body felt like I was lying on a cloud.

I was placed gently on what felt like a bed. I opened my eyes to see my bedroom curtains and then Hemi appeared in front of me. I smiled.

"Hemi," I whispered. I pulled her to me, her warmth comforting me even more, and I drifted back to sleep.

Light shining in from my bedroom window had me squinting. I went to stretch and stopped when I felt the pain in my side.

"Shit," I mumbled as I managed to get myself out of bed. The smell of coffee and bacon filled the air. My mother must have been making breakfast.

Walking slowly, I headed into my bathroom and brushed my teeth. A quick splash of water on my face caused a start as I stared at myself in the mirror.

"I look like death."

A quick ponytail and better wash of my face to remove the dirt and make-up from yesterday made me realize I needed a lengthy shower.

"Mom! I'm jumping in the shower," I called out as I turned on the hot water.

I wasn't sure how long I stood in there before Hemi came running in.

"Hey there, beautiful!" I said as I stepped out of the shower. My rib was killing me and as much as I wanted to reach down and pick up my new puppy, I knew I couldn't.

"Hank. Crap, I need to pay him for Hemi."

I dried off and wrapped the towel around my body. I needed to get my cell phone back. I was positive Toby had texted to confirm about tonight. I hated to break the news to him that things weren't going to work out between us, but the sooner I did it, the better.

"Come on, Hemi. Let's go see what your grandma is making for breakfast. Have you met Lady?"

I walked down the hallway and noticed the guest bedroom door open. The bed had been slept in last night, and I was surprised my mother hadn't made the bed before starting breakfast. That was one of her biggest pet peeves. It was so late when we got home from the hospital, she probably overslept and wanted to get a quick start on breakfast.

As I walked into the living room, I headed to the landline phone. Paxton had teased me for having it, but it was a good thing I did. I started to dial Tripp's cell. After calling it over and over for years, I

had the damn thing memorized. His number would forever be en-
grained in my memory. I'd always thought it was strange he didn't
change it. I figured for sure he would have gotten tired of me calling
him so much.

"Mom, that smells so good," I said as I took out the Oak Springs
phone book and looked up breeders to get Hank paid for Hemi.

That's when I heard it. A cell phone ringing. In my house. And
not my cell phone.

Closing my eyes, I turned while saying a prayer.

Please don't be his. Please.

It stopped ringing the moment I heard Tripp's voice. In stereo.

My eyes sprang open and standing before me was Tripp.

"Oh my God. What are you doing here?"

He kept the phone to his ear. "You've been asking me that question a lot lately."

I hung up and walked over to him. "Yeah, well, this time you're
in my house. So, again, what are you doing here?"

"Taking care of you," he said as he put the phone in his pocket.

I laughed, then stopped, my face pinched when the pain hit me.
"Really? I don't need to be taken care of, thank you very much."

His eyes moved down my body and there was no denying the
look of lust in them. I realized I was standing naked with only a towel wrapped around me.

Tripp's tongue ran over his bottom lip like it often did when he
was turned on. Some things never changed. My core pulled tight,
and I wanted to accidentally pull my towel off.

Squeezing my eyes shut, I chastised myself for thinking that
way. I needed to take back the power in this stand-off. I came to my
senses.

My fingers snapped in Tripp's face, causing him to look up at
me. "Um, hello? My eyes are up here?"

A sexy grin moved over his face, and I was pretty sure I let out a
small moan.

Ugh. Asshole.

"Why are you in my house, Tripp? Didn't you have to meet your girlfriend last night for a late night fuck session?"

He jerked like I'd just slapped his face.

"Ah...no. Not sure where you heard that."

I scoffed and made my way toward my bedroom to get clothes on.

"From her. Y'all didn't hide your conversation too much in the barn yesterday." Glancing over my shoulder, I added, "Remember? The nanny was there last night."

Anger moved over his face.

"You didn't get the whole conversation then. I told her I was staying at my folks' place last night."

I pressed my lips together as I walked to my dresser. It was hard to hide my joy over hearing that Tripp had turned Mallory down. I took a moment to revel in that bit of news before turning around to him. "I'm sure you'll make it up to her tonight."

He didn't say a word and that shot down any happiness I had briefly felt.

I grabbed the first thing I saw in my drawer, and damn it all to hell if it wasn't a pair of red panties.

The second drawer down wouldn't open. I tried jerking it. The pain shot through my entire body causing me to wince.

"Let me. Don't hurt yourself."

Tripp gently moved me. I couldn't help but notice how his thumbs brushed over my skin as he touched me.

"I can get it," I insisted as I tried to push him out of the way. All that did was cause another shooting pain, and I bent over, which caused more pain. And made my towel come apart.

"Ohmygawd," I cried out as I was hit with the pain twice over.

"Harley," Tripp said, his arms wrapping around me and lifting me up. My entire body flamed at his touch. It didn't help my stupid libido when I realized that the towel fell away, and I was stark-ass naked.

"Put me down," I yelled.

"Let me get you to the bed so you can rest."

"Tripp! Put me down now! I'm naked!"

He froze when he realized. Slowly, he set me down and stared at me, his eyes roaming over my body with nothing but desire swimming in them.

We stood there like two idiots. Me, naked, and Tripp staring at me. This time, I let my eyes roam over his body and realized he had on thin sleeping pants and a T-shirt that said, *I'm hot for pancakes.* I couldn't miss the outline of his erection through those thin pants.

God, why are you so cruel?

My mouth watered, and I wanted more than anything for him to pull his pants down and demand that I take him in my mouth. I always loved how demanding and strong Tripp was in bed. He was the only man I had ever been with who knew what he wanted and wasn't afraid to tell me. He was the only man who ever tied my hands to his bed post, blindfolded me, and made me come more times in one evening then I had in the years we'd been apart.

Darting my eyes back to his, we continued to gaze at one another. My body was desperately waiting for him to do something. When he didn't move, I remembered my robe on the bench at the end of my bed. Turning, I put it on. My breathing was heavy as I kept my back to his, trying to get the fog out of my head. I had been so close to begging him to touch me. So close to wanting to touch myself while he watched me with that veiled look of lust in his eyes.

How pathetic am I?

When his hands touched my shoulders from behind, I jumped, and the entire world felt like it stopped. It was only the two of us, and my body hummed with the delicious memories of Tripp making love to me.

"Harley." His breath was hot against my neck, but he didn't kiss me. Instead, he moved his hands and I felt the instant loss of heat from his mouth and hands.

"Breakfast will be ready in a few minutes."

Tears fell down my cheeks. When the door *click* echoed in the room, I let my sobs quietly spill…ignoring the pain in my ribs, suffering in silence.

CHAPTER 19

Tripp

My head dropped against her door, and I squeezed my eyes shut. My stomach rolled when I heard her sobs.

Fucking hell. What the fuck do I do?

Seeing her naked brought every single memory of us back in one fell swoop. It took everything I had not to pick her up and put her on the bed and make love to her. But I couldn't do that to Mallory. I couldn't cheat on her...I *wouldn't* cheat on her. We were exclusive, and even though I had every intention of breaking things off with her, I wouldn't be that much of an asshole.

I pushed off the door and headed to the kitchen. Grabbing my phone, I hit Steed's number and waited for him to answer as I put the last of the bacon on a paper towel to dry.

"Hey, what's up?"

My brother's voice seemed to calm the whirlwind of uncertainty twisting around in my head.

"I need your advice."

"You sure you didn't mean to call Dad?"

"No, Papa Smurf can't help me with this one."

Steed laughed. "Hit me with it."

Glancing back over toward the hallway, I swallowed and headed for Harley's sliding door that led to her patio.

"I'm at Harley's."

"Oh hell, it's early in the morning, what did you do?"

"Nothing. She fell asleep on the way back from the emergency room, and I didn't have the heart to leave her alone. Her mother said both her and Harley's father felt like they were getting sick and couldn't come over. I couldn't leave her alone so I stayed in her guest room. Nothing happened…but…"

He sighed. "But is never a good place to leave off on a sentence, dude."

"Something happened between us this morning, and I'm pretty sure Harley wanted the same thing I was wanting."

"You didn't sleep with her, did you?"

"No, I wouldn't do that to Mallory."

I could almost hear the relief in his voice. "Good. I'm glad you didn't do something stupid."

"Steed, I'm so fucking confused, yet I'm not confused."

"That statement doesn't make a lick of sense."

Running my hand down my race, I let out a frustrated groan. "I've never stopped loving her. I'll always love her."

"Then what's wrong? Are you having a hard time forgiving her?"

I scoffed. "Fuck, I think I forgave her the moment she told me the truth, but my damn pride and anger got in the way. I've only ever seen a future with one woman, and right now I don't know what my future looks like. Hell, I don't even know what I want anymore."

"Tripp, you've always been the one who had your future planned out right down to the damn day you were going to retire. Even I remember you talking about how you and Harley were going to finish school, get jobs, work a certain number of years, have kids, run for mayor. Fuck, you've had every damn life event planned out. But life isn't like that. Things happen, people change, feelings change, plans change. Harley knew that, but she didn't have the heart to ruin your dreams. Life is about taking risks, jumping off the ledge every now and then and praying like hell it all works out. If I learned anything from my time away and my return to Oak Springs, it was that what you love and want shouldn't come sliding to you on a silver platter. It doesn't come neatly tied up in a package, waiting for you to open it when you think it's time. It's about fighting for what your heart truly wants."

I nodded, even though I knew he couldn't see me. "What if my heart already knows it wants one thing for sure?"

"Is it Harley?"

It didn't even take me a nanosecond to reply. "Yes. What do I do, Steed?"

"You go slow. Y'all have been apart for a long time. I know the temptation to fall into each other's arms is strong. Hell, it killed me not being able to be with Paxton the moment I saw her. But I knew I needed to win her back. I needed to repair the past and that's what you and Harley need to do. Go slow. Show her you've forgiven her, show her she is worth the wait and get to know each other again."

I heard a noise from inside the house. Turning, I saw Harley mixing something in a bowl as Lady and Hemi sat on either side of her.

"Thanks, Steed, for talking it out with me."

"You already know what to do, bro. Just do it."

I watched as Harley poured ingredients into the mixing bowl, talking to both Lady and Hemi in only the way that animals would understand. My chest squeezed. "Yeah, I know exactly what I need to do. Thanks, Steed. Kiss the girls and Gage for me."

"I will. See you tonight."

The line went dead and I continued to stare into Harley's house as I watched her pour the batter onto the griddle.

"I know exactly what I have to do," I whispered as I lifted my phone and hit her name.

The phone rang a few times before Mallory answered it. "Hey there. Did you get some sleep last night?"

Facing away from Harley, I walked a few feet from the house. "I got some sleep, tossed and turned most of the night. Mallory, are you free for lunch today? I have something important I need to talk to you about."

"Sure, I need to pick up my dress for tonight from Clair. She did a few adjustments for me since the dress was too long. How about around one?"

"One sounds good. See you then."

"See ya later."

I walked back into the kitchen. Harley spun around and stared as I walked through the sliding glass door.

"I thought you left."

My lips twisted into a smile. "Before we have our pancakes?"

She laughed and let her eyes roam over me again. "So, do you always have pajamas with you?"

I looked down and laughed. "I swung by my house after I got you home and in bed."

With a nod, she turned back and flipped the pancakes. Slipping onto the stool at her island, I watched as she slid the pancakes on the plate and poured two more onto the griddle.

"Do you remember the first time you made me breakfast?" she asked with a chuckle.

I laughed. "How could I forget? We almost burned down my parents' guesthouse."

Her smile faded some, and she looked away. The memory was strong for both of us and I was instantly taken back in time.

"Tripp, we're going to get into trouble!" Harley whispered.

"Nonsense," I said, turning the key in the lock. "My folks are out of town and your folks think you're staying the night with Paxton."

We stepped into the guesthouse, and I turned on the lights.

Harley shrugged off her coat and laid it over the back of the sofa. All it took was one glimpse of her hard nipples through her thin sweater and I was all over her. My mouth pressed to hers as I lifted her up, and she wrapped her legs around my body. A moan slipped from her mouth as I pressed my cock into the warmth between her legs.

"You drive me fucking crazy, do you know that?" I whispered against her soft lips.

She drew her head back and stared into my eyes. "Show me how much I drive you crazy."

My tongue slid over my lips as I set her on the back of the sofa.

"Let me start breakfast first."

"Tease," she playfully said before cocking her head to the side. "Breakfast, huh? That's going to be the first meal you make me?"

"Bacon and eggs are my specialty."

She gave me a hard look. "Aren't they the only things you know how to make?"

"Minor details."

I moved into the kitchen and got everything ready while Harley stayed in the living room.

"Need help?" she called out.

"Nope, I've got this."

I found a frying pan and opened up the bacon I had grabbed from the house. I settled the bacon in the pan, turned the fire to low and headed back to the living room. Harley had hopped off the sofa and was standing in front of the fireplace looking at photos.

Fuck if I didn't want her every single time I looked at her. I was like a crazed, horny bastard when she was within a few feet of me.

She must have felt my stare because she turned around and faced me. I ached to be inside her. I stripped out of my clothes while she watched. Even though we had made love in the back of my truck earlier, I needed her again. She was an addiction I would never be able to break.

Her mouth opened slightly. She watched me with heated eyes as I stroked myself.

"Tripp," she barely whispered. "I want you."

The corner of my mouth rose in a cocky smile. "Then come take what's yours."

With one quick movement, she lifted her sweater over her head and made her way to me. I pushed the lace bra over her breasts and took a nipple into my mouth as I twisted and pulled the other one.

"Oh God," she whimpered.

"I want to fuck you, Harley."

"Yes," she hissed as she grabbed my cock.

My fingers and hands worked fast to get her jeans and panties off.

"Tripp, please..." she begged.

Slipping two fingers inside of her, we both moaned. "You're always so wet for me, baby."

Our mouths crashed together as I finger fucked her. Her hips riding hard against my hand. The sounds of her moans into my mouth as she came nearly had me coming myself. I lifted my mouth from hers. "Turn around and put your hands on the back of the sofa. I want you from behind."

Her tongue slid over her bottom lip before she bit down on it and did what I said.

I looked at her perfect ass sticking up, waiting for me to push my cock into her pussy. My heart slammed against my chest. Bending down, I grabbed my wallet from my jeans and took out a condom. I tore it open and quickly put it on.

When I grabbed her hips, she looked over her shoulder. A sexy-as-fuck grin moved over her face as she purred, "Show me, Tripp. Show me what I do to you."

One quick push and I was filling her all the way. Her gasp made me stop, worried I'd hurt her.

"Don't. Don't stop." She was panting, the need rolling off of her in waves.

Leaning over, I kissed her back. "Tell me what you want me to do."

Her body shuddered. "Fuck me," she gasped—either from hearing herself say it or from me filling her completely.

I smiled. I loved hearing those filthy words from her perfectly beautiful mouth. My sweet little church girl on Sunday and my naughty girl every other day of the week.

The sounds of my body slapping against hers fueled me to go harder. Faster.

"Fuck," I groaned as I reached around her and played with her clit. Harley was so responsive to my touch that she exploded within seconds. With the way she pulsed around my cock and how deep I was, I came right along with her. Both of us, calling out each other's names.

"Jesus Christ," I exclaimed as I leaned over her. Pressing a kiss on her back, I softly said, "I love you so much. I can't get enough of you."

Her body started to sink so I wrapped my arms around her, but stayed inside of her. One of these days I would make love to her with no barrier. It was a moment I fucking wished for every single time I was inside her. I dreamed of what her body would feel like surrounding mine.

"I want you...with no condom, Harley."

Her body tensed, and I quickly pulled out. Discarding the condom, I reached for the blanket that was laying over the sofa and wrapped us both in it.

Her gaze was downcast, so I placed my finger on her chin and lifted her eyes to mine.

"Look at me. I don't mean now. Or tomorrow, or hell, even next week. But one of these days I want you with nothing separating us."

She smiled and her cheeks flushed. "I want that too."

"Promise me something, right here and now."

Her soft emerald eyes searched my blue. "Anything."

"That no matter what happens, I will be the only man who gets to have you that way."

Harley's eyes filled with happiness. "Tripp, you're the only man who will ever have that, and so much more. You are the only man I will ever love."

She lifted up and our lips softly touched. The kiss was sweet and gentle. Just like the woman in my arms.

The smell of something burning had us both pulling back.

"Oh my God. Tripp! What's burning?"

"Fuck!" I shouted. "The bacon."

The alarms in the guesthouse went off and smoke poured out of the kitchen.

Harley and I rushed into the kitchen. The frying pan I had been cooking the bacon in was now a pool of flames.

"Fire!" I screamed as Harley screamed next to me. "The fire extinguisher." I had no idea why I shouted it as I ran into the kitchen. It was under the sink. My parents had always made sure we knew where they were in our house and the two guesthouses.

I pulled it out from under the sink and yelled for Harley to get out of the kitchen. For some reason, it was then I realized we were both naked.

Don't burn your dick, Tripp.

I chanted it over and over in my head.

"God, please don't let us die and have my parents find out we fucked in the guesthouse," I said in reverent prayer.

"Tripp! Pull it and get that out!" Harley screamed.

Doing what she commanded, I soon had the fire out and the pan in the sink. Standing there, I dragged in one deep breath after another. My hands shook with fear.

Harley took my hand in hers.

"Holy shit. We almost burned the whole damn place down."

She shook her head. "Your parents are going to kill us!"

That was when we heard sirens in the distance. Turning to look at each other, our eyes drifted down. We ran as fast as we could back to the living room where we grabbed for our clothes. Harley was dressed within seconds but was struggling to get her sneakers back on as I was trying to get my fucking jeans back on. The front door of the house burst open, and Steed and Mitchell came rushing in. Their eyes bounced from me to Harley before they landed back on me and they both started laughing their asses off.

"Uh, holy shit!" Mitchell said, bending over at the hip, his body shaking. "I fucking wish like hell the fire department had gotten here first."

"Fuck off, you asshole," I said as I gave another hard jerk and finally got my jeans on.

"Where is your other boot, Tripp?" Harley asked in a panicked voice.

"Right here, next to what I'm going to guess are not our last guest's panties."

I nearly punched Steed in the face as I grabbed Harley's panties and pushed them into my pocket. By the time I slipped on my boots we heard the fire department walking up the porch steps.

"I sure hope it was worth it, dude, and you were able to finish," Mitchell said.

"It was and we did, if it's any of your business," I said in a hushed voice.

Mitchell laughed. "Good, cause when Mom and Dad find out what you did, your ass is going to be confined to your fucking room until you graduate!"

"Tripp?"

Harley's voice pulled me from the memory.

"Sorry, I was thinking about a case."

A slight smile formed on her mouth. She knew what I was thinking about, and I knew she knew. "Here are some pancakes. Do you want more?"

I shook my head. "No. This is good."

A lump formed in my throat as I thought about how many amazing memories Harley and I shared. I still had the panties from that day tucked in the back of one of my drawers. That probably made me seem like a fucking creeper, but it was one of the few things I had from Harley that I had kept. Most were tucked away in a box in my parents' attic. But those panties and a handwritten note she had written and given to me at our high school graduation were the two things I had always kept close at hand.

"How are your ribs feeling?"

"They hurt."

"Well, be sure to take your pain pills and rest today."

She nodded. "Hopefully they'll feel better by this evening for your mom's dinner."

Our eyes met and there were unspoken words between us.

My phone beeped, and I pulled it out. It was a text from Mallory asking if we could meet early…a late breakfast because she had to get her hair done for tonight.

I stood. "I need to leave."

Her eyes watered and she turned quickly. "Just leave your plate. I'll get it."

"Harley, about earlier."

Holding up her hand, she shook her head. "It's okay, Tripp. Don't worry about it."

"You don't understand."

She faced me, her face in a hard, neutral expression. "Just don't. Please don't. Not when you just got a text from your girlfriend. I can't do this...not right now."

Her voice cracked, and it about killed me. My stomach twisted in knots. I walked over to her and placed my hands on her arms. She pulled away, wrapping her arms around her body. I knew it had to hurt because she winced.

"Promise me one thing, Harley."

She swallowed hard. "What?" she whispered. Her voice barely audible.

"Promise me we'll talk. Soon. I need you to understand about what happened earlier."

Her eyes dropped to the floor. "I think it's pretty clear where we stand on things, Tripp." Jerking her eyes back up to me, anger turned them almost black. "You can show yourself out."

And like that, she walked down the hallway to her bedroom. When I heard the door shut, I scrubbed my hands down my face. I wanted to fix things with Harley, but I needed to get things straightened out with Mallory first.

Time to face the music.

"Fuck," I groaned as I picked up my truck keys and wallet. My feet felt like lead as I made my way to her front door. Turning the handle, I glanced over my shoulder.

"I love you. I'll always love you," I whispered before walking out her door and closing it behind me.

CHAPTER 20

Harley

"You did what?" my mother asked as she gently placed my shoes next to my bed.

"I told Toby I couldn't go with him tonight. It wasn't fair to continue to date him when I had feelings for another man."

She was attempting to hide her smile and failing. Big time.

"Don't act like you're not happy, Momma. I see it in your eyes."

With a simple shrug, she motioned for me to sit in the chair in front of my vanity.

"You don't see a thing in my eyes, Harley. Now, if you were in my head, you'd be hearing a heck of a lot things."

I chuckled.

Sitting in the chair—carefully because of my ribs—I stared at my reflection. My grin faded as I looked at myself. I looked tired. Stressed to the max, and more confused than I had ever been in my entire life. The once-determined woman looking back at me who'd had it in her mind she would move back to Oak Springs and get the life she wanted, was nearly an empty shell. Ready to give up and pack her bags.

My mother brushing my hair instantly relaxed me, even more than the hot bath I had taken after Tripp left to go meet with his... *girlfriend*.

"Do you want to talk about it?" my mother softly asked.

My chin trembled and I pulled my lip between my teeth, gently biting down to keep my emotions in check. My mother knew Tripp had stayed here last night because he had told my parents he was going to. The moment she walked into my house, she was chomping at the bit to get me to tell her what happened.

I closed my eyes, feeling a single tear slip down my cheek.

"Oh Momma, I think I'm more in love with him now than I was the day I left him with that stupid lie."

She paused what she was doing. When I opened my eyes, she was smiling at me. There was no pity, just plain ol' happiness.

With a gleam like she knew something I didn't, she replied, "I believe he feels the same way."

The lump in my throat grew bigger, and I found it hard to form any words... so I shook my head.

When I was finally able to speak, I told her. "Earlier this morning, there was a moment between us, an intense moment, and I wanted more than anything for him to act on it, but he didn't," I choked out.

"Did you think he didn't act on it because he's seeing another woman?"

I wiped at my wet cheeks. "I thought of that. Tripp isn't the type of man to cheat, but I also know we wouldn't have let it go that far. I just wanted something from him. Anything that told me he *might* still feel the same way about me as I do him."

Burying my face in my hands, I found myself crying yet again.

Holy shit, I've cried more in the last few months than I have in the last ten years.

"Oh sweetie, don't cry."

My hands fell to my lap in defeat. "I don't think he feels the same way as I do, Momma. I think he's attracted to me, but that's it. He brushed it off and acted like the moment never happened. That one brief moment when I swore we both felt something from our past and maybe a hope for a future. *Oh God*, how could I be so stupid to think I could show up and things would fall back into place?"

The brush started to move across my long brown hair again.

"The first thing you need to do is take a deep breath and let it out. Then, you need to get yourself fixed up and walk into the benefit dinner like you don't have a care in the world."

I laughed. "Even though my world is falling apart?"

She scoffed. "It is not falling apart."

I stared at her like she had lost her damn mind. "Where have you been the last few months? I'm going to lose the vet clinic, I've lost the only man I've ever loved, and I just broke up with a *really great guy.*"

I let out a long groan.

"You're not going to lose the vet clinic, not with Tripp helping you. And don't give up hope, Harley. We never raised you to be a quitter. Now, as for Toby…"

She placed her hands on my shoulders and leaned in. Our eyes locked in the mirror. "You wouldn't have been satisfied with that boy. He looked like he wasn't packin' a big one."

My cheeks heated, and I turned to face her, my Latino heritage taking over my astonishment at what she'd just said. "Momma, dios mío! Eres increíble!"

"Don't chastise me in Spanish, young lady. You know I don't know what you're saying!"

We both laughed. "Mom, you're married to a Mexican man. When will you learn Spanish?"

She rolled her eyes. "He refuses to help me learn."

My father used to tell me he refused to teach my mother because when he complained about her in Spanish, she had no clue what he was saying. There were so many times my father would complain about my mother for one reason or another, but he would smile at her when he spoke. She would melt on the spot and kiss him, thinking he had just said something romantic to her. It saved many a fight in his mind.

"You know…you could learn on your own."

Giving me a wink, she shook her head. "Now where would the fun be in that?"

I stood in the front of the floor-length mirror. A small smile lifted the corners of my lips. I looked damn good, if I said so myself. I took a pain pill to hopefully get me through this night. A dull ache in my side was currently the only reminder that I had a bruised rib.

"You are stunning."

My eyes lifted to my mother. Her light brown hair was pulled into a ponytail and her blue eyes looked into my green. *She* was stunning. The fact that she didn't look a day older than forty gave me hope that I would be blessed with the same gene of looking younger than my age.

"You have to say that. You're my mother."

She nudged my shoulder. "You look like me when I was your age."

I turned to face her. "You were and still are beautiful."

I was rewarded with a wink. "And so are you. I would have killed for your sun-kissed skin." Her fingers twirled one of the curls that framed my face. "I need to say just one thing. Don't get mad at me or curse me out in Spanish like your father does."

My smile widened.

"When you walk into that room, Tripp Parker's eyes will not leave you the entire evening."

And like that, my smile faded. "Then I'm sure his date will be rather pissed."

Again, she looked like she was privy to information I was not. I wanted to quiz her…but I didn't. What good would it have done to my broken heart?

Dragging a deep breath, ignoring the pain, I turned back and gazed at myself again. I had splurged on this gown a few months back in Dallas. It was very rare that I spent this sort of money, but it was a gift to myself, and I'd known I would be wearing it to this event.

My hands ran down the dress. There were two things you noticed first with this dress. The leg-flaunting slit that ran up the side of my left leg and the plunging neckline that was framed with intricate beadwork. All hand sewn. The silk felt smooth against my hands.

"Touche finale!" my mother said in French as she placed the ombré-looking Jimmy Choo shoes on the floor. They were the most expensive pair of shoes I had ever bought, but when I purchased the clinic, I splurged on them. I loved how the light mocha blended in with the black. The glitter look made them even sexier. At least, I thought it did.

Slipping them on, I took another look at myself. From my pinned-up hair, dangling diamond earrings, and sexy-as-hell dress all the way to my expensive ass heels, I looked like a damn movie star.

Admit to yourself, Harley. You want his eyes all over you to-night.

"Do you think the red lipstick is too much?" I asked, leaning in and licking my lips.

"No! It's sexy."

My eyes darted over to my mother. "Are you hoping I hook up tonight, Momma?" I asked with a lifted brow.

"You said it, not me. I don't know how much you'll enjoy it with your rib being hurt, though."

I shot her a frown, but a small grin lifted at the corners of my mouth.

"I better go so I'm not walking in late." Turning to face my mother, I tilted my head and pouted. "I can't believe you and Daddy aren't going. You've never missed this dinner."

With a sad face and a long sigh, she replied, "I know. But your father has the flu. I already called Melanie and told her we couldn't make it, but we'll send in a donation."

Last night my mother had told Tripp she thought they were both coming down with the flu. She wasn't fooling anyone. She was feeling fine and could have stayed with me last night.

I kissed my mother's cheek. "Well, wish me luck. I'm going to be the only pathetic person to walk in without a date."

She laughed. "You'll be fine. Enjoy your evening."

The last time I had come to one of Melanie and John's benefit dinners I walked in on the arm of Tripp Parker. I was young and naïve. Not a care in the world.

Tonight I was walking in alone. No longer the clueless girl, but a grown woman who was both heartbroken and scared to death of what her future held.

My, oh my, how time can change things.

As I pulled up to the front of the house, a teenage boy came up to the car. I smiled when he handed me a ticket.

"Here you go, ma'am. May I get your phone number?"

After giving him my number, I made my way into the Parker house. It was the same set up each year. You were walked through the house by a host or hostess, again, a young teenager who was volunteering their time. After being taken into the den where you could leave your donation and your coat, you were escorted to the back-yard. I could see the giant tents set up as we walked into the den. The floor-to-ceiling windows showed three giant tents. I couldn't help but gasp at the sight on the other side of the windows. It was exactly like I remembered. People had worked non-stop all last night and today to transform the Parker's backyard from yesterday's Spring Fling barbeque, to an elegant, breathtaking sea of white twin-kle lights. It was a warm evening so the sides of the tents were up, giving you a view of the people inside. It looked like a five-star res-taurant and not a tent in the backyard of someone's home.

I dropped my donation in the box and wrote a small note in the journal that Melanie had set out. Each year she put a new one out and notes were written to someone you had loved and lost to cancer. I wasn't sure what Melanie did with all the journals, and for years I had wanted to ask. Maybe this year I would get the chance to.

"This way, Ms. Carbajal," the young girl said with a smile.

I followed her through the French doors in the den. A pathway led from the house to the first tent. It was the mingling area that also contained the bar—which would be my first destination. I was going to need to a stiff drink to get through this evening. Especially after I saw Tripp and Mallory together.

Ugh. I thought about what would happen later, when it was tra-dition for all of the Parker family members to dance the first dance. I would have to find an excuse to either leave before then or conven-iently head to the bathroom. My stomach twisted as I thought about it.

Over the years I had been absent from the benefit dinner, my mother had still managed to tell me that Tripp had always danced with either Amelia or Waylynn. Even if he had brought a date, he always danced with one of his sisters. It had brought me to tears be-cause I knew why he never danced with his dates.

The memory of that last dance together rushed to me.

"You look beautiful, Harley."

"And you look very handsome, Tripp."

His blue eyes seemed to shine brighter under the twinkle of the hundreds of lights that were strung up around the inside of the tent.

"This first dance is so important for my mother," he said, glancing over to Melanie.

"You've never told me why y'all always start the dance off before any of the guests."

Tripp gazed down into my eyes. "My grandparents met in a jazz club. My grandfather asked my grandmother to dance to this very song, and during the dance he told her he would never dance with another woman for the rest of his life. She was it. The love of his life. His future."

I smiled big. "That's so romantic."

"That's why my mom's only request from us is that we dance to this song with the one person we love with our whole hearts. If we haven't found them yet, we either don't dance or we dance with one of our sisters."

My stomach dropped as our eyes stayed locked.

"I love you, Harley. And just like my grandfather made that promise to my grandmother, I'm making it to you."

The tightness in my chest caused me to take a deep breath, which reminded me of my rib.

Damn cat.

"Oh my gosh! Harley!" Waylynn's voice drew my attention to her.

She made her way over to me. She was dressed in a beautiful blue strapless gown that was covered in what looked like small crystals. Her hair was swept up into a French twist and she was carrying two flutes of champagne. The sight of the pale cream, sparkling wine made my fingers itch for it. I was for sure going to need a few more of these…in case I got stuck and had to watch Tripp and Mallory dance.

"You look stunning, Harley," Waylynn stated, handing me the glass.

Taking it, I gave her a wink. "So do you, Waylynn. You look like you just stepped off the red carpet."

She laughed. "Well, living in New York all those years I bought my fair share of gowns."

"I bet," I said, taking a sip of the liquid courage.

"Where's Jonathon?" I asked, glancing around, hoping to catch a glimpse of Tripp but not having any luck.

"He's with Steed and Tripp."

And that was all she said. I nodded as I looked back over our surroundings. "It's so beautiful. I had forgotten how amazing this all is."

Waylynn looked back with a huge grin. "My mother does a great job with this event. Dad lets her go crazy once a year, and let me tell you, she takes advantage of it. Wait until you see what's for dinner."

The cost to attend the benefit dinner was three hundred dollars a plate, and was also your donation. Those who didn't attend the dinner still made donations. My parents had bought three plates every single year since I had turned thirteen—the age when the kids got to join the grown-ups at the big fancy party the Parkers threw every spring.

"I'm starving," I said, taking another long drink of my champagne.

Waylynn's brow lifted. "Do you need something stronger?"

"Is it that noticeable?"

The corners of her mouth lifted into a grin. "Slightly." Hooking her arm with mine, she guided us through the room and toward the bar.

We stopped a few times to say hello to people either Waylynn knew, or we both knew. Most welcomed me home and almost all wished me good luck on my fight for the clinic.

Yep. Small town living. Everyone knows everyone's business.

As we made our way past the local town gossips, I saw Corina, Paxton, and Amelia standing with Melanie. They were talking to some men I didn't recognize.

"That is the Worthington family."

"Who are they?" I asked.

"They are a family from Austin who bought about five thousand acres outside of town off of Ranch Road twenty-three."

"Please tell me they're not going to make it into a subdivision."

She shook her head. "They want to raise cattle on it. They've been trying to talk my father into helping them get things started by hiring him as a consultant."

"Wow. Do they know anything about cattle?"

Waylynn chuckled. "Not a goddamn thing. Which tickles Daddy. But they're loaded and were all too happy to throw down some serious money for this event. Hence why my mother and sisters are all currently kissing their asses right now."

We laughed before Waylynn turned us away from the group. We walked up to the bar and Waylynn motioned for me to order.

The bartender gave me a smile, his eyes falling to my cleavage and then back up to my eyes.

"Are you able to make a Death in the Afternoon?"

"Jesus, you do need a drink," Waylynn laughed.

"I am," the bartender said. "Is that what you'd like, ma'am?"

I nodded. "Yes."

I turned to look at Waylynn, who was wearing a smug smile.

"What?"

She half shrugged. "That's a pretty powerful drink."

I shot her my own smug grin. "I'll take baby sips. Besides, I need it."

The bartender slid the drink over to me then looked at Waylynn. "Long Island Iced Tea."

After making Waylynn her cocktail, the bartender told us to enjoy the evening. We held up our drinks and Waylynn made a toast.

"To having you home again."

My smile faltered a bit before I pulled it together. The last few weeks I had wrestled with my decision to come back to Oak Springs. It *was* home, and I had wanted to return for so long. Now that I was here, though, my heart ached more and more.

I forced the words out. "To being home."

We each took a drink, and I let the burn of the alcohol run down my throat all the way to my stomach.

Shit. I probably should have actually eaten something today besides the one pancake this morning.

"Come on, my mother is going to want to see you."

I nodded. "Who is watching Liberty?"

"Lori, Paxton's babysitter she uses for the kids. Liberty is up in my old bedroom sound asleep. She goes down pretty early, so Lori really only has to deal with Chloe and Gage."

"It's nice the kids can all stay here at the house."

"It is," Waylynn agreed.

As we approached the rest of the Parker women, I was struck by how beautiful each of them were. The way the lights danced off each of their faces I swore they looked like angels.

Amelia wore a stunning green gown that showed off her long red curls. Half of her hair was pinned up and the rest was left to flow freely around her shoulders. Paxton wore a red gown that was completely backless. I had to wonder how Steed managed to let her out of the house dressed so sexy. If those two were anything like they were back in high school, I wouldn't be surprised if Steed snuck a little playtime in before they left the house.

Corina was dressed in a gorgeous teal gown that showed off her baby bump and her amazing figure.

Christ above. I hope when I'm pregnant I look that good.

Melanie wore a stunning white gown that hugged her body in all the right ways. The woman was like my mother; they could both pass for being much younger than they were.

"Oh hell, hold onto your drink. Here's Aunt Vi."

I turned to see Vi walking toward Melanie. There was a man next to her with his hand around her waist. He looked younger than me.

"Is that…"

"Her date. Yes."

I giggled. "He looks like he's Amelia's age."

Waylynn tilted her head and studied the man. "*If* that."

We laughed and Melanie turned to us as we approached.

Her mouth opened and her eyes quickly swept over me before our gaze locked.

"Lord above. Harley Carbajal, you look beautiful. Every man in this room must have had their tongues to the floor when you walked in."

I felt my cheeks heat.

"That she does," Vi said, walking up and pulling me into her arms. Her mouth was next to my ear as she said, "Every man in this room is going to have a woody looking at you in that gown."

I busted out laughing, as the pain radiated in my ribs.

"Good Lord," Melanie said as she moved Vi out of the way. "Even I heard you, Vi."

Vi gave me a wink and then looked down at the drink in my hand. When our eyes met, her brow lifted. "Feeling anxious this evening?"

With a smile, I replied, "Slightly."

"Sweetheart, there is no reason to be nervous." Melanie looked around. "Where is Toby?" Her question felt forced. Almost like she already knew the answer.

Pulling my lip between my teeth, I bit down for a moment before saying, "I told him I didn't think things would work out with us."

Every single Parker woman standing in front of me smiled.

I snarled at them. "Y'all could at least hide your excitement."

Melanie tilted her head and gave me a sympathetic smile...sort of.

"We're all very sorry to hear that." She cleared her throat. "Um, when did this happen?"

My eyes darted among all six of them. "Earlier today."

"Interesting," Vi purred before letting out a laugh. "Oh, this evening just got a hell of a lot better."

Pinching my brows, I started to ask what she meant when Melanie grabbed my hands.

"Like I was saying before, no need to be nervous. Every single man in this place will be fighting for a place on your dance card."

I forced a smile. The need to tell her my card only had one open spot and that would always belong to her son was eating at my stomach. I was regretting my drink choice now. Especially with no food in my stomach.

Oh shit, the pain pill I took. Well, this is nice. What a great combination you've made for yourself, Harley. Drugs and booze. This should be fun.

"Come on, I want to introduce you to a few of my friends," Vi stated. She held her arm out for me to take it.

Paxton leaned in. "Don't leave with Vi. And if she mentions something about JuJu, come find us."

With a confused look, I responded, "Um, okay."

Vi and I walked around the room. Her young date followed closely behind, looking me over with hungry eyes. Vi didn't seem to care, though.

"I believe my acquaintance is having dirty thoughts about you, sweet Harley."

Glancing over my shoulder, my eyes caught his. The way his tongue swept over his lips, I would have to agree with Vi.

My head turned forward quickly. "That doesn't bother you, Vi? That he's openly staring at me?"

She scoffed. "Why should it?"

"He's your date?"

Vi stopped walking. "He's my *acquaintance*. Like I said before," Vi looked back. "Roger understands my needs, and I understand his. But he's currently barking up the wrong tree."

Roger cleared his throat. "Noted, ma'am."

With a nod of her head, Vi guided us back to walking. I couldn't help but chuckle. "So what exactly is an *acquaintance* of yours?"

"If it's a woman, she is a friend of mine whom I see every now and then. We exchange small talk and politely move on with the knowledge that I may or may not say hello to her the next time we see one another. If he is a male, my age? The same holds true. But, if he is a male around Roger's age….well…things are little more…"

Her eyes looked up in thought. As if she was trying to think of an elegant way to say that Roger was her fuck buddy.

"He's your fuck buddy?"

Roger let out a choked laugh from behind us.

"Jesus Christ, Harley. Tell the whole place."

Scanning the room, I looked at Vi. "You do know they are all thinking the same thing."

She wore an evil little smile. "Touché."

We walked up to an older group of people. I was positive this was Vi's crowd.

"Well, who do you have here, Vi?" an older woman with silver hair asked. Each of the women were dressed in simple, yet elegant gowns. They were all beautiful with hints of worldly experiences on their faces. I couldn't help but wonder if any of them had had any work done. As I looked closer, I smiled. No. These were all southern women. They owned their age and wore it like freaking rockstars.

I smiled as Vi introduced me to her group of friends. Two of the women had dates who seemed to be only a few years older than Roger. The other woman stood next to a handsome man who was her age. His salt and pepper hair made him look regal—or it could have been the overpriced tux he had on.

"Harley owns the veterinary clinic in town," Vi stated with pride in her voice. She had always treated me like I was family. Guilt wrapped around my chest and squeezed as I thought about all the people I had hurt when I lied to Tripp. I began to feel sick to my stomach and lightheaded.

"If y'all will excuse me, I think a need a bit of fresh air."

They smiled but Vi gave me a concerned look. I pointed to the drink. "No food today mixed with a pain pill."

Her shoulders relaxed. "Get some food, water, and fresh air. But don't hide. You need to show off that curvy figure of yours, my dear. From the look on Roger's face, Latino woman are highly desired."

I laughed and rolled my eyes. "I'll try to remember that."

As I made my way through the room, I felt the heat of Tripp's stare. I didn't dare look because the moment I saw him standing next to Mallory I was sure to lose whatever was left of this morning's pancakes.

I saw the exit at the far end of the large tent. Picking up my pace, I headed toward it. But something stopped me. With a quick glance over my shoulder, I sucked in a breath.

There he stood, in a black tuxedo, looking handsome as fuck.

Tripp Parker.

My knees weakened, and I had to fight to keep myself from dropping to the ground at the mere sight of him. He hadn't shaved and his five o'clock shadow made him look even more dashing. No. He looked utterly fuckable. The heat between my legs was instant. The lightheadedness and the ache in my stomach were replaced by the throbbing between my thighs. My heart pounded so loudly it was drowning out the light music in the background.

"Christ above," I whispered. This man could turn me into a puddle on the floor.

Tripp let his eyes roam over me before they locked with mine. Even from across the crowded room, I could see the desire in them. Or was I imagining it?

He's here with another woman, you idiot. Smile and walk away, Harley.

Before I could do that, Tripp smiled at me, the dimple in his cheek evident from across the room. My eyes burned with tears, and my heart ached as I forced one in return. I dared to look to either side of him, expecting to see Mallory. When I didn't, I let out a sigh of relief. She must have been in the restroom, or possibly talking to Melanie.

When my eyes captured his again, I had to remind myself to take a damn breath.

Turn around, Harley. Turn. Around.

Forcing my feet to move, I spun and headed outside. A cool rush hit me in the face, causing me to take in some much-needed air.

I dropped my chin to my chest and let out a long sigh.

I was never going to be able to move on... Never would I be able to love another man like I loved Tripp Parker. One single tear trailed down my cheek as I let the reality of this into my heart.

He was the only thing I was certain I wanted in my future...and he was lost forever.

CHAPTER 21

Harley

After spending too much time hiding outside, I mentally prepared myself and headed back in. I had worked things out in my head the best I could and decided I need to pull my big girl panties up and make it through this night. Once Tripp finished helping me get the clinic back I would move on with my life. I wasn't sure if that meant finding someone to spend the rest of my life with, or casually dating, or maybe living out the rest of my life surrounded by animals. Whatever my path would be, I would be happy for Tripp. He had moved on and found happiness and feeling sorry for myself wasn't making anything better.

Squaring my shoulders, I moved about the room. I spoke with people I knew, and people I didn't know. A number of people at the dinner were not from Oak Springs. Most of them were rather intriguing, and I found myself passing the time by making up stories of who they could be.

I smiled and scanned the room, letting the drugs and booze take over as I played out their pretend lives in my head.

The young, tall sandy-blond man with the beautiful redhead on his arm was an investment broker from New York City. The woman was an actress, trying to make her way on Broadway but happy to be on the arm of a rich man who kept her sexually satisfied and well-kept with jewels and expensive clothing—not to mention a BMW.

Then you had the dashing thirty-something-year-old man with the English accent. He was a Duke of something or other. A rich family history of old money and fast cars. The blonde on his arm was his mistress because the bastard's poor wife was most likely back in England, pregnant with his heir. The mistress looked utterly bored having to mingle with everyone in the room and made no attempts to hide her distaste for Americans.

I giggled as I pulled a drink from my glass of champagne.

"What's with that smile on your face?" Melanie asked as she stood next to me.

With a roll of my eyes, I shook my head. "I'm letting my overactive imagination run wild as I make up stories about the strangers in the room."

My eyes nearly came out of my head as I saw Trevor with a stunning young woman on his arm.

"Who is *that* with Trevor?" I asked, taking another glass of champagne as a waiter walked by, replacing it with the empty glass I had just drained. I was for sure feeling it as the room spun slightly.

Melanie grinned from ear to ear. "That…is Scarlett Littlefield. She's the daughter of one of my very best friends, Lynn."

"She is stunning!" I said, taking a drink.

"Trevor is refusing to speak to me because of her."

My eyes traveled over to look at Trevor and Scarlett. Trevor was always a bit of a rebel, at least from what I remembered. The hint of his tattoos on his hands gave him a bit of a bad boy persona. His buzzed hair and unshaven face made him even more attractive. And I wasn't the only woman in the room who thought so.

Scarlett Littlefield was staring at Trevor, trying not to seem smitten with him. Of course, she herself was unbelievably gorgeous. Her soft brown hair had subtle hints of blonde highlights in it. She was tiny, and had a body to die for.

"They look adorable together," I gushed.

"They do."

"How long have they been dating?"

Melanie sighed. "They're not. I pretty much had to threaten Trevor's life…and inheritance…to get him to bring Scarlett this evening."

I let out a giggle. "Oh no, Melanie, you didn't?"

She nodded. "I did. I'm tired of hearing rumors about my youngest son sleeping with nearly all the women in this town. It's time for him to settle down a bit."

Chewing my lip, I looked over at them. Trevor placed his hand on Scarlett's lower back and ushered her on to the next group.

"They sure look like they're comfortable with each other," I observed.

We looked at one another and a mischievous smile grew across Melanie's face. "Indeed, they do."

My brow lifted. "Why do I get the feeling you're playing matchmaker, Melanie Parker?"

She placed her hand over her chest and gasped. "Me? Interfere in my children's' lives?"

A gentleman wearing a white tux approached us. "Mrs. Parker?"

Turning, she gave him a polite grin. "Did you take care of that request, Smith?"

He nodded. "I have, ma'am. The seats at the family table have been adjusted like you asked."

"Thank you." Melanie faced me and laughed. "Now, what makes you think I would meddle in my kids' love lives?"

There was a look in her eye that screamed she was up to something. She lifted her glass to mine and said, "A toast. To butting in."

Laughing, I replied, "To butting in."

Little did I know, Trevor and Scarlett weren't the only peoples' lives Melanie was meddling with.

CHAPTER 22

Tripp

For the last fifteen minutes I had stood there and listened…or pretended to listen…to Bobby Hansen's discussion of the budget for the Oak Springs City employees Christmas party. It was fucking April, and he was worried about a damn party that was eight months away.

"What do you think, Tripp?"

I had been scanning the large tent hoping to get a look at Harley again. The moment I saw her my cock went rock hard, and I'd had a hell of time hiding it. I glanced around looking for her. She must have moved to the next tent to find her seat for dinner.

"What do I think about what, Bobby?"

The older man groaned. "The budget. Honestly, Parker, for a man running for mayor you need to be more involved."

Slapping him on the back, I gave him the smile I knew could charm any woman or man. "Bobby, tonight is not about that. It's about enjoying the company of family and friends and making a difference in a cause close to my mother's heart. The budget for a party eight months away is not something I think I need to focus on right now."

I glanced around at the other men in our small group, who all nodded. Some even raised their whiskey glasses to me. I was positive they wanted Bobby to shut up as much as I did.

"Now, if you'll excuse me, gentlemen, I'd better find my mother. We'll be sitting soon for dinner."

Bobby seemed to be angry at first, until I mentioned the reason we were all gathered in my parents' backyard under tents that were made to look like they were ballrooms in a five-star hotel.

He gave me a slap on the back in return, and I walked away. I took a long pull from my rum and Coke. I was going to need a shot of something straight if I wanted to make it through this night. I hadn't seen Toby with Harley yet, but I had seen them separately. The thought of him dancing with her this evening had my stomach in fucking knots.

"Who's the lucky lady who will have the honor of dancing with you this evening, Tripp?"

I turned to see Claire Montigo standing there. She was the younger sister of one of my best friends from high school, Scott Montigo.

Giving her a kiss on the cheek, I looked down to her rather large, pregnant belly.

"I heard you were expecting another baby. Scott told me a few months back."

Her cheeks blushed. "Baby number three."

I grinned. "Exciting."

She nodded. "It is. So are you going to answer me?"

Leaning my head in a bit closer, I asked, "Answer what?"

"Who are you dancing with? I noticed you didn't come in with anyone. Rumor was you were dating that woman who owns the little shop on Main. Mallory, I believe her name is."

Jesus H. Christ. The people in this town. Even when they don't live here they are in on all the gossip.

"Now how in the world would you know all that, Claire? You don't even live here anymore."

She laughed. "The gossip mill is high tech now. Text messaging and email make it easy for us out-of-town folks to keep up, my sweet Tripp."

It was my turn to toss my head back and let out a round of laughter.

"Well, considering both my sisters are married and their husbands are here this evening, it looks like I'll be sitting that dance out with Trevor and Cord."

Everyone in town knew how that dance worked. It was special to my mother, and the fact that Claire was asking pissed me off. "If you'll excuse me, Claire, I need to get to my seat."

"Of course. Have a good evening!" she called out to me as I walked away.

By the time I'd made it into the tent where all of the tables were set up, I was in a foul mood. The idea of sitting on the sidelines had never bothered me before, so I had no clue why tonight it was grating on my nerves.

As I walked toward the family table, I saw her.

Harley.

She was walking with Paxton, and they were both laughing. Harley was glancing down at the name plates as she walked around one table. My heart felt like it was about to leap out of my chest when I didn't see Toby next to her.

Steed walked by, and I grabbed him by the arm. "Steed, wait."

He looked at me and then over to Paxton and Harley.

"Shit, how fucking lucky am I?" he stated as he gazed at his wife with a look that screamed he was head over heels in love.

I smiled. "Paxton looks beautiful."

"So does Harley."

He slapped me on the back. "I bet you're glad she's here alone."

My head jerked to the side. "What do you mean she's here alone?"

The corners of his mouth pulled into a smirk. "You don't know?"

I balled my fists to keep from grabbing him and shaking the fuck out of him. "No, Steed, please enlighten me."

"Dude, Paxton said Harley told Toby things wouldn't work out between the two of them."

There was no way I could hide the stupid ass smile on my face. "Did she say why?"

He shook his head. "I'm afraid you're going to have to ask her. But don't worry, you'll have plenty of chances, especially since Mom moved her seat next to yours."

With a wink, he bumped me with his shoulder and made his way to Paxton. I quickly followed.

"Hey beautiful. Let me escort you to your seat," Steed said to his wife. When Paxton looked at me, she gave me a knowing look. She knew where Harley was sitting but was playing along.

"I'll see you in a bit," Paxton said, giving Harley a quick hug. When they both walked away, I let my eyes finally get a good look at the woman I loved.

"You're the most beautiful woman in the room, Harley Carbajal."

Her cheeks flushed and all the blood ran straight to my dick.

"And look at you, Mr. Parker. You look quite handsome this evening." Her eyes roamed my body before her eyes met mine. When her tongue licked across her lips, I nearly pulled her into me for a kiss.

"May I show you to your seat?" I asked, extending my arm.

She looked confused, and then glanced over my shoulder and around the room. "Um...sure. That would be great since I can't seem to find it."

When her hand slid across my arm, my body shook with antici-pation. Just having her this close had my cock pressing against my zipper, begging to come out and play.

I guided her to the family table.

"Tripp, that's your table."

Ignoring her, I stopped and leaned down to kiss Amelia on the cheek. "I haven't had the chance to tell you how beautiful you look this evening, Meli."

Her eyes swung from me to a very confused Harley. "Thank you, but I dare say, Harley seems to have captured every eye in the room."

Harley's hand gripped my arm tighter, and I saw her looking around.

We started walking, but only long enough to stop and kiss Aunt Vi. "Aunt Vi, as usual, you're the hottest woman in the room."

"Damn straight I am," she replied with a wink.

I spied the two empty chairs. I knew they were for me and Har-ley.

"Tripp," Harley said, pulling my arm back to get me to stop walking. "Tripp, those seats belong to you and…"

I cut her off before she said Mallory's name.

"Waylynn, you're breathtaking." Leaning down, I kissed my sis-ter who was attempting not to laugh. I could see Harley looking around the room for what I could only guess was Mallory.

"Why, thank you, little brother. I would say you're the most dashing man in the room, but my husband holds that honor."

Jonathon chuckled.

I gave her a wink. "I'll let that slide this one time."

Harley was still pulling on me as I practically dragged her to the two seats. I found my mother staring at us as I came to a stop in front of the name tags. One read Tripp Parker. The other, Harley Carbajal. I narrowed my eyes at my mother. She flashed me a dimpled grin and then blew me a kiss. God, I loved that woman as much as the woman who was on my arm right now.

"I'm going to go ahead and find my seat while you take yours," Harley said, her voice cracking.

"Harley, sit down."

She looked at me, confusion not only on her face, but in her eyes. When tears started to build in them, I wanted to pull her into my arms.

"It's...not my...seat." Her chin trembled.

I reached down and picked up the tag that read her beautiful name.

"Baby, this is your seat. It's always been your seat."

Her breath hitched. She didn't even bother to look down at the name tag. She searched my face as the words settled in. When a tear slipped from her beautiful eyes, I reached up and wiped it away.

"You're not here with Mallory?"

"No," I whispered.

Before I had a chance to explain everything, they were announcing for everyone to take a seat. I held out Harley's chair as she sat. Waylynn leaned over and gave Harley a quick hug.

My mother stood next to my father as everyone else took their seats.

"I'll be brief, as I'm sure everyone smells that delicious food," she said with a huge grin.

Chuckles echoed across the room.

"Thank you to everyone here this evening. Many of you have been attending this benefit dinner and dance since the very first one almost thirty years ago. I lost my mother and father to cancer, so this is a cause very near and dear to my heart. For those of you here this evening for the first time, let me tell you how the rest of the evening will go. We'll eat..."

Cheers erupted and my mother tossed her head back to laugh.

"Then, my husband, John, and I will make our way to the dance floor where we will be joined by our children. It's the first dance, and I only have one rule for my kids as they take the dance floor. If they dance with anyone other than one of their siblings, it must be with someone they intend to dance with for the rest of their lives. You see…"

Her voice cracked a bit and my father wrapped his arm around her waist, pulling her close to him. When he kissed her head, she took in a breath and went on.

"You see, this dance will be to the very same song my father danced with and made a promise to my mother to love her for always. They died within days of one another. I choose to believe that they did everything together after that dance. Even when they died."

My mother wiped a tear from her cheek. "Now some of my boys—" She turned and looked at Trevor and Cord. "Will be sitting this one out."

The crowd laughed, and I couldn't help but notice Trevor give a tight smile. Cord made no attempt to hide that he was happy with sitting out the dance.

Continuing, she said, "The rule doesn't apply past the first song, so men, don't panic out there!"

Another round of laughter lifted the somber mood that had settled in.

"Now that you know what to expect, let's eat!"

CHAPTER 23

Harley

Dinner flew by in the blink of an eye. I was starving, but the moment I realized I was sitting next to Tripp, and Mallory was nowhere in sight, my stomach decided to go haywire. I forced myself to eat, though. I needed it with the damn booze I'd been drinking all evening. The slight buzz I had felt from the bubbly and the pain pill combo couldn't compare to the way my chest was fluttering while I sat next to Tripp. I wasn't even sure he realized he had reached for my hand twice and held it for a few brief moments. It was exactly like the last dinner I attended. Like I had fallen through a time machine and traveled back to when I was his and he was mine. The slight touches on my leg, the way he would take his hand in mine and give it a light squeeze.

Was I dreaming? Was this really happening right now?

"Are you okay?" Waylynn whispered.

I nodded and took a sip of water.

"I see we moved to water."

"Yep." Facing her, I quietly asked, "What happened with Mallory?" The question had been burning at me since I sat down.

She gasped, bringing her fingers to her lips. "Has no one told you? Tripp broke up with her."

My mouth fell slightly open. "Wait, what?"

"I'll let Tripp tell you."

"Waylynn!"

She giggled and reached for her glass of water.

"I thought you were my friend," I added.

"I am. But it's not my story to tell. It's Tripp's. Just like I'm sure he would like to know why you're not here with Toby. Well, Toby's here, but you're clearly not *with* Toby in that sort of way because if you *were* then you would be sitting next to *him* and not next to *Tripp* which you are *for sure* sitting next to Tripp and..."

"Oh, for the love of God!" I whispered as I hit her on the leg. "You're rambling! How much have you had to drink?"

She lifted her champagne glass. "A lot."

"I can tell," I stated with a roll of my eyes.

Heat rushed through my body as I felt Tripp's arm on the back of my chair. When his thumb moved over my exposed neck, my entire body erupted in goosebumps.

This man is going to cause me to explode with a stroke of his thumb across my neck.

I swallowed and tried to focus on other things besides the heat pooling in my lower stomach.

My eyes landed on Trevor and Scarlett. I studied them carefully. They were both in conversations with other people at the table. Trevor was talking to Wade who sat next to him, and Scarlett spoke with Corina. I moved my eyes past Corina to find Mitchell talking to Cord. I didn't recognize the young lady sitting next to Cord. When I had seen him earlier I was bummed he wasn't with Maebh. I'd spotted Maebh and her father just after they arrived. She looked stunning in a dark green gown with her brown hair pulled up. I knew it was a long shot, but they *would* look cute together. My eyes darted over to Melanie—and I remembered the waiter coming over earlier and saying he had taken care of the request she had made at the table.

That little sneak.

She had moved my seat next to Tripp's. Taking another sip of water, I shook my head. Melanie must have sensed me staring because our eyes met. I could see her happiness as she lifted her water glass to me. I couldn't help but return her smile.

I wondered if she knew about Maebh. I was going to have to talk to Paxton and Waylynn about it. Those two seemed to be on the same wavelength as Melanie. They were all trying to play Cupid in one way or another.

"Are you feeling okay?" Tripp asked.

I buzzed from his hot breath against my ear.

"Y-yes. I'm fine."

"You're only drinking water."

I let out a nervous laugh. "I've reached my limit on alcohol this evening."

Our eyes met and our mouths were inches from one another. There was no denying the heat between us. This man sitting next to me, looking at me with nothing but pure love and desire was the king of my heart. He'd been able to take me to places no other man had been able to since. Not just between the sheets, but by a simple taste of his lips. A brush of his thumb across my skin, a smile that made my knees tremble when I wasn't even standing.

If I was lucky enough to get a second chance with Tripp, I was never letting him go.

A bell rang to notify that dinner was over and the first dance was about to start. Tripp was still staring into my eyes. There were so many things I wanted to say. To do. My hands were shaking as I fought to keep them tucked together in my lap.

"Ladies and gentlemen, please allow the Parker family to take the dance floor before joining them," an announcer said, pulling my gaze from Tripp's.

Melanie and John stood. He kissed her, then whispered something to his wife before escorting her out to the dance floor. The rest of the family stood except for Cord and Trevor. I gasped when I realized Tripp wasn't sitting but standing next to me, holding out his hand.

My mouth dropped open but nothing came out.

"Now that you're back. I don't have to dance with one of my sisters or sit this one out."

"Tripp..." I whispered as I stood.

He guided me around the table before placing his hand on the small of my back and leading me out to the dance floor.

When Tripp gently drew me into his body, I took the chance to look around: smiles on every single face. Some whispered, some had tears in their eyes, and some looked like they were falling in love with the idea of love as the familiar jazz tune of Bobby Darin's "More" filled the air. This song meant so much, not only to Melanie's parents, but to the entire Parker family.

I shook my head to clear my confusion. If Tripp had asked me to dance to this song, then he had forgiven me. He was giving us another chance. Squeezing my eyes shut, I prayed this wasn't a dream. The moment hit me so strongly, my legs went weak and Tripp held me tighter.

His fingers lifted my chin so our eyes met.

"Your mind is racing when it doesn't have to, Lee."

"What about Mallory? Why is she not here with you? We're dancing to this song. Tripp, I know what this song means to your family. To your mother. What about earlier in my room? I'm so confused..."

His smile was gentle and sweet. His eyes were filled with the same love I'd seen the last time we made love so many years ago.

"I met Mallory for lunch today and told her things would never work between us, not when I was in love with another woman. Not just another woman...*the* woman. The woman I have been in love with since the first moment I laid eyes on her."

A small sob slipped out. "Tripp," I whispered.

"It's always been you, Harley. Always. And it will be for the rest of my life."

Attempting to swallow the lump in my throat, I forced the words out. "But I thought y'all were..."

He placed his finger on my lips. "I was never in love with her. I never saw a future with her."

When my tears fell, he brushed them away with his thumbs and then his lips. The warmth caused an explosion of tingles to race over my body.

"Now what?" I asked, my voice shaking in anticipation of his answer.

A beautiful smile spread across his handsome face and my body trembled. Tripp leaned down, his lips inches from mine. His breath made my heart race faster than it had in years. It hadn't pounded like this since the last time he had leaned in to kiss me.

"Now? Now I get to kiss you, Harley. Finally."

My smile dawned before his lips slid against mine. His fingers laced in my hair, drawing me closer, making me moan into his mouth. Tripp's hand moved to the small of my back, pulling me to him. The feel of his hard length on my stomach nearly had my legs buckling.

Tripp's mouth withdrew. His eyes pierced mine with such intensity I was almost frozen still. "Let's show them how to dance to this song before it ends."

I giggled. Soon we were gliding across the dance floor. As I danced in the arms of the man I loved, I realized I'd never been this happy in my entire life.

When the song ended, and Tripp drew me to him for another kiss, I knew everything was finally going to be okay. No matter what happened with the clinic or how things went with Tripp running for mayor…we were together at last.

The sounds of "It Had To Be You" brought everyone out of their seats. With a spin, Tripp and I danced like two silly teenagers staring at one another while gliding across the makeshift wooden dance floor.

My eyes caught Melanie's, and I could see her tears as she lifted her hand off John's back to give me a wave.

I returned the gesture before Tripp spun me again.

"You know, your mother is pretty sneaky."

He laughed. "Tell me about it. I'm positive the moment she saw us both walk in alone she went to work."

I buried my face into his chest as I smiled. Drawing back, I looked up into his beautiful eyes.

"I'm sorry we lost so much time together."

Tripp cradled the side of my face. Leaning into it, I closed my eyes as I felt his lips brush over mine. "It just means we have a lot to catch up on."

My lower stomach clenched. When I opened my eyes, we were lost in each other. A few more songs and I was in need of water and a rest. I couldn't ignore the throbbing at my side.

Tripp guided us back to the table where we both sat down. I scanned the dance floor to find Cord and his date.

"Who is that with Cord?"

"That is Tammy. The manager of Cord's Place. Or I should say, his go-to girl when he needs a date for an event like this."

"Anything going on between them?"

Tripp let out a hearty laugh. "Hell no. Cord knows better than to sleep with her. She helps keep that place running and the last thing he wants to do is mess that up."

I took a sip of water. "Does she feel the same way?"

"I think so. She's never seemed interested in Cord that way. Of course, she has a front seat view of his ways so that probably keeps her at bay."

I watched as all the couples danced and laughed.

"Everyone looks like they're enjoying themselves," I stated.

"Look at Trevor. I think the little bastard has finally met his match."

"With Scarlett?" I looked around, searching out over the dance floor. "Where is she?"

Tripp pointed to Scarlett in the arms of Aunt Vi's date. I covered my mouth and laughed.

"Oh. Roger got to her."

"Yeah, look at my brother. He's pissed."

Trevor looked rather upset, indeed.

"Do you think he likes her?" I asked.

With a shrug, Tripp looked at me and grinned. "Oh, yeah. And I'm sure that confuses the hell out of him. He'll act like he doesn't care that another man asked her dance, but he can't hide the seething."

"Are we talking about our lovestruck baby brother?" Waylynn asked, sitting down next to me.

"Yep," Tripp and I said at once.

Waylynn stared for a brief moment at Trevor before she lost it in a fit of laughter.

"Christ Almighty, look at the poor bastard. He doesn't know what to do."

Tripp started laughing next.

"He looks like he wants to knock the shit out of Aunt Vi's poor boy toy!" Waylynn added.

"Are y'all talking about Trevor?" Steed asked, sitting down at the table with Paxton.

Paxton shook her head. "Don't be mean. I think it's cute Trevor has finally fallen for someone."

"Lord, don't let Mom hear you say that," Waylynn said. "She'll make it her mission in life to get them together. She's already worked her magic on these two."

She jerked her thumb toward me and Tripp.

Mitchell was now at the table with a very miserable looking Corina. She forced a smile, but I could tell she wasn't feeling well.

"I say we throw Cord and Maebh to Mom, while we're at it," Mitchell said with a chuckle.

Waylynn cleared her throat as everyone turned to her.

Jonathon let out a groan as he said, "What did you do now, Waylynn?"

Her eyes widened, and she pretended to be shocked. Her hand went to her chest while she said, "Me? Why all I did was happen to point her out to our mother and possibly let it slip that Cord couldn't keep his eyes off our new Irish friend."

We all laughed.

"Those poor bastards," Tripp said as he took my hand and kissed the back of it. When he winked, my stomach felt like a million butterflies were flying around in it.

"Boys!" Melanie called out. "I need a picture of all my handsome men. Come on. That means you too, Jonathon...Wade. Come on!"

All of them groaned as Melanie smacked Mitchell on the back of the head, only because he was closest to her.

"Stop acting like that. You know this happens every year."

As they all got up, Melanie turned to the table.

"Girls, you're next." Melanie pointed to me. "And that means you too, Harley."

"Yes, ma'am," I said with a nod.

Waylynn grabbed her drink. "The annual family pictures. I swear if she could do this once a month, she would."

My eyes glanced to Corina. She looked pale. I stood and made my way around the table and sat down next to her. Taking her hand in mine, I squeezed it.

"Corina, what's wrong?"

She swallowed hard. "I don't feel good. My head is spinning, and I feel hot."

Placing my hand to her forehead I shot my eyes over to Waylynn. She was watching us with a concerned look on her face.

"You have a fever, Corina."

"I feel like I'm going to pass out."

I grabbed her water and poured it over a napkin. I dabbed it on her forehead and cheeks.

"Drink this," I said as I took Mitchell's ice water that he hadn't touched. "Small sips. Have you been drinking lots of water?"

She shook her head. "Probably not enough."

Amelia walked up. "Mom stole Wade from me and…what's wrong?"

Paxton was now up. "I'm going to go get Mitchell."

"My body hurts so bad," Corina softly said. She was weak, and for the first time this evening, she wasn't trying to put up a front.

"Sweetie, we're going to get you to a bed." I pointed to my clutch. "Waylynn, reach in and grab my phone."

She did as I asked.

"I saw Dr. Peterson saying goodbye to your parents earlier. I have his number in my phone. We might be able to reach him before he gets too far away."

Waylynn pulled up the number and started talking.

"What's wrong?" Mitchell asked as he rushed up and took the seat next to Corina.

"I think she might have the flu," I said.

Mitchell's head snapped up as he looked at me.

I stood, motioning for Mitchell to do the same. "Let's get her into the house so she can be comfortable. Waylynn's calling Dr. Peterson now."

Mitchell and I helped Corina stand. We were soon surrounded by the entire family and Tripp had taken over my spot.

Mitchell called out over his shoulder. "Paxton, can you call Dr. Buten?"

She nodded and rushed in front of everyone, making her way to the house.

"That's Corina's OB," Amelia told me, taking my hand in hers.

I gave it a reassuring squeeze. "Don't worry. She's going to be okay."

Amelia gave me a tight smile, but I could see the fear on her face.

As we all walked toward the house, Aunt Vi gave an announcement that things were going to wrap up early due to a family emergency. I hated that my fairytale evening had to end, but I was more concerned for Corina and the baby.

Mitchell carried Corina up to the guest bedroom where he and Amelia attended to her. Luckily, the girls had all gotten ready here at the house, so Corina had a change of clothes.

Sitting in the living room, I watched as members of the family paced or sat looking scared.

I stood. "I'm going to go put on some coffee and hot water for tea."

Tripp's head lifted as our eyes met. I hated to see him worrying, and I wished there was something more I could do.

"I'll help." Tripp reached for my hand and we walked into the kitchen in silence.

Nothing about the kitchen had changed. Appliances had been updated, but the coffee pot was still located in the same exact spot. I got to work adding the coffee and water and putting on a kettle to boil.

Warm arms found their way around my body. I stopped moving and spun to face Tripp.

His eyes searched my face before he lifted his hand and tracked my jawline with one finger. "I love you."

My heart soared. "I love you too."

"Is it wrong that I want to take you and hide away for a few weeks?"

I smiled. "I don't think so. We sort of have to get to know each other again."

He nodded. "I promised Steed I'd go slow, but I've missed you so goddamn much."

My eyes burned with the threat of tears. This time happy ones. "I missed you too. I wish I could..."

His fingers pressed to my lips, and he shook his head. "The past is in the past. All I care about is our future. Yours and mine. The only thing I want right now is to be with you. And the only memories I want to talk about are the happy ones because those far outweigh anything else."

I swallowed the lump in my throat. "That's all I want too."

Tripp's head dropped and he let out a worried sigh. "Is she going to be okay?"

Taking both his hands in mine, I pulled them to my mouth and kissed each one.

"Yes. She's going to need to rest and do what the doctor says, but I think she'll be okay. I know it's scary because she's pregnant, but I have no doubt in my mind that both Dr. Peterson and Dr. Buten will take care of her."

The way Tripp gazed so intensely caused a shiver to race through my body. If we were alone I was positive I would be dropping to the floor and begging him to take me right here.

His tongue ran over his bottom lip, and I groaned quietly.

"Have I told you how fucking beautiful you look tonight?"

My mouth opened, but nothing came out.

"I wanted to take things slow. Get to know each other again, but the second we get news that Corina is okay, I'm taking you home."

I did the only thing my stupid body would let me do. I nodded.

"Then I'm going to slowly take this dress off of you."

The throbbing between my legs was so intense I had to press my thighs together to ease the ache.

"Then…then what?" I asked as I fought for breath.

The left side of his mouth lifted. "Then I get to explore what's mine, what's always been mine…from top to bottom. Slowly."

CHAPTER 24

Tripp

"Go home," my mother said to everyone as she stood in the den and looked around the room.

"Is she going to be okay?" Waylynn asked before letting out a long yawn.

"Yes. Both Dr. Peterson and Dr. Buten said Corina will be fine. They tested her for the flu, but Dr. Peterson thinks she has a virus and she's not been resting enough. She is on strict bed rest for the next few days. Once we find out more I will be sure to let you all know. Mitchell is on his way to pick up Milo and some clothes. They're going to be staying here for the next few days."

I was positive we all let out a collective sigh when my mother said Corina was okay.

Harley's fingers were laced with mine as we listened to my mother bark out orders. My mother walked up to Scarlett, hugged her, and thanked her for staying as long as she did. Trevor had offered to take her home earlier, but she'd said she wanted to make sure Corina was okay. The fact that my little brother couldn't seem

to keep his eyes off the brunette beauty amused me, Steed, Cord, and
Mitchell. The bastard was going to be catching hell for this.

Tammy, Cord's date, had driven her own car and had left over
an hour ago.

There was no fucking way I was going to take Harley home.
Fuck that. She was coming back to my house and I was going to peel
that black dress off of her and bury myself inside her all damn night.
I'd already called her mother and asked if she could keep Hemi and
Lady for the evening. She was more than happy to, and said they
were both already at her house.

"Harley, sweetheart, thank you for being so observant and noticing Corina wasn't herself."

With a sweet smile, Harley hugged my mother. "Of course. She
did a good job of hiding it for quite a while."

I wrapped my arm around Harley's waist while my mother's
eyes bounced between us.

"Does this mean you've finally gotten your head out of your ass,
son?"

"It does, Mother. With your help, I might add."

She acted like she had no idea what I was talking about. "Whatever do you mean?"

Leaning over, I kissed her on the forehead. "I'll see you tomorrow, Mom. Thank you."

"Goodnight, Tripp." My mother turned her attention back to
Harley. "You looked stunning this evening. Enjoy the rest of the
night."

"Thank you so much, Melanie," Harley said with a kiss to my
mother's cheek. After saying goodnight to everyone and giving my
father the usual handshake and quick hug, I led Harley outside.

"Your folks said not to worry about Hemi and Lady. They have
everything taken care of," I stated as Harley leaned against her car
door.

"I'm sure they won't mind watching them for a bit longer. Besides, I already sent my mother a text and told her what was happening with Corina."

My finger brushed a curl from those stunning emerald eyes of hers. "And did you talk about what was happening with us?"

Her teeth dug into her lip. "That part I kept to myself or I'd be currently on the phone with her giving her a play by play of this evening."

Sliding my hand to the nape of her neck, I drew her mouth closer to mine. "Would you like a play by play of how the rest of your evening is going to look?"

Her smile made my stomach drop. "Yes, I'd very much like that."

"First, you're going to follow me home, then the moment you step into my house I'm taking that dress off of you. Then I plan on burying my face between your legs and tasting what I've waited ten years to have again."

The small moan that fell from her lips had me wanting to skip the driving part and do it right this moment.

"Then...then what?" Harley asked with a shaky voice.

"After I make you come on my face, I'm going to bring you up to my bedroom and do it all over again."

"Tripp," she panted, her body trembling as I spoke to her.

"How does that all sound so far, baby?"

She nodded.

"Then, those pretty red lips are going to wrap around my cock because it's been too fucking long since I've been inside your mouth."

Her eyes closed while her tongue swept over her lips. My dick was so fucking hard I almost felt the urge to release it and let her suck me off here...if only we weren't standing in front of my folks' house.

"I think...I think you should finish telling me once we get to your house," Harley whispered.

"'Night, Tripp! 'Night. Harley! Use protection!" Waylynn called out as she walked with Jonathon over to his truck.

Rolling my eyes at my sister, Harley and I both called out our goodnights to Waylynn and Jonathon, as well as the rest of my siblings.

"Follow me back to my house," I demanded. Leaning in, I pressed my mouth to hers. Our tongues danced together as Harley opened up and let me in.

The drive back to my house felt like it took forever. Pulling into my driveway, I opened the garage and pulled in, leaving room for Harley to pull her car in next to my truck. There was no way I could hide the smile on my face seeing her car parked next to mine.

Quickly getting out of my truck, I waited for her at the door.

"Your house is beautiful, Tripp."

I'd built this two-story house a few years back. It was the house I'd drawn when I was in college. The dream house that had been part of my grand plans. I was curious to see if she would recognize it from the little drawing I'd made on the back of a Sonic drive-thru napkin so many years ago.

Over the last few days it was becoming clearer to me that maybe those plans needed to be altered. That I needed to start living my life without thinking and planning out every damn move. I needed to live on the edge.

"Thank you. I had it built a few years back."

I opened the door from the garage and stepped into the mud room. We walked past it and down the hall that led into the kitchen.

Harley was looking up at the ceiling as she walked. "There's wood on your ceiling."

With a chuckle, I replied, "Yep, I did that."

"You did?" she asked in a stunned voice.

"Don't act so surprised, Harley. I'm pretty handy when it comes to things like that."

When we walked into the kitchen, I set my keys down in a small bowl on the counter. The kitchen was open to the informal dining and living area with a large rock fireplace at the opposite end of the large space. A wall of windows and one set of French doors showed the view out back.

"Wow," she whispered as her fingers ran along the white marbled quartz counters. "I love the white cabinets."

"So do I. Makes everything look clean and simple."

She turned to me. I could see it in her eyes…she knew I had designed this kitchen like the one we used to talk about. With a slight smile, she walked to the alder wood door.

"Let me guess. Pantry?"

I nodded. She *did* remember.

She opened it and stepped into the large walk-in pantry. "Tripp, there is no food in this pantry and it's as big as my office at the clinic!"

Laughing, I pulled her out of the pantry.

"A quick tour, then I'm taking you to bed."

She giggled. "What happened to your plan?"

"I've changed it."

"I see."

Pulling her behind me, I walked into the living. "Dining room. Living room."

I turned the corner and walked down another hallway that brought us to the formal dining room. Harley gasped when she saw the table.

"Christ above! That table is huge. Is that from a real tree?" she asked.

"Yep. The table seats ten. Let's keep moving."

We walked up to a spiral staircase. This wasn't in the original plans, but my builder thought it would look cool, and I agreed.

"This is stunning!" Harley stated as we walked up the steps and into the large game room. A huge leather sectional sat up here along with a pool table, a shuffleboard table, and my favorite part of the room—the fully stocked bar.

"Holy serious game room."

I chuckled and showed her the two guest bedrooms and the bathroom before bringing her back downstairs, using the back staircase that went straight to the hallway to my office.

"This is my office."

We walked in and the first thing you saw when you stepped in was the floor-to-ceiling knotty alder book cases. My large wood desk sat in the middle of the office with a large leather desk chair on one side facing the white stone fireplace, and two smaller leather chairs.

"Tripp, this is all so beautiful. You've designed a beautiful home. Just like the one you drew on the back of that napkin." She rewarded me with a sexy wink.

I smiled. For some reason her remembering made me so happy. I wasn't sure why it did, but it had my chest doing that damn stupid fluttering shit.

"Looks like the only thing left to show me is your bedroom." She approached me with a predatory gaze in her eyes.

They grew darker the closer she got. My hands itched with anticipation.

"Follow me," I ordered.

Walking into my room, I stepped to the side so Harley could take it all in. It was a large room with a big sitting room at the back. Large windows looked out toward the backyard. Two elegant white chairs sat in the area with a round marble table that contained my grandmother's oil lamp and one single book. Harley made her way over to the area in silence. She picked up the book, clutching it to her chest as she spun around. Tears streamed down her face.

"You kept the book?" she asked, her voice cracking as she spoke.

"It was your favorite book," I replied.

Her head shook back and forth. "Tripp, this is the bedroom we talked about having together someday. This is it down to the...to the..." she held out the book.

"Down to your favorite book sitting on the small round table in the sitting area. Waiting for you to sit down and read it."

"But...I don't understand," she managed to get out as she cried just a little harder.

I walked up to her and wiped her tears away. "Deep down in my heart, I was never ready to give up on the idea of us, Lee."

She chewed on her lip and looked at the floor. "I don't have the right to ask this, but have you had very many...um...very many..."

I lifted her chin so she could look me directly in the eyes. "I've never once brought a woman into this room. Not even Mallory."

Harley sucked in a breath. "What?"

Glancing at the book in her hands, I smiled. *"Sense and Sensibility,"* I said as I ran my fingers over the title. My eyes lifted to hers. Taking the book out of her hands, I set it back onto the small table. Cupping her face in my hands, I pressed my lips to hers. When Harley opened to me, I poured every ounce of love I could into that kiss.

Her hands moved up and around my neck, and her fingers laced into my hair. She moaned when I pressed my hard cock into her.

I picked her up in one quick move and carried her to the king-size bed, gently placing her down on it. I dropped to my knees.

"As much as I want to rip your clothes off and fuck you seven ways to Sunday, I need to take my time. I need to love you, Harley." I realized after showing her the home I'd built—the home I'd subconsciously built for her—that I had all the time in the world with this woman. She was my past, my present, and my future.

She smiled and placed her hands on the sides of my face. I knew she was still in pain from her ribs, and I tried like hell to be careful with her.

"Then love me, Tripp. I'm all yours."

CHAPTER 25

Harley

My hands shook as I smiled at Tripp. The way my stomach knotted you would think this was my first time. The throb on my side was no match for the one between my legs.

Tripp stared at me with hungry eyes. He pulled me into a standing position. "Turn around," he softly ordered.

I did as he said, feeling the wetness on my panties.

When Tripp's hands touched my shoulders, I jumped.

Soft lips kissed my neck.

"Are you nervous, Lee?"

A small chuckle slipped out as I answered. "Yes."

"Why? I've made love to you before. Many. *Many*. Times." His lips moved down my neck and across my shoulders. "I've fucked you plenty of times and plenty of ways."

My chest rose and fell with each word he spoke. The feel of his hands unzipping my dress had my libido screaming, *Move faster!*

"My mouth has been on your pussy, tasted you so many times. My fingers have explored every inch of this perfect body. And tonight, I plan on taking my time and learning you all over again."

"It all feels so new, Tripp… Ten years is a long time but I'm here and I'm not going anywhere. Make love to me, stay with me." My breath caught in my throat as he pushed the dress off my shoulders, letting it pool at my feet. No man had ever touched me or made me feel the way Tripp had. To say I had a good sex life after Tripp was laughable. I'd been with a few other men, but nothing like what I'd experienced with Tripp. He had taken me to a place of pure delight.

Heaven, if you will.

I couldn't help but wonder how many women Tripp has been with since I left. I'd heard rumors, some of which I believed, others I chose to ignore. None of that mattered and I needed to push it to the side. What mattered was the here and now.

The past was just that.

The past.

Tripp's fingers brushed down my sides as he dropped to his knees. I hadn't worn a bra with this dress so my bare back was on display. The only thing I had left was my black lace thong. Tripp let out a low growl as he slowly peeled it off.

"Fucking hell," he whispered. I stepped out of both my dress and panties while Tripp placed soft kisses on each of my ass cheeks. He cupped my ass and groaned. Anal sex had always been something he told me he wanted, but I had always been too nervous to go that far with him.

His hand moved up my back while he stood.

"Lean over and put your hands on my bed, Harley."

I did as he said. Tripp reached around and cupped both of my breasts. He squeezed them gently before moving on to my nipples.

"I've missed your body so much, baby."

My head dropped, and I let out a moan as I felt his hard cock pressed against my ass. When had he undressed?

Glancing back, I saw he had his pants undone, his impressive hard-on jumping with anticipation.

"I've missed...you...too."

Christ. I sound so needy.

The words barely came out between hard gasps of air.

He dropped back down, his hands kneading my ass cheeks again.

"Is this still mine, Harley?"

My teeth sank into my lip so hard I was sure it would be swollen tomorrow. "Yes."

"Good. Someday...soon."

I could hear the smile in his voice and my entire body shook with the thought.

"Get down on your elbows, baby. I want to taste you."

Doing as he said, I leaned over more. My heart was beating so hard I could hear it in my ears.

Tripp lifted my leg and my whole body jumped when he licked between my lips.

"Oh God!" I cried out, gripping the comforter. When he pushed his fingers inside of me, we both moaned.

"Fucking hell, Harley," Tripp said. "You make me crazy. I need you to lie on your back."

I stood and gave him a smirk. "So bossy."

He lifted a brow and pointed. "Now, before I fucking explode in my own pants."

There was no awkwardness between us. It was as if we had picked up right where we left off. I watched Tripp as he stripped out of his tux. It was the hottest damn thing I'd ever seen in my life. My legs rubbed back and forth as I tried to keep from slipping my hand between them.

"Are you turned on, baby?"

I let out a harsh laugh. "To say the least. You're teasing me, Mr. Parker."

"It's called payback."

My brows lifted. "Really?"

He nodded as he crawled onto the bed next to me. "For leaving me and trying to decide what was best for me. For us."

The ache in my chest pulsed.

Tripp's hand on my stomach forced it away. "Look at me, Harley."

Trying to keep the guilt and sadness at bay, I turned my head and our eyes met.

"Don't ever do that again. You're here. Your mine. And we are going to spend the rest of our lives together making decisions…together."

"Trust me, I learned my lesson."

The way he smiled released butterflies in my stomach. When his hand moved south and his fingers slipped into me, his eyes turned dark like a storm building in a beautiful summer sky.

"So fucking wet."

He moved quickly, spreading my legs and settling between them. After peppering me with a hundred kisses up and down my thighs, Tripp did as he promised, tasting me after all these years.

Finally.

My hands didn't know what to do. I went from grabbing the bedspread to running my fingers in his hair, back to the comforter. My body squirmed and jumped as Tripp brought me right to the edge of an orgasm, only to back off. I was dizzy with the need to come. Dizzy with the knowledge that Tripp was between my legs. Driving me on to what would be an explosive orgasm.

"Tripp!" I cried. "Please!"

It didn't take long after my plea for him to bring out the most intense orgasm of my life. With my eyes squeezed shut, bursts of light matched the pulse inside my pussy. It was intense. Beautiful. Earth-shattering. If I survived this night, it would be a miracle.

When I finally settled back into my mind, Tripp was over me. His hard length pressed against me, creating friction when I lifted my hips to him. I needed more. I needed him.

It had always been this way with Tripp. We could never get enough of each other, and so many years apart only added fuel to the wildfire of our needs.

"Are you on the pill?" he asked, his lips brushing mine. The roughness of his five o'clock shadow was already causing my lips to swell. My entire body was going to be chafed from his unshaven face, but I didn't care.

"Yes," I gasped, lifting to feel him against me. "I'm clean. I haven't been with anyone in a few years."

Tripp stopped kissing my neck and pulled back to look at me. The guilt in his eyes was evidence of his past relationships. He closed his eyes and I could feel him pulling away. I wrapped my arms around his neck.

"It doesn't matter. Everything is in the past, remember?" I whispered. He opened his eyes and my breath caught in my throat when I saw his tears.

"I'm sorry, Harley."

I knew he was apologizing for Mallory. For that day in his office.

With a shake of my head, I stared into his beautiful sky blue eyes. "It's in the past."

"I've never been with another woman without a condom."

"And I've never been with a man without one," I replied.

He smiled. "Are you sure about this?"

Hooking my legs around him, I drew him closer. "I'm sure."

Tripp pressed his mouth to mine as he pushed himself into me. I gasped when he filled me and the beauty of this moment settled into my heart.

I was finally home.

"You feel so good, Lee. God, you feel so good." I could have sworn I saw his eyes tearing up, even as my own emotions threatened to spill from my eyes. This moment was a long time coming… It was where we belonged… It was perfection.

My fingertips moved lightly over his back, our bodies moving together as one. When I felt another orgasm building, I dug my nails in and called out his name. In that same moment, Tripp lost control. He moved faster. Harder. Our bodies slapped together, echoing in his bedroom. Tripp's mouth crashed down on mine. My name poured from his lips along with promises to love me for always. And I made the same promises as his body slowed, and he buried his face into my neck. I would never tell him my side was aching. If I did he would get off of me and not do this again. And I *so* wanted him again.

The moment was everything I had dreamed it would be, and then some. Our hearts felt like they were beating as one. All the lies, the broken hearts, the years we lost…they faded to nothing. This was the beginning of our future.

The beginning of us.

Again.

Hot breath hit my face, causing me to turn my head.

The bed moved and a wet kiss swept over my face. I jerked up and looked around the room.

Where am I?

The memories of last night came rushing back. My cheeks heated as I thought about all the ways Tripp had made me come last night. His mouth, fingers, and dick had taken me on one hell of a ride last night. My body was going to need a long soak in a hot bath.

A small howl made me fly out of the bed and land on the floor. I groaned in pain from my bruised rib. When I looked up, Hemi was staring down at me.

"Hemi?" I asked with a smile on my face. "What are you doing here, girl?"

She leapt off the tall bed and landed right in my arms. I hugged her close and kissed her on the head. I hadn't been looking for a dog, but thanks to Chloe, I was the proud mother of a daredevil pup.

"I see she finally got you to wake up. Why are you on the floor?"

Tripp stood at the end of his bed, a glass of orange juice in his hand. His eyes swept over my naked body and I could see he was ready to take me again. My stomach growled and I felt my cheeks heat.

"Food. I need energy and I have a feeling I'm going to need a pain pill with the way you're looking at me right now, Mr. Parker."

His eyes turned sad. "You're right. You do need food and your pain meds. Shit, I sort of forgot about your rib last night."

Reaching down, he took Hemi and placed her next to me before taking my hands and pulling me up.

"Let me get a hot bath going for you. Then we need to talk."

My breath caught and fear ripped through my body.

"Don't look at me like that, Harley. I meant every word I said last night, you and I are forever now. This isn't about us. It's about the vet clinic. Karen sent me over something this morning from Gerald Harris's attorney."

"Oh," I said, my shoulders sagging. From the look on Tripp's face, it wasn't good news.

"That bad?"

He nodded. "He is planning on tearing down the clinic. He plans on building something else on the land he owns."

My mouth fell open. "Can he do that? I thought Doc said he had paid him back for the land!"

When his gaze fell to the floor, I had my answer.
I was about to lose my dream.

CHAPTER 26

Tripp

A few weeks later

I sat in my office looking over the paperwork. After trying to find a loophole, I came up with nothing. There was no proof to show that Doc Harris had paid his brother back for the land that the Oak Springs vet clinic sat on. Harley owned the clinic, and Gerald owned the land the clinic sat on. It was a fucked-up situation to say the least.

Karen knocked on the door, and I looked up. "Don't forget, you have lunch plans with your brothers today."

"Right," I said with a nod. "Thanks, Karen."

She started to leave but stopped. Clearing her throat, she took a few steps back into my office. When I looked up at her, I gave her a questioning look. "I only wanted to say that I'm so happy for you, boss. I don't think I've ever seen you so happy."

My chest tightened. "I don't think I've been this happy in a very long time, Karen."

A large smile appeared on her face. "You'll make beautiful babies."

I laughed. "Thank you? I think."

She blushed. "Now, go to lunch. You know how cranky Cord gets when he has to wait for his food."

"True. I'm leaving now."

I reached for my phone and sent two texts. One to Cord, and one to Harley.

Me: *I'm on my way. Order if everyone is there.*

Cord's response was almost immediate.

Cord: *Trevor just walked in. We're waiting on you, so get a move on!*

Rolling my eyes, I ignored his text and typed to Harley.

Me: *I can't stop thinking about you this morning.*

Her reply didn't come, and I figured she was busy with patients. Glancing down, I shook my head. Hemi had crashed on the giant ass dog bed Harley had bought when we had made a trip to PetSmart in San Antonio.

"Spoiled ass dog."

Hemi lifted one eye at me. I tried to hide my smile. This damn dog had somehow managed to wrap me around her little paw. I pretended I didn't care, but the little stinker knew I was falling for her.

"I'm going to meet your uncles for lunch."

She lifted up and watched me get my suit jacket on.

"Do not tear up anything or I will throw your ass outside tonight. Got it? Remember, I'm the boss."

Hemi howled in argument, then did a little whimper that made me roll my eyes. She didn't do it very often, but when she did, Harley melted and usually gave her a treat. I, on the other hand, wasn't as affected by her cuteness. The last thing I wanted was for her to start howling to get a damn treat.

"Behave, mutt," I called out.

Hemi didn't bother to answer. She simply laid her head back on the bed and pretended she would sleep the entire time. Both of us knew that was not going to happen.

I shut the door to my office and made my way out. "Karen, before you leave for lunch, will you put Hemi in her crate? I already took her out to pee."

"Why do you always make me put her in the crate? You walk out and leave her all happy on the bed and then I have to go in like the mean aunt and lock her up in jail."

Staring at her, I shrugged. "Cause I'm the boss."

Hemi barked from my office. I swear Harley had taught the damn dog to do it every time I said that.

"The boss!" she scoffed. "Huh!"

I decided to not engage with Karen on this one. "I'll be back in a few hours. Enjoy your lunch."

Karen mumbled something as I headed out the door, the word *asshole* standing out.

As I walked over to Lilly's place, I saw Mallory outside her store. She was talking to a man in a business suit and her hands were flying all over the place. She didn't look angry, more determined. We hadn't talked since that day at lunch before the benefit dinner. I had figured she was going to be angry. I hadn't expected she would tell me she saw it coming. Especially since I hadn't touched her since that last time we fucked in my office.

The bell on the door of Lilly's rang as I stepped inside. Glancing to my left, I saw my brothers, plus Wade, all sitting at the large round table in the back corner.

I pulled out a chair and looked at each of them. They wore cowboy hats and smiles on their faces. Almost as if they knew something I didn't.

"How's it going? Y'all look like you're up to no good."

Cord spoke first. "I finally fucking figured out your Smurf name."

I rolled my eyes. "Christ, not this again."

"Yes. This again. You joined the rest of them. You're a fucking Smurf."

"Welcome to the mushroom, dude," Steed said as everyone else laughed. "We only have two more to go."

"Fuck that," Trevor said. "No, thanks. Women are nothing but a goddamn pain in the ass."

All eyes turned to Trevor.

"Oh hell," Cord whispered as he closed his eyes. "Son-of-a-bitch."

With a frown, Trevor stared at Cord. "What's wrong with you?"

"You fucked her, didn't you?" Cord asked.

We all leaned in to watch Trevor's reaction.

"What?"

Mitchell jumped back and pointed to Trevor. "Oh hell! Dude! You did!"

"What are you talking about? Let's move on," Trevor said, and I could have sworn I saw beads of sweat appear on his brow as he tried to derail the conversation.

"Don't even try to hide it, Trev. They can smell it," Wade said before taking a bite of the loaf of bread the waitress must have brought out.

Trevor looked confused. "Smell what? There's nothing to fucking smell. All I said was women are a pain in the ass."

"It's the *way* you said it," Mitchell replied. "Clearly, you slept with Scarlett. She got under your skin and now you don't know what to do about it."

Our baby brother's mouth dropped open. "The fuck?" he whispered.

Cord reached for the bread and broke a piece off and used it to point to Trevor.

"You see, normal girls we sleep with? They don't get under our skin. We fuck 'em and move on."

I shook my head. "Real nice, Cord."

The bread pointed my way. "No judging. That was you a year ago, so no comments from the peanut gallery."

My hands came up in defense. "You're speaking the truth, but can you keep it down, and maybe not be so damn blunt?"

Cord lifted his eyes in thought before agreeing. "Yes. I can do both."

He focused back on Trevor. "Alright. The way I see it is, you promised yourself you wouldn't sleep with her. One, because you actually felt something for her. Two, she's Mom's best friend's daughter and you wouldn't do anything to hurt Mom."

"But…you did sleep with her," Mitchell added. "And if I were a betting man, I'd say you've slept with her more than once."

All our heads turned to Trevor.

"I hate you. Both of you fuckers." He tried to hide the smirk, but failed.

We all laughed.

"Ah hell. Another Parker brother has been bitten," Wade said with a laugh. "Hell, I knew you liked her, Trev, but I didn't think you liked her that much. Why didn't you tell me?"

Trevor shot Wade a dirty look. "I don't tell you every time I fuck a girl."

Wade chuckled. "You pretty much do, dude. But this one you didn't utter a word about."

Trevor huffed. "So what? We fucked. It wasn't a big deal, but she is making it something it's clearly not."

Cord jumped and pointed to Trevor. "I knew it! I freaking knew it!"

Rolling his eyes, Trevor let out a frustrated sigh.

I leaned in and looked at my younger brother. "Trev, listen to me. If you don't see anything happening with Scarlett, clear it up with her. Sleeping with her more than one time is going to send her mixed signals. That's not your normal thing. This isn't like a one-night stand with a girl who's in town on spring break or a local girl with a crush. Don't lead her on. I already warned you about this shit."

We all exchanged looks as Trevor stared at his coffee. He didn't say a word, but we left it where it was. Let him marinate on that sage advice for a day or ten.

"So, back to your Smurf name," Cord said.

With a heavy sigh, I leaned back in my chair. "Tell me this isn't why you wanted to meet?"

Mitchell laughed. "Just humor him. Cord clearly has a secret obsession with the Smurfs."

"Oh, like you weren't pissed when I gave Jonathon the Handy Smurf title."

"Fuck you, Cord," Mitchell spit out

Cord pointed to Mitchell. "Hey, I'll change yours to something else if you don't watch it."

Mitchell went to fire something back when I cleared my throat.

"You do realize there is a group of women sitting right there looking at you idiots like you're crazy."

Cord and Mitchell turned to see a group of women smiling at them.

"Can we get to the reason we're meeting for lunch?" I added.

Wade chuckled. "I thought y'all met once a week to feed off of each other."

"Feed off of each other?" Steed asked.

With a half shrug, Wade said, "You know, rub that Parker shit off on each other."

We glanced at each other and then back to Wade. "Dude, what are you talking about?"

"Please. Don't act like you don't know what I'm talking about. It's like you all possess some weird magical power. When you're together it gets stronger."

"What the fuck are you talking about?" Steed asked.

Wade exhaled. "For example? I could walk up to that table right now and strike out with every single one of those ladies…not that I would, because you know…I'm happily married to Amelia. But any one of y'all could walk up and score at least one number."

This seemed to intrigue my brothers.

"What you're saying, Wade, is we have swagger," Cord said with a grin. "Parker swagger."

"Call it what you want, dude. Whatever it is, you have it and when you're all together, it grows. You feed off each other."

"I'm up for trying this game," Trevor said with a mischievous grin. He stood.

"What are you doing?" I asked.

He looked around the table and then to Wade. "I think I can score *two* phone numbers."

I glanced back to the table of six women.

"You're on," Wade said.

It didn't take Trevor long. He walked over to the table, said something that made them all laugh. Then he leaned in and said something else that caused a few of them to blush.

"Boys, now that you're all here, what can I do you for lunch?" Lilly asked.

We each ordered today's special. Hamburger and fries.

"And Trevor?" Lilly asked.

"He'll have the same," I said.

Less than a minute later, Trevor walked up and tossed two pieces of paper in the middle. "That is how it is done, gentlemen."

Cord huffed and made his way over to the table. When he pulled
up a chair and sat down with the women, we all laughed.

"What did you say to them?" Mitchell asked Trevor.

"Dude, I'm not telling you my secrets."

"Seriously? You do know I'm married and my wife is having a
baby. It's not like I'm going to use your moves."

Reappearing at our table, Cord laid three numbers down and sat.

"You were saying, Trev?"

Trevor shot Cord daggers. "Go to hell, Cord."

"Steed? Going to give it a try?"

He held up his hand. "Hell, no. With my luck Paxton would
walk in and see me talking to a group of women trying to score
numbers. She'd kick my ass all the way back to the house."

Mitchell turned it down, and so did I.

Wade stood. "Just so we know. I love your sister. This is simply
proving a point."

We all nodded and motioned for Wade to give it a try. He
walked over. Said something that made them all laugh. When he
looked back at our table, he winked.

"Bastard," Trevor said.

The next thing we knew, all six of them were giving Wade their
phone numbers.

"What in the hell?" Trevor said with a shocked look. I couldn't
help but laugh. When Wade sat back down, he sprinkled the numbers over Cord's and Trevor's.

"How in the hell did you manage to get all of their numbers?" I
asked.

"It was simple," Wade replied with a huge grin. "I told them it
was a bet, and I didn't want to look like a loser."

Steed, Mitchell, and I all busted out laughing as Cord and Trevor gave Wade the finger.

There really wasn't a reason why we all met for lunch. I simply wanted to spend time with my brothers. To laugh, talk some smack and throw in serious talk every now and then.

When we were finished, we said our goodbyes while Trevor scooped up all the numbers and pushed them into his jeans pocket. On the way out, he stopped at the table and whispered something to one of the girls, causing her to blush and chew on her lower lip. She got up from the table, put money down and waved goodbye to her friends as she followed Trevor out. After giving her what I would have guessed was his phone number, they parted ways. She went to her car, and Trevor bid a final goodbye.

"I'm heading out. Talk to y'all later."

I gave him a knowing look. "Trevor. Really?"

He slapped me on the arm. "Hey, just because you've got Harley back doesn't mean the rest of us have to stop playing."

"What about Scarlett?" I asked.

His eyes turned dark. "What about her?"

I shook my head. "Okay, if all you want is to hook up with random girls. Go for it."

"A random, hot-as-fuck girl. Later, big bro."

He quickly headed over to the girl's car and climbed in.

I shook my head. *Stupid bastard.*

"He's going to regret it," Steed stated, standing next to me.

"Yeah, he is."

With a frustrated sigh, I turned to Steed. "Do you need to head back to the ranch? I really need some advice and could use the ear."

"Sure, want to meet at your office?"

"Yeah, let's do that."

"I'll see you over there," Steed said, slapping my back and walking toward his truck.

After saying goodbye to Cord, Mitchell, and Wade, I made my way over to the office. My phone buzzed in my pocket and I pulled it out to see Harley's name.

Harley: *I can't stop thinking about you too. Sorry, we had an emergency surgery come in. I'll call in a bit!*

I typed out my response.

Me: *No rush. About to talk to Steed at the office. Love you, Harley.*

Harley: *Love you back!*

The front door was locked, so Karen must have been out to lunch. Unlocking the door, I stepped into the lobby and was hit by a horrible smell.

"What the hell is that?" Steed asked from behind me. "Is that...dog shit?"

My fists balled up and I made my way back to my office.

"Why is she shitting in her crate? I thought they didn't do that." I threw the door to my office open. The sight before me had me rocking on my legs, fighting to stay standing.

Steed let out a hearty laugh. "I'm no dog expert here, Tripp. But I think in order for them to be crate trained...they actually have to be *in* the crate."

My office was completely torn apart. Papers were everywhere. Clumps of white were all over the place. What was that from? The smell of dog shit was overpowering and had me pinching my nose.

Sitting on my desk, with one of my Berluti dress shoes in her mouth, was Hemi. Her little tail wagged with a purpose. With each swish she pushed papers aside. She dropped the shoe and let out that little howling bark of hers.

I closed my eyes and counted to ten before speaking. "Steed, call Harley and tell her if she wants to ever see this dog alive again...she better come get her. Now."

CHAPTER 27

Harley

"What a crazy morning." Dropping in my desk chair, I let out a breath.

Julie, my vet tech, sat in one of the chairs opposite me. "I don't think we've ever been that busy, Harley."

I gave her a tight smile. Even though my vet clinic was thriving, I was about to lose it. Tripp had been going back and forth with Gerald for a week with offers to buy the land that the clinic sat on, only to have him decline time and time again.

"Any luck with Doc's brother?"

"No," I said. "Doc keeps calling me, saying how sorry he is. He swears he paid his brother back for the land, but he can't find any paperwork stating it, and the deed was never transferred to his name."

"It was so long ago, maybe he thought he paid it."

Shrugging, I nodded. "Yeah. Probably."

"Tripp's been trying to figure out how the sale of the clinic went through with the land not even being in Doc's name. We think it was just pushed through and not checked."

"What are you going to do? Ask Doc for the money back for the clinic and let him and his brother duke it out?"

"No. I couldn't do that to him. Tripp and I will think of something." I tried to keep my voice positive, but I knew she could hear the doubt in there.

"Speaking of Tripp, y'all have been the talk of the town."

My eyes widened. "We have?"

"Yeah, of course. The whole second chance romance thing. The hot attorney who is running for mayor and the equally hot new vet. It's like a love story waiting to be written."

I chewed on my lip, trying not to giggle. "Well, I can honestly say I haven't been this happy in years."

Julie scrunched up her nose. "See! It is a love story. Did you hear about Mallory, though?"

My heart dropped and I moved around in my chair. Tripp had told me she seemed all right with the break up, but I couldn't stop thinking about how she'd acted at the spring fling. I had a feeling she was still hung up on Tripp.

"No. Is she okay?"

Julie looked at me like I had just asked the stupidest question ever. "Oh my gawd... You don't know, do you?"

"Know what?" I asked, leaning forward, my curiosity getting the best of me.

"Mallory sold the store. I guess she had been sort of seeing another guy while she was with Tripp. Well, not really *seeing* him. They knew each other. Had a past. It's rumored she was sleeping with him, but you know how small towns are. Karen claims her sister walked into the store once after closing. The sign was still turned to open and the door was unlocked. She heard a noise in the back and tried clearing her throat. Mallory called out a man's name and it wasn't Tripp. A few minutes later, Mallory came walking out and claimed she was in the back with a sales rep."

It felt like a rock had settled in my stomach. "What?"

"Some guy she knew from her hometown. He had come to Oak Springs a few times to do 'consulting' for her." Julie used air quotes around consulting. "Guess he had stayed a few times at her house, but Tripp never knew about it."

"Wow." That was all I could say. I wasn't one to get into the gossip mill, and I certainly wasn't going to gossip about Tripp's ex.

My phone rang, saving me from the present conversation.

"Hello?"

"Harley? It's Steed."

"Steed? Hi! What's going on?"

He let out a chuckle. "Are you busy? Do you have time to come to Tripp's office?"

I pulled up the schedule. "I've got a clear schedule for the rest of the day. Is everything okay?"

When he laughed again, I did too. I couldn't help it. I had no idea why I was laughing, but I did.

"Yep. Everything is great. Tripp just needs your help with something. And I'm pretty sure Karen is fixin' to get fired."

I stood up quickly. "Oh my gosh. I'm on my way!"

Hitting End, I pulled my desk drawer open and grabbed my purse. "Julie, I hate to do this to you, but I have to leave."

She stood. "Don't worry about it."

"If anyone calls needing an appointment, tell them it will have to wait until tomorrow. If there's an emergency I'll have my phone. Just call me."

"I will. Don't worry, I can hold things down here."

Rushing out the door, I walked to my car. I pulled up Tripp's name and hit it.

"Hello?"

"Hey, is everything okay? Steed called me."

"Did he tell you I'm about two seconds from letting Hemi out the door and wishing her good luck in life?"

I gasped. "Oh no, what happened?"

"Karen happened."

I frowned. "Okay, now I'm sort of confused."

"She didn't put Hemi in her crate when she left for lunch. Do you know what happens when Hemi wakes up from a nap and wants to play? And is left out?"

I pressed my lips together. I didn't dare tell Tripp I had found out this past weekend when I ran to the store and left a sleeping Hemi in the game room. When I came back she had chewed both of Tripp's remotes. The one to his giant screen TV and the one for DirectTV. Luckily, it only took me one phone call to Trevor to order two new ones quickly.

"Um, I can only guess." I braced myself to hear what damage she had caused.

"Then I'll let you be surprised. Like I was."

By the time I pulled up and parked in the driveway of Tripp's office, I had already come up with three different ideas to get him to forget about Hemi. They were all sex-based, and involved a new outfit from the lingerie store that had opened on the square.

I walked into the office, and Karen sat behind her desk. The look of fear on her face spoke volumes.

"What happened?" I whispered.

She went to talk when Tripp's voice boomed from down the hall, causing us both to jump.

I started for his office when Karen grabbed my arm. "If I get fired, I just want you to know it was worth it. That dog was the only one who was able to get rid of those God-awful dress shoes Tripp insisted on wearing all the time."

I covered my mouth to hide my laughter.

"Good luck," Karen said as I headed toward Tripp's office.

The door was partially open, and the smell hit me first.

"Oh no," I whispered.

Pushing the door in, I took one look around the office and bit down on my cheek to keep from laughing. Tripp was near the windows and I had to do a double-take.

"You're seeing this all correctly," Steed whispered from beside me. "He's wearing a ski mask while cleaning up dog shit."

I tried holding it in, and failed. A burst of laughter broke out, and Tripp turned to face me.

"Oh thank God! Your dog pooped!"

Rushing over, I grabbed the paper towels and the cleaner from his hand and cleaned up the mess Hemi had made. I noticed how he had called her my dog. I'd let that go...for now.

Tripp had already opened the windows to his office, and Hemi was sitting on one of the chairs with her nose up against the screen.

"There. All better," I said as I bagged up the trash and handed it to Tripp who tried to hand it to Steed.

Lifting his palms, Steed took a few steps back. "Hard pass."

Tripp looked like he was about to come undone. "You listen here, this is all your fault."

"My fault?" Steed asked. "How is *any* of this my fault?"

"Chloe! She's your daughter, she dognapped Hemi and then hid her out in your office, and *your* wife guilted my girlfriend into taking the dog."

My heart soared when Tripp called me his girlfriend. I loved hearing that come from his lips.

Steed stood there in silence before nodding his head. "I see your point, but—"

"No buts!"

"*But*," Steed went on, "You were the one who left and didn't make sure Hemi was in her crate."

Tripp balled up his fists and was about to let loose.

"Steed, I think I can help Tripp from this point on with the clean-up."

"Oh, I didn't come here to help him clean, he wanted to talk to me. Speaking of, what did you want to talk to me about?"

Pushing Steed out of his office, Tripp said, "Never mind. Just get out of here before I punch you in the face."

Glancing back over his shoulder, Steed dumped a bit of fuel on the fire. "Now how would that look? Attorney running for mayor hits brother and kills dog."

"I didn't say I was killing the dog."

"You did about ten minutes ago."

"Get out, Steed!" Tripp yelled. He slammed the door shut and then looked over to Hemi who was now sitting in her crate with one of her toys in her mouth.

His entire body sank, and he let out a defeated sigh.

"I can take Hemi to work with me from now on. I'll keep her in my office and make sure I have a crate at both places. It'll be fine," I said.

"She ate my favorite pair of shoes."

A slight chuckle slipped out, but I pulled it back in when his eyes snapped up to mine.

When his mouth twitched with a smile, I returned one. His hands reached for me, and I let him pull me to his lap.

"I've been thinking," he softly said.

"Oh yeah? While cleaning up dog poop?"

His body shook when he laughed. "No, before that. I think I have an idea that will get you out of the clinic and into another one."

My brows pulled in tight. "Tripp, I used every bit of my savings on that clinic."

He nodded. "I think we take Gerald up on the offer to buy you out. Let him give you the money back that you paid Doc. He would have had to buy Doc out anyway. I'm pretty sure we can get him to pay the full price you paid Doc. He's getting pissed and wants his place."

"Then what do I do?"

He brushed a piece of hair back that had fallen from my pony-tail. "Do you know how fucking sexy you are in these kitten scrubs?"

I looked down at my scrubs and rolled my eyes. "I'm glad to see you're easy to please when it comes to my clothes."

There was no denying Tripp was turned on, even though his office was a mess. I could feel his hard length pressing into me.

"I want to make love to you."

I smiled. As much as I wanted to straddle him and ask him to take me right now, knowing he had been with Mallory in his office—probably on this very sofa—turned my stomach.

"Then we should head to your house or mine," I said, trying to keep my thoughts out of my eyes.

He frowned slightly and then lifted the corner of his mouth in a slight grin. "Mine's closer."

I stood and clapped my hands together. "Okay! Let me get this place cleaned up and…"

Tripp pulled me to him. Cupping my face with his hands, he stared into my eyes. "Talk to me, Harley. You're holding something back."

Swallowing hard, I closed my eyes and let out a breath. "I know you were with her here, and I can't bring myself…" I gazed into his beautiful baby blues. "I'm sorry. I know it's stupid and I have no right to feel that way."

"You have every right. If I knew you had been with a guy in your office at the clinic I wouldn't like it either. I'm sorry I was insensitive to that just now."

The corners of my mouth turned up. "I love you, Tripp."

Heat built on my cheek where his thumb rubbed lightly back and forth. "I love you so much, Lee. More than you will ever know."

His lips pressed to mine and I reached up to grab his arms. Tripp's kisses always left me dizzy. When he pulled back, I let out a soft moan.

"More?" he asked.

"Always."

Hemi barked, reminding us we still needed to clean up the office.

"Let's get this place cleaned up," I said, giving Tripp a quick kiss before setting off to clean.

An hour later, the office was back to normal. I shut the window and was about to say something when Tripp's office door busted open and Bobby Hansen burst in. Karen was hot on his tail.

"What do you mean you're not coming to the city council meeting tonight? You're always there. You have to be there. You're running for mayor! And speaking of, when are you going to be actually campaigning for the spot, Tripp?"

"Bobby, I announced it a month or so ago. I've had a few things going on and some cases that have kept me busy."

"Well, are you an attorney or a..."

Before Bobby could finish, Tripp interrupted him. "I'm a human being with a damn life. And if you'll excuse me, you caught me during a meeting."

Bobby's eyes swung over to see me standing there, Hemi in my arms.

"A meeting? With your girlfriend and her dog?"

"Our dog," Tripp corrected.

Karen and I exchanged glances.

"What is the meeting about?"

With her finger shaking in Bobby's face, Karen lost her cool. "You hold on here, Bobby Hansen. You may have barged your way into Mr. Parker's office, but it is none of your business who he is meeting with or what the meeting is about."

"He's running for mayor, Karen. Everything he does now is the town's business."

Tripp looked like he was about to blow his top. I walked over to Bobby and flashed him a big smile.

"Mr. Hansen, your wife stopped by the vet clinic yesterday. Your Boxer, Bruce, is so adorable."

I knew from the way Mrs. Hansen had talked yesterday, Bruce was the apple of both of their eyes.

"He is cute, isn't he?"

"We have to get Bruce and Hemi a play date when she has all her shots. I'm sure she is going to fall in love with Bruce."

His face blushed. "He is quite the flirt."

I ushered Mr. Hansen out of Tripp's office while I kept talking about his dog. "Then let's get something set up soon. I know Mrs. Hansen is dying for Bruce to meet Hemi and Lady."

"We will. For sure, Harley. It's great having you back in Oak Springs."

"It's great to be back. See ya soon!" I called out as I ushered him out and shut the door behind him.

Turning, I saw Tripp and Karen staring at me.

"The wrong person is running for mayor," Karen mumbled as she headed back to her desk.

I focused on Tripp. "I need my purse and Hemi's blanket."

Tripp held them both up. It was pretty clear he was ready to leave.

"How about if we leave your car here at the office. I'll drive you back later if you want it or we can get it in the morning."

I had brought some clothes and toiletries over to Tripp's after it was clear I would be spending a number of days there at any given time. I wasn't sure how Tripp felt about it, but he didn't seem to mind. At least, he didn't act like he minded. We lived in such a small town and no matter what we did, people were going to talk.

When we walked into the house, I expected Tripp to attack me and drag me to his room. He didn't. He took Hemi from me and told me to take a seat on the sofa.

"There are a few things I want to talk to you about."

My hands wrung together as a million things crossed my mind. None of them good.

"Is…everything okay?"

He set Hemi down at his feet after he sat across from me. "With us? It's amazing."

I let my shoulders drop in relief.

"I've been doing some thinking about our future."

Tripp was always the planner. I wasn't the least bit surprised he would be thinking about our future, especially since I was walking into the middle of one of his major plans.

Kicking off my shoes, I tucked my legs up under me. I replied with a simple, "Okay."

His eyes looked so sad, and for a minute I had the urge to get up and go to him, wrap my arms around him and tell him not everything in life had to be planned out. But this was Tripp, and I loved him. If planning our future made him feel better, then I would sit and listen.

"For the longest time, I've lived my life by my agenda. I had it all figured out for both of us at one point, and then I kept on with that same plan, only adjusting a few things."

I glanced down at my hands. Guilt filled my chest and made my breathing heavier.

"The last few weeks, though, since we've been together, everything seems to be changing. The things I thought I once wanted, no longer seem to be important."

Swallowing hard, I held my breath as I waited for him to drop a bomb on me. "What don't you want?" I asked.

"This life."

"This life?" I repeated, as a question.

"I mean, I want this life with you, but the planned life I had laid out so carefully? I don't want it anymore. I don't want to run for mayor."

My jaw dropped. "What do you mean? Tripp, you've always wanted to get into politics."

He shook his head. "No, the twenty-one-year-old who thought he had it all figured out wanted that. I'm thirty-one now, Harley, and what I want is sitting in front of me. You've always been my dream. The one thing that stayed constant. I think I kept on with my agenda after you left because it was the only thing I knew to do. Stay the course."

"And you don't want to stay the course anymore?"

The corners of his mouth lifted into a wide smile. "No. I want to shake things up, and I know exactly how to do it. I had the beginning of the idea earlier, and then in my office today, the rest of it hit me."

"What hit you?" I asked.

He got up and moved to sit next to me. "Just listen to me and let me get this all out before you say anything, okay?"

I nodded.

"There's some land outside of town, not very far, that my father owns. Steed takes care of the taxes and manages the place. The only thing on there is a barn from on old ranch back in the day. I talked to Steed earlier to see if he thought my father would be interested in selling it to me. We didn't get a chance for me to tell him why because of the whole Hemi disaster."

The intense way my heart was beating had me both nervous and excited. I had no idea what he was about to say, but I couldn't wait to find out.

"Here's what I'm thinking. You let Gerald buy you out. We take that money and build a new vet clinic on the land."

"What?" I gasped, my eyes nearly popping out of my head. "Tripp, I don't have enough money to start a vet clinic from the ground up."

"You have a good portion of money to get it started. You just need an investor."

"An investor? And who is that going to be?"

"Me. Because there's something in this for me as well."

The room started to spin, and I stood up, trying to let all of his words settle. "Wait. You want me to build a new vet clinic, let you invest in it, and there's also something in it for you? What could there possibly be in it for you?"

"A new office."

I stared at him like he was insane. "You have an office."

Tripp stood and made his way over to me. "Earlier when we were in my office, and I told you I wanted to make love to you. I saw it in your eyes. The idea of us being together in there made you feel physically ill."

"Tripp, I—"

"Let me finish."

Snapping my mouth shut, I motioned for him to go on.

"We've only been together for a few weeks, but I already know if you let me, I'd marry you today, Harley."

I gasped and covered my mouth with my hand.

"I want to marry you. I want to have babies…as many as you want. I want to help you make your dreams come true and call me selfish, but I want to be minutes from your office so I can fuck you anytime I want to. And I sure as hell don't want to be mayor. People getting into our business and telling me what I can and can't do? No. That's not for me. Not anymore."

Tears filled my eyes as my hand dropped to my side.

"Tripp," I whispered. "Did you say you want to marry me?"

He tossed his head back and let out a roar of laughter. "Is that all you heard, Lee?"

Shaking my head frantically, I replied, "No! I heard it all, but that part stuck out. That and the part about babies."

Tripp took my hands in his. "We can do this. You and me…together."

I didn't need time to think about any of it. It all felt right. "Do you think we can make it all work?"

"I do. It's fifty acres of land. If you wanted to, we could even build a house on it."

Chewing my lip, I glanced around the living room. "But I love this house. It feels like...home."

Tripp's eyes felt like they were burning into my soul. He crashed his mouth to mine and picked me up. Walking us into the bedroom, he gently laid me on the bed. "Are we doing this?" he asked.

I nodded, my chest rising and falling with each breath.

"Will you marry me, Harley Carbajal, and let me try to knock you up while building a new vet clinic and a law office?"

Squeezing my eyes shut to make sure I wasn't dreaming, I let out a squeal of delight and stomped my legs like a crazy woman.

Tripp cleared his throat. "I'm not really good at this, but was that a yes?"

I opened my eyes and sat up, throwing myself at him.

"Yes! It's a yes to everything!"

CHAPTER 28

Tripp

"What do you mean you're withdrawing from the race?" Charles, my campaign manager, said.

The ten men and women who sat in my office stared at me like I had lost my damn mind.

"I'm taking myself out of the race for mayor."

"But why?" Mrs. Lords asked. She was the owner of the *Oak Springs Gazette* and one of the city council members.

"I decided that I want to go a different path. I'm focusing on my future with my fiancée and making *her* dreams come true."

"Her dreams?" Bobby Hansen asked.

"I know you all know about Doc's brother. He was making life difficult for Harley, but he finally bought her out last week. I'm buying some land from my father right outside of town and Harley's building a new vet clinic."

"A new vet clinic! Oh my goodness, this is so exciting!" Kenzie Lewis said. She was already writing like crazy in her notebook. "Is this something we are keeping under wraps or can we publish this in the *Gazette?"*

Kenzie...always wearing her reporter hat. "You can publish it with an interview showcasing Harley as the new town vet. Give her a chance to talk about what the new clinic will have."

Bobby let out a huff, acting like he was more upset than he really was. "I guess if we have to have you pulling out of the race, it's for a good reason."

"Thanks, Bobby. I also want to focus on my law practice. It's been growing steadily the last few years, and now that I'm moving my office next to the vet clinic, I think it will be a nice change."

All the women in the room gasped.

"Oh, this just turned into a happily ever after piece," Kenzie said. "I want to interview both of you. Featuring the new vet clinic and why you're moving your office."

"Umm, me? You want to interview me as well? Why?"

Kenzie and Mrs. Lords both looked at me like I had asked the dumbest question ever. "Tripp Parker, you are a major influence in this town. Not to get caught up in the gossip, but it is part of my business. Everyone knows the story of you and Harley. Besides, the whole second chance romance thing is beautiful. We can focus on how the town is growing by you expanding your law firm and Harley doing the same with the vet clinic. I think it would be best to leave the drama out of why Harley is building a new space. Let's keep it on the growth of the town, with the twist of the happily ever after Kenzie mentioned."

"Do we announce the withdrawal separately?" Lori Durham, another city council member and owner of the one and only grocery store in town, asked.

"We need to take care of that today," Charles said. "I'll call a press conference for around three. Does that sound good?" He scanned the room for objections. I was a bit surprised he wasn't putting up a fight about it, but I think a part of him always knew my heart really wasn't in the race.

Everyone nodded in agreement.

As they stood, I pulled Lori back and asked to speak with her. Once the room cleared out, I sat down on the edge of my desk as she took a seat in front of me.

"Lori, there's two things I wanted to discuss with you."

"Okay, shoot."

Lori wasn't that much older than me. Her grandparents had opened up The Springs Grocery back in the early forties. It had been passed on to Lori's folks and now to her. They also owned a small ranch a few miles outside of town that housed a barn worthy of the king of England's prized horses. Lori was an avid horse lover and had pretty much shown horses her entire life. Harley and Lori had been good friends when they were younger, both into the horse scene.

"Your family's barn. Do you rent it out?"

She looked thoughtful for a moment. "We never have, but then again, no one has ever asked."

A slow smile moved over her face.

"I think you might know where I'm going with this?"

"Yes, I believe I do. If I remember correctly, Harley used to say her dream wedding would be in our barn."

My chest tightened at the thought of marrying Harley there. Hell, marrying Harley anywhere made my body tremble.

I pointed to her. "Bingo. I'd love to hold our wedding there, if you and your folks agree to it."

"Tripp, I think that is a wonderful idea. It's large enough to hold a number of people."

"Perfect. I haven't officially given Harley a ring and or done the whole drop down on one knee thing yet, so maybe I can do that, as well as break the news to her we're getting married in the barn while actually being in the barn."

"I love that idea. I'll give you the gate code. Give us a day's notice to make sure the barn is cleaned up."

Laughing, I raised my brows at her. "Lori, that barn is so damn clean you could eat off the floors."

She chuckled. "I wouldn't go that far." She paused for a moment. "What's the second thing you wanted to discuss?"

"You."

"Me?" she asked, pointing to herself.

"Yes. I think you should run for mayor."

She scoffed. "Please, you can't be serious, Tripp."

"I'm dead serious. You love this town, you want the same things I want for it and you're respected in the community. You'd be perfect."

Lori fiddled with her hands in her lap as she let my words sink in. "I have the kids…"

"Josh would help out, I know he would. He's a damn good father."

Chewing on her lip, she looked down.

"Think about it, but I was sort of hoping I could pass the torch to you this afternoon at the press conference."

Her eyes shot up to look at me. "Wow. Okay. Let me talk to Josh about it. Can I get back with you in a few hours?"

Glancing at my watch, I smiled. "If it's a yes, just show up. If it's a no, I totally understand."

Lori stood and I followed her lead. She took in a deep breath and blew it out. "Okay, well, you've given me a lot to think about in a short amount of time."

I walked her out of my office to the lobby.

"As far as the other thing we discussed. Would tomorrow be too soon to head out there?" I asked.

"Nope. I'll make sure everything is ready for you. I'll text you the gate code."

We shook hands. "I hope to see you later."

The corners of her mouth rose, and I had a feeling I would for sure be seeing her this afternoon.

"Tripp, where in the world are we going?" Harley asked, her legs bouncing up and down in the passenger seat of my truck.

"You are terrible with surprises, do you know that?" I said with a chuckle.

"I can't help it! Are we going to the land?"

"No."

"Um, are we going to San Antonio?"

"No, why would we be going there?"

She giggled. "I don't know. It feels like we have been driving forever!"

I had been driving around town for the last thirty minutes. Mrs. Johnson was now standing outside on her porch staring at me as I drove by. I was waiting for Sheriff Miller to show up behind me any second. The last time I drove by, I reached my hand out the window and waved to Mrs. Johnson. She held up a pie like she wanted me to stop for some.

"Are we almost there? This blindfold is making me claustrophobic."

"How? It's only covering your eyes."

After one more drive around the square, I headed to Lori's place. It was fifteen minutes outside of town.

"We're almost there. Another ten minutes or so."

Harley went on and on about her meeting with the architect earlier this morning. I listened as she told me how she wanted a rustic feel to the new vet's office, but with modern technology. We had decided my office would be in a separate building, but not far from the vet clinic. Even with sound proofing, Harley thought barking dogs might be disruptive to my office. After talking to Jonathon about it, he also agreed with Harley.

I pulled up and rolled the window down and punched in the gate code.

"What's that noise?" Harley asked when the gate started to swing open.

"Nothing," I said, driving over the cattle guard.

"Cattle guard. We're still in the country."

"Harley Carbajal, stop trying to figure it out."

"Fine! I'll stop."

When I finally reached the barn, I put my truck in park and turned it off. "Wait here, I'll come around to get you."

She nodded and folded her hands in her lap to wait.

As I walked around the front of my truck, I took in a deep breath and felt for the ring box in my jeans pocked. I'd bought this ring over ten years ago and kept it in my safe. I'd only pulled it out once the entire time—when I had gotten the letter from Harley that I never read.

I took my cowboy hat off and ran my fingers through my hair, trying to get my damn heartbeat and breathing under control.

"This is it," I whispered, opening the truck door and reaching for the love of my life. After I helped her down, she took in a deep breath.

"Horses," she whispered.

"Yep."

"Are we going riding?" she asked, excitement in her voice.

"Baby, the kind of riding I want to do wouldn't be appropriate for where we are."

She laughed and tried to hit me, missing me by a mile.

I guided her to the barn and my knees almost buckled. Lights were strung up across the barn and a small round table sat in the middle, flanked by two hay bales.

Lori walked out from one of the rooms and gave me thumb up.

"Did you do all of this?" I mouthed to her.

She nodded and made a heart shape with her hands as her mother appeared at her side.

"Thank you," I mouthed to them. They walked quietly past us as I led Harley farther into the barn.

Harley did a little jump as I brought her to a stop. "I hear horses."

"You ready?" I asked.

"Yes! Take it off already!"

I removed the blindfold. She stood there with her eyes squeezed shut.

Leaning in, I placed my mouth to the side of her ear. "Open your eyes, Lee."

I took a step back to see her reaction. It didn't take her any time to realize where we were.

"The Durham's barn!" she exclaimed as she spun around in a circle.

While she was taking everything in, I dropped to one knee and held the ring box out.

"Harley," I said, trying to keep my voice strong and steady. When she turned to me, she gasped and covered her mouth with both hands.

"I've waited so long for this moment. Dreamt about it almost every night."

Her body started to shake with sobs.

"You've always held my heart, since the first day I looked into your beautiful emerald eyes. You were always the one. I'm so sorry I was blind all those years, but if you'll do me the honor, I swear to you I'll make every single day the best day of our life."

Harley dropped to her knees. Tears streamed down her face as she nodded.

"I love you," she choked out before throwing her body against mine. She wrapped her arms around me and held me tightly while she shook from crying.

"I love you too, baby. More than you'll ever know."

When we finally drew back, I took her left hand and kissed the back of it. "This ring has waited for ten years to be on your finger. Let's put it on, shall we?"

My hand shook as I slid the ring on her finger. The princess cut diamond was surrounded by ten smaller princess-shaped diamonds. The band was engraved while gold and was breathtaking.

"Tripp, this ring is stunning. I don't...I don't even know what to say."

Cupping her face with my hands, I replied, "Say you'll marry me, in this barn, with our family and friends watching."

Her eyes widened. "In this barn?" Her tears came again, and I saw the happiness dancing in her beautiful eyes.

"Yes! Whenever you want, I've already talked to Lori about it."

Harley shook her head, unable to form any words.

"Are we going too fast? Just tell me if we are."

"No, this is all so...beautiful. Amazing. Wonderful. You're making all of my dreams come true, Tripp, and I...I want to stand on the tallest mountain and scream how happy I am."

I chuckled as I stood and brought her with me. I pointed to the table that had been set up. There was a chilled bottle of champagne and a fruit and cheese plate. She gazed up at the strings of lights with tears in her eyes.

"Did you do this?" Harley asked, taking a seat.

"I'd love to take credit for it, but Lori and her mom did it."

"Oh my God, it's just so perfect. What a thoughtful thing for them to do."

I poured us each a glass and took a seat. "What do we toast to?" I asked with a wink.

She looked up as if in deep thought, before her eyes swung back to mine.

"Let's toast to our future."

"Our somewhat unplanned, go with the flow, future?"

A wide, beautiful smile appeared on her face as she lifted her glass to mine. "Yes! To that future!"

"Tonight is family dinner at my folks' place. Should we have a date in mind when we drop the news to them?" I asked.

Harley set her glass down and popped a grape in her mouth. "Let's see, it's early May. Corina is due July 19. We could do it after the baby is born? But then we risk it being really hot."

I agreed. "A wedding in July or August in a barn in Texas is going to be hot."

We both let out a breath of air. "How fast can we throw this thing together?" I asked with a wiggle of my brows.

Harley pulled out her phone and started texting someone.

"Who are you texting?"

She looked up and winked. "Paxton. I can trust that she won't say anything to anyone."

After Harley typed out a long text message, we sat there and waited for her response.

Harley stood and started walking around the barn. "The way it looks right now, with the lights, it's perfect. We only really need to add a trellis and altar and places for people to sit."

She spun around and looked at me. "Hay bales. With blankets on them!"

I smiled. "I love that idea."

Chewing on her lip, she started walking again. "We could set up tents outside for the reception if Lori and her folks agree to it."

Her phone beeped with a text. When she read it, a huge grin spread across her face.

"What did she say?"

She flipped the phone for me to see it.

Paxton: *May 26. Two weeks. It's doable.*

We both looked at each other.

"Two weeks."

"What about a dress?" I asked.

Tears filled her eyes. "That's not a problem."

"The cake and food?"

"That's not a problem!" Lori shouted as she rushed in. "I can take care of all of that."

Harley and I stood there, staring at Lori.

"Sorry! I couldn't help but overhear y'all. I was walking back to get my phone! I left it in the tack room."

"Lori, y'all are okay with this? We'll keep it small, family and friends only."

"Are you kidding? Yes! My mother is going to be over the moon. Do you know how much fun she had setting this up today for y'all? She was already making plans for the wedding. I think my mother just found a new job…event planning!"

"This is it, then. We're getting married in two weeks!" Harley exclaimed, jumping up and down along with Lori.

I leaned back against one of the stalls as I watched my future bride running around with the possible future mayor of Oak Springs. Both of them acting like two little girls blurting out ideas and squealing in delight after each one.

Best fucking day of my life.

CHAPTER 29

Harley

I stood with Waylynn on one side and Paxton on the other. The three of us stared down at an old trunk my mother was trying to get unlocked.

"How old is the dress?" Waylynn asked in a whisper.

I was positive my look of horror answered her question.

"It's going to be okay. Vintage is...in...right now," Paxton added.

Waylynn and I turned at her. I snarled as she shrugged. "What? It is!" she softly said.

"Gosh darn it. Why won't this thing unlock?"

"It's a sign!" Waylynn declared as Paxton reached around and hit her.

My mother twisted and tugged on the padlock.

"Mom, honestly, I can buy a dress."

"Nonsense!" she exclaimed, glancing at me over her shoulder. "I know the second you see your great-grandmother's dress you'll love it."

"Great-grandmother?" Waylynn gasped. She pulled me and Paxton back and out of earshot of my mother.

"That means it's going to cover you from head to toe. Like… one of those dresses that buttoned all the way up the neck, complete with a chastity belt!"

My fingers brushed over my neck as I swallowed hard.

"Look at your figure! You have boobs! Hips! Skin that looks like the sun god himself kissed you. We cannot have you in an old timey gown. It's got to be against your Latino roots!"

Paxton nodded. "I agree, not necessarily with the whole Latino roots thing." She shot Waylynn a weary look. "I think it's time to tell your mom you want to buy a gown."

I took in a shaky breath. "Crap. I guess I have to break the news to her."

"You do!" Waylynn added.

Paxton took my hands in hers. "You can do this. Remember, it's your wedding and you've waited a long time for this day."

Chewing on my lip, I closed my eyes and dug deep down for the courage to tell my mother I wasn't wearing Great-Grandma Rose's wedding gown.

"I got it!" my mother exclaimed.

"We're too late!" Waylynn whimpered, her hands running down her face as she let out a groan.

The three of us walked toward the old trunk like something evil was going to jump out at any second. My breath caught in my throat as my mom opened the trunk. We all gasped.

"What is that?" Paxton exclaimed.

"It's beautiful," Waylynn and I both said at once.

The light-gold lace caught my eye first. Small pearls were hand sewn into it, with a different pattern lining the sweetheart neckline and the shoulder straps.

My mother pulled the dress out, letting the champagne-colored tulle fall to the floor.

"Goodness, how long is this train?" Paxton asked, gathering the fabric up in her hands.

"Grandma Rose had exquisite taste. She had fashioned a designer in Paris make this one-of-a-kind gown. Of course, because she was ahead of her time, it was considered risqué."

I stared at the beautiful vintage gown. "Momma, why didn't you wear this for your wedding?"

She chuckled. "When my mother showed it to me, I fell in love with it. Tried it on, and it didn't fit. I was heartbroken and refused to let my mother take it in somewhere and have it altered. So we tucked it back in this trunk and I've waited until the day you told me you were getting married to take it out."

"Did grandmother wear this dress?" I asked, my fingers brushing the delicate lace.

"No. Grandma Rose didn't care for my daddy and made it clear to my mother. So, being the stubborn fool she was, she refused to wear the dress. She, of course, regretted it."

I looked past the dress into the trunk. "Holy shit!" I said, reaching down and pulling out the lace boots. Turning, I held them up for Waylynn and Paxton.

"I'm so wearing these," I declared.

"Can you imagine Tripp's face when he sees you in nothing but…" Waylynn looked at my mother. "Cover your ears, Maddi."

Mother chuckled. "Girls, I'm not ignorant of what will happen on Harley's wedding night. And I agree with you, Waylynn. Tripp is going to trip all over his tongue when he sees you in these boots and your wedding lingerie."

My cheeks heated.

"I can't believe my great-grandmother dared to wear such sexy pieces for that time period," I gushed.

"She was a rebel, to say the least. Now, this lace lining the back will need to be removed, exposing your back. Some of the buttons feel a bit loose, so we'll need to get those adjusted, as well. Mindy

Crawford is a fine seamstress. She'll be able to do it, and I know she will use extra care and caution."

The gown was placed up against me by my mother as we all gazed at my reflection in the attic's long, floor-length mirror.

"What if it doesn't fit?" I whispered.

"It will. Your body is exactly like Rose's. I'll need to find her wedding picture. You are the spitting image of her, just dark hair and darker skin."

"Really?" I asked, my eyes lifting. I remembered my great-grandmother Rose. I was seven when she passed. Closing my eyes, I pictured her, sitting in the rocking chair of our house. Even in her eighties she was beautiful. I can still picture the elegant dress and hat she wore as she took tea from my mother.

Paxton leaned in closer to me. "Let's try it on. I'm dying to see it on you!"

When I agreed, Waylynn and Paxton nearly ripped off my clothes. My mother laughed while taking a seat in an old antique chair.

"Mom, what's all this furniture doing up here?" I asked.

"It all belonged to Rose. When she passed, Momma stored it up here."

I'd only been in our attic once, and that was when Tripp was trying to get a bat out. I swore I saw a women looking back at me through this mirror. I screamed, running downstairs and past my father who was walking up the attic stairs to help Tripp. That was the first and last time I set foot up here until my mother begged us to come look in this trunk. Now I was thanking the Lord above I let her talk us into it.

I slipped into the dress. It hugged my body like a glove. Waylynn began to button up the back and when she got to the last one, we all let out a sigh. My mother was now standing next to me, tears rolling down her face.

"It's like it was made for you, Harley."

My hands ran over the lace and tulle. I could smell faint perfume on the dress all these years later. It hadn't been kept in a special bag or treated. It simply was laid in an old trunk with the shoes, along with a stunning veil that Waylynn was now placing on my head.

"You look like a princess," Paxton whispered.

Waylynn smiled while she adjusted the veil. "Tripp is going to fall on his knees when he sees you."

When I looked myself over, I swore I saw a different version of myself. Blonde hair. The same emerald green eyes and the same flutter in my stomach.

I stood at the window in my old bedroom at my parents' house. I'd been poked and prodded for the last three hours. At least, it felt like it had been that long. My hair was in a beautiful swept up-do, cascades of copious curls hanging down to frame my face. The perfect amount to make me look walkway ready, or at least that's what the hairdresser said. I couldn't even remember her name. It was French, and she was a friend of Waylynn's. I was positive the woman was from France, but Waylynn remained tight-lipped. It went the same with the young lady who did my make-up. She somehow managed to make me look like I wasn't wearing make-up, even though she put a shit ton of it on my face. Everything was natural looking, from my eyes to my lips. The shades looked like they were made just for me.

Turning from the window, I stared at my reflection. My father and Tripp had brought the full-length mirror down from the attic and placed it in my bedroom. I had already told my mother I wanted the mirror. I had the perfect place for it to stand in Tripp's bedroom.

I pulled in a deep breath and slowly let it out. My eyes drifted up and down my body. Rose's wedding gown fit me like it had been made for my body, not my great-grandmother's. I lifted the dress and saw the lace boots. A smile spread across my face while my stomach flipped with anticipation.

The knock on the door jerked my eyes up.

"Do you need anything, Harley?" Paxton's voice rang out.

"No, I'll only be a few more minutes."

"Take your time! We have plenty of time before the cars arrive."

I blew out another deep breath. After I getting dressed, I had asked for a few minutes to myself. I needed to gather my thoughts. The last two weeks and gone by in a blurry rush. Hell, the last few months had. Everything was happening all at once, and I needed time to slow down, even if only for a few minutes. All of my dreams were coming true at once and a part of me needed to make sure it wasn't all a dream. That I wouldn't wake up standing outside Tripp's house, wondering when he would be back in town so I could explain everything to him.

My eyes closed as I thought about the day he asked me to marry him. When I opened my eyes, my reflection seemed to change for the briefest moment. A strange feeling rushed through my body. It was almost like it was hot and cold mixed together. Leaning in closer, I stared into the old mirror. I could actually feel Rose staring back. My eyes glanced at her old wedding picture sitting on the table. My mother wasn't kidding when she said I looked like Rose. Everything about us was the same, except our hair. Her hair was a dirty blonde, mine was brown. Even our eyes looked the same. Rose had light emerald eyes, the same as me. When I was little, my grandmother used to tell me when she looked into my eyes she was looking into her mother's eyes, and now I understood why she said that.

"So, Grandma Rose. How do I look?"

A breeze lifted my curtains and caused my entire body to erupt in goosebumps. She was here with me. I could feel it. And it didn't feel like it was just her. It was the strangest feeling.

I gathered up the long train and turned toward the door. The entire room turned cold, which was crazy because it was warm outside. Not too hot, and not too cold. When I woke up to a clear blue sky and a high of seventy-five, I nearly cried. It was going to be the perfect day.

My feet stopped walking. I couldn't explain why my heart had all of a sudden started beating so fast. Deep down, I knew. If I turned around, that same reflection I saw all those years ago would be looking back at me through the mirror. My body trembled at the thought. It wasn't fear this time, but something entirely different.

With a quick glance over my shoulder, I saw her. Standing in the very gown I had on…a beautiful smile on her face. It only lasted a moment and then she faded away, another breeze filling the room.

The corners of my mouth lifted and my teeth bit into my lip. "I'm going to take that as your blessing, Rose."

Turning back to the door, I opened it and looked at my mother and Paxton. Both waiting patiently for me.

Paxton handed me a beautiful bouquet of pink roses. She held something in her hand and when I looked at it, my brows pulled tightly together.

"What is that?" I asked.

"I found it, in the bottom of the chest. I think it might be the perfume Rose wore on her wedding day."

My chest fluttered with delight.

"Shall I?" she asked, holding up the vintage-looking bottle.

"Yes," I whispered. When the aroma filled the space around us, I nearly cried. I didn't know my great-grandmother Rose, but somehow she knew exactly what her great-granddaughter was going to need on the most amazing day of her life.

"The cars are here!" Waylynn called up.

Chloe came running up the stairs, dressed in a beautiful ivory-colored gown we had found. Her brown curls bounced as she came to a stop. She was the spitting image of her father. She looked up at Paxton and then swung those sky-blue eyes over to me.

"As your flower girl, I take this job seriously. It's not my first rodeo, so I know what to do, Aunt Harley. Follow me."

I had to fight to keep my laughter in as I turned to Paxton. "She is, for sure, a Parker."

"Tell me about it," Paxton said as she gathered up my train, and we headed downstairs.

Two Rolls-Royce cars were parked out front. Tripp had clearly remembered our conversations when I'd dreamed about the type of wedding I wanted. Even down to the type of car I wanted to show up in.

"Your brother is going to spoil me," I said, slipping into the back of the car.

"Let him," Waylynn replied with a wink. "Y'all have got a lot of making up to do."

After my train was carefully placed into the car, I folded my hands and took in a deep breath.

"Aunt Harley, do you need me to ride with you?" Chloe asked.

I could see the hopefulness in her eyes.

"I would love for you to ride with me, Chloe."

She grinned. "I thought so."

When the drive to the barn was filled with Chloe's chatter, I silently thanked God for her. She was keeping my mind off of everything.

"Oh! We're here! Do you feel like you're gonna puke?"

I frowned. "No. I mean, I didn't until just now."

She chuckled. "You've still got time if you need to. You can go behind the car and throw up. I've seen Aunt Meli do it a couple of times already today. She tries to hide it, though. Nothing's coming out, but she sure sounds like she's throwing up.

My eyes widened, and I wanted to ask Chloe more about this little bit of information she'd just handed me. But I couldn't. I was fixing to walk down the aisle and get married. I filed her comment away to revisit later.

The door opened on Chloe's side, and she stepped out. "Let's do this!" she shouted and fist-pumped. I giggled and turned to see my father opening the door. He reached in and helped me out. Waylynn and Paxton were right there, gathering the long train out and spreading out so it wouldn't wrinkle.

I looked up at my father and my breath caught. He had tears in his eyes and was fighting to hold them back.

His thumbs brushed lightly over the back of my hands.

"Estás lista, Corazón?"

My chin trembled. "I'm ready, Daddy."

I'd never been more ready for anything in my entire life.

CHAPTER 30

Tripp

When I spotted the two white Rolls-Royces driving by the barn, my stomach dropped. I ran my hands down my black tux and tried to breathe.

Steed placed his hand on my shoulder and gave it a squeeze. "It's about damn time."

I let out a sharp chuckle. "Sure is."

After another quick squeeze, Steed dropped his hand. I glanced past him, and Mitchell gave me a wink. It was hard trying to decide which of my brothers I wanted to stand with me. Harley only wanted one matron of honor and one bridesmaid. She didn't want a large wedding party, and I agreed with her. When I broke the news to my brothers, the fight for who was going to stand with me began. In the end, we all ended up at Cord's Place, drank one too many beers, and they drew straws. Steed and Mitchell won.

Harley asked Paxton and Waylynn to be in the wedding. It was expected, since the three of them were good friends growing up. Paxton was her matron of honor, and Waylynn the bridesmaid.

Chloe appeared from around the corner of the barn first. She came skipping down the aisle in her flower girl dress, tossing rose petals in the air. Everyone awwwwed at the sight. It shouldn't have surprised me when she stopped and looked behind her. We all followed her gaze.

"Come on, Hemi girl! Come on!"

My mouth fell open when Hemi came bounding into the barn, a giant pink bow wrapped around her neck.

Everyone laughed, and I could hear Steed groan. "How did she get that dog here?" he said as I turned to face him.

"I'd rather have the dog than a goat," I whispered.

"Amen," Mitchell and Steed said at once.

Chloe walked over to her spot, Hemi hot on her heels. When she told the dog to sit, Hemi did, and I grinned from ear to ear. Glancing back to Steed, I whispered, "Better start saving up for college. I see another vet in the family."

The music changed, and I looked back to see Waylynn entering the barn, with Paxton following her. They looked stunning. Both of them were wearing a more adult version of Chloe's dress. Steed inhaled sharply when he saw his wife walking toward us.

They smiled and nodded to family and friends who were all seated on blanket-covered hay bales. At each end of the rows sat beautiful potted plants that the girls had made over the course of the last two days. Harley was worried her fingers would be stained black from digging in the soil.

The music switched again, and the guitarist and violinist started to play "Jesus, Joy of Man's Desiring."

My knees nearly buckled when I saw her turn the corner with her father.

Tears pooled in my eyes. "She's beautiful," I choked out to no one in particular.

Steed put his hand on my shoulder as I fought to stay on my feet. It was a reminder that I wasn't dreaming. That my dream was coming true right before my eyes.

Harley walked toward me, a vision so stunning I had to keep blinking back my tears until I finally gave up and let them fall. When our eyes met, her body jerked with a sob, which did something to my heart I would never forget. Words couldn't even begin to describe the happiness that bubbled up within me.

Gus held onto Harley a little tighter as they made their way to us. My eyes never broke away from hers.

"Are you breathing?" Steed asked. "You're wobbling, bro."

I drew in a deep breath as Harley's smile grew bigger. When they stopped next to me, I couldn't pull my gaze off of her while Gus lifted her veil and Paxton straightened it from the back. Wiping a tear from my face, I leaned in closer to her.

"You are absolutely the most stunning woman ever. You look beautiful."

My knees shook at the look of pure love in her eyes.

"And you look handsome as ever."

The pastor cleared his throat, asked who was giving Harley away, and the rest was a blur.

Before I knew it, Harley and I were tucked away in one of the tack rooms. I thought my father's prized main barn was insane, but this barn put his to shame. The tack room felt more like a parlor you'd find in a house. It had been converted to a room where Lori's family could relax. It had a sofa, TV, small sink with a coffee pot sitting on the counter and a large cooler filled with water. It was the perfect place for us to catch our breath after the ceremony. The photographer was waiting for us, but I insisted that I got to spend at least five minutes with my new bride.

She was breathtaking in the gown. The way it hugged every one of her curves nearly drove me insane. How I was able to keep my cock from going hard as stone during the ceremony was beyond me. It probably had to do with her father standing by her side.

Our eyes met and Harley dropped her bouquet onto the sofa, making her way to me and into my arms. When she reached up for a kiss, I cupped her face and let my gaze roam across her face.

"Let me look at you. You're my wife. My entire world. You are my corazón."

Tears spilled from her eyes as she barely got my name off her lips. "Tripp."

Pressing my mouth against hers, I poured every ounce of my love into her. For every year I foolishly left town when she would come home. For the letter I ripped up and never read. For fighting my love because I was too fucking stubborn to let her back in. We had so much time to make up and I intended on starting tonight.

Our tongues danced with each other, and I nipped at her lip as she let out a low moan.

"I could fuck you right now, I'm so damn turned on."

"And I would let you…if our family wasn't on the other side of that door."

"Who cares?" I said, pulling the dress up and running my fingers along her inner thigh.

"Tripp…we…can't," she said, her voice heavy with want.

"We can. Just be quiet."

Her chest rose and fell as my fingers moved lightly along her lace panties.

"Five minutes. We said we only needed…five minutes," she panted.

"I can be quick."

Harley's eyes turned dark, and I was on the cusp of getting to taste my wife.

The knock on the door and the sound of my mother's voice deflated my hard-on within seconds. Harley let out a giggle and took a few steps back, adjusting her dress.

"Come in, Mom."

My mother rushed through the door, shutting it quickly. Her eyes bounced between us and it didn't take long for the dam of tears to break.

"Melanie!" Harley gasped, making her way over to her.

In some weird language I couldn't understand, my mom started talking to us. Her mumbled words had us both leaning in to try and figure out what in the hell she was saying.

"What? Mom, what are you saying?" I asked.

"I think she said the words…happy…in love…new beginnings."

"How in the hell did you get any of that?"

Harley shrugged.

"Mom," I said, gripping her upper arms gently. "I need you to take a deep breath and talk slowly."

"I…I…I…" Between each word was a sob. We'd be here all night, at this rate.

"Mom! Get it out!" I urged.

Waving her hands, she finally said, "I'm just so happy!"

Harley chuckled as I pulled my mother into my arms. "So am I, Mom. So am I."

I motioned for Harley to join us and we stood there in a circle, hugging. When my mother was finished crying, she got herself together and let out a refreshed breath.

She placed one hand on my cheek, the other on Harley's. "Five down. Two more to go."

Harley and I both laughed.

After kissing us both, she took a few steps back and a mischievous smirk appeared on her face.

"Mom? That is the face of a woman who is fixin' to butt into someone's life."

"Me?" she asked, pointing to herself. "Nonsense. Now, let's get those pictures going so we can get to the reception and y'all can get on out of here. I need more grandbabies."

Harley and I glanced at one another and I winked. That process had already begun.

The red dress she had on was driving me fucking insane. I'd adjusted my cock at least four times while watching her get ready. There was no way I was going to make it through this dinner.

Harley stood next to me, my arm around her waist. I pulled her possessively against me. I loved the way she leaned her body into mine. Like she needed me to keep her upright. She chatted about some excursion that the young couple had signed up for tomorrow. I wasn't paying attention, and I was positive the husband of the girl talking was on the same page as I was. I would have been happy staying in our bungalow tonight, but Harley insisted we go out for dinner. I couldn't argue with her. I'd had her holed up in our little slice of heaven for the last three days. Room service had been the only thing we'd eaten, and she deserved a nice night out.

My hand pressed slightly against the small of her back, giving her the signal I was ready to get to our table. The faster we ate, the faster we got back to our room.

Our room. I smiled. It was more than a room. It was fucking paradise. Harley's fingers landed on The Maldives when we randomly picked a honeymoon destination. I had no idea how we lucked out getting into the Anantara Veli Resort, but we did. Our first night was spent making love in the hot tub. The second night we went for a swim and made love in the crystal-clear water lit by the moonlight. I somehow managed to talk Harley into that. Hottest damn moment of my life—especially knowing we could have been caught at any moment. Today was spent exploring. I voted for the hot tub again, she voted for a nice dinner out, with the promise of the hot tub later.

"Where are you from again?" the redhaired girl asked for the second time.

"Sweetheart, let's let them go to dinner. Tripp looks…hungry."

"You have no idea," I replied.

He nodded. "I'm sure I have some idea."

I gave him a knowing grin. Poor guy. Today was their first day on their honeymoon and his new wife had already dragged him out of their bungalow. *Sucks for him.*

My phone went off in my khaki dress pants.

"Excuse me," I said, pulling it out. Cord's name splashed across my screen.

Cord: *You need to come home. Now.*

I typed out a quick response.

Me: *Piss off. I'm on my honeymoon, dickhead.*

Cord: *Listen here, Grumpy Smurf, Mom has lost her damn mind. I need you here to distract her from her current mission.*

Damn. He'd piqued my interest.

Me: *What is she doing?*

Cord: *She is butting into my life. That's what she's doing. I guess she got bored with Trevor, so she's coming after me.*

I chuckled.

Me: *How exactly is she coming after you?*

Cord: *She thinks I've grown a fondness for the Irish. I opened my refrigerator today to find three tubs of Irish butter in there!*

I laughed, and Harley glanced my way. Her smile nearly sent me to the ground each time. I had pinched myself a dozen times over the last few days, making sure this wasn't one of my dreams where I dared to think Harley and I would ever get back together.

Me: *My wife is giving me fuck-me eyes...later.*

Cord: *DUDE! Too. Much. Information.*

Slipping my phone into my pocket, I cleared my throat. "Honey, we better get to our dinner reservation."

Harley nodded. "Enjoy your trip tomorrow! I hope you have fun."

The young woman clapped her hands in excitement while her poor bastard husband forced a smile.

"So they seemed nice."

"They'll be fighting in less than twenty-four hours."

She looked up at me and frowned. "How do you know?"

"It's easy. You can tell by the poor guy's body language he hasn't been able to have sex with his wife yet. She's probably kept him going since they landed on the island."

Harley covered her mouth to hide her laughter. "She did mention they've been on the go exploring all day."

"See? Poor bastard."

Hitting me in the stomach, Harley laced her fingers in mine as we made our way to dinner.

After an amazing meal and another round of conversations with yet another couple on their honeymoon, I practically dragged Harley back to our bungalow.

The moment we walked into the room, I had her pinned up against the door. My mouth on hers. I knew my unshaven face was rough against her mouth and face, but she didn't complain. Instead she wrapped her hand around my neck and pulled me in closer. My hand went behind her leg, lifting it at the knee while I pushed my hard cock into her stomach.

"I can't get enough of you," she whispered against my mouth.

"Good, because I feel the same way."

Her hands slid under my polo shirt. When she squeezed my nipples, I bit her lip. We both moaned. Two seconds later, my shirt was off and her hands were exploring my bare chest.

"Your body is so damn amazing."

My fingertips trailed across her cleavage. "So is yours. This damn red dress is driving me fucking insane."

"As insane as when you saw me on our wedding night?"

My eyes closed. I pictured Harley standing in front of me dressed in nothing but a baby blue lace bra, matching panties and those fuck-me shoes that laced up her legs. I had her whimpering on the bed of the hotel as I slowly took them off.

I let out a deep growl. My eyes snapped open and our gaze locked.

"More insane."

Her teeth sank into her lip and I pulled it out, gently sucking it. Grabbing her hips, I walked backwards, kissing her lips, down her neck, then back up to her lips.

When my legs hit the sofa, I spread out over it, motioning for her to crawl on top of me.

"Why, Mr. Parker. Are you wanting me to take control this evening?"

The lust in her eyes was unmistakable.

"If that's what you want."

She nodded, and crawled on top of me. Placing her finger under my chin, my gaze met hers. I could easily get lost in those eyes.

Those light green eyes that were the color of emeralds. The slight specks of golden yellow seemed to sparkle when she was turned on.

As she lowered her body, my hand went to her thigh.

"What I want is for *you* to take control. I want you fast and hard, then slow and gentle."

My cock strained against my zipper, making me moan. I was so hard it was almost painful.

"Fucking hell, Harley."

Her finger traced my lips before she pushed it into my mouth.

"Did I mention I wasn't wearing any panties?"

And like that, I was lost. Flipping her over, I acted like a madman. One hand pushed her dress up, exposing her sweet, wet pussy, while the other hand managed to get my dick out of my pants.

"Hard and fast?" I asked, pushing my fingers into her, priming her for what she'd asked for.

"Exactly."

One quick move and I was buried balls deep inside of my wife. A hissing *yes* came from her mouth with each pull out and hard thrust back in. I gave her exactly what she wanted. What I needed. We'd had some pretty intense sex over the last few days, but each time we were together was better than the last.

Her hands rubbed against my chest as she arched her back.

"Harder, Tripp," she demanded. "I'm so close."

My body was covered in sweat, and I realized we both still had our damn shoes on. When her nails dug into my back and her eyes closed, I knew she was close. One move of my hips, and she was calling out my name. Fuck, I loved hearing it fall from her lips. Especially when they were swollen from kissing.

The feel of her pulsing around my cock made me come so hard I swore I saw stars. Stilling inside her, I held my body up while we both caught our breath.

"Shower?" I asked, slowly pulling out of her.

Her mumbled response made me smile. My wife had been thoroughly fucked, and she looked like it. I stripped out of my shoes and the rest of my clothes before taking off her high heels and pulling that fucking sexy dress off her even sexier body. I couldn't wait to see her pregnant with our baby. It was an image I had dreamed about many times over the past few weeks.

We stood in the hot water for the longest time, her body up against mine. I shampooed her hair then conditioned it. After I washed her head to toe, she returned the favor. When I lifted her up and slowly sank her down on me, she gave me the most beautiful smile I'd ever seen. We made love slowly. The moment was beautiful. She was beautiful.

CHAPTER 31

Harley

July

"Progress is good." Jonathon said, walking Tripp and I through both the vet clinic and Tripp's new office.

"Do you think I'll still be able to get in by early fall?" I asked, chewing on my nail.

"Once everything gets framed in, weather won't be a problem."

I breathed out a sigh of relief. It had already been a wetter-than-normal start to the summer, and we couldn't afford delays. Gerald had turned down our proposal to rent the space from him to keep the vet clinic open until I was able to get mine up and running. The day after the money was wired to my account, he had the building knocked down. The land now sat void of anything. How that man was Doc Harris's brother was beyond me. Rumor had it he was planning on building a house there. Doc had apologized a dozen or more times. I assured him in the end, everything had worked out. If it hadn't been for Gerald, I might not have gone to Tripp's office that day. We wouldn't be married, and I wouldn't be getting ready to tell my husband I had missed my period.

The pregnancy test was tucked safely in the middle section of my purse. I had peed on it, slipped it back into the box and hadn't looked at it since.

"That's great, Jonathon!" Tripp said, slapping his future brother-in-law on the back. "Now, when is it exactly you're going to be marrying my sister?"

Jonathon's face turned a few shades whiter. When he took a step back, Tripp let out a low grumble.

"You didn't," he said with a touch of anger, but even more amusement in his voice.

"It was Waylynn's idea. We had your folks, my folks, and Liberty there with us."

I gasped. "Y'all got married!"

A smile bigger than the state of Texas spread over his face. "Yeah. It was just to make it official. Once Liberty gets a little bigger, we're thinking a beach wedding."

"Oh! I love that idea!" I said, rushing into his arms. "Congratulations!"

"Thanks, Harley."

Tripp extended his hand. "As long as my folks were there, I'm good with it."

"We plan on announcing it tonight at the family dinner," Jonathon said. His happiness shone. I was surprised Tripp and I hadn't noticed it before now.

A car door shut behind us, making us turn around. Mitchell jogged around Corina's car and helped her out.

"Holy shit!" Tripp whispered. "She's huge."

I hit him. "Hush up, Tripp Parker."

They made their way over to us. Well, Mitchell made his way, Corina sort of wobbled. She looked miserable.

"Hey there!" I said, rushing to her so she didn't have to keep walking. I hugged her, while her stomach had me arching to get my arms around her.

"How are you feeling?"

She sighed. "Big. Hot. Big."

I tried to give her a sympathetic smile, and she returned one, but it didn't touch her eyes. Something was off.

"Wow, this place is really coming along," Mitchell said.

Tripp, Mitchell, and Jonathon walked off to talk about everything men talk about on a construction site.

"Come on, let's sit in the chairs."

Corina looked at the camping chairs. "I won't be able to get back up if I sit in that."

I laughed. "Yes, you will. Let's get you off your feet."

After making our way over to them, I decided to see if Corina knew anything about Amelia.

"So the day of my wedding, Chloe mentioned something to me."

Corina was fanning herself with a piece of paper she had brought from the car, a makeshift fan. Poor thing. I was secretly hoping I was pregnant. If so, I'd be giving birth in the winter and wouldn't have to deal with the Texas heat at nine months pregnant.

"What did she mention?" Corina asked.

"It was something about Amelia."

The fanning stopped and our eyes met. She knew something… or at least she suspected something. Leaning toward me, her brows pulled in tight.

"What do you know?" we said at once.

"I don't know anything!" we exclaimed in unison.

Falling into a fit of laughter, Corina rested her hands on her stomach.

"Honestly, I don't know anything, but we all suspect it. She hasn't said a word, and Mitchell and Steed have started to ask Wade when they thought they would start a family. The man is like stone. He responded with something like, *'In a few more years. We want it to be just us for right now.'* Or something like that."

Chewing on my fingernail, an idea occurred to me. "Corina, what if Amelia is pregnant and hasn't told Wade?"

Her face dropped.

"You don't think so, do you? I know Wade said that, but he would be over the moon if they were having a baby."

"I don't know. I can't imagine she would be able to hide it. I mean, I can't wait to show Tripp the pregnancy…"

Stopping abruptly, I tried to cover my mistake. "The, um, the progress of the vet clinic."

Corina slowly shook her head. "No way. You cannot hide that blunder, Mrs. Parker."

"Why, Mrs. Parker, I don't know what you mean," I said, placing my hand over my chest in a fake shocked way. Okay…that had to be a Parker gesture. Once you married into the family it wore off on you.

"Harley! Are you?" Corina whispered. Her body jerked and she let out a quick breath.

"Are you okay?" I asked.

She nodded. "Just got too excited."

I watched as she rubbed her stomach. Placing my hand on it, I felt her belly tighten and watched her breathe heavily until the contraction subsided.

"Braxton Hicks, I'm sure," she said.

"That was a pretty strong contraction from the look on your face, Corina. And I felt it."

She chewed her lips. First the bottom, then the top. Tears formed in her eyes. "I'm not due for another few weeks. I'm scared."

I dropped down in front of her. "Sweetheart, it's okay to be scared. I would be too."

"What if the baby isn't ready to come out?"

"He or she is. I promise." Reaching for her hands, I pulled her out of the chair. "Is everything packed up?"

"Yes. My bag is in the car already. Mitchell likes being prepared."

I giggled. "Smart guy."

"He's going to panic. I know he is. It's all for nothing. I'm sure it's just a false alarm."

"Nah. He was a cop, he'll be fine, and better to be safe than sorry."

We made our way over to the guys. When we stopped in front of them and stood there in silence, the three of them turned to us.

Mitchell looked at Corina and frowned.

"It's probably nothing," Corina said with a light-hearted laugh. Then she looked down at the ground. "Or…it is something." Her head jerked up, and I knew.

"Your water broke, didn't it?"

She nodded.

"Wait! What?" Mitchell yelled. "Water broke! Now? It's time? You're in labor?"

We stared at Mitchell as he spun in a circle to the left, then to the right. His hands pushed into his air and then down his face.

"Right now? It's not time!"

Jonathon grabbed him. "Mitchell. Dude! Calm down, you freaking out isn't going to help Corina."

That seemed to snap him out of it. In one second, he calmed. Rushing to Corina, he cupped her face within his hands and gave her a sweet smile. My God. Every single one of the Parker brothers were handsome. Each of them had a smile that was sure to melt any woman's heart. The way Mitchell was looking at Corina right now was even melting *my* heart.

"Are you okay to drive to the hospital, Mitchell?" I asked.

Tripp's gaze bounced among all of us. "Hold on. You're going to have the baby? Like…right now?"

I laughed. "Not right now, but her water broke so we need to get her to the hospital in Uvalde. How about I ride with Corina and Mitchell? Tripp, you follow me, and Jonathon, you get on the horn and alert the family."

"I'm on it," Jonathon said, pulling out his phone. He kissed Corina on the cheek. "See you soon. You've got this!"

Turning to Mitchell, he gave him a hard look. "You're fixin' to be Papa Smurf."

We all laughed and Mitchell's shoulders relaxed. He wrapped his arm around Corina and guided her to the car.

"Tripp, can you get the towel in the backseat of your truck? Oh, and grab my purse."

He nodded and took off. Mitchell made it to Corina's car, and I glanced over to see what was taking Tripp so long. He ran up and handed Mitchell the towel. He laid it in the passenger seat and helped Corina back into the car.

Handing me my purse, Tripp kissed me on the lips quickly. "Y'all be careful driving, and I'll meet you there."

By the time we got to the hospital, Corina's contractions were getting closer together. I was proud of how calm Mitchell kept himself. By the time the entire Parker clan arrived, Mitchell and Corina were checked in and had disappeared to their room. Waylynn held a sleeping Liberty in one of those front pouch things. She was still so tiny at three months old. My chest fluttered at the thought I might be pregnant. I remembered the test in my purse and sighed.

Looks like I won't be sharing any possible news tonight...

I wasn't sure how I was going to keep my hands off that test. But I had to. I wanted us to find out together.

Amelia and Wade sat in the corner. I wanted desperately to pull her to the side and demand she tell us whether or not she was pregnant. She looked tired, and my heart ached for her for a reason I wasn't clear about. I could see sadness in her eyes, though, and that made my stomach knot up.

Paxton sat on the floor and played with Gage. He was walking now, and it kept Paxton and Steed on their toes.

Steed sat next to his parents, Chloe in his lap, as he softly read her a story.

Melanie and John sat with their hands intertwined. John's leg would jump up and down every now and then, until Tripp leaned over and said something. Whatever he would say, John would calm him down for about ten minutes. Then his leg would jump again.

Melanie's eyes scanned the room, landing on Waylynn and Liberty for a few moments before moving on to another one of her loved ones. This time it was Jonathon and Paxton who were both trying to keep Gage interested in the game they were playing. Then her eyes locked on mine. I smiled and she returned the gesture.

"Harley, stop pacing, honey. Come sit down," Melanie said.

"I can't seem to sit still."

Tripp stood. "Let's go find some coffee."

I nodded. "Good idea."

We walked off, and I glanced back over my shoulder. "Don't you need to see who wants some?"

He chuckled. "No. It was an excuse to get you some fresh air."

"Oh, I could use some fresh air."

The elevators closed, and I wrung my hands together. The thought of the test sitting in my purse was driving me crazy. Wondering how Corina was doing only added to the insanity.

"I don't know why I'm a wreck," I stated with a nervous chuckle.

When we stepped off the elevator, Tripp took my hand in his.

"I know why."

CHAPTER 32

Tripp

It took everything out of me to act normal.

Breathe in. Breathe out.

When I grabbed Harley's purse it fell over and everything spilled out. I saw the pregnancy test box. When I picked it up and saw it open, my curiosity got the better of me.

When was she going to tell me? How long had she known? Was she planning on a special dinner to tell me?

Pregnant. Harley's pregnant. With our baby.

The test was in my pocket. With every move I made I felt it. My heart was ready to burst at any second. Sitting in the waiting room with our entire family, I wanted to stand on my chair and yell....

"We're having a baby!"

But I didn't. I sat there, calm. Collected. Trying to remember to breathe each time I felt the stick in my pocket.

Harley was as calm as a cucumber until after we got to the hospital. Then it set in. She paced, her eyes lifting to meet mine every two to three minutes. She would give me a smile, then her focus would flitter away to someone else. But it always ended up back to me.

She was anxious, and I couldn't help but wonder if she had just done the test today and was waiting for the right time to tell me. She could have told me on the drive over to see how Jonathon was doing with the construction. Or, hell, earlier that morning when I made love to her.

I pulled her along behind me, searching for a place where we could talk in private. There was no way I could wait for her to tell me. I was probably about to ruin some special plan she had, but I didn't care.

After stepping out of the hospital, I saw a park across the street. I headed that way.

"Tripp, you're about to pull my arm out of its socket. Is everything okay?"

When I didn't answer her, she got agitated. She rattled something in Spanish and I smiled. When my sweet Harley got pissed, she bitched in Spanish—exactly like her father did to her mother. Little did Harley know, I'd taken Spanish classes for three years in college. I knew everything she was saying to me.

"I'm not trying to irritate you, Lee. I just want to be alone."

Coming to a stop, Harley's big eyes looked at me in shock. "How did you know what I said?"

With a wink, I replied, "I might have taken some Spanish classes in your absence."

"What?" she gasped. "So…that day in my office…you definitely knew what I was saying?"

Guilt bubbled up before I popped it with my grin. "Every. Word. Well, almost every word. You and your father talk fast."

"Tripp Parker! You sneak!"

We walked to a park bench, and I motioned for her to sit down.

My heart hammered in my chest. My hands started to sweat, and there was no way I could hold it back a second longer.

"When were you going to tell me?"

She looked at me confused. "Tell you what?"

I laughed. "Ha ha. You know."

Harley chuckled and shook her head. "No. I don't know."

"Dinner? Did Corina throw everything off?"

Her head tilted slightly, and she gave me a concerned look. "Tripp, what are you talking about?"

I exhaled. "We're having a baby?"

Her expression turned to utter shock.

That's right, baby. I found your little secret.

"We are?"

My mouth opened to say something, but her reply caught me totally off guard.

Oh, shit. What if the test wasn't hers!

Fuck. Fuck. Fuck.

"Are we?"

She went to speak, then clamped her mouth shut. Opened it again, then closed it. "I…I don't know. I haven't looked at the test yet."

We stared at each other for a good two minutes. Finally, I shook my head. "Wait. Hold on. Was the test in your purse?"

Her throat swallowed hard. "Yes. Did you see it?"

I whispered, "Yes."

When her eyes filled with tears, I held my breath. "You didn't look at it yet, did you?"

"No," she choked out, a sob slipping from her beautiful lips. "I wanted…to look at it together. To find out at the same time."

The way my heart slammed against my chest made me physically ill. I'd ruined the moment for her.

"*Fuck…*" I said, dragging out the word.

My hands pushed into my hair and I tugged hard, punishing myself for ruining this moment.

You stupid idiot!

"It's okay!" Harley said, pulling my arms down, pressing her palms on my chest.

"It's not okay. I ruined it for you because I had to be a snoop."

When the corners of her mouth rose, I felt a flutter in my chest. "The only thing I care about right now is that I have our baby growing inside of me. We're having a baby, Tripp."

Another round of emotions hit me. Christ, I was going to be exhausted from my mood swings.

"A baby," I whispered, placing my hand on the side of her face. Sliding my hand to the nape of her neck, I drew her in closer.

"Are you happy? Truly happy?" she asked against my lips.

I blinked rapidly, attempting to hold back tears.

"I've never been so happy in my entire life."

She grabbed my T-shirt. "It's not too soon? We've only been married for a few weeks. I can't be that far along."

"Not too soon at all. Let's keep this between us for now. At least until we go to the doctor. We should get used to the idea before we share it."

She agreed. The way her eyes looked, I swore she seemed a bit scared.

"You okay?" I asked, lifting her chin to mine.

With another brilliant smile, she wrapped her arms around my neck.

"I'm more than okay. I'm blinded by our love."

This Love Sneak Peek

"You're not going to the grand opening of Aisling?"

I shot Tammy a death look. "Why do you think I'm not going?"

"Because you're sitting here reading the newspaper. Who reads a newspaper anymore? It's a beautiful place. Maebh gave me a sneak peek of the inside."

My brow lifted. "First off, lots of people still read newspapers, and are you, like, friends with Maebh now?"

Tammy, who was pretty much third in command of my bar, smirked. "If I said *yes* would that bother you?"

I shrugged. "Why would I care?"

Tammy sighed. "For fuck's sake, Cord. The bar is closed tonight. Don't act like you didn't do it because you knew it was her big opening. Which, by the way, was a nice thing to do."

"Don't know what you're talking about."

She let out a frustrated sigh. "Fine. Make yourself look like an asshole when you don't show up."

"I'm going! *Fuck*. Stop nagging me."

A triumph smile spread over her face. "Then come with me. I don't want to walk in alone."

I was already done up in dress pants and a button down shirt. I claimed earlier I had been dressed nicer than usual for a meeting, but it was because I had planned on making a quick appearance at the grand opening of Maebh's new restaurant.

"Fine," I mumbled, grabbing my suit jacket and slipping it on.

Ten minutes later, Tammy and I were walking into Aisling. I'd been here a few short days ago when Jonathon gave me a tour. Maebh had gone into Austin to look for a dress, according to her father, so I knew I wouldn't run the risk of seeing her. I did get to talk to her father some. Nice guy. Hard as fuck to understand, but nice.

My eyes scanned the place. It was packed, and I could hear people making comments about the elegance and how this was just what Oak Springs needed. The twitch in the corner of my lips made Tammy elbow me in the ribs.

"You think it's pretty amazing, don't you? I see the smile tugging at your mouth."

I nodded. "I won't deny the place is beautiful. I think she's going to do really well."

"I love the books! Look at the books, Cord!" Tammy said, grabbing my hand and dragging me through the sea of people. It was more of a reception than a dinner party. It wasn't "sit down and enjoy the food," but more about getting to know the staff, sampling some of the menu, and drinking. The Irish certainly liked to drink.

Tammy pulled a book down and shoved it in my face.

"Look! Romance books!"

I rolled my eyes. "Oh, joy."

I glanced at the cover and realized it was one of the titles Amelia had bought for me to read last year. I wanted to chuckle.

A few people approached me and we made small talk. Everything from how the weather was and how good the fish were biting, right up to it was about time an elegant bar came to town. That was about when I lost interest in the conversation.

Assholes.

My eyes scanned the room, and they locked on the most breathtaking green eyes I'd ever seen in my life.

Maebh.

Holy shit. She looked beautiful. More than beautiful. She took my breath away in that dress she had on. My mind instantly went back a few days to when those legs were wrapped around me and my cock was pushing into her hot core.

Fucking hell.

Her gaze jerked to Tammy next to me, who was going on and on about another book she had found. Every now and then she punched me in the arm.

Maebh looked back to the person she was talking so. She said something and then headed up the steps to the reception area, otherwise known as: the bar with the whiskey. Just what I needed.

Tammy was buried elbows deep in books, and I slipped away upstairs.

The second I got there, I found my family. Well, most of them, anyway. Mitchell and Corina were absent, since Corina had just given birth to Merit a few weeks back.

Then I saw my mother. A huge smile spread over her face and an expression that said she was on a mission.

Fucking great.

"Cord!" my mother exclaimed. "You made it."

Leaning down, I kissed her on the cheek. "Of course I did."

She pulled me close and put her mouth next to my ear. "Thank you for showing up."

Smiling, I replied, "Why wouldn't I?"

Her brow lifted like she knew something I didn't.

"Mom, may I ask you a question?"

She tilted her head and tried to look innocent. "Of course."

"Why did you put the Irish butter in my refrigerator?"

She wanted to laugh, I could see it all over her face. "Well, I read that it's much better for you. Just ask Maebh."

And there it was.

"Mother, don't be butting into my business."

"Cord Parker, I have no idea what you're talking about."

I balled my fists at my side. "I'm telling Dad!"

She spun around and glared at me and then laughed as she patted my chest. "Oh, good luck with that, son. I need to go say hello to someone."

Groaning, I made a mental note to stop by my folks' place. I needed my mother to keep her nose out of this.

I glanced around the room, searching for her. Maebh was standing behind the bar, laughing alongside some good-looking bastard whom I was hoping was the bartender.

"Maebh!" Waylynn called out. "Show everyone the proper way to take a shot."

My dick strained in my pants when I saw her cheeks flush.

The things I could whisper in her ear to make those cheeks turn pink like that.

I shook my head, clearing my wayward thoughts.

Maebh poured herself a generous shot. Right before she brought the shot glass to her mouth, her eyes met mine. I shot her a smirk and shook my head slightly. No fucking way she was going to down all that.

She winked at me, tilted her head back, and took the shot in one fucking gulp. My knees actually trembled.

What in the hell?

"A round for everyone!" she called out. Shots were poured and handed out to everyone in the reception area. Maebh's father stood next to his daughter and lifted a glass.

"To Aisling!" he cried out, and everyone followed his lead.

I swallowed hard as I watched Maebh take another shot with ease. She was soon walking around the room, mingling with everyone. I needed to find an escape before she got to me.

"Where you going?" Tripp asked, pulling me to a stop with his hand on my shoulder.

"Fresh air."

"Why are you so afraid of her?"

I laughed. "I'm not afraid of her. I can't fucking understand a word she says."

He looked at me like I was full of shit.

"Maybe you should go hide out on the rooftop patio," he said with a smirk.

"She has a rooftop patio?" I gasped like a fucking girl.

"Yep!" Harley stated. "It's stunning."

My eyes narrowed. I had a rooftop patio, but it was only for my own private use.

"How do you get to it?" I asked.

Tripp cleared his throat. "I don't think they're allowing anyone up there tonight. It's to rent out for special occasions. But you just keep going up those stairs. There." He pointed back to the set of stairs I had just come up on. Sure enough, the stairs went farther up.

"Well, I'm going to go check it out. I need some fresh air."

They didn't even bother to stop me as I made my way to the bar, ordered a Murphy's Irish Stout and took the steps two at a time before someone saw me heading to the rooftop.

The door was open, and I stepped out onto the patio. A light breeze was blowing, making this July night feel more like a spring evening.

I made my way over to the edge and looked out over Oak Springs. It was pretty much the same view from my rooftop, but it felt more like a romantic scene out of one of Amelia's books. Not like my place, with the oversized chairs, Jacuzzi, and outside bar with a big screen TV.

Sitting down, I finished off my beer. When I knew I couldn't hide out any longer, I stood and found Maebh watching me.

"Is everything all right?" she asked, a sweet smile on her beautiful face. Her thick Irish accent made my head spin, and my heart pound in my chest. Or maybe it was her smile. Or her eyes.

Fucking hell. What's in this alcohol?

"Everything's fine. This is nice up here. The whole place is really nice. Beautiful." I swallowed hard.

"Thank you."

I grinned. I loved it when she said thank you, because it sounded like she was saying, tank you. It was adorable as fuck.

She took a step closer, and all I wanted to do was run. Run to her. Run from her. Run and jump off the top of the fucking building.

No woman had ever made me feel so messed up inside, yet Maebh O' Sullivan had the ability to smile at me, and I was like a sixteen-year-old idiot not sure what in the hell I should do next.

"I'm glad you came. I didn't know you had a girlfriend."

My brows pulled in tight. "What?"

"The woman you came with?"

"Tammy?" I said, laughing at the idea of her being anything more than a pain in my ass. "She's the manager of the bar. We only walked down here together, that's it."

There went that goddamn smile again. I couldn't stop looking at her mouth. My cock grew harder in my pants. A sure sign I needed to leave…right now.

"What are you doing up here?" I finally managed to say.

"I needed a moment to myself. Why are *you* up here?" There was a playful edge to her voice and I found myself liking it. I wanted to hear her talk more, even though half the damn time I couldn't understand her.

There was no way I could tell her the truth. That simply being in her presence made me turn into a stupid idiot. I needed to stay far, far, far away from her.

"I, um, needed air. I wanted to see your view."

"It's not the same as your view?"

Fuck. Busted.

I smiled and let out a chuckle. Her mouth dropped open, and her eyes seemed to light up. She liked it when I laughed. I needed to remember that.

"You got me on that one. Truth be told, I'm feeling a bit off. I think I'm going to call it a night."

She nodded. Was that a flash of disappointment on her face?

Dragging in a breath, I headed toward the door. Maebh reached out and lightly grabbed my arm, halting me in my tracks. My stomach fucking dropped like a rock thrown into the river.

Our eyes met and some weird fucking feeling hit me right in the chest. My breath caught, and I swear to God it sounded like hers did too.

What in the hell is this woman doing to me?

"Thank you for coming this evening," she said softly. "It meant a lot to me."

My mouth opened but nothing came out. Clearing my throat, I got my shit back together and winked. "No problem. See ya around."

Her hand dropped to her side, and I quickly headed to the door. I loosened the tie that felt like it was cutting off my breathing while I picked up my pace. When I got to the reception area, Steed took one look at me and asked what was wrong.

"Nothing. I'm going home. Tell everyone I said goodnight."

I headed down the steps, not giving him a chance to respond to me or say goodnight.

The second I made it out of the restaurant I picked up my pace and damn near ran to my place. Sprinting up the steps, I unlocked my door, stepped inside, and shut it like the apocalypse had happened and a zombie was trying to get in.

Bending over, my hands rested on my knees and I fought to pull in a few deep breaths. My arm still felt like it burned where she had touched it.

I stood as soon as I felt like I could breathe again. Leaning against my door, I dropped my head against it. When I closed my eyes, I saw her smile. Her emerald eyes staring at me. My stomach felt like I was on a rollercoaster going a hundred miles an hour.

I let out a laugh and jerked my fingers through my damp hair.

Am I sweating?

My phone buzzed in my pocket. Taking it out, I found a text from an unknown number.

Unknown: *You dropped your wallet when you were on the rooftop terrace. I'll bring it by the bar tomorrow. – Maebh.*

I swallowed hard. I had her cell phone number. I quickly added a new contact and typed out her name with shaking hands.

"Wait, she has my wallet? That means…I have to see her tomorrow," I said to myself.

Walking to my couch, I dropped face down into the oversized pillows and groaned.

"I'm so totally fucked."

THIS LOVE coming October 9th

PLAYLIST

Contains Spoilers

Chris Young – "Where I Go When I Drink"
Harley walking away from Tripp.

The Pussycat Dolls – "Buttons"
Harley dancing with Toby at Cord's Place.

Taylor Swift – "New Year's Day"
Harley and Tripp at Lilly's Café when tells her they are just friends.

Miranda Lambert – "Tin Man"
Harley going back to Tripp's office after she drops her key.

Florida Georgia Line – "Dirt"
Parker spring fling.

Shania Twain – "Is There Life After Love"
Harley telling Tripp the truth about why she left.

Kelsea Ballerini – "Legends"
The girls on girls' night out.

Dierks Bentley – "Say You Do"
Tripp with Harley the morning after the spring fling.

Cody Johnson – "With You I Am"
Tripp leaving Harley's house the morning of the benefit dinner.

Ariana Grande – "My Everything"
Harley at the benefit when she thinks she's lost Tripp for good.

Taylor Swift – "King Of My Heart"
Tripp and Harley at the benefit dinner.

Bobby Darin – "More"
Song the Parker family danced to at the benefit dinner.

Taylor Swift – "Dress"
Tripp and Harley the night of the dinner at Tripp's house.

THANK YOU

A huge thank you to Tanya for first, giving me the idea to have Harley be part Latina! And second, for your help with the Spanish!

Laura – Thank you for letting me use Hemi's name!

Kristin, Laura, and Tanya – Thank you for your input as I wrote BLIND LOVE! You girls are the best!

Elaine – Thank you so much for polishing up the manuscript! You're the best!

Cori and Amy Rose – Thank you for your mad skills with editing! It's been fun doing these books with y'all.

Danielle – I couldn't do this without you! Thank you for everything you do for me and your mad skills at coming up with titles!

Darrin – I love you. I couldn't do this without your support and love. Thank you for the endless material I use in my books!

Lauren – I really want you to write that book...I know you can do it! I love you and I can't wait to see what your future holds. Love doo!

To my readers – Gah!! I love y'all to the moon and back! Thank you for letting me share these crazy stories that are floating around in my head. I honestly love writing and the fact that I can do this and share them with you is such a huge blessing. Thank you!

Thank you, God, for the blessings you've given to me. You leave me speechless with your endless love..